Praise for *The Woodcock*

'Quietly enticing ... but this is not a small novel because Smyth knows how to use setting, metaphor and memory to deepen and expand his scope ... The period detail and the sensibilities and prejudices of the time are portrayed with great deftness' *TLS*

'An unusual and enticing beast, reminiscent of the early work of John Fowles ... *The Woodcock*'s greatest strength is Smyth's evocation of place and nature, which is imbued with a compelling sense of closely observed realism' *Literary Review*

'Smyth's compelling characters ... are awash with a discombobulating surge of conflicting emotions and motivations' *Daily Mail*

'Accomplished' inews.co.uk

'This is a beautiful, beautiful book that mesmerised and transported me; I would quite happily have read about the lives of Harriet and Jon forever. Highly recommended' *The Historical Novels Review*

'Subtle, insightful (as if under a naturalist's microscope), surprising and memorable' *The Countryman*

'A sensitive and beautif   emotions of
the various characters si   final chapter
is strangely and quietly (

D1439694

'Smyth is a master of tension; it is thick and languid, simmering below the surface' *Northern Soul*

'Quite unlike anything else I've read this year, *The Woodcock* is an unmitigated delight' *ReadListenWatch*

'If you're looking for a beautifully written, richly detailed ... historical novel that will gently tug at your heartstrings, *The Woodcock* by Richard Smyth is a must read' *Reading World* blog

'Smyth has a true eye for magnificent detail, I was captivated' *Armadillo Magazine* (via Instagram)

'A well written, slow burning domestic drama with beautiful descriptions of the coast' @emma_bookshelf (via Instagram)

'Smyth's gift for finely grained and sentiment-free observation, of the human and animal worlds both, is on full display in this rich and rewarding novel' Stanfords Bristol Staff Picks

'A novel of shifting, silted landscapes and relationships laid bare, with quiet urgency *The Woodcock* reveals the complexities of desire, instinct and faith' Eley Williams, author of *The Liar's Dictionary*

'An astonishing piece of literary ventriloquism – Smyth revisits the period novel with a contemporary sensibility and an incredible sense of place' Owen Booth, author of *The All True Adventures (And Rare Education) of The Daredevil Daniel Bones*

'Observing the consequences of the arrival of strangers through the salty prism of a small, northern English coastal town, Smyth has a naturalist's eye for detail, and turns it here upon human nature. *The*

Woodcock is beautiful and unsettling in equal measure' Jon Dunn, author of *Orchid Summer*

'This is a funny and thoughtful novel. Sardonic sometimes, mordant at others; it is always witty, fast, and smart' Tim Dee, author of *Greenery*

'A quietly astonishing novel ... a beautifully patterned and morally serious inquiry into desire, modernity and catastrophe' Peter Mitchell, author of *Imperial Nostalgia: How the British Conquered Themselves*

'There are echoes of DH Lawrence in this novel, most obviously in its overwhelming concern with sex, both repressed and expressed, but also in its attention to nature and its inter-war period setting. Smyth does a lovely job of evoking time and place ... The sense of symbolic structure and resonance is unmistakable' David Wharton, author of *Finer Things*

'A really engaging charming novel that I got really involved in, and didn't want to stop, to the point where I read it all day one Saturday until I'd finished it ... The book very much exists in the playful historical fiction zone, inhabited by *The French Lieutenant's Woman* and *The Essex Serpent* for instance, challenging our assumptions about the past' Emma Townshend, author of *Darwin's Dogs*

'I bloody loved this. Warm, a bit weird, full of vivid life (human + non-human). Reads like an instant classic' Tom Jeffreys, author of *The White Birch*

'Beautiful sentences! Apocalyptic dread! Really good nature writing! An ending that knocks you for six!' Rob Palk, author of *Animal Lovers*

'The combination of rockpooling, brutal fisticuffs, and a metaphysically tinged love triangle is one you won't find everywhere. Highly recommended' Sammy Wright, author of *Fit*

'An elegantly written, finely observed and poignant novel' Jamie Delano, author of the *Leepus* series

'A truly great read' Douglas Cheape, author of *Mokum* (via Twitter)

'[An] incredible novel ... The books I love the most are the ones which compel me to put them down for a moment, so that I may recover. I'm still recovering' Gareth Durasow, author of *Endless Running Games*

'Brilliant' Alom Shaha, author of *Mr Shaha's Marvellous Machines*

'By crikey, what an astonishing novel' Rory Ffoulkes, author of *Sarah The Spectacular Squirrel*

'*The Woodcock* is a lively, intelligent novel which affectionately explores human folly, vanity and ambition. The world Smyth evokes with his vibrant prose leaps off the page – every character lives and breathes, and beneath its ordinary surface, 1920s Gravely teems with beauty, complexity and mystery' Jenn Ashworth, author of *Fell* and *Ghosted*

'Beautifully written – I could almost taste the salt' Carys Bray, author of *A Song for Issy Bradley*

The Woodcock

RICHARD SMYTH

Fairlight Books

First published by Fairlight Books 2021
This paperback edition first published by Fairlight Books 2022

Fairlight Books
Summertown Pavilion, 18–24 Middle Way, Oxford, OX2 7LG

A CIP catalogue record for this book is available from the British
Library

1 2 3 4 5 6 7 8 9 10

ISBN 978-1-912054-75-6

www.fairlightbooks.com

Printed and bound in Great Britain by Clays Ltd.

Designed by Emma Rogers

This is a work of fiction. Names, characters, business, events
and incidents are the products of the author's imagination. Any
resemblance to actual persons, living or dead, or actual events is
purely coincidental.

For Daniel

Few, very few, are at all aware of the many strange, beautiful, or wondrous objects that are to be found by searching on those shores that every season are crowded by idle pleasure-seekers. Most curious and interesting animals are dwelling within a few yards of your feet, whose lovely forms and hues, exquisitely contrived structures, and amusing instincts, could not fail to attract and charm your attention, if you were once cognizant of them.

—Philip Henry Gosse, *A Naturalist's Rambles* (1853)

In her murderous hold this frigate earth is ballasted with bones of millions of the drowned.

—Herman Melville, *Moby-Dick; or, The Whale* (1851)

I

I was on the beach the first time I saw them. I had a crab struggling in my right hand and the jar in my left.

There was a rain, a dense rain of fine, cold particles. Turnstones poked around at the weed-strewn tideline. Visibility can't have been good, the view of the grey North Sea fading into the mist within a hundred yards – and yet I saw them, the two of them. They were on the cliff edge. A big one and a little one; a big man, as I was later to learn, and a slender girl (she could be said to be short only in relation to him).

The crab, with that strange strength of crabs, managed somehow to pivot in my grip, and I was diverted by a fierce pinch in the webbing between my forefinger and thumb. When, having subdued the little swine, I looked back towards Priory Bluff, they were gone. But their image lingered: she had been standing still, quite still, at the cliff edge and he, the larger figure beside her, had been gesturing with a wildly waving arm across the bay, towards the sparse masts of the harbour.

It's a wonder that I could see them at all, in that rain or mist, or whatever you want to call it. But in fact I can still see them.

I slipped the crab, safely jarred, into my satchel and turned, as the tide was turning, back towards the land. It was a Sunday, around lunchtime, and the townspeople, as they issued from the chapel at the harbour end, strolled in twos and threes, in good hats and sober suits, up the sea road towards their homes or Holroyd's pub – or towards nowhere, just towards the end of the sea road, where it turned inland at the priory. At this point, having completed their promenade, they would turn on their heels and return the way they came.

As I laboured through the soft ankle-deep sand between the tideline and the road I tried to pick out Harriet and her mother in the crowd. I couldn't see either of them – only a stream of indeterminate faces turned narrow-eyed towards the sea. Besides, my eye, or my mind's eye at any rate, was still distracted: those figures on the cliff, in the rain—

And my hand hurt. A crab can easily draw blood when it wants to (and in this case I couldn't blame it in the least for wanting to).

Someone's hat blew off: it went pinwheeling along the sea road. I laughed to watch the young men haring after it, their own hats tumbling as they ran.

Harriet wasn't there when I got home. On a Sunday she often went to her mother's for lunch, an arrangement that suited all three of us. On the occasions when we took Sunday lunch together, Harriet was embarrassed by my absence, so fresh in the memory, from Mr Aldridge's Sabbath sermon. Her mother found it a painful strain, indeed almost a *physical* strain, to keep from jibing at me with regard to the same subject; and I – well, I spent the meal wishing that I was in my workroom, pickling shore life.

I was in my study, applying a gummed label to the dead crab's jar, when she returned.

'Hello, darling.'

'Hello, my sweetest,' I called. I set the jar on the appropriate shelf and rinsed my hands in the cold-water basin. While I towelled, she came through hat in hand and, balancing her weight on the ball of one foot, reached up to kiss me.

'Another crab?'

'*Portunus puber.*'

'That's "another crab" in Latin.'

'Indeed.' I tapped the jar. 'Velvet crab. It has a sort of a fur all over it. And if you aren't quick, the fur – like the bloom on a delicate fruit – just vanishes when the crab is dead.'

She held my arm and eyed the jar, and the crab within, with unease.

'Perhaps the poor thing oughtn't be dead at all, Jon,' she said.

'This one had it coming, my dear one.' I opened my right hand and showed her the pincer wound. She made a small noise of pity and dropped at once to her knees to press her lips to it. I was surprised to find that my wife had the capacity to arouse me even here, in this room that reeked of formalin, iodine and salt. With my left hand, while she knelt, I stroked her roughly pinned beech-blonde hair.

Then she stood.

'Mr Aldridge spoke very well about forgiveness today,' she said, making a moue.

With a gentle sigh: 'I should hope he did. That's his trade.'

'Jon.'

'Very well.' I addressed the crab in its jar: 'I forgive you, my little friend. You knew not what you did.'

Again: 'Jon.' But she laughed, and put a hand on the back of my neck. The other hand she put frankly between my legs, and I drew in a sharp whistle at the cold touch of the mist-sodden corduroy.

I kissed her despite the curious beady-eyed gaze of the crab in its jar. There are, I dare say, good wives and bad wives. Harriet was a good wife.

*

'There were some people on the cliff earlier.' I was lying on the unmade bed in my underthings. I held a cup of tea that was as yet too hot for me to drink.

Harriet glanced over from the corner, where she was folding or unfolding or refolding a pile of linen.

'People?'

'Yes. Two of them.'

'That's not like you, Jon. Taking notice of *people*. Were there no ragworms or sea slugs around to catch your attention?'

'No sea slugs north of Mablethorpe, my dove,' I told her, and tried the tea: still too hot.

'Where were they?'

'On the cliff. Priory Bluff. Standing in the rain and having a set-to.'

'Not a very nice spot for a set-to.' She swung a bedsheet expertly over a bare forearm.

'No. But then maybe it wasn't a set-to. Maybe he was just *theatrical*.' I watched Harriet folding for a second and then I added: 'Like Mr—'

'Mr Aldridge is *not* theatrical,' she snapped.

I think I was permitted only a certain quota of remarks at the expense of our long-bearded minister. Beyond this quota Harriet would not even smile. But he *was* theatrical, that preposterous Aldridge. His beard was of Trollope length and he wore a suit of plain wool, the smell of which was unholy regardless of the good-hearted piety of the minister within. He was much given – or at least *had* been much given on the two or three occasions on which I had seen him sermonise – to the use of extravagant hand gestures to emphasise such words as 'wicked', 'devil', 'damnation' and 'error'.

I sipped my tea, scalded my tongue and sucked my teeth in exasperation.

'There was a strange new woman at church,' Harriet said thoughtfully.

'Strange?'

'American. But that wasn't the strange thing.'

'It was surely *one* of the strange things, in Gravely. An American, here? I've never heard of such a ridiculous idea in my life.'

'No, she—'

'You don't mean an American *wigeon*? Sort of duck. We had one over here once. But that was in Middlesex, I think.'

'*Jon*. We aren't *quite* the rude fisherfolk your imagination likes to paint, and we're perfectly able to accommodate a Daughter of the Revolution should we find one in our midst. As I said, that wasn't the strange thing about her.'

'Then go on.'

'We just couldn't find out what she was *doing* here.'

'Breathing the healthful sea air. Enjoying the views. Hearing the good word from Saint Aldridge of Withy Passageway.'

Harriet dumped the linen into the linen casket with a tired sigh. I watched her walk quite bare-bottomed from the bedroom and heard her sink with another, softer and happier, sigh into the sofa cushions. I heard her take up a newspaper.

My tea was now drinkable. I drank it.

I was always regretful after I had been facetious with Harriet. I was never regretful after sex, as I gather we're supposed to be, as a species; I never felt ashamed or anything about all that, and I don't mean to say that I was shame*less*, either, because I wasn't. I was very proud of my wife, of myself, and of what we together made as wife and husband. I can't see any reason on earth why I shouldn't have been.

But there *was* something shameful in the way in which I often spoke to Harriet. I was probably worse – I certainly was that day – after we'd made love; I don't know why. But I *do* know that that sickly jocularity, that compulsive levity, left me feeling – well, as though I were the most dreadful *beast*. As though I'd deflowered a shop girl in some appalling novel.

It may have had something to do, after all, with Harriet and her damned church. It may simply be that the hairy minister Mr Aldridge brought out the bully in me.

Or perhaps – on that day, in any case – it was to do with those two figures, up on the cliff, by the priory, in the rain. One big, one small.

I was born here. I grew up here. A Gravely lass – whatever that means, and I suspect it doesn't mean anything much. Dab hand with a filleting knife, know all the words to 'For Those in Peril on the Sea'. Would I have been very different if I'd been born in Bradford, like Jon?

Well, David McAllister was born in Bradford like Jon and he isn't anything like Jon, so you can see how far that goes.

If I hadn't been born here we would never have moved here. Or who knows, maybe we would. Maybe the rock pools would have called to Jon from afar, across the moors and wolds.

From here I can see the sea, just about. It's a short, fat strip of grey lurking between two houses; our driveway wall hides the breakers and the beach. Black-headed gulls go up and down, up and down. There must be sprats on the tide.

It's funny, sitting without any clothes on, looking at the sea. I like it. I like it in a way that hasn't got anything to do with sex. I like the feeling of contact – even though the sea is far away and behind glass, I feel like I'm in it, even though at the same time I know I'm sitting in the altogether on our second-best settee.

Glad I'm not in it, though. Frigid.

It's quite cold enough here in the cottage. I should put something on but I don't feel like it. I suppose I'm perverse. I fold my arms and carry on watching the sea.

In the bedroom Jon slurps his tea. Everyone thinks he's so cold and rational but he's not rational enough to wait for his tea to cool before he drinks it. That tells you something. He clears his throat, and I hear enough of his voice in the sound to make something in my belly, right down deep, ripple like a fish. It's a miracle how I love him, it really is. Literally a miracle.

I get up and go back in and start putting on my underthings. Jon watches me. I hear him take a breath and I know it's going to be a crack about Reverend Aldridge. Jon thinks it's fun to wind me up like a watch spring and see if he can make me snap – but the thing is, he's never even got close to making me snap, not really, and if he ever thought he was getting close he'd cut it out sharpish. It's just this or that about the reverend's beard or the way he talks. Nothing real.

'What will you do today?' I ask him as I fasten my skirt.

'Dissertate on crab kind until David's train comes in,' he says, and sets his teacup down on the bedside table. 'You?'

'Nothing that can match the doings of crab kind for drama and excitement,' I say.

I have to call on Mother, and update the household accounts, and fetch in some additional groceries because David McAllister is coming to stay (though I suppose he's the type who lives on nothing but cold cuts and absinthe).

Jon smiles. He has the sort of smile that always looks relieved.

I put out a saucer of fish trimmings for Josephus, kiss Jon goodbye, put on my shoes, collect my purse from the dresser and leave the house. The fret hasn't cleared but at least it's not raining. There are puddles in the driveway. It's murder on shoe heels, this driveway.

Two things on my mind today – that is, apart from the bills to settle and the groceries to buy. Mother said at dinner yesterday that she wished my father could have lived to see me come home. I've been home quite some time – we've been in Gravely, Jon and I, for two years – and besides, Dad wasn't here to see me leave, he's been dead since I was fourteen. So what did she mean? I asked her straight out, what do you mean? – but she just made one of those faces. One of those 'mother' faces. I could've pinched her. So that's one thing on my mind today.

The other is that girl at church.

Alice Reynolds, the doctor's wife and to all intents and purposes empress of Gravely and district, took the girl by the elbow as we were leaving church and said: 'Are you staying with us long, Miss—'

Which raised a few eyebrows, being on the pushy side, but that's Alice all over. Not backward in coming forward – and besides, weren't we all dying to know? Someone had to ask.

And this girl, she just smiled (she had a lovely smile, we all thought so), and said: 'I honestly couldn't say for sure how long we'll be here – but you really do have a beautiful little town.'

I've been thinking about that all afternoon.

Not many people out on the main road. There are some fellers walking up to the horrible pub and I see Kath Connolly, who lives two doors up from Mother, pushing her pram on the opposite pavement, but I've not got time to natter.

Who was we, for one thing? No wedding ring, you see. Tap mine with my thumbnail. Best pewter money could buy, Jon jokes. He's not far off the truth, of course. But it was the best his money could buy.

And then Gravely, a beautiful town. Well. It's like when people used to say I was a beautiful little girl, and Dad'd grin, showing his missing teeth, and say, 'You don't know her.' I'm not saying anything against Gravely – it's my town, it's mine, it's me – and I suppose in a lot of ways it is beautiful. All I'm saying is that if you say it's a 'beautiful little town', and you say it like that, then you don't know it.

Jon's like that with his birds and butterflies sometimes. I think he knows what their life is really like – because it's not nice, life, for wild things, and I think he knows that, how could he not? But he finds it beautiful anyway. Can't help himself.

II

Waiting at the railway station that afternoon, while Harriet remained at home, I was reminded of my own arrival in Gravely two years previously. I'd travelled alone – work had detained me in Bradford until the Thursday after our wedding, so Harriet had travelled up with her mother on the Monday morning, promising that in the intervening days she would dust the cottage and acquire us a pet cat.

I hadn't been north of the Tees before. I had travelled only infrequently on the intercity railway. I knew when the gleaming tracks swept us along the bay's very edge, and for a few moments (moments fixed for me thereafter in the clearest spirit) I was able to watch the skuas, the pirate birds of summer, harrying Arctic terns against the high cirrus, that I could live here. I could still be *me* here, I knew – though of course what we had come here to be was *us*.

Perhaps forty minutes prior to those moments on the sunlit southbound line, I had been hurried, almost smuggled, in and out of Newcastle, hastened with my cases along mile-long platforms by scrawny porters and their skew-wheeled trolleys. It had been as though they thought that, if they were quick enough and sufficiently furtive, I might not notice the great smoking city beneath which the station buildings cowered – as though Newcastle were a dirty family secret, like an abortion or a brain sickness, to which they would not readily admit.

On the train I craned my neck to watch it retreat. I watched until all that was left in view was the city's smoke. It reminded me of home. Bradford stank, too.

'Jon Lowell. You damn sea creature.'

McAllister stepped down from a train that I hadn't noticed had arrived. He had a square-edged suitcase under his arm and carried a hat, an umbrella and a newspaper in his hands.

'Can't shake your damn hand,' he apologised as he approached, gesturing with the items he carried.

'That's all right. You know how we sea creatures are.'

'Yes. Clammy.'

'But you could ease your burden, David, if you wore your hat on your head.'

'Waste of energy putting on a hat at the seaside,' he said, but put it on anyway. I took his case. Heavier than it looked. 'Wind'll only blow it off,' he added gloomily. Then he shook my hand. A firm shake but firm only because it wanted to be, not because it had to be. Not a test or a challenge.

I suppose there was no need for David to test me because he knew already that he was better than me. But that wasn't the reason why his handshake was the way it was.

If he'd known I was giving so much thought to a bloody handshake he'd have ribbed me fiercely. He might have changed since we were boys, but a fellow can change only so much.

We walked out of the station archway. To our right, to the east, was the sea, and to our left, west, was Station Parade, a narrow and clean-looking run of shops and guest houses that stretched for perhaps two hundred yards away from the coast and led to the narrow-spaced black railings enclosing Quebec Park.

'Nice-looking town,' said David politely, linking his arm with mine.

To me, looking westwards at Station Parade was like looking into a rock pool on a clear day. On the surface of the water you can see with astonishing detail the reflections of surrounding rocks, the clouds above, perhaps one's own net or hand, or curious, benevolent, hollow-cheeked face. But of course the thing to do is to blink and refocus, to look *beyond* that. And beyond that you see a different and perhaps a better world.

At sunset the canal of sky above Station Parade would fill with sunlight as though someone had opened a lock gate. Perhaps tall, fluorescent clouds would tower above the park. Perhaps the sky would turn to the colours of a wheatear and the clouds would be thin and lateral and dark grey like blotted lines of ink.

When someone said something like 'Nice-looking town' it made me want to say 'You are not looking at the right *thing*.'

But I was pleased that David liked the place, so instead I said: 'Do you want to go straight to the cottage, or do you want to see a bit of the town?'

He looked at me in counterfeit surprise.

'You mean this isn't it?'

'This is most of it. But there's a bit more. There's the beach, and the priory. And the pub, of course.'

'I think I'd enjoy seeing those things, only with their order reversed. Will there be girls?'

'You can't bring girls back to the cottage.'

'Good Lord, no. I wouldn't want to take them anywhere. I just thought it would be nice if there were going to be girls there.'

'It's not really,' I said, 'that sort of place.'

But, as it turned out, there *was* a girl there.

*

Bradford's technical school, late in 1923 or early in 1924. The pavement outside. A young man appeared hatless out of the slanting snow with his hair plastered across his brow. A girl with him: wool cap, dark stockings, T-strapped shoes. I would have walked by them but the young man touched my shoulder. Just a light touch, but enough to make me stop in spite of the weather.

'You're Lowell, aren't you?'

I nodded, ducking my chin and blinking my eyes against the snow.

'I'm McAllister. You have rooms nearby, don't you? I've seen you.'

'I, yes, sort of. Laburnum Road.'

'Yes, that's not far.' He looked at the girl and gave an encouraging nod. 'That'll do. And' – looking again to me – 'how's your landlady, Lowell?'

I hesitated. I must have gawped, because McAllister clarified: 'I mean, is it a case of *here be dragons*, you know, or is she a liberal, broad-minded type?'

'We really are *very* cold,' put in the girl, smiling apologetically with a sort of half-curtsey.

'I, she—' I faltered, and swallowed, then, feeling my cheeks burn, said: 'She's my father, I'm sorry to say.'

I walked off into the snow. I expected at any moment to hear caws of derisive laughter behind me, but I didn't hear anything.

The girl in the public bar of Holroyd's could have been the elder sister of the girl on David McAllister's arm that night. Like that girl, she had wide eyes, dark stockings and T-strapped shoes. That girl's hair had been hidden beneath her wool cap but this girl's hair, knotted in a chignon, was rust-red. Both had a mill-girl slenderness. This one was no mill girl, though the other might have been.

In the public bar of Holroyd's the red-haired girl stood out like an anemone in an empty rock pool. Or, rather, not empty – there were men standing at the bar, others by the dartboard, one at a table in the corner with a folded racing paper, so not empty, but rather peopled apart from the anemone with beings as blank-eyed as blenny fish, as insular as limpets, as crusty and sharp-clawed as crabs.

David lifted his hat to the girl as soon as we entered.

'Good evening, madam,' he said.

'Good evening,' she quietly replied, barely lifting her eyes. She was reading a book, a cloth-bound book. Too slim to be a Bible, I was pleased to see. There was a glass of tonic water or something on the table.

David caught my eye when I turned away from the girl.

'What'll it be?' he said, although the look he gave me said something else.

'Pale ale,' I answered. More quietly, I added: 'Mr Holroyd doesn't keep anything else.'

'A pale ale will go down very well.' He smiled and dug in his trouser pocket, as fat Clement Holroyd appeared behind the bar. 'Evening, landlord. Two pale ales, if you would.'

Holroyd nodded and exhaled a phlegmy breath. Taking hold of a glass with one hand and the pump handle with the other, he looked first at David, then at me, and then, with a long, chinny leer, at the girl at the table, and said: 'I would indeed.'

I smiled politely. I couldn't see David's face.

Through the bay window by which we took a table I could see little but the grassy lip of the cliff and, beyond that, the grey sea. The crooked vertebrae-like rocks of Adam's Middens broke the sea's surface in a perpendicular line that led a quarter-mile out into the bay. At the limit of my eyesight the lighthouse at Fossmouth showed a warm light.

David, of course, wasn't looking out of the window.

'American,' he said, and sipped his beer. Over the rim of his beer glass his blue eyes were reverential.

'Did you think?' I murmured. 'I thought Irish. We get quite a few of them. Hard to be sure, of course, just from—'

'No, American.'

The beer was tepid and good. I wiped my moustache with finger and thumb and said: 'Well, you could be on to something, now that I think of it. Harriet said there was an American girl in town. She was at church this morning.'

'Not this one.' David shook his head with a curious smile. He was still watching the girl. The girl was still reading her book. 'This one,' David said, 'doesn't go to church.'

I drank more of the good beer. I would have said 'How the devil could you know that?' or 'What on earth makes you so sure?', but I knew David, and I knew that, in asserting so confidently that the girl was an American or a non-conformist or whatever else, he wasn't seeking to tell me anything about the world as he thought it *was* – he was simply telling himself stories.

David had written his first novel while he was still at the technical college. It was a rather swooning love story. I, of course, adored it; I was a lonely and sensitive adolescent, and lonely and sensitive adolescents are little better than lonely spinsters – or, I suppose, lonely *any*bodies – where cultural discernment is concerned. Tosh of that sort I positively lapped up.

I was friends (and rather proud to be friends) with David by then. I went with him to a photographer's studio in Leeds, where he had the necessary publicity snaps taken.

'Both of you?'

'No, just me.'

'Two shillings.'

'It's for a book I've written, you see.'

'Still two shillings.'

The grimy fellow in the studio with his moth-eaten screens and pre-war kit knew his business, though. Those pictures: the McAllister jaw square, the mouth a firm line, the dark eyes humorous, the blond hair swept back and showing a fine grain like turned wood. The knot of the tie a fraction off-centre. When the pictures arrived at the publisher's office the publisher must have heard in his ears the ringing – joyous as wedding-day church bells – of booksellers' cash registers.

But that isn't to say that David had no talent as a writer. And I do know that telling stories was a thing that David would have done whether he was a writer or not.

'Should I go and speak to her?' he asked me, smiling and leaning forwards over his beer glass. 'Would that be all right, do you think? With the locals, or whatever. Think of the *talk*, Mr Lowell's reputation in *tatters*, that sort of thing.'

I returned the smile.

'I think my reputation could sustain the blow.'

'But remember, Lowell, you aren't *from* here.'

'No, but I'm a respected local limpet-botherer and husband of a ninth-generation Gravelian.'

'Ninth? What were they before that?'

'Barbary pirates, but we don't speak of it.'

'All right.' He made a motion as though to rap the table with his knuckles but stopped short of the tabletop. 'Here I go,' he said, and stood, and winked, and went.

I looked out of the window. Three flickering turnstones scudded low across the surface of the sea. I heard David say: 'Good evening, madam. My name's McAllister. My mournful-looking friend over there and I would be delighted if you'd like to join us at our table and make our acquaintance. Or perhaps you prefer to be alone?'

I expected some sort of demure murmur or mumble.

'That'd be absolutely lovely, *Mr McAllister*,' she said instead, in a loud, clear voice – and David, damn him, had been right in one thing at least, as her accent was, when heard in full stride, unmistakably American.

Some people enter one's life by stages, by imperceptible progression. Like a tide that catches the beachcomber unawares, all of a sudden they are among you.

Others break upon your life as decisively as a wave. In this way did Cordelia Shakes break upon us.

Just me and the cat in the house. Look at him. Josephus: a daft name for a cat but it fits him. Sleeping with his feet and nose, his white parts, all puddled together. I like it when he sleeps. They're worriers, cats. That's all there is to them as long as they're awake, just worry. A little black worry on four white feet. So it's nice when he's sleeping because I think that's as close as you can get to happiness when you're a cat.

But then I like it when he's outside, too. Stalking starlings in the driveway. Just a wild thing, really, once he's over the doorstep.

He stirs, makes a funny noise: 'murp', something like that. Don't wake him. Leave him be. Things to be done.

It's well and good being bohemian and not caring a damn about what people think of you but no one wants to stay in a place where there's no tea and cat hairs in the bed. Jon tells me not to worry, that David wouldn't want us to go to any trouble, which might be true but only because men don't know what trouble is. 'Oh, don't go to any trouble for me *– as long as the house is clean and there's food on the table and a fire in the hearth, I'll get by.'*

No idea.

I run the iron over the second-best bedsheets and wonder about this David. Feels like meeting the family, only more important than that. When it came to meeting the family, there was only

Mr Lowell, a stuttering little sheep of a man in an old-fashioned overcoat, and I wasn't the least bit scared of him. It's like Jon says about spiders and mice: they're more afraid of you than you are of them. *This David, though. I* am *a bit scared of him.*

I'm sure he'll be all right. People generally are.

Bedsheets on the spare bed. It creaks but he'll have to put up with it. And I can't do corners but he won't notice and if he does, well, he can put up with that, too. Or tuck in his own corners. Vegetables out the pantry. Peel, peel, chop, chop. Hands pink like they've been skinned. Pan on. Empty out the teapot. The old leaves go on the compost, though I don't know why we bother, we don't grow anything, the compost doesn't do *anything – it just sits and rots.*

One year Jon found a family of lizards or something living in it. Made his summer, that. Gave me the willies.

Dusting. I can't bear dusting. I do it, of course – skirts, coving, ceiling, lampshades, tabletops – singing merrily as I go, but I can't bear it really. Jon'd say, then why bother? And I'd say, well you would *say that, and carry on dusting.*

Pheasant feathers on a bamboo cane. Like something a jester would tickle the king with. Bish, bash, this way, that way. Cobwebs rent asunder. Spider on the sitting-room ceiling makes a run for it. I can *hear* him *saying it, 'More afraid of you…', but nuts to it, pardon my French – bash him with the duster end. Curls into a ball and drops to the rug.*

Tread on him. Cruel really but not compared to what Jon does to crabs and things. It was in my house, after all. I don't think God would mind and anyway he's done worse. Look what he did to the Midianites, if it's the Midianites I'm thinking of.

Four o'clock already. Hardly anything done.

*

'Mrs Lowell! Good afternoon.' Hand extended in a pretty little lace glove. Recognised the glove from church. Recognised it before I knew the face.

'Miss Shakes, how do you do?' Almost curtseyed. You'd think she was visiting royalty. Not her fault, I don't suppose, but still it's the impression you get.

'Very well, thank you – but please, call me Eleanor.' Smiles. Meets my eye but not in a rude way. She's not being what Mother would call bold. Shy, I think. Watching me watching her. 'I'm the most awful housekeeper – I hadn't realised we've practically nothing in for dinner, so thank goodness Mr Souter was still open. Or we'd have had to go foraging on the beach.' A laugh, and in the laugh the clear desire that I should laugh, too – so I do. Who's 'we'? It's killing me, nosy parker that I am.

Souter butts in, all pink cheeks and salesman's grin, What can I get you this afternoon, madam, but I know he's just in a hurry to close up, so I just tell him a pound of sugar, please, and he grins double, pinker than ever, and says: 'You're sweet enough already, Mrs Lowell,' and I look at Eleanor Shakes, just quickly, and she looks back at me and rolls her eyes, just a bit, but she rolls them – and I think, hey up.

I laugh partly because I want to and partly because I feel as though if I don't she'll cry. I can see she's grateful when I do. I take my bag of sugar from Souter and we leave the shop together.

'Do you take sugar in your tea?' Eleanor says as we turn on to the coast road.

At first I think she's just making conversation and not doing a very good job of it but then I remember that of course she's not from round here. To say the least. They don't have tea, the Americans – they chucked ours into their harbour, didn't they? – so it's only natural she should wonder about things like that. If I was in France I'd want to know whether they put salt on their frogs' legs. You want to fit in, don't you? And it's the sort of thing no one tells you unless you ask.

'Actually it's for a guest,' I tell her. 'A friend of Jon's – Jon, that's my husband, Mr Lowell. Neither of us takes sugar so we don't generally keep it in. But this Mr McAllister does, only I'd forgotten till just now. Nick of time. They might be there now, actually – gasping for a cup of sweet tea and us with not a grain of sugar in the house. The shame!'

She laughs – she does have a lovely laugh, a toothy, tongue-y American laugh – and asks if our friend is staying long. I start to say: 'He's not my friend,' but that'd sound funny. So instead I say he's here for a little while.

'You're local, aren't you? I can tell – I think – by your accent.'

Which is pretty sharp of her, because all I can tell from hers is that she's American. She might be from Alabama or Alaska for all I can tell. I nod and say, 'Yes, born and bred. Though I travelled about a bit in between.'

Meaning Bradford.

'Oh, wonderful. Are your family still in Gravely?'

'My mother is. My father passed on. Some time back.'

'Oh, goodness. I'm sorry. That must be difficult.'

'It was. Now it's not so bad.'

'Was it the war? No – I'm sorry for asking, I oughtn't be so curious.'

'I don't mind. It was before the war. I was only young.'

She nods, and looks absolutely heartbroken. It's all right, I want to say. I'm all right. Don't be sad, pet – give us a smile. Like my dad would have! Daft.

We stop where the road turns off to our driveway, and say all those things you have to say about having tea some time. I mostly mean them this time, I think.

'You must tell me all about your travels,' Eleanor says. Heck. I blush. Bradford beck. Jenkin's mill. Canal Road. Manningham Park.

'They're nothing compared to yours,' I say, and we smile and shake hands again and she's off.

Later on, waiting for Jon and this bloody David McAllister, I think you can hardly blame us for not having travelled more, after all those boys, all those boys and men went off abroad and didn't come back.

Another thing I think later on is that I told Eleanor Shakes all those things about my dad, and I still don't know the first thing about her. Still don't know who 'we' is. Don't know if she has a mother or a father.

But Eleanor knows my dad's dead and I don't take sugar in my tea.

III

I, like David, first made it into print in that summer of 'twenty-four. In a diffident letter to the *West Riding Naturalists' Journal* I logged the immortal observation that, in the towns of Airedale, the house martins had returned from their migration far earlier than in previous years. I suggested timidly that it had something to do with the pupation of insects.

In the next issue my theory was rigorously discredited by an entomologist of Hanging Heaton, but it didn't matter, not to me – what mattered was that not only my name but my *thoughts* had been rendered into print upon a page. Someone had considered them – as I might consider, turning it over in my hand, a pear in a greengrocer's – and found them worthy.

A week later I wrote again, and then again and again, my authority increasing in small increments each time, about ants, harebells, sparrows, spiders, bulrushes, hares, kestrels, damselflies, hoverflies, sandstone, snails, clouds, cornflowers, cuckoo pint.

In September I received a letter, handwritten and so elaborate in its politeness that it might have been dictated by a Japanese, inviting me to contribute not a letter (I dare say they had had enough of my letters) but, by God, an article to the *Journal.*

Away I went – launched, so to speak, as a writer (though I had no two-shilling publicity pictures).

David, mischievously, told the girl – 'Cordelia, Cordelia Shakes,' she had said her name was, offering an ungloved hand – that I was a scientist.

'My *good*ness,' she said, thinking, I suppose, that I was a sort of seaside Einstein or Edison of the rock pools.

'Mr McAllister has a writer's gift for embellishment,' I said. 'I'm hardly a scientist. You might say that I'm a naturalist, though I'm hardly that, either. I write about natural history. Articles. Books. That sort of thing.'

'The man is a positive Boswell to the shore crab and the lugworm,' David smiled. 'Not a sea squirt sneezes on the Gravely beaches but Jon Lowell knows about it. And if that isn't science I don't know what is.'

'It's Mr Hubble measuring the miles between galaxies,' I said. 'It's Mr Dart digging up a new species of prehistoric man. It's emphatically not Mr Lowell writing homilies about herring gulls.'

'*Homilies about herring gulls.* That's rather good. Poetic. Perhaps I'm wrong. You're no scientist, but an artist after all.'

I laughed, shaking my head.

'I'm as much of an artist as you are a scientist.'

'Well, why not? Aren't I an astronomer, of sorts, mapping the comings and goings of stars?'

'If by stars you mean your characters then that makes Bloomsbury Square your galaxy.'

'Yes, that sounds about right.'

'And mapping stars that never existed sounds like a quixotic sort of astronomy.'

'Oh, they exist, all right,' David said. 'For me, at least – for me, they're every bit as real as any damn stars *you* can see.'

Miss Shakes was watching our sparring with a half-smile.

'You gentlemen certainly know how to talk,' she said.

'Talk rubbish,' I said, a little abashed – it had sounded like a rebuke.

'Apologies,' smiled David, 'but we only banter like this to keep ourselves from betraying our curiosity. Otherwise we'd have to be terribly rude and ask you lots of questions about yourself.'

Cordelia showed her long white teeth in a laugh.

'You English. I guess I should be glad we aren't talking about the weather.'

Taking this as permission, David asked: 'What brings you to Gravely?'

He pronounced it as the locals did: *gravelly*, not *gravely*. Cordelia lowered her eyelids and shrugged one shoulder.

'My *father*,' she said wearily.

'And,' David put in confidently, looking sidelong at me, 'your churchgoing sister.'

She had picked up her glass but now set it down again and, wide-eyed, said: 'Well, aren't you a regular Pinkerton, Mr McAllister.'

'Small town.' He shrugged. 'People gossip. You were saying. Your father.'

'My father.' Cordelia took a mouthful of her drink. I had decided by now that the tonic was surely spiked with gin. 'My father brought us here.'

'And what brought him here?'

'A *dream*.' She smiled rather fiercely. 'All three of us bundled on a boat to England because Maurice Shakes had a dream.'

'Oh, come,' David objected, as I suppose, being a writer, he felt he had to. 'You oughtn't speak so dismissively of a dream. *Any* dream.'

I cuffed his arm with the back of my hand.

'Stars and dreams, for God's sake, David, you sound like a writer in a bad play.'

Over Cordelia's loud laugh, David, laughing too, said: 'Noted. But still, the point stands. I'd like to know about Mr Shakes's dream.'

She stopped laughing, and quickly gulped at her drink, and shook her head, and poked out her coral-red lower lip.

'No,' she said. 'No, I couldn't do it justice. Only my father should tell my father's dream.'

We all thought about that for a moment. I don't know if we all thought of our own father's dreams. I only know that I did.

I imagine that, as a small boy, my father, Arthur Lowell, dreamed of playing county cricket. Perhaps later he dreamed about girls or about the church (or, of course, both). But in what came after I can't discern any traces of a dream. He was a soldier, of course, but I'm quite sure he had never dreamed of being a soldier – though he dreamed of it enough afterwards. He owned a confectionery business for a short time. He taught maths at a small private school. He enjoyed playing lawn tennis.

Perhaps, as Cordelia said, only he could have told his dream. Perhaps, after all, what my father ended up with *was* my father's dream. But it seemed to me, as I considered it, like rather a dereliction of a dream.

'When,' asked David, 'might we meet this Mr Shakes?'

'Town this small, you'll meet him soon enough,' Cordelia said.

*

I left them to it, after a while. I headed for home and Harriet. Before I got there, however, an impulse overtook me – some small, domestic variety of *wanderlust*. When I was within perhaps fifty yards of the end of our driveway I hesitated, took a turn seawards, and before very long found myself on the beach, the north end, descending through the silent dunes to the sand at the point at which six long barnacled breakwaters stretched out towards the sea. I felt all right but my mouth was musty from the three or four pale ales I had drunk.

Out in the dark somewhere an oystercatcher said *kleep*. There were stars and a moon overhead. I sat down in the sand. I breathed deeply the seaweedy air. The distant sea breathed with me.

I might have guessed – but didn't, I don't think – that I would not be alone for very long. Here they came, arm in arm, in silhouette against the moonlit sea. Beer and gin had made them a little louder than before.

'We have no whalers here, my dear,' David said, 'for we have no whales.'

Heaven only knew what sort of conversation had led to this. But naturally I knew what this was leading *to*.

I was seated in the darkness at the foot of the low dunes, some way to their landward side. If they had looked, or if I had moved, they would have seen me. But of course they did not look and I did not move.

'There was a tradition, you know, in old New Bedford,' Cordelia said, 'whereby a whaling vessel returned from a successful hunt would donate the whale's penis to the preferred brothel of the officer who lanced the whale. And the brothel *madame* would boil it up into soup.'

David laughed.

'And what if it was a lady whale?'

'No dick soup for the whores of New Bedford.'

And again David laughed. I wanted to chip in – make him laugh, and her, too – because I had read *Moby-Dick* and remembered the part where a fellow wears a whale's prepuce as a mackintosh. But of course I said nothing, and only sat in the dark and watched.

They stopped before the first breakwater. Cordelia reached up and took off David's hat.

'It's bad luck,' she said, 'to be kissed by a man in a hat.'

Bare-headed, David kissed her. He hardly had to stoop, she being almost as tall as he. In the broken moonlight the shadows were impenetrable. Cordelia's chignon trembled. David's white right hand showed for a moment and then was gone. They seemed almost a single figure, black and odd-shaped, like a chess piece.

They subsided together into the dry sand. Two white buttocks were bared starkly to the moonlight. There were small sounds: their breathing, the mutter of buckles being unbuckled, something Cordelia whispered. A shoe heel clunked against the breakwater.

I looked up at the moon. It was then that I saw the man.

He was standing on the dune that rose to my right, and his wide-brimmed hat was black against the moon. I didn't know if he had just arrived or if he had been there all along. His dune was in the shadow of a cloud: had he been sitting down, I would not have been able to see him, even if I had looked (and I hadn't looked).

A large man, as heavily built as a bear, and bearded. His shoulders sloped. More than that I couldn't discern. But that he was Maurice Shakes, Cordelia's dream-driven father, I didn't for a moment doubt.

He stood quite still and watched his daughter rolling in the sand with David McAllister.

My instinct was to cry out – for David and Cordelia surely had to be warned. But to cry out would have been to betray myself, and in doing that I should have betrayed a good deal more than I wished. Instead, uselessly, I held my breath. The man on the dune let out a low, choleric wheeze that merged in my ears with the far-off soughing of the sea.

My second instinct was to run. I heard Cordelia moan and I mustered my feet beneath me.

Cowardice was a family trait and one with which I had long since come to terms. There are few battles from which I would not run. To look in the eyes of a man who has watched his daughter being fucked on a beach by a fashionable novelist – this was a thing that I knew to be beyond me. I would as soon have looked in the eyes of a man in whose belly I was twisting a bayonet. Even, in a mirror, to look in my own eyes – even that took what I called courage.

I was rising to my feet when I heard the man laugh.

I paused, frozen on my haunches. The laugh persisted: a staccato series of explosive snorts emitted from the man's nose. I looked and saw that his shoulders were shaking. He swung his heavy head from side to side and drew in more breath and then the strange laugh began again. The shoe, down on the sands, was now banging at a mounting tempo against the wooden breakwater. I heard David say 'oh God' with his voice on the brink of breaking.

The man on the dune – how *could* he be Maurice Shakes? And yet I knew that he was – scratched at his beard. Once more he shook his head, and the wide brim of his hat eclipsed the moon. Then he turned, and walked away with a stomping gait through the stiff grass and flyaway sand. I heard him say what might have been 'my, my, my'.

I suppose he heard Cordelia's drawn-out climactic whimper. He had to have done. From the far-off shoreline an awoken bird echoed the noise.

Awake because I'm not a bit tired. In bed because who makes a fire in September? And there's only me in – still only me, though it's gone ten. But it's cold, so lie under the blankets and wonder about this David McAllister, who's keeping Jon out late. Not worry, wonder.

At night sometimes all wondering feels like worrying. But this David McAllister will be nothing to worry about, surely. Such an old friend of Jon's. A good-looking lad, I gather. There's something to worry about in itself.

Listen at you: your mother's daughter.

David McAllister – I think of him by his full name since I saw it in the newspaper, something about his new novel – didn't come to our wedding. Such an old friend, and a Bradford lad, too, or near enough – why was that?

He wrote a charming letter. Well, of course he did. How these writers start out, isn't it? Writing charming letters to daft lasses. Then it's writing charming books for daft women. Something about commitments, he said. Inescapable commitments. I ask you. Our wedding day, and he's telling us about inescapable commitments.

'Do you mind?' I asked Jon.

'Mind? Of course not. He's a busy man.'

I could have slapped him. Are you not a busy man? I wanted to ask. Am I not a busy woman? Because I bloody am. But if David

McAllister had decided to get wed you can be sure we'd have been there in London, with our best hats on and our hair in a braid.

Can't take it personally because he'd never met me. Still hasn't for that matter. How long does it have to go on before I can take it personally?

Half ten. The veg can be reheated. Just as well the sausage'll keep till tomorrow or David McAllister'd be getting a butcher's bill.

There's tea in. Yes. I checked the tin. There's tea in. Reverend Aldridge coming by in the morning. He's really only coming for a cup of tea so what would it look like if I hadn't any in? What would be the point?

As bad as me going to church and him having no hymn books out, no hassocks, no Bibles.

Then there's Jon. Maybe he'll be out on the rocks collecting periwinkles or maybe he'll go buzzard-spotting with David McAllister. Or maybe they'll still be down the pub at eleven tomorrow morning.

But he'll probably be here and that's another thing. Jon and the reverend. Jon and the reverend and David McAllister and his bloody sweet tea. At least I know I've not to worry about that.

And there's tea in. I checked the tin. There's tea in.

IV

'I find great peace in the sea, Mr Lowell,' said the long-bearded Reverend Aldridge. 'I find a great sense of timelessness. Intimations of the infinite.'

'Very deep,' I said.

He looked at me as though surprised.

'Hm?'

'Very deep,' I repeated. 'The sea. Nearly four hundred fathoms in the Norwegian trench. Only around five fathoms hereabouts, though that's quite deep enough for me.'

Aldridge gave me a look of polite incomprehension. One of the bristles of his gingery beard, I noticed, was trailing in his tea.

I could sense Harriet giving me a severe stare. I declined to look at her. Instead I half-turned in my seat and set my face politely towards the latest Shakes to have entered our little sphere – to have somehow landed in our lives.

Eleanor Shakes said: 'You don't have a spiritual response to the ocean, Mr Lowell?'

She shared with her sister an unembarrassed clarity of speech. A good school, I supposed; a good Massachusetts school that made it its business to turn out confident, unembarrassed, clear-spoken and frightening girls. Sipping at my tea gave me a moment to gather my thoughts.

I hadn't been prepared, that morning, having risen from an unfulfilling sleep with a head full of rather sharp-edged clutter, for this – for the arrival of this second Miss Shakes, respectful in the train of the hirsute Aldridge.

'Mr Lowell is a scientist,' Aldridge smiled.

'Yes,' I said. 'I look at the sea and see only a grey agglomeration of atoms.'

The minister's eyes twinkled nastily behind the pebble lenses of his spectacles. A bead of tea hung suspended on the bottom-most bristle of his beard.

'A scientist is no less entitled to a sense of the spiritual than a layperson – or for that matter a minister,' Eleanor said.

'Jon would sooner commune with shore crabs than consider the eternal mysteries,' Harriet put in, laughing so as to pretend that she didn't think it true.

'Maybe the shore crab *is* an eternal mystery,' I said. I wondered, returning to my teacup, if Miss Shakes would again rally to my side – but she remained, this time, well-manneredly silent.

Sitting beside Harriet, Eleanor Shakes did not look pretty (perhaps even Cordelia Shakes, whom I had thought rather beautiful, would not have looked pretty sitting beside Harriet). She was tall and upright in her chair. Her hair was of an autumn shade, though far less vivid than her sister's, and wrapped at the nape of her neck in a smooth bun. Her eyes were large. She wore no lipstick.

'The Almighty will not be revealed by the lenses of a microscope,' said Aldridge.

I wished that David were there to dismantle the minister with easy wit and metropolitan cleverness, but, it being barely ten in the morning, David hadn't yet risen from bed. It wasn't, of course, that I couldn't address Aldridge's banalities myself – my fear was that I couldn't do so without becoming indignant, shrill and generally uncivilised.

I opened my mouth to say something that would, no doubt, have been unwise, but I was interrupted by a slow triple knock at the outer door.

Aldridge ignored it. Aldridge employed, in his tall house in Withy Passageway, a maid, and so for him knocks at the door were a thing customarily dealt with by others. He continued to watch me attentively. He was a man not readily diverted from his purpose.

We, however, had no maid. Indeed we had no staff of any kind. With a pray-remain-seated gesture to Harriet, who had set her hands on her chair arms preparatory to rising, I put aside my tea and rose.

'One moment,' I said.

'Of course.' Aldridge indulged me.

In the hallway Josephus the cat sidled about my ankles. As I negotiated his slinkings I prayed that the visitor at the door would occupy me for far longer than *one moment* – that he might be, say, a local with news of an osprey sighted off the shore or a sand shark caught in a trawlerman's net. They knew, the shore folk of Gravely, that news of such freaks and phenomena was always to be brought urgently to the door of Mr Lowell, who could then be relied upon to add greatly to the gaiety of village life by squeaking some sort of excited exclamation ('Good golly!', 'Great heavens!'), dashing into the back parlour, and emerging, pink-faced and dishevelled, with a butterfly net, or a pair of binoculars, or a rock-pooling hook, or a satchel of jars and cases, or most probably some clattering and unwieldy combination of three or more such objects, and making a beeline at speed for the beach.

But as soon as I saw the high, sloped shoulders of the silhouette visible through the door's window-glass I knew that this was not a local man.

*

For all his formidable physical bulk, it was the eyes of Maurice Shakes that most strongly commanded the attention. They were his daughters' eyes. He sat on a stool in our drawing room (for we had run out of chairs) and cupped a teacup in the palm of his hand. It looked utterly incongruous, like a paper hat on a bull or a baby's rattle in the hands of a tamed bear. He wore a suit of pearl-grey broadcloth, a wide-brimmed black hat and a blue cotton scarf. When he smiled – as he did repeatedly, showing slab-like grey teeth – his eyes were lost in a morass of crow's feet and unkempt eyebrow. But when he wasn't smiling his eyes were enormous and tea-brown. Like Eleanor and Cordelia, he had a baby's eyes.

He had come, he said, to pay a neighbourly visit. He had heard of me, from the 'folks' thereabouts – and had heard, too, that the local minister was also to be found at the cottage – and hated to pass up an opportunity to pay his respects to a minister.

All this in a thick, foresty, smiling Yankee baritone. Of course I had ushered him in. He had paused in the hall for a full two minutes to tousle the bobbing head of Josephus the cat.

'Mr Lowell has been entertaining us,' said Aldridge now, 'with some details of oceanography. He tells us that the North Sea is – *how* deep did you say it was, Mr Lowell, at its deepest extremity?'

As I child I was not good at dealing with teasing. Now I dug a fingernail into my palm and mildly answered: 'Four hundred fathoms.'

Shakes turned a broad grin on me.

'Is that so, sir? "Fifteen cubits upward did the waters prevail, and the mountains were covered." You gentlemen will surely know: how deep *is* fifteen cubits?'

'Less than four fathoms,' I supplied with a smile. 'Shallower than the sea just offshore here.'

'Deep enough to float an ark, though, sir,' he joshed back at me.

Aldridge, stirred into a rare sincerity, leaned forwards in his chair and said: 'You know your Scripture, Mr Shakes.'

'That I do,' Shakes nodded. 'I'm a student – though I believe a poor one – of all the literatures of the world.' He pronounced *literatures* as four full syllables: *lidder, itchers*.

'Then it's a great pity,' said Aldridge, making his thin face mournful, 'that you weren't able to come along to our service yesterday.'

'No doubt, no doubt.' Shakes smiled.

Harriet piped up to say that Mr Aldridge had taught a marvellous lesson from the story of the prophet Jonah and the great fish prepared by the Lord to swallow him up.

Shakes scratched at a grey-bristled jowl.

'What *is* the lesson of Jonah?' he asked. 'That would be very interesting to know.'

'Redemption,' said Harriet.

'God's love,' added Aldridge with an oily sort of authority. 'God's love for the sinners of Nineveh, a love such that he restored life to the dead Jonah and summoned him from the bowels of the great fish to go to Nineveh and preach God's word.'

I had forgotten, myself, that Jonah *died* within the great fish. But Shakes showed no surprise.

'Indeed, Reverend, indeed.' He nodded, thoughtful beneath the shadow of his hat. 'A great love most surely, I suppose. To draw a dead man from a fish's belly, and restore to him his life.'

'Indeed,' Aldridge echoed.

'But I wonder.' Shakes turned his teacup through a quarter-circle in his palm. 'I wonder at something, Reverend Aldridge. You see, there was a man I knew, not all that many years ago, in a town called New Bedford, back in Massachusetts. A pretty town. A whalers' town. The bar-rooms smelt of whale blubber 'cause they burned it in their lamps. This man was a friend of mine, and he worked a whaling ship.'

I exchanged a glance with Harriet. She was a shore person; she had a keen eye for changes in the weather. And I was a student of clouds.

'The ship, in the cold spring of eighteen ninety-five, sailed to the South Atlantic,' Shakes went on, sharing his innocent gaze with each of the four of us in turn, 'and in the lee of the Falkland Islands the lookout spied a whale, broaching the surface two miles to the starboard. The whaling boats set out boldly in pursuit – and my friend, Mr Lowell, Reverend, ladies, was right there among them.'

Aldridge's eyes were wide with excitement at the yarn. He was leaning forwards intently and again without noticing he had dunked the tip of his long beard in his tea.

'They met with the beast?' he prompted.

'Indeed!' Shakes chuckled. 'Indeed they did, and at first it seemed sure, most sure, that it was the whale who would have the better of the encounter: he was a great fish, a mighty fish. He flailed in fury and the sea boiled. But the harpoons bit deep and the whale grew tired, and they knew, the brave men of New Bedford, that the fight would soon be done with, and the officer readied his lance.

'Then with one dying swipe of his great black flukes the whale tossed one of the boats high up in the air, and the sailors all spilled into the blood-red sea.'

Aldridge gasped like a little boy. I looked at Eleanor. She was quite composed. She wasn't watching her father. Instead, she stared out of the window, seeming to watch the herring gulls yelping on the neighbours' chimneys. I supposed that she had heard the tale before.

'And your friend?'

'He fell into the sea,' said Shakes, 'and was swallowed by the whale.'

A sort of thrilled giggle escaped the Reverend Aldridge. I heard a slow, quiet sigh from across the room – Eleanor, still watching the window.

Shakes drank what remained of his tea and set the cup carefully on the carpet before he resumed.

'I was there,' he said, 'when they cut that damn whale open, for I, Reverend Aldridge, was aboard that whaler, too. From the second boat I watched my friend fall into the water. When, with the whale slain, we couldn't find him, well, we supposed he'd simply drowned, and we each after our fashion said a simple prayer for his soul – for whaling men are simple men.

'Then, on the deck of the *White Star*, we dug that whale open. With spades, you see – you use spades to break open a whale, you dig into its blubber like you'd dig into the earth. And in due time we reached the whale's gut, and, in due time, we found, as you will have guessed, my friend.

'I saw his body fall from the whale's rent belly. It lay on its back on the blood-drenched deck. An eye was missing from his face. The other eye stared up at us. It said, "Your prayers, friends, did me no good." The acids of the whale's gut had burned his skin, not like the sun burns it or even like the burning of a fire. His skin was as white as paper, and wrinkled, like an old man's, though my friend was barely twenty years of age. And the worst, the worst of all: his fingers were all broken, at the middle knuckle, and they were caked in the stinking grime of the whale's belly-lining. For he had been alive, this man who was my friend – he had been alive in the belly of the great fish. He had clawed at the walls of that foul prison until his fingernails split and his knuckles broke.

'I remember the sound, all along the line of whaling men with their blubber-spades, of vomit spattering on the deck,' Shakes said. He was speaking only to Aldridge now. The squeamish Reverend had covered his mouth daintily with his fingertips.

'There are ladies present, sir,' he said in a muffled tone.

'A lady can stomach the truth as well as any man, Reverend.' Shakes smiled. 'In any case I'm coming to the meat of the matter. *I* wasn't sick. I always had a robust constitution. But something else was vomited up from me, as I looked down on my friend's dead body – I was purged, in that moment, not of the day's breakfast, but, Reverend Aldridge, of my faith. My *faith*, sir.'

Aldridge regarded him with an expression that seemed quite spent of feeling.

He said: 'I'm sorry to hear that.' As though a local lady had told him that she had lost her pet cat or a small boy had told him he had lost a ha'penny.

'So you may carry on,' Shakes said, 'telling your nursery stories about men who emerge from the bellies of whales preaching the glory of the God that put them there. You may carry on, as you please, telling tales of the saved and forgetting the lost, though it's a question of one to a thousand, by my guess. But don't ask me, Reverend Aldridge, to come and listen to your tales. Don't ask me to share your slavery. Don't ask me,' he finished, still smiling (he had not stopped smiling), 'to pray to your goddamn murdering God.'

He tipped his hat to us, thanked us for the tea and our company, and left. We all sat quite still for a moment. I watched a bead of tea drop from the reverend's beard and make a brown coin on his trouser leg.

'The man is an absolute Ahab,' he said weakly, mustering a smile.

For a moment, replete with pity, I almost liked him.

Following, then, in Shakes's wake into the hall, I found a tableau: by the door the huge American, once again bent double, murmuring endearments and tousling the black fur of Josephus the cat, and, on the stairs, paused in bleary-eyed puzzlement, David McAllister, tieless and open-collared.

And then that night, in the bedroom, as we undressed for bed, Harriet remarked that I had found in Mr Shakes something of a kindred spirit, though rather a fierce one.

'Any kindred spirit of mine would have known that a whale is no *great fish*,' I said.

He was the same. He was no better. His letters: 'I must say Captain Rickard seems a very sound sort of fellow. A real gent I must say and he always does his bit and is always very fair to us lads even if sometimes he has to take us to task! You can understand how it is Harriet. We do crab about the top brass I know but they are here doing a job just the same. Captain Rickard does seem the best of the lot I must say. You know he played cricket for his county, I shouldn't like to face him out in the middle I must say! He is a big fellow, bigger than me even though he has brains too. I think we are in safe hands Harriet with him in charge.'

Rickard this, Rickard that. And look how that turned out.

I don't know which of them to watch. The reverend making a fool of himself. This is a man who talks to God every day, or reckons to. Look at him now, like a schoolboy in morning assembly.

And Jon. Not quite so daft-looking but not far off, and it's worse with him because he's my husband.

And they're both clever men! This is the thing. We've seen that, with their jabbing at one another – I mean, Miss Shakes has seen that, and I'm glad about that, I'm glad she's seen how bright Jon is, even if him and the reverend don't always see eye to eye – I'm glad she saw that before she saw this.

'They met with the beast?'

Reverend Aldridge – like a little lad having a serial from a comic read to him. Glance across at Eleanor Shakes and she's looking out the window. Bored. I ought to feel bad because I'm the hostess but I don't feel like the hostess any more. That's men for you. Get a few of them together and you've no chance.

Jon's watching himself. Inside I reckon he's agog just like the reverend but he knows a little bit better because he's watching himself and he's not letting his eyes go wide or his jaw go slack and he's not – oh, goodness – dipping his chin in his blasted tea.

This is it, with men. If I was some silly lass maybe I'd be appalled. The scales would fall from my eyes! But I already know what they're like. They've always been daft – daft in some ways, and in other ways brave and handsome and bright and good, but daft underneath.

Jon's got it about right. Daft enough to go running about the fields with his butterfly net for all to see. Bright enough to watch himself – to know how daft he is.

Reverend Aldridge doesn't watch himself at all and I suppose that's why he's a minister. You can't say it's a bad thing. It's just love, really.

'This has been a hard week Harriet I can tell you that. If Captain Rickard wasn't such a brick I don't know how we would have stuck it. But we did stick it and who knows what the coming weeks will bring, whatever it is we are ready. But he (Captain Rickard) is a brave fellow I must say.'

Him and his rifle and his country and his Captain Rickard. Jon and his butterflies. The reverend and his God. And now this fat fellow spouting about heaven knows what. A good posture and a big voice and a way with words and an overdose of self-confidence – well, it's girls that are supposed to lose their heads in the face of that, but as far as I've ever seen it's fellers more than us that can't help themselves. To call a spade a spade it's seduction, plain and simple. Only they don't get 'ruined' or in the family way or what have you. They do things like going off to war. 'Great men.' They're a menace. Look at Kitchener. That swine.

Eleanor beside me a model of forbearance, and it's funny, looking at her, knowing her (even if only a little bit), thinking that she came out of him. So to speak. But then these things are never how you expect. These things often work out funny – if they work out at all.

He's got them on a ruddy string. Putting the cat among the pigeons and no mistake. Makes a habit of it, I expect. Thinking like your mother again: Trouble, this one. *But Miss Shakes here lets it all drift by like it was nothing but a light sea breeze.*

V

'Why don't we swim?' said David.

'Swim?' We were bare-footed on the rocks below Priory Bluff. 'I haven't a costume.'

He laughed.

'I know. Neither have I. I mean – you know. In the altogether.' He grinned at the foolishness of the phrase. 'There's no one around.'

'*You're* around.'

'Ah, come now, Lowell. Let's have none of your slum prudery.' He slipped his tie through its knot and began unbuttoning his shirt.

I'd never seen him naked. I'd never seen anyone naked, as far as I could remember – anyone male, that is, and grown-up. I'd seen Harriet naked a lot of times. And of course there had been plenty of nudity at school in Bradford: underfed bare boys with their ribs showing, pushing and shoving and yelling and whipping wet towels on cold floor tiles. You couldn't avoid it even if you didn't really go in for sport.

I stood, shaking my head with a wry smile fixed on my face, as David quickly stripped. His body was as pale and slender as a schoolboy's. I watched him limp over the barnacle-rough rocks to the edge of the sea, and cautiously dip his right foot.

'Oof. Bloody hell,' I heard him say.

'I'll stick with the rock pools,' I called to him. 'Rock pools are warmer.'

Over his shoulder he smiled: 'Sod you and your tame seas.'

He stumbled out up to his knees and then half-dived, half-fell head first into the water. He swam three body-lengths entirely submerged. I could see his white body, marbled and refracted, undulating like a flatworm. Then his drenched blond head broke the surface.

I turned away. I was here, after all, to work.

We had walked perhaps two hundred yards out across the spit of uneven rocks that reached out into the sea at the foot of Priory Bluff. My satchel and net were propped against the steep wall of the bluff. Between them and where I now stood was a trench that I thought of, with private joviality, as the Challenger Deep. It was the largest rock pool in the bay, though even from where I stood I could see clear to the bottom. A good-sized shore crab was sidling across the sand. Red anemones in full venomous bloom crowded the waterline.

I hopped the Deep adroitly – it wasn't more than three feet wide – and took up my satchel. I wasn't concerned, today, with the Challenger Deep. In a letter I'd received that morning my editor had asked me for a piece on birdlife – in fact, he had asked for 'fewer bloody invertebrates, Mr Lowell', if I would be so good – so my business was not in the rock pools but, rather, up on the bluff itself.

From the seaward side, the slope to the top could be scrambled up easily enough. I pulled my boots on over my wet bare feet and picked my way round to where the gradient was least challenging.

The wind from the sea gusted up the back of my jacket and carried to me the sound of David shouting something, I couldn't hear what, as I clambered through the loose soil and sparse grasses of the bluff. If I looked back, I knew, vertigo would overcome me. Even as it was, the high blue unoccupied sky was enough to produce a painful quiver of unease in my perineum.

At the top I rose carefully to my feet, feeling my way into this new air, this new altitude. I had always been that way – every new position had always called for a reassessment, a recalibration.

I looked down at the rocks and the sea. David was doing the Australian crawl through the gentle swell perhaps twenty yards out. Where the rocks met the beach, herring gulls were gathering around some luckless dead or dying thing – a crab, a bird, a rabbit that had strayed from the dunes. Pipits danced between the rock pools.

I had known this place, at least by name, for years. When I was a young boy my parents took me on holidays to the seaside very regularly. Usually we'd go to guest houses in Bridlington, or Flamborough (where I was very taken with the lighthouse), or Filey, and from road signs and local talk I picked up a limited but evocative vocabulary of place names further up the coast: Runswick, Ravenscar, Scalby, Saltburn, Gravely. I never supposed that I would end up married to a Gravely girl. And if you had told me that I would be, I wouldn't have cared, except that I might have been excited to think that we would be able to live together by the sea, and together go rock-pooling.

Above me an Arctic tern called *ee-ahh*. I looked up, watched it bob swallowtailed on the updraught from the bluff as if on elastic until it bobbed out of sight beyond the priory wall, and then looked instead at the priory. It had not been whole, not been anything but a ruin, since the last King Henry had had his way with it. Lichen, moss, bramble and the patient work of earthworms had subsumed it. There were four walls, still, or at least four sets of buttresses, but no roof above, and nothing within the walls but rubble, fungus, slow-growing brambles, a gypsy's derelict fire, a mouldy smell of pigeon mutes. There was neither frame nor glass in the huge east window, only sea and sky. Between the foot of that east wall and the brink of the bluff a hawthorn grew; attached to the hawthorn was a fable.

I approached it now and gingerly fingered the thorny lower branches. The berries already looked dark, withered and pinched, though it was barely mid-September. Most of the leaves had been whipped from their stems by the sea wind; many lay heaped in a damp drift against the priory wall. When the wind gusted, the drift of leaves shifted with an uneasy sigh, as though the drift were a blanket and the sleeper beneath had rolled over in his bed.

Like any hawthorn on a hill, the tree was crooked as a crippled man. In Gravely they knew this as the nun's hawthorn.

It was in the twelfth century, I had been told many times, that the monks of Gravely Priory arrived here. They were Cistercians: hard men, severe men, who worshipped a stern God. They came here to suffer and they suffered indeed. How near they were, here, to their fearful God – to the teeth and claws of the wind and rain and sea.

If the suffering of these foolish monks were all there was to this fable it would have been a bleak enough tale. But there was more suffering to it than that.

It was in the days of that wanton King Henry that a young woman found her way to the Gravely Priory. A rainy night, as the storyteller usually has it. She was, she told the hard-faced prior, a daughter of Barnoldswick. She had been visited by visions of the Christ, and of the Virgin; she had been called to Gravely Priory, and to Gravely she had walked, bearing on her back the sins of her pagan forefathers – and she would, if the good brothers would take her in, devote her life, from that day forth, to penitence and to the service of almighty God.

The good brothers took her in. For all the closeness of the sea and sky, these men had strayed far from their God.

What uses they made of her, this girl, what penances they extracted from her virgin pagan flesh, varied from storyteller to storyteller (all that was consistent was the relish with which the storyteller dwelt on the wickedness). What was agreed – what was, one might say, canonical – was that, after her ruined body had been cast into the priory yard and a spadeful of dirt thrown over it, a hawthorn sprouted on the spot.

It had never seemed to me to be much of a memorial. I turned from the tree and looked out across the bay. From here, the harbour – a thrush's nest of chiming masts incompletely encircled by a retaining sea wall – looked fragile, painfully so, fearfully so.

The sea before it might swallow it so easily. From here, to me, the harbour seemed a bold and needless venturing forth.

From the rocks below, where he was climbing naked out of the water, David shouted: 'Madam! Avert your eyes! My shame!'

I could hear the smile in his voice. I turned and saw Eleanor Shakes approaching along the bluff edge.

*

I greeted this Miss Shakes with a courtly 'good morning'. She was dressed in a suit of soft tweed, tan court shoes and a brown-banded hat. She smiled and bade me the same in return. We pretended that we were simply not aware of David McAllister clambering into his trousers down on the rocks.

'And what brings you,' I ventured, 'to this blasted promontory?'

She shrugged lightly and looked out at the sea.

'I enjoy the view.'

'Perhaps we could walk a little?' I suggested. In the periphery of my vision I could see David hopping with one shoe on and the other off, and I could hear him swearing at his shoelaces; I did not trust myself to be able to keep a straight face if we stayed at that spot.

Eleanor Shakes assented, and took my arm. Her fingernails were unpainted and convex. When I drew aside a low-trailing branch of the hawthorn so that she might pass by – and she thanked me with another smile – I thought of telling her the tale of that abject priory tree. But, I supposed, it was no story for a gentleman to tell a girl. Besides, she had no doubt heard a sufficiency of savage stories from her strange, smiling, heathen father.

Rather at a loss for words as we walked along the bluff edge out to sea, I dared to ask: 'Were you here on Sunday? Around lunchtime. It was a beastly day – but I was down on the rocks, hunting for specimens, and I saw, or I believe I saw—'

'Not me.' She shook her head and over the smell of the sea I smelt a mild perfume. 'My father, and my sister. You've met my sister, I believe – she spoke of you. You and your friend Mr McAllister.'

I glanced at her but there was no *innuendo* in her expression. Instead she was looking out to sea.

'Yes. Yes, we ran into her.'

Did American sisters speak to one another of their boyfriends, their sex lives? Did *English* sisters? For that matter, did anyone? I hadn't spoken to David about that night on the beach. I would have been surprised if he had spoken about it to me – although not perhaps as surprised as all that.

'I was up here the day before,' Eleanor said. We were approaching the point of the bluff, and we dawdled, blinking into the trade wind. Eleanor held on to her hat with her free hand. 'My father likes to bring us up here. He likes to talk about his – his *vision*.'

'Miss Shakes – your sister, I mean – mentioned a dream.'

'Yes. You must think him an extraordinary man.'

'I—'

'He *is* extraordinary, of course. Anyone with eyes in his head can see that.' She looked up at me from beneath her trembling hat brim. 'I'm sorry for the way he tossed and gored your minister yesterday. He has – strong feelings about these things.'

'He isn't *my* minister.'

She looked, I thought, a little put out by that. Her expression suggested that I had been rude but, even if I had, I was surely still some way to the credit side of *goddamn murdering God* and what have you.

'Your town's minister, then.'

'That I can't deny. But I shouldn't worry, Miss Shakes. Our reverend is perhaps more resilient than you imagine.'

'He may have to be,' she said. There was a minerality in her voice;

something like the rub of a thumb across a flint-face in the *h* of 'have'.

I began to say something horribly humble about having perhaps spoken out of turn, or having caused inadvertent offence, quite without meaning to, *quite quite without* – but all at once Eleanor Shakes was smiling again, a smile that wasn't (I thought) wholly without derision. Perhaps she had wanted me to have been a little bruised, at least, by her father's rampage. Perhaps she was not as sorry as she had said (perhaps she had sensed that *I* was not sorry at all to have seen Aldridge so rambunctiously mauled).

'My father,' Eleanor said, turning her face again to the sea, 'lost his brother. It affected him profoundly.'

I murmuringly observed that all losses of that sort must do so. Then Eleanor said: 'You have a very beautiful wife.'

The non sequitur left me unable to think of anything to say except, with ghastly proprietorial pride, that yes, indeed I had.

There was a sudden noise behind us; together we turned. David, open-collared and unsocked, pink in the face and breathless, was scrambling to the brink of the escarpment. On reaching the level ground he straightened and with a somewhat dramatic gesture brushed his wet hair from his brow: flying motes of seawater glittered in the chalky sunlight.

'Good day, Miss Shakes!' he grinned.

Eleanor nudged me lightly and unexpectedly in the ribs.

'Is this Mr Mallory,' she said in a stage whisper, 'or Mr Irvine?'

David laughed, but only, I could see, because he had to. I laughed in earnest.

My father wore a black armband over the sleeve of his tweed coat on the day we read that Mallory and Irvine had been lost on Everest. I was still seated at the breakfast table; Father was leaving for the library, and paused self-consciously at the dining-room door to straighten a crease in the black crêpe. As he took up his briefcase he looked at me, nodded, and said: 'Brave men.

England's lost two of its best.'

I watched him go. I had a lump in my throat.

Later that morning, over tea with David in the refectory of the technical college, I repeated – like an actor mouthing another's words – my father's grave sentiment. David, chewing on a mouthful of toast, had looked at me sardonically.

'Balls,' he said, on swallowing. 'Mallory was a bloody good climber I suppose, but it doesn't take a bloody hero to die on Everest. A bloody *idiot* can die on Everest.'

He took another bite out of his slice of toast. I sipped at my taupe-coloured tea. I wanted to follow David's lead (I always did), but the thing was that I was sad about Mallory. Irvine, too, though less so. Of course neither of *us* had ever met either of *them* but we knew them through the newspapers. I say that you can know a person through the newspapers and know them well enough to grieve for them.

'Hard on their people, though,' I suggested diffidently.

'Life is hard,' David said. He was finished with his breakfast now. He had pushed back his chair and was standing up, pulling on his blazer. I didn't say anything – I just watched him gather up his watch, notebook, the keys to the groundsman's hut. His cricket bag was packed and ready by the door.

He paused before he headed out. He looked annoyed. He put one hand on the back of a chair and the other on his hip.

'I know I must sound like I don't give a damn,' he said, rather fiercely. 'I see that. It isn't true, of course – it *is* hard for their people, isn't it?'

I nodded mutely, and David, encouraged, nodded back.

'Of course it is. But all the same, life *is* hard, and terrible things *will* happen – and to put it quite simply we haven't got *time* to cry and wear black armbands, Jon, because we've got things to do ourselves.' He seized the straps of his bag and straightened up. 'See you tomorrow.'

He went out. The door banged. I half-turned to see him pass the window: the cricket bag like a child's coffin hoisted on his shoulder, the wind stirring up his uncombed hair.

Now he shrugged off Eleanor Shakes's derision and stepped forwards to offer her his hand. They hadn't, he said as she took it, been properly introduced; they hadn't, Eleanor rejoined, previously met.

'But I've heard a lot about the two enigmatic American ladies who have taken Mr Lowell's village by storm,' David said, 'and, as you aren't the one I *have* met, you must be the one I haven't. Seeing as you aren't Cordelia, you must be Eleanor.'

Eleanor acknowledged that this was so.

'This is David McAllister,' I said, mostly for the sake of the thing. 'You may know his novels.'

'No,' smiled Eleanor, 'but it's a real pleasure to meet you, Mr McAllister.'

David, though now as pincushioned with darts as Saint Sebastian, continued to smile, there on the bluff edge.

'This vision—' I began.

'My father can tell you about it himself. In fact just you try *stop*ping him. Here he comes. I can feel the ground trembling.'

And indeed we saw, looking back towards the mainland, that Maurice Shakes, immense in a charcoal greatcoat and carrying a shoulder-high staff, was picking his way towards us through the shadows of the priory.

'Gentlemen, gentlemen, gentlemen,' he cried, lifting his black hat.

Shakes's approach startled a woodcock from its hiding place in the brambles. The fearful bird burst into the air in a drama of panicked wings, climbing with a clatter into the safe pale blue of the sky above the ancient stones.

No one else paid any attention to it. I looked at David, who was watching Shakes come nearer. From his face I inferred that if he could have flown from the bluff, as the woodcock had flown, he would have done so at that moment.

Might I have quite liked Cordelia, if Mother hadn't been with me?

I'd certainly have felt more ready to admire the sit of her stocking-silk about her ankle, and perhaps even to ask how she got her eyebrows so full and dark. I might have quite liked her. But we'll never know now, will we?

It's different when there's someone else there. It's like being in the music hall when there's a turn on and there's a friend sitting beside you who doesn't find it the slightest bit funny – even though, if you were on your own, you know you'd be screaming with laughter, you somehow can't manage to even raise a smile. It's spoilt somehow.

This was the same, only instead of the poor comedian with a striped suit and a thin moustache, looking out at a sea of stony faces, it's this Cordelia Shakes looking at us, me and Mother – her with a face like she's sucking a pickle and me looking like goodness knows what.

Not much of a welcoming party.

We ran into her on the high street. We'd been shopping – I had a bag of crabs and fish bits, Mother a roll of lace and a pound of bread flour, and we were heading back towards the coast road. I was on my way to see the minister. We'd arranged to meet for tea. There were a few things I wanted to talk about. Some Scripture things; some village things.

And here she was: one of the village things.

I noticed her, of course. Hadn't the first idea who she was but I did wonder about what Jon'd said the other day, about the theatrical couple on the cliff. She wasn't doing anything theatrical – she was just walking along – but I thought, looking at her, that if she was ever minded to be theatrical she certainly had the face for it. The figure, too.

I heard Mother's 'tut'.

But then it was her *that stopped* me. *It was one thing with Eleanor because at least she knew me a bit from church. Cordelia didn't know me from Eve, but here she was, laying a gloveless hand on my forearm and saying: 'Pardon me, but is it – would you be Mrs Lowell, by any chance?'*

She said she recognised me from her sister's description. She said her sister had been talking about a blonde lady named Mrs Lowell with the most dazzlingly beautiful blue eyes and – 'My gosh,' she said – there couldn't be more than one set of eyes like that in this little town.

Well, you know what Americans are like, and it's not like no one's ever paid me a compliment before. But I could almost feel my head getting bigger under my hat. Mother lost for words, at least for the minute. 'I gather our father behaved abominably yesterday,' she said. She smiled when she said it, like some mothers smile when they talk about how little Timmy pulled poor Margery's pigtails.

This one I could imagine being that man's child. The physical resemblance was there in the eyes and the proportions of the profile, but it was more than that. What would you call it, that look they both had about them? Daring, maybe – but no, not daring, because you can't be daring when you can't see the danger, and that's the look they both had, the look of just not seeing *the danger – a kind of innocence, in a roundabout sort of way.*

But the Shakeses are hardly alone in that. Our own David McAllister, by that measure, might have been this girl's brother.

We'd been avoiding each other like folk in a French farce, me and him. Me abed when he and Jon came home; he not yet stirring the next morning, until after Mr Shakes made his big exit, and then Jon sent him back upstairs to dress properly, so as to avoid frightening the ladies – so it wasn't till all the Shakeses had left that I had the pleasure.

It was a pleasure, too. I know his sort, all right. But still you can't say it's not good fun meeting a nice-looking young fellow with a bit of dash and charm. I'd choose Jon over him any day of the week, but still.

We didn't say all that much to one another. Him with the compliments: me, the house, the town. Me with the heard-so-much-about-yous. I liked him, I think.

Much as I might've liked this Cordelia, given half a chance.

'Thinks summat of herself, that one,' Mother said once we'd bidden Miss Shakes goodbye. 'Americans for you. What a lot of flannel.'

I didn't say anything. She looked sideways at me. I didn't look at her but out of the corner of my eye I could see her looking me up and down.

'There but for the grace of God,' she said, half-laughing.

Normally it's there but for the grace of God go I *but it wasn't that, it was* you, *it was* there but for the grace of God go you. *Loud and clear.*

VI

A foaming blue Atlantic, a robin's-egg sky, a merry smell of fried food, the strident and quavering music of a barrel organ. Laughter, sailors' songs, delighted screams from the daredevils riding on the Mangels machinery. It was easy to picture, when one heard Maurice Shakes speak of it.

We sat on the bluff, me and David and Shakes, in the teeth of the autumn easterly. Eleanor had been dispatched home to the terraced house that the family rented at the north extremity of the village. As the three of us talked, a bottle of rye whisky, drawn with a wink from an inner pocket of Shakes's greatcoat, passed back and forth between us.

'And you propose to rebuild this paradise here at Gravely?' I prompted.

'I do, gentlemen.' Shakes nodded heavily, staring out across the bay.

David laughed lightly, emboldened by the rye. There had been no mention of Cordelia, of moonlit fornications in the sand – he felt safe, therefore.

'This is not Coney Island, Mr Shakes,' he said.

Shakes grinned, and swigged from the bottle.

'Once, Mr McAllister, Coney Island was nothing but a Puritans' village and a stretch of barren beach,' he chided gently. 'And I tell you so true, for I knew it then. And I know what it became, too.' He nodded again, and repeated the syllables as though they were sacred: 'Co-ney Is-land.'

This, to my surprise, was Shakes's dream. In my imaginings he had come to Gravely to write a rollicking novel of seafarers, or perhaps to invest misguidedly in some new chophouse, brewery or railway enterprise. Not so. Instead, he had seen in his dream a pleasure ground, here on our remote and rocky shore.

'A pleasure ground,' he had said, 'such as these storied ocean kingdoms have never known.'

I had told him that there was a rather grand pavilion at Brighton, on the south coast, and that there were notable piers, much in use for promenading and such, at Blackpool, Hastings and Cromer.

He hadn't really responded. Instead he had made a rumbling noise of assent in the back of his throat and murmured: 'A pier, yes. There will be, sir, a pier.'

Across the bay the harbour looked ever more fragile. A light burned aboard a moored trawler, for dusk was gathering, and it seemed to me a flame preserved in cupped hands.

Something, perhaps the raw rye whisky, made me ask: 'Your daughter – Miss Shakes, I mean – *Eleanor*, I mean – mentioned a younger brother.'

Shakes frowned.

'Yes,' he said. 'A brother, a younger brother.' He looked sideways at me – I sat to his left – and his eyes widened in a momentary show of anger. 'My *excuse*, sir. In my daughter's eyes the gallant death of Lawrence Shakes is my *excuse* for behaving as monstrously, as irreligiously, as I am known to do.'

'I am sorry,' I muttered, 'to have spoken of it.'

'My displeasure is not with you,' Shakes said. 'And you shouldn't be sorry to speak of my brother, Mr Lowell, for in spite of everything he was a gentle and kind man.' He smiled down at the mouth of the whisky bottle. 'I'd be glad, by God I'd be *proud*, to tell you of him – only I'm afraid, sirs, I've already wasted enough of your time.'

'Our time,' said the courtly David McAllister, 'seems a fair exchange for your good whisky.'

Shakes laughed, and said: 'This isn't any good whisky.' He took another mouthful, wiped his mouth on his cuff and, sighing, passed the bottle back to me.

'The war took Lawrence,' he said.

I glanced across at David. Not only Lawrence Shakes but George McAllister, David's father, too – plus the many thousands besides.

David only said: 'It took such a lot.'

'Indeed, sir. I'm sure you fellows, too, suffered greatly in that forsaken time. The war told a million sad stories. But Lawrence's story – the story, I mean, of me and Lawrence, the story that ended with my brother dead in a Montfaucon ditch – that story began a little way before. When in the springtime of nineteen-fourteen Lawrence met a girl named Grace Derbyshire.'

'Another marriage,' suggested David, 'sundered by the conflict?'

Shakes shook his head.

'Not quite.'

My own parents' marriage survived the war but not the peace. My mother died in the autumn of 1918, from the Spanish influenza. I was twelve.

I remember her perfectly well, of course – a busy, fretful, nervous woman, lean-bodied, with a frizz of brown hair and dark-pink hands – but the picture of her that predominates in my mind was taken a year before I was born. It is of my parents on their wedding day: they stand side by side, arm in arm, awkward and unsmiling in the light of the brand-new century. My veiled mother looks terribly young. In my father's face I see my own face.

'Lawrence and Grace were never married,' Shakes said. 'They were engaged, it's true, properly, formally, and with all appropriate consent and what have you – but they were never married.'

'The war intervened, I suppose,' I said.

'Not quite,' Shakes said. Slowly, stupidly, I began to understand that this was not a story about the war.

Still, even in 1928, there weren't very many things that were not, in some way, about the war. We were all, it was supposed, foundering in its wreckage. David, when he spoke of the writers with whom he unenthusiastically mixed in London, could be scathing on the subject. That morning, indeed, as we walked to the beach, he had spoken sourly of Wells and Woolf, Lewis and Eliot – of their high-minded and precious pessimism.

'A bunch of bloody gloomsters,' he had said. 'Grieving for the loss of their beloved *civilisation*. Not one of them with the wit or imagination to look beyond the bloody newspaper headlines.'

Even in the far north-east we had not escaped. The Reverend Aldridge, no less than David's gloomsters, was prey to an overpowering anxiety for this same civilisation, and was wont, I gathered, to harp on the matter rather fearsomely in his sermons. Christendom, by the minister's reckoning, hung in the balance; the peoples of the West, I had heard him say, stood on the brink of downfall.

David, of course, would have none of it. He had things to do himself.

'Grace fell pregnant,' Shakes said.

I felt myself colouring and despised myself for it.

'Unfortunate,' David said carefully.

Shakes snorted.

'Unfortunate? The conjuring of life, unfortunate, Mr McAllister? The flowering of a young couple's physical love, unfortunate?'

'Inconvenient, then.'

Shakes laughed, and nodded.

'Indeed, but not how you might think, sir. The Derbyshires were a freethinking family – and if they hadn't been, well,

Grace wouldn't have given a good goddamn. They could've been Cabots or Vanderbilts or Lowells and she wouldn't have cared, that girl Grace – saving your presence, Mr Lowell,' he added with a weary chuckle.

'The Bradford Lowells are a cadet branch at best,' I managed.

'I'm sure they're a more honourable family than our Boston neighbours. But what I meant, gentlemen, was this: the baby, Grace's blameless baby, was an inconvenience to no one but my brother.'

He stopped. We sat in silence. What could be said? It was perhaps five o'clock. Down on the half-submerged rocks three redshank started up a raucous bickering.

'My brother,' Shakes said eventually, 'quailed.'

'A child is a great responsibility,' I offered.

'It is a *gift*, sir. It's a goddamn *privilege*.'

The whisky bottle was four-fifths empty. I wondered if the whisky – this whisky – was the only drink Shakes had drunk today.

David stepped in: 'Your brother did not welcome the baby?'

'He did not, sir, he did not. My brother was a coward. From his home in Plymouth, he fled, to me, to my home, my very home, there in Bedford. On my doorstep I found him standing in tears.'

Again a silence, a stage pause.

I provided the cue: 'And what was your counsel?'

'I ordered him – for our folks were passed on, and I was the elder brother – to go back, goddammit! To return to Plymouth, to go back to Grace. To face the consequences of his actions, like a man.'

David said: 'He refused. You told him again, and still he refused.'

'That's right.'

'And when you saw that he would not comply, perhaps *could* not—'

Shakes interrupted him with a hoarse sigh.

'If only he had, if only he had,' he said. He reached up and removed his broad-brimmed black hat. Turning it over in his hands as he spoke, he said: 'I told him, gentlemen, that he was a coward.

I told him, however, that he was my brother yet – he was my little brother Larry, yet.' He lifted the hat and for a long second held it over his face. Then he resettled it on his head and gruffly, shortly said: 'I told him I would handle the business. I would make sure that everything was seen to. On one condition. On condition that he prove himself no coward. On condition that he enlist.'

And with those words the war rose up before us once again.

I never cared for world affairs. My business was always with birds and butterflies – that is, I saw to it that those things were my business. I couldn't, therefore, side with those who saw, in the complex patterns of diplomacy, democracy, politics and war an impending disaster, an inevitable doom – and yet nor could I, with David McAllister, shrug off the pessimism that in the wake of the war overtook the Western world like a sea fret.

I was afraid. Indeed, I think that I was always afraid. I think that I have always been afraid.

'And so he enlisted, and died,' David said gently.

'He did, he did. Montfaucon.'

'My father,' David said. 'Mons.'

'Uh-hm, uh-hm,' murmured Shakes in a tone of agreement.

I, having no lost soldier to mourn, looked out to sea, noting a cormorant, another yawing trawler approaching the harbour, the unbroken stratus cloud stretching to the horizon, until David, recalling himself to himself, said: 'Your pleasure ground, then – it will allow you, perhaps, to forget your grief – or at least to try.'

Shakes let out an unexpected shout of laughter.

'No, sirs, no,' he wheezed, and scrambled noisily to his feet, and then stood over us, whisky bottle in hand, as we sat cross-legged on the grass and looked up at him like schoolchildren.

'This is not about *forgetting*!' the giant American cried. 'I wear no black armband, Mr McAllister, I sing no sad songs, Mr Lowell, I will not mourn, I will not lament, I will not *grieve*. My pleasure ground,' he laughed, 'will be a *remembrance* of my brother. The Lawrence Shakes Pleasure Ground – in my brother's name, by God!' He shook his massive head. 'A forest of lights. A carnival of noise. A pier, electric-lit, decked out with wonders, stretching a clear half-mile out to sea. *Pleasure*, gentlemen. Pleasure, the greatest thing of all.' Again his huge laugh rang momentarily among the priory ruins before it was swallowed by the sky.

Pleasure. The word made me think of my Harriet – of her body, of course, her hands and eyes, and of her quick and unembarrassed instinct for it – but also of Harriet the child of Gravely, this shore, this stretch of sky and reach of sea. One has a deep and stratified feeling for one's own place. A pier and a pleasure ground? I had not yet fully fathomed Harriet's feeling for Gravely but this, I thought, was a bad match for it, an awkward fit. Still less was I sure that Harriet's housewifely practicality would swallow any scheme as ramshackle as Shakes's seemed to be.

'I'll drink to *pleasure*, sir, if you'd be so good,' said David, grinning and reaching up a hand for the whisky bottle.

Shakes looked down at him and smiled in the shadow of his hat brim.

*

I came home to an empty house. This in itself didn't trouble me a great deal – and yet I was troubled. I walked from room to room and my footsteps sounded thunderous. The footsteps of the cat Josephus, as he followed after and around me, sounded thunderous.

I needed Harriet. I needed her there to calm me, reassure me, restore to me my equipoise.

'I'm sure you will, Mr McAllister,' Shakes had said, there on the bluff, his face to the declining sun. 'I know you.' He chuckled saltily. 'I know pleasure, sir, and I know that you know it, too.'

He had lifted his head, taking the shadow from his face. The low sunlight had imparted a terracotta glow to his skin. His wrinkles had seemed drawn in black ink. There he had stood, grinning, at the foot of his tall shadow.

In the bathroom I splashed my face with cold water, and then slurped a mouthful from my cupped hand. It tasted of the peat through which the water ran to Gravely from the high inland moors, and did little to wash my mouth clean of the flavour of Shakes's whisky. I shook my hands dry and addressed myself in the mirror. The face I confronted was long, hollow-cheeked and raw-shaven. In large part it was my father's face. Even my hair, severely short and left-hand parted, followed my father's lead.

Had my father, I wondered, been a good man? I pictured this face white and flinching beneath an infantryman's helmet.

'Pleasure?' David had queried. He had shifted position, awkwardly, as though to rise.

'Yes, sir. The profoundest, Mr McAllister, of all the pleasures!'

I had pictured them again, and, I have no doubt, flushed in so doing: David and Cordelia, descending like a sigh to the sand, and those buttocks so rudely bared, and that shoe heel banging against the breakwater—

'I saw! I saw! I saw!' Shakes had declared, or perhaps testified, as I am told the faithful testify in the enthusiastic churches.

David, in no doubt that he was surely now to be assaulted – flung from the bluff, or brained with a whisky bottle – had scrambled to his feet and staggered backwards, holding out one hand to protect himself. Hardly had he risen before he had fallen again, with a grunt, on to his behind – and Maurice Shakes had loomed laughing over him.

'Jon!' David had cried.

Having stalked all about the house, I returned to the bedroom and sat upon the bed. I wanted Harriet. I wanted to make facetious remarks and tease her for her foibles. I wanted to watch her undress, and demonstrate in so doing her easy affinity with nakedness. I wanted her to help me fill our empty home.

I am, as I have said, resigned to my own cowardice. I would have let David be brained or thrown to his death. What could I after all have done to prevent it, even if I had tried? Shakes would have tossed me into the sea with a flick of his great flukes – he would have gulped me down like the whale that swallowed his friend.

But Shakes did not kill David.

No – he only grabbed him by his wrist, and hauled him to his feet, and pounded, laughing, on his back.

'Sir, sir,' he choked, from in the deeps of his laughter, 'fear not, fear not! I am sincere – your joy is my joy, I swear it.'

David, uncertain, wavering upon trembling knees, stammered: 'Joy, Mr Shakes? My joy?'

Shakes stooped to put his smiling lion's face close to David's.

'I watched,' he said, agreeably. 'I watched you, Mr McAllister, achieve union with my eldest daughter, in the blessed sands above which we stand. No, do not quail, sir, never quail' – David had again taken a backward step – 'for I am not angry. Joy is so rare a thing. I revelled in it, my boy, my handsome Mr McAllister. I *swam* in your shared delight.'

I was not sure whether I found Mr Shakes's turn of phrase more or less offensive than the sentiment he expressed. What was more, the man was an atrocious ham. And yet I could not turn from his performance. In the few times I have visited the theatre, I have found that this is often the way with even the worst hams.

Bold David swallowed down his fear and said: 'It is funny, sir, but I had almost rather you were angry. I would almost rather be beaten, in a strange way, than – than *this*.'

Shakes released him.

'Perhaps happiness is not for everyone.' He smiled ruefully. 'Did you know, gentlemen, that though a man must breathe oxygen in order to live, if he breathes *only* oxygen, oxygen and nothing else, then that man will suffocate – that man will *drown*?'

I opened my mouth to say that indeed I did know that but Shakes went on: 'The air a man breathes must contain dilutants, impurities. It must, if you prefer, be adulterated.' And on this final word he seemed to look at me and, though it may only have been a grimace or quirk of expression reflexive to the bright setting sun, seemed to wink.

'So it is,' he said, 'with happiness.'

'Sometimes it is safer,' David said drily, straightening his shirt collar, 'to take one's whisky with a little water.'

'And yet,' Shakes rejoined, 'you took your pleasure of my darling Cordelia, though that was not *safe* – why, another father would have had your blood, if not your head. *Safe*. A weakling's word. Sometimes to be happy takes courage, gentlemen.'

The way Shakes then turned to me – no, turned *on* me – reminded me of the occasions at school in Bradford when a bully had detected, there in the corner of the corridor or changing room, a boy who did not play football, who perhaps collected pressed butterflies or steam-engine numbers – a boy with whom there was sport to be had.

'What of you, Mr Lowell?' he demanded, smiling.

I tucked my hands into my trouser pockets, and smiled blandly back.

'What *of* me?' I said.

'Your pleasures, your joys.' Shakes waved a hand. 'Aside from your birds and your butterflies, aside from your studies – which, I must say, I would not deprecate. But man cannot live by birds and butterflies alone.'

'I'm fortunate,' I said, with a dignified inclination of my head, 'to be a married man.'

'Fortunate is the word. Your wife,' he said, serious at last, 'is a great beauty – and not only by England's standards.'

David laughed at this last jibe. It is the way of the bullied to suppose, after a while, that every laugh is a laugh at their expense. I could feel my face burning.

'Thank you,' I muttered.

At home later, I lay on the bed, my hands linked on my stomach, and listened for the sound of Harriet's footsteps on the shale driveway.

'You need only,' Shakes had said ruminatively, looking out across the darkening bay, 'consider the way in which your reverend, Mr Aldridge, looks upon Mrs Lowell when he thinks he is unobserved, for proof of the pleasure that a fine woman can bring to a man. Oh, the pleasure he would have of her, sirs, if only he could! And you need not colour, Mr Lowell' – though by now I had not only coloured but had turned away, feeling for a way back down the escarpment to the beach – 'for you are a fine-looking fellow yourself. And I have after all a second daughter, and I have seen the way *she* looks upon *you*, sir! If you would only ask, Mr Lowell, I am sure, despite the fear of God, which is as nothing beside the love of life, she would roll in the dunes with you – oh sir, if you would only ask!'

I was clambering down the slope as he spoke the words. I blushed and fumed and was hurt and felt mocked – but even then, and later as I waited for my wife, and even now, I could not say that I truly heard mockery in Shakes's voice. *I am sincere*, he had said.

I had grabbed my satchel from where it lay on the rocks and hastened home.

Harriet's footfall on the driveway must have sounded at some point in the evening. I didn't hear it. When I awoke, deep in the night, I found her naked beside me in the bed, and I held her to me tightly until again I fell asleep, and when once again I awoke, and it was morning, she was gone.

I was sixteen. Dad a couple of years dead. Cleaning fish down the quay. Only had to stick at it till a husband came along, Mother said. For her a husband was a different thing to a feller, though even then I knew better, knew that every husband started off as a feller, and that fellers, even if they stayed fellers and nothing more, weren't anything to be scared of. Mother terrified of fellers. What sort of husband wants a wife whose hands smell of herring tripes? I said. She laughed. One'll come along, she said. That's how it is in a small place like this. Say that to the lasses in Bradford they'll think you're touched. Big place like that, people come and go, always someone new, and the lasses'll fight tooth and nail for a man. Not here. Just wait around and one'll come along.

When he did come, I have to admit it, a feller was all I wanted, and all he was. All he'd ever be as it turned out.

Does his name matter? I don't think it does. You can find it if you look. His father – and his father's father, and all that – were lobstermen. But of course I didn't give a fig what his father was. He had big thick forearms and was missing a finger. Dark hair neat as a pin. Long face that went from tea-coloured in summer to fuchsia pink in winter. Liked church more than I did. That was when church seemed more important than it does now (God forgive me saying so). Then when country became more important than Church he cared a lot more about that than I did, too.

I was gutting a fish, actually right in the middle of pulling out the poor thing's innards, when he came over and said hello. Next day he came round for tea. Mother liked him. Not in the same way I did! And after that I saw him most days. Me always red up to my wrists with that horrible thin fish blood, him always shattered from hauling up pots. What did we talk about? I hardly even know.

We did kiss. Of course we did. In the shadow of his dad's boat. Behind the market house. On the beach if no one was about. That was all, though. And it's not as though – well, we never had an Understanding, as they call it.

Did he want to marry me? I dare say he might've done but it doesn't really matter much if there's other things you'd sooner do – like join the blasted army.

I don't know if I wanted to marry him. I don't know if I even loved him. I suppose I must have done but what does that even mean when you're sixteen? Come to that, what does it mean when you're twenty-seven?

Of course he died.

I say all this, all of it, the whole story apart from maybe the bit about Church not mattering as much as it did, and I don't say about the kissing, but apart from this I say the whole story, and I honestly couldn't tell you why – it just all comes out, somehow. I say it all and he sits there looking at me with those eyes of his.

The funny thing is that their eyes are the same, even though you could hardly imagine two faces more different. So serious! And because they're serious they look strong, or rather they look like they want *to be strong – even if they're not strong, in the end, they want to be, because they think that things matter. And they'll go on thinking things matter even as they get swept aside.*

'I'm glad you told me,' the reverend said, and smiled. His smile spoilt it a bit.

It must be easy being a Catholic because you've got rules about talking to the Father. You can climb into that box and say whatever you please and they can't say a thing back to you except Hail Mary or whatever it is.

And here's me without even a father, small eff.

'It was a terrible time,' says Mary.

You can be blooming sure that if I went into a Catholic priest's confessional I wouldn't have to contend with the priest's housekeeper perched on a stool and sticking her oar in with a face like a gravestone. That's how we got on to it, of course – Mary saying something about her husband, lost at Arras.

The reverend's stopped smiling now and again his eyes look like James's. That was his name, for what it's worth. James.

VII

I was suffering from a mild anxious headache, and remained in my study all morning. I had work to do (Harriet and I had accrued a number of due bills). I spent the morning writing and thinking about the woodcock – the bird, the wise bird that had fled in fear at the sound of Shakes's approach.

There are many legends about the woodcock. Some may be true. Generalities are unhelpful in natural history – one can't say 'no woodcock ever carried a gold-crested wren upon its back', to take one example, any more than one can say that no man ever did this or that – for the next day, or the day after, you can be sure, a man *will* do this or that.

No man ever travelled from America with a dream of establishing a pleasure ground in a fishing outpost of two thousand souls. A case in point.

It's said – and, in fact, it's very probably true – that the woodcock will sit tight upon its nest even as the wheels of a forester's cart pass by either side of it. It's also said that the woodcock develops a fast attachment to a given location: that like a swallow it will return again and again, year after year, to the same nesting spot.

I wrote, in my piece for the journal, that for all that we associate wild birds with freedom, flight, escape, they are in fact specialists in remaining still – in staying put. Think of a bird that sleeps perched upon a branch: thanks to some miracle of anatomy, some feat of weights and balances, check and countercheck, though the bird sleeps, the bird doesn't fall – in fact, the sleeping bird clings more tightly to its perch than before.

One more thing about the woodcock: by those who know birds, it is spoken of as an exceptionally stupid bird.

'You'll come to London soon, of course?' David McAllister had said to me, long ago.

'Of course, of course,' I had replied.

I was to be a novelist too, naturally. I would craft fine stories in a high style. I would tease out the delicacies of sensitive hearts with the precision of an artist painting with a woodcock's pin feather.

I do wonder what would have happened if I *had* written in that way (because of course I never did – never have). What stories might I have told? Dreadful ones, I have no doubt. Perhaps they would be about taciturn country types whose trousers are fustian and whose gypsy souls are restless. There would have been tall, dark-eyed hill women. It would all have been appalling.

David, in his letters from London, used to badger me.

'How can you bear not to *know*?' he demanded. 'To at least *try*? It's as though you have never sung – no, never so much as *spoken*. It's as though you have never spoken and, sitting silently, cannot understand why we, your friends, keep hectoring so: "Won't you just *try*, dear Jonathan? How can you bear not to know what will come out when you open your mouth?"'

He stopped bothering me about it after a while. Once it became clear, I suppose, that other things had happened to me – above all, that Harriet had happened.

I finished my piece on the half-witted woodcock and pulled the final page from the platen. With the typewriter fallen silent, the emptiness of the cottage visited me again like an intimation of doom. Harriet must be with her mother, I supposed, as I shuffled the paper and carbons, or out shopping (she was an astute and busy housekeeper).

I took the top piece of paper, richly ink-smelling and cobbled with the imprints of the typewriter keys; I ran my fingertips over the text. I was, after all and in any event, a writer of sorts.

Outside, the air was full of salt water. I blinked and buttoned my collar under my nose. On my way to the post office I would call at Mrs Holloway's, at Harriet's mother's house. I would merely pop my head in at the door and ask if Harriet were there; I would decline the cup of cheap tea I would probably be offered. The house was barely any distance from the high street.

The slight detour would also take me past the end of Withy Passageway. Why shouldn't Harriet be there, rather than at her mother's? She didn't hide – I wouldn't have *wanted* her to hide – her admiration for our hirsute reverend. Why shouldn't she be there, brushing up on Scripture, gleaning insights into the prophecies?

I truly had no suspicion. Perhaps Aldridge did covet his neighbour's wife – perhaps, indeed, he looked on her to lust after her, and committed adultery with her in his heart. Harriet was beautiful. Her eyes were a bracing blue. She *shone*, like a sea-wet pebble.

Had I not looked on plenty of other women in just that same forbidden-by-Matthew way? Of course I had, beginning with the girls at St Margaret's School when I was a boy and proceeding in the usual fashion from there.

Had I ever betrayed my wife's trust? I had not. I was a good husband. Harriet was a good wife. As far as I was aware, the Reverend Hugh Aldridge was a good Christian.

I set off for the high street and the wet wind off the North Sea tousled my hair as I walked.

In my head I carried a memory as perfect and as self-contained as a teasel head set within a glass paperweight: my first memory of Harriet Holloway. I carried it with care, knowing that, over the years of our acquaintance, it had never been touched – not by David, even, and certainly not by the Reverend Aldridge, and most certainly not by any Shakes of either sex. It wasn't even a Gravely memory, that first meeting with Harriet; no, it was a memory of Bradford – of a dry, chalky day in January, beneath a boiled-linen sky.

It happened in Manningham Park, a little way out of the town proper. I was on my knees, prying beneath the bark of a fallen larch in search of grubs.

'Goodness!'

I looked up in surprise. The knees of my cream-coloured trousers would have been brown from the dirt of the path; I wore no hat, as a hat only encumbers the grub-seeker, and I would not, even by my own standards, have been well dressed: I had come seeking rose-chafer larvae, rather than a wife. I clutched a magnifying glass in my unclean right hand.

She had stopped, the girl who had said 'Goodness!', just short of the fallen larch. I could understand her surprise. We must have made an unexpected tableau, the larch and I, as she had rounded the bend: the larch lying stricken across the footpath, and I, unkempt and wild-eyed, astride it – perhaps as though I had just that minute wrestled it to the ground.

The first word Harriet heard me say was: 'Entomology!'

'Pardon?'

'Insects,' I clarified.

'Ah,' said Harriet.

She would tell me, later, that I had cried *entomology!* in a tone of fearful innocence, as though in anticipation of being charged with some much darker business: witchcraft, devilry, blasphemy. In rec-ollection the scene brings to my mind a chafer larva when one *does* unearth him within the mouldering larch – how, as one prises away the bark, he shrinks like a contracting white heart from the light, and would, one is forced to feel, plead his own innocence if he could.

I stood, brushing my hands on my trouser front. I said I was sorry to have startled her, and she said that that was all right. She

asked me what *enter-what-is-it* was all about and I told her that by
and large it was all about butterflies and ladybirds.

'And woodlice and spiders and cockroaches and – and whatever it was you were grubbing about in that tree for, too, I'm sure,'
she said.

'Grubs, actually,' I smiled. 'And yes, those too. You're an awful
cynic, madam.'

'I know enough about men,' she said darkly.

I laughed.

For all her bluntness and all her beauty – for I had now shaken
off my squint-eyed preoccupation with the chafer hunt and was
aware, quite aware, of how beautiful she was, there in the filtered
off-white light – I felt emboldened somehow by this girl.

She was wearing a tilted narrow-brimmed hat and her corn-
coloured hair was bundled in a complicated knot at the nape of her
neck. Her eyes were large and a very clear light-blue (a holly blue butterfly has wings of roughly the same shade); when she blinked she did
so slowly, presenting and withdrawing her pale-lashed eyelids with
easy deliberation. Of her facial features only her chin wasn't perfectly
ladylike, though that isn't to say that it wasn't very fine-looking: it
was just perhaps a little long, and she held it high – it made me think
of an elbow (that of a nymph or Sabine, say) carved in white marble.

I noticed, too, the neat fit of her teal-blue dress to the curves of
her fashionably trim bosom and unfashionably wide hips, and the
fragile daintiness of her ankles, which she crossed and uncrossed
as we stood and talked. Her feet were very little.

'My name's Lowell,' I said, extending a hand. 'Jonathan Lowell.'

She took my dirt-streaked hand gingerly between her thumb
and finger, and I felt the point of her index fingernail, and she told
me that she was Harriet Holloway.

I fancy that, as I walked the seafront road south to where the
high street turned towards the west, my tread was tentative, as

though I were afraid that the memory might spill from my mind, and I might never be able to regather it.

Withy Passageway was a narrow whitewashed ginnel between two houses of red brick and green woodwork, leading westwards off the sea road up three flights of stone steps. The walls of the ginnel were patterned with the stubborn brown aerial roots of ivy (the ivy itself having been ripped away some time since). A violet ground beetle picked its careful way across the dead prints. Up ahead, on the second flight of steps, a black-faced tortoiseshell cat sat and preened. Herring gulls howled on the roof of Aldridge's tall house.

A very Saint Francis, I thought.

As I waited at the door for the minister's maid to answer my knock, another memory came unbidden to mind. Bradford again – the Interchange, the train station. A weekday morning, too late for anyone with an office to go to, perhaps half past nine or ten o'clock. Sunshine. And once again her, Harriet: in a two-piece suit of pale-blue tweed, and a hat tilted to the right. I saw her first, and boldly trespassed on her shadow.

We each said 'hello', or 'good morning'. We each asked where the other was off to. I said that I was going to Keighley to seek nesting lapwing on the moor; she laughed and said that I always seemed to be on the lookout for *some*thing or other. She, she said, was bound for Bingley, to visit an aunt. It thus became clear that we would both be taking the same train.

At that moment Harriet's heavy-lidded eyes were of the same immense and terrible blue as a cloudless sky, and as I gazed upon their blueness, just as when I at other times had gazed upon the sky, I felt the imminence of an awesome, an infinite inevitability – I was helpless, a bug pinned, a rabbit entranced, in that tremendous moment.

I had to go and buy a ticket. Harriet said that she would see me on the train. Later it seemed very funny to me that I thought, in asking her, then, which carriage she would be sitting in, I was being most magnificently *forward*.

She answered: 'The one with all the blinds pulled down.'

In fact, it turned out there were *two* carriages with all the blinds pulled down. In one, an obese man sat snoring amid the golden motes of dust with a newspaper open on his knee. In the other, Harriet sat by the window, with her hat on the seat beside her, blinking sedately to herself in the narrow strip of light from the window.

We smiled at one another as I removed my own hat and took the seat opposite. Harriet's knees were pressed together. I sat with my hands folded in my lap and considered the way the light played on the fine gauzy knit of her stocking rayon where it was stretched tight across her knee bones. And I watched her fidget: she stroked the ball of her thumb with her index fingertip, over and over, as though she would rub away its print.

We were a little way out of Bradford when Harriet leaned forwards and – in a queerly low, shivering and somewhat stagey voice – said: 'I find the worst thing about train journeys is trying to think of a way to pass the time.'

The blue eyes blinked (they, at least, retained their poise) and when they opened they seemed as endless as the sky.

We would disagree, later, on the question of whether I made a gauche lunge for her or she threw herself at me (I insisted the former, Harriet the latter). In any case we met more on my side of the carriage than hers; together we subsided into the dismally protesting springs of what had been my seat.

My groping left hand found in sequence her tight-wrapped right breast, her right buttock, the tendons at the back of her slender right knee. The smooth, hard toe of one of her shoes moved across the muscle of my calf. I heard her shoulder joint gently click as she straightened her arm and I felt her open hand press into my crotch.

Her movements were in rhythmic step with the motion of the train. Soon I had to pull my mouth from hers and whisper, breathlessly, that she ought to stop, that really she *must* stop – or my pale-coloured trousers would be stained.

She didn't stop. For the rest of the day, as I strode about the sun-drenched moor in pursuit of whooping, jeering lapwings, I was mortifyingly conscious of the florin-sized stain on my trouser front.

I didn't, of course, regret its provenance.

*

The Reverend Aldridge opened the front door himself. My stomach pulsed like a heart when I saw, on his pale trousers, a faint coin-sized stain – but this was only the ghost of the bead of tea that had dripped from his beard on the Sunday foregoing.

'Hello!' he said, with false heartiness.

'How d'you do, Reverend? I was only passing by, and I wondered—'

'Wonder no more,' Aldridge said with a smile. 'Please *do* join us, we'd all be delighted. The two ladies really are *most* able students – and the fastest of friends now, I think!'

He turned with a gesture and I followed him. The house smelt of boiled root vegetables. He ducked into a chamber, off to the left, and again I followed. Within sat Harriet and Eleanor Shakes, each on a wooden kitchen chair and each with a Bible open in her lap.

Harriet pressed her lips momentarily together at the sight of me.

'What,' I asked, diffidently, 'is today's lesson?'

Brown-eyed Eleanor's smile seemed self-conscious when she replied: 'The Lord taketh pleasure in them that fear Him, in those that hope in His mercy.'

'I shan't stay,' I said, even as Aldridge resumed his seat and took up his Book. 'I shan't stay – goodbye, Miss Shakes, goodbye Reverend. I hope your studies are rewarding.' I smiled at Harriet as I walked backwards out of the door.

Then I did something that in doing I surprised myself. I walked to the home of Mrs Holloway. When Mrs Holloway answered the door, I asked, in a mild subterfuge, if Harriet was there. When Mrs Holloway told me (as I already knew) that she wasn't, and asked if I'd like to come in for a cup of tea anyway, I, knowing that the tea would be both cheap and weak, said yes.

*

'There was a cachalot washed up, when he was a boy, right here, right on the beach. And oh he wept over it, he did, Jonathan. He *wept*. Prayed and wept.'

A cachalot is a whale, a sperm whale. I don't know how the word gained currency in Gravely; Mrs Holloway pronounced it *catch-a-lot*, as though the great leviathan were no more than equivalent with a good boatful of herring.

'And yet the beast perished?'

'Of course it did. They always perish. Though young Hugh poured bucket after bucket of seawater over it, for all that his parents told him it was no good. I remember seeing him on his knees in the sand, praying, his empty bucket beside him, and all tears on his cheeks.'

A touching recollection of the boy Aldridge.

We sat in Mrs Holloway's drawing room, which was tiny and filled with oil paintings of the ocean. These she bought, relentlessly and without discrimination, from local amateurs, visiting professionals, roving bohemians – practically anyone, in fact, able to muster enough slate-blue pigment to paint the North Sea, and a daub of zinc to furnish a white horse.

When she brought the tea she said that I had a gruff look on. 'You've a gruff look on, today, Jonathan, if I might say so' – meaning that I appeared gloomy, sullen, ill-tempered.

'It's the March wind,' I explained (truthfully, I thought). My being out in the wind and sun and sea spray so often imparted a habitual grimace to my features.

'Scowling won't help that,' she said, and poured the tea from an ugly blue pot.

Then he arose, and rebuked the wind and the raging of the water; and they ceased, and there was a calm. I refrained from voicing the quotation. Mrs Holloway would have sniffed mockery. It was marvellous, she continued, that Gravely had such a minister, such a *muscular* minister (describing his Christianity, rather than his weedy person), at just the time that Harriet was finding her way back into the fold. The gist was that Aldridge was a good shepherd and my wife a strayed sheep. I sipped my tea unperturbed. I had long known that, in Mrs Holloway's eyes, Harriet had departed from the true path when she had left Gravely.

Mrs Holloway usually alluded to Harriet's Fall with the words 'went down to town': 'Of course, *that* was before she went down to town'; 'There is no *talking* to that girl since she went down to town'.

What was worse was that she had not gone down to just any town, not to a decently salt-washed town like Whitby or Scarborough (and nor had she gone *up,* to Hartlepool, Middlesbrough, Sunderland). No, she had gone to Bradford, the type specimen of the satanic-mill metropolis. Even the nearby presence of that Bingley-dwelling aunt – Mrs Holloway's elder sister – hadn't calmed the anxious mother's qualms.

'There'll be *men,*' she had warned Harriet fervently.

'No, no,' Harriet had reassured her. 'I shall be staying with three girls, and it's all girls that work in the office (the clerical division of Marshall's Mill, that is, where Harriet had secured a situation) – even the supervisor. A Missus Bent.'

'There'll still be *men*,' Mrs Holloway had said. 'They get everywhere.' As though men were woodlice or silverfish.

But of course, there *were* men, one of whom was me. Harriet fell right into my clutches.

Thus, in any case, Mrs Holloway and I had arrived at the subject of the boy Aldridge. He'd grown up here, as Harriet had, although of course they never knew one another as children (I suppose that Mrs Holloway considered boys scarcely better than men, and was accordingly vigilant).

'A studious boy, I imagine, as well as pious,' I ventured, and sipped at the vile tea.

'Clever, aye.' Mrs Holloway squinted thoughtfully. 'But you'd not have called him *bookish*. The beach, that was his place. Always about the rock pools, putting a crab in a jar or getting himself stung by a jellyfish.'

She smirked at me. *You are not so different, you and he*, the smirk knowingly observed.

'I take your meaning, Mrs Holloway,' I said urbanely, 'but we are really not so alike, the Reverend Aldridge and I. He found sermons in stones. I, though I looked at the same stones, dug them out, broke them apart and fingered the ammonites and belemnites within, found no sermons.'

'That isn't to say they weren't there,' said the obtuse Mrs Holloway.

I resorted again to the unpleasant tea, seeing that the alternative was an unseemly argument with my wife's mother. The bitter cup drained, I rose to go. As she helped me perfunctorily with my coat, Mrs Holloway asked about the young man, Mr McAllister – would he be staying with us for much longer?

'Mr McAllister is a law unto himself,' I said with a light laugh. 'But as a house guest he demands very little of us – he is in bed most of the morning, and in his room writing all afternoon. Three meals out of four he takes at an inn or a tea room.'

I refrained from adding that he was usually in Holroyd's pub all evening and that three nights out of four he spent – not very discreetly, but just about discreetly enough – at a rented terraced house at the north extremity of the village. Still, Mrs Holloway's lined face wore a scandalised look as I bade her good day.

Hoping not to see anyone I know and now this. Not that I know him exactly but still.

Had to leave the reverend's. Too much to do. Anyway I felt awkward after the reverend's crack about me and Eleanor being fast friends. I'm not saying we're not, I mean maybe we will be, maybe we won't, but it's horrible being put on the spot like that. She was embarrassed too, I could tell. It was a question of which of us made her excuses first. It was me: said I'd to go get dinner on. Which was true, but only part of the whole truth (but then isn't everything?). You can't say oh, I've got to go, sweep the carpets, dust the hall, black the stove, take out the ashes, scrub the bathtub, wipe the windows, scour the step, feed the cat and get the dinner on. So I just said that about getting the dinner on, and went home.

Fingers swollen from scrubbing that blasted stove-top. Had to take my ring off. And black right into the fingerprints. Had a quick go with the nail brush but no good. Red raw under the black anyway.

Hair's a state. Pinned up any old way. Shoved a bonnet on before I came out but it's a summer bonnet. Stockings probably in a state too, daren't look at them. Can feel them bagging round my ankles.

Wonder what Eleanor's up to now. Maybe still ploughing through the Book of Isaiah. More like sitting at home with her feet up and a pot of tea. And never mind her, where's Jon? He's *not here. Calls this his office sometimes; 'Going down the office,' he'll say with a wink, when he heads out with his nets and jam jars. Funny. I grew up here, if this is anyone's beach it's my bloody beach, but it still feels strange me being here and him not.*

Cat took a swipe when I put down his dish. Caught me on the forearm but didn't break the skin. Thin white scratch like a white whisker showing through the dirt. 'Sick to death of fish trimmings!' maybe he's saying. But I know he doesn't mean anything by it. It's just the worry. That's all they do, cats.

They must enjoy it sometimes. I want to tell him: 'Sometimes the anxiety is good, Josephus. Sometimes it's good and then we call it excitement.' But I suppose that's a terrible thing to say to a cat or anybody.

Back's twanging like a banjo-string. That's bending over the bath. You'll be old before your time if you don't watch it, Harriet Lowell.

Of course he's going to say hello. He's not the type to pretend he's not seen you. And he'll make out like he hasn't even noticed my hair or my hands or my bagged stockings. But he will have noticed, make no mistake – he's that type, and all.

'Mrs Lowell!'

Same lord mayor's suit, same big hat. He looked enormous in our little parlour. You'd think out here he'd look small but if anything he looks even bigger. I don't mean fat (though he is a bit fat).

'Good afternoon, Mr Shakes. What are you doing out here?'

'Taking the air, Mrs Lowell, taking the air! I may paddle in the breakers later. It's a wonderful place, my goodness. Do you know it puts me in mind of Gravesend Bay, back in the States. But of course why would you know a backwater like that? It's the sense of space, you see, Mrs Lowell – and the sense of possibility.'

Which is all very well, but notice he doesn't ask me what I'm doing out here.

'People generally prefer it in the summer,' I say.

'I dare say they do,' he says, and does his funny laugh.

'They certainly will once your pier's up, Mr Shakes, is that right?' I think why not bring it up. It can't be a secret. From what I gather he told Jon all about it freely enough. A pier and a whole lot else. Jon had called it 'Mr Shakes's vision'.

I didn't much like that. 'Vision'. Something a bit spiritualist about it. I suppose that sort of thing has its place but I don't think that place is here.

I thought saying the words aloud out here on this beach might help blow away the whifty-whafty stuff, the vision, the dream, all that. I'm not altogether against the idea, I don't think, but let's let the sand and wind and salt at it for a bit – then we can see what's left of it. If anything.

'Oh indeed,' Mr Shakes says, not a bit abashed. Pink in the cheeks, a grin from one ear to the other. I can't rightly say he looks like a man who's had a vision. More like a schoolboy who's found a bag of toffees. 'A grand thing that will be to see in the summer sun, Mrs Lowell.'

'I wouldn't bank on too much of that here.'

'Joy can be its own summer sunshine, I would say, madam.'

Answer for everything.

'My husband and I were wondering,' I say, partly because it's true but mainly because I can't abide being steamrollered over by fellers who know it all, 'if these marvellous plans of yours have got by our town council yet? They can be sticklers, I understand.'

'Oh, I shan't let any paper-pushers of that sort—'

'Because the law is the law, of course.'

He opens his mouth, then shuts it. Pauses. Raises one big hand halfway, like I've just played a good shot in lawn tennis.

'I will be sure to proceed by the book, as they say, Mrs Lowell,' he says, and nods at me with a smile. A travelling salesman's smile.

I've seen enough of those. I won't buy their cheap brush sets that fall apart after five minutes and I won't buy this.

I look at the sea. The thing about the sea is, there's always more going on there than you think.

I say: 'I do hope you'll be careful, Mr Shakes. These can be treacherous waters.'

'Mrs Lowell—'

'What I mean to say is, Gravely's not a place you ought to take for granted.' And I give him a look so he knows what I'm getting at. Or anyway I hope he does. I know how dense fellers can be. I want him to know I don't just mean the waves and the tides and the weather and the seabed. When I say Gravely I mean us. And when I say us I mean me.

I don't mean to be rude to the man, I've nothing against him really. It's just there's right ways of doing things and there's wrong ways. A lot of the time it doesn't matter much which you do, the right or the wrong, but sometimes, of course, it does matter. The trick isn't knowing the right from the wrong. The trick is knowing when it counts.

Better not say that in front of the reverend.

Again Mr Shakes pulls this face, half respectful, half making fun.

Then there's a little spot of quiet, save for the weather and waves – a little moment of hesitation, like the conversation is wondering which way to go. A few specks of spume come skipping past my ankles.

We're slap in the middle of the sands, halfway from sea to road and from bluff to harbour. The sand's just damp enough here for a man's shoes to leave faint footprints. Of course you can see my square little heel-points like a train track all the way from the tideline. I see he's looking at them, Mr Shakes. Like a man reading a code.

Now he looks straight at me.

'You've a smut, Mrs Lowell,' he says.

First I wonder what the heck he's getting at.

'Pardon me?'

He grabs his right earlobe and says it again, and I put my own hand to my own ear and it comes away with a smear of stove-black.

'Oh, crikey.'

Work at it with a hankie. He says I've got most of it off – and besides, what's the harm in a smudged earlobe? I have to laugh at how he says it.

'You came out here to get the smell of caustic and washing-flakes out of your nostrils, I suppose?'

'Something like that, yes. It can get under your skin, housework.'

'Worth the trouble, though, my dear Mrs Lowell.' As if the big clown's ever done a day's scrubbing in his life. 'Some folks say it's trivial. Trivial! My goodness, Mrs Lowell – the sense of freedom one finds in a clean house.' Laughs and waves an arm. 'As on a beach scoured clean by the tides and winds.'

Well, I still say he's a travelling salesman. And I still don't suppose he's over-familiar with the inside of a cleaning cupboard. But sometimes someone says something you've been thinking and have never got round to putting into words.

VIII

At the evening low tide I was once again on the lower shore, sifting through straps of wet kelp in search of blue-rayed limpets, when I heard David's jovial cry of: 'Hulloa!' I turned and saw him approaching unsteadily across the rocks.

'What is it this time? A shark? An electric eel? A sea serpent?'

He seemed somewhat drunk.

A little testily I told him that, with luck and the opportunity to conduct my work undisturbed, it would be a blue-rayed limpet. He slapped my shoulder and laughed in my po-face.

'Not just *any* limpet, but a blue-rayed one!' He squatted beside me and a wavelet sloshed over the toes of his shoes. 'Tell me, Professor Lowell, of its life and habits, its tastes and predilections, its phylum, class, family, genus, species.'

As David well knew, I wasn't able to retain much ill humour in his presence.

'*Mollusca, Gastropoda, Patellidae, Patella, Patella pellucida,*' I recited easily (and pridefully). 'There *is* an interesting thing about its habits, you know. It lives on this kelp' – I ran my hand through a hank of the stuff – 'which keeps it anchored in place. But sometimes, it seems, the limpet starts enjoying its dinner too much, and absent-mindedly gnaws all the way through its belt of kelp. With the result that the kelp breaks free of the land – and the limpet is washed out to sea.'

'Much to the limpet's disadvantage, I dare say?'

'Very much.'

'Well, well.' David nodded gravely, regarding the kelp. 'Well, well.' Then he smacked his hands on his thighs, rose and said: 'In any event, I discovered a rather interesting specimen myself this afternoon.'

'A girl, I suppose,' I said, affecting boredom. 'Won't Miss Shakes be put out? But I expect she's too *modern* to be disconcerted by such things.'

'Churlish, Lowell. Besides, he isn't a girl. This specimen of mine. I couldn't tell you much about his phylum, class, family and so on except that he seems to be human and his name's Furlong, but he's certainly worth taking a look at. I came down here to fetch you. Come and see.'

'*Come and see.* And I looked, and beheld a pale horse, and the name of him that sat on him was Death, and Hell followed with him. And power was given—'

'Oh, for God's sake.' David shook his head helplessly and laughed. I laughed with him. He had always been amused by my facility for reciting Scripture (I had been known more than once to show it off as a parlour trick). He thought it amusing in an atheist. I had learned it all in childhood: I was a bookish boy, even if the Reverend Aldridge wasn't.

'Now, am I to leave you here preaching Revelation to the limpets,' David demanded, arms akimbo, 'or are you going to come back to Holroyd's with me and look at this fellow Furlong?'

I sighed. The sea slopped over the rocks. The tide was turning, after all; there would be no blue-rayed limpets for me today.

I began to gather up my jars and glasses.

'Who is he, this Furlong? *What* is he?'

'A man of iron, forged in flame.'

'No riddles, please.'

'Very well, you bore. By forged in flame I mean that he was born and reared in infernal Newcastle. And by man of iron—'

'A blacksmith, I suppose.'

'So much more. An authority on the truss, the girder and the steel-rolled beam. An artist of the rivet and screw. An architect, of all things. A conceiver, designer and builder of piers, Lowell – piers just such as that splendid Mr Shakes plans to thrust out a statute half-mile into your bleak northern ocean.'

I looked at him, and then followed his gaze out to sea. It was as though the pier stood there already – the green weed and barnacles already made fast to its great oaken pilings, the black iron already whitewashed with the fishy mutes of herring gulls, the corroding salt of the sea already at work—

And then it was gone, and there was only the sea and the sky.

'I just saw Mr Shakes's vision,' I remarked, hooking my satchel strap on to my shoulder.

'I fear Mr Shakes's vision goes further than you or I can comprehend,' David said.

*

He had a beaked, lipless mouth and the insolently gaping eyes of a grouper or wreckfish.

'Bradford, is it?' he said, after a sip of the beer I had brought from the bar. 'Well, even if you count the Bowling works there's been nothing smelted worth the coal there since the fifties and the Crimean. Thwaites and Carbutt ran themselves into the ground before the war, and even at Leeds there's only Kirkstall and that bastard Butler at Stanningley. It's just not iron country, I'm afraid, boys.' A thin and condescending smile. 'I'd not build a doghouse out of West Riding steel.'

I glanced at David and we both, laughing within, made chagrined faces, as though we had the first idea what this fellow Furlong was talking about.

He saw through us a little, at least.

'You boys don't know what you're at,' he said. 'Writers, or whatever you are. And yet you ride my railways. You stroll on my piers with your wives and children.'

We both nodded, and slurped our own drinks.

Furlong was a man of perhaps thirty-five or forty – half a generation older than David and me. His face was long and haggard; he wore (or, rather, affected) a workmanlike shirt and cap. I had been studying his hands: they were strong, long-fingered and thick-knuckled, and a scar seamed the ball of his left thumb, but they were not raw as fishermen's hands are raw; these hands had had time to heal. Time spent working at the draughtsman's desk.

'And you're here—' I began, knowing already, of course, why he was here.

'For the American's grand pier, aye,' Furlong nodded. 'A bloody folly for sure, but a grand one, I'll give it that. If a man has to be a fool he'd best be a grand fool.'

'His plans are ambitious?'

Furlong slapped the tabletop.

'*His* plans, man? *My* plans. How is Mr Shakes to build a pier, who doesn't know a truss from a buttress, who can't tell a bolt from a rivet, how is Mr Shakes to build a pier?' He subsided a little. 'The money is to be furnished by the American. But the plans are mine.'

'Will you bring in your own men for the job?' David asked.

'Aye. Good Newcastle men.' He eyed David humorously. 'Or were you angling for the work yourself, son?'

'I could build no pier, it's true,' David confessed with theatrical airiness, 'though I could write you a fine tale of one.'

'Aye, you build yourself a fairy-tale pier' – Furlong smiled – 'while we're busy with the iron and steel of the real thing.'

Again David and I exchanged arch glances. The man seemed to think of little other than applied metallurgy.

Having swilled another mouthful of beer, the architect shook a finger and said: 'But while you're busy telling your tales you'll want to keep an eye out for what your wives and daughters are up to.'

This was David's territory.

'Indeed!' He grinned. 'Fancy themselves as romancers, do they, these Geordie steelmen of yours?'

Furlong made a wry face.

'Nay, Mr, McAllister is it. All good Christian men, my lads, true to their wives and sweethearts. You've nothing to fear from them.' He hawked and gulped and snatched a drink of beer. 'It's them others. Mr Shakes's boys.'

I was quite lost.

'Boys?'

'The what is it, *service personnel*. He's going for the glamorous touch, is your Mr Shakes. A proper bloody Yorkshire riviera, he wants to make. This place won't know what's hit it when those fellers roll up.'

I shifted uncomfortably on my stool.

David, intrigued, leaned forwards: 'Who? Come on, Furlong, tell us before we die of old age.'

Furlong looked shiftily to left and right, wiped his lips with two fingertips and, propped on one elbow, said: 'Foreigners.'

'Great God,' David breathed. I bit my lower lip to keep from laughing.

'No word of a lie. A whole bloody regiment of Eye-talians.'

Shakes would be bringing Scots Italians down from Glasgow or somewhere, I supposed, to grind organs, sing arias and sell ice cream in his pleasure grounds. In this, at least, he would be imparting a dash of Coney Island – or in any case Coney Island as I imagined it, or New York as I imagined it. I said as much.

'Aye, that's about it,' Furlong said sourly. 'As if you can't teach a Geordie lad to make ice cream or grind a monkey organ or whatever it is. There'll be wops left, right and centre – a woman won't be safe to walk the streets. Of course, it's all Mr Shakes's idea of charity.'

'Charity?' I put in. 'Surely these Italians will be expected to do a decent day's work for their pay?'

'Oh aye, I didn't mean that. If you can *get* a decent day's work out of an Eye-talian I'm sure Mr Shakes will. I meant – well, maybe you don't know.'

We were both rapidly wearying of the glee Furlong transparently took in knowing things we didn't.

'Know *what*?' David sighed.

'He's recruiting nobody but veterans. All of them veterans, of the war, like. Or I should say all of *us*, shouldn't I? All of us fought, you see. I suppose Mr Shakes doesn't want to see such brave fighting men' – he said the words, as he seemed to say most words, with bitterness – 'queueing down the labour exchange.'

David and I took to our ales as we absorbed this. *That again*, I thought glumly. When one was thinking of ice cream and arias and organ grinders, it was easy to forget the dead of Isonzo and Caporetto. But it seemed that Mr Shakes would never forget the dead. There seemed no limit to his capacity for penance.

'I suppose you men who saw the war are more likely to share in Mr Shakes's sense of mission,' I suggested.

'Mission?'

I faltered, worrying that I had spoken out of turn. I had drunk perhaps a pint and a half. I knew that it didn't always take a great deal of beer to loosen my tongue.

'That is – perhaps you've heard of Mr Shakes's brother?'

Furlong pushed out his lower lip and said: 'Aye, I have. The poor bugger that died at Montfaucon. But I think you're under a misapprehension, Mr, Lowell is it. Us that *saw* the war – and we did more than see it, believe you me – aren't so much the sort that are inclined to believe in anything very much.'

'The foxholes are crammed with atheists, you mean?' David said.

'I'd not go that far.' Furlong frowned. 'And I'd not use that word – that's a big word, that. But I do say that Mr Shakes's soldiers aren't coming here because they believe in any bloody mission. I'd say they're coming here because – well, because they don't believe in owt very much.' He sucked noisily at his beer.

'On such foundations,' David murmured drily, 'will Maurice Shakes build his Babylon.'

Furlong looked up sharply.

'*Foundations*,' he sneered. 'Don't talk to me about foundations. Round here, they're nowt but sand and water.'

This was true. Our lives in Gravely were lived amid eternal erosion. The sea breeze, the sea spray, the persistent rubbing of the particles of the sea itself were devouring our village, or rather they were gnawing at the roots by which the village was held in place. An old man in the pub once told me that when he was a boy the southern sea cliff, the very cliff on which the pub was built, reached fully thirty yards further out to sea than it did now.

There was a boy of perhaps nine or ten who played with a stick and a dog on the beach most mornings. By the time *he* is an old man, the sea cliff will have fallen into the sea – and the old man who was once the boy will have to find a new pub.

Harriet would sometimes remark to me as she climbed from bed: 'Today my hair is a little longer and England a little smaller.'

What Furlong said rang true to me. Nowt but sand and water.

In a bid to make David smile I said: 'Every one that heareth these sayings of mine, and doeth them not, shall be likened unto a foolish man, which built his house upon the sand: and the rain descended, and the floods came, and the winds blew, and beat upon that house; and it fell – and great was the fall of it.'

David did indeed laugh, temperately, a breathy *ha ha ha ha* that dishevelled the froth of his beer. But Furlong squinted at me.

'You're a funny bugger, you,' he told me.

I had no ready rebuttal.

We drank on, the three of us, in the empty pub that smelt of Mr Holroyd's unpleasant pipe tobacco – I guiltily, thinking of my abandoned limpets (and of my abandoned wife), David carelessly and Furlong, it seemed, unthinkingly, or mechanically, as though he were some contraption (of iron, naturally) built only to hoist, empty and digest glasses of pale ale. Not long after the lamps came on, David excused himself vaguely, and Furlong and I fell into conversation about our respective home towns.

He was a child of the district of Sandyford, I learned, in the crowded east end of Newcastle. Father a puddler (an important role, I gathered, in iron manufactury), mother a charlady. This Peter was the sixth of eight Furlong children. He and two elder brothers had worked, first on the fish quay at North Shields and then later, and in Peter's case only briefly, for war had soon called, at the same ironworks that employed their father. A younger brother had gone to sea (and been lost, though whether that was in the war or in peacetime Furlong didn't make clear – the poor boy being to him, I suppose, neither a drowned sailor nor a drowned trawlerman but only a drowned brother). The rest were sisters – all, Furlong told me with a proud nod, successfully married off.

I politely expressed expectation that they had all *made good marriages*.

Furlong sneered.

'Is there such a thing?' he said, and showed his brown teeth. I told him that indeed there was, that indeed my own marriage was evidence of it, but he acted as though he hadn't heard me.

'One to a pitman, one to a fishmonger, one to a schoolmaster, one to a riveter,' he recited. It had to me the ring of a nursery rhyme, of 'This Little Piggy' or 'Baa Baa, Black Sheep'. Thus – like bags of black wool – had the Furlong girls been disposed of.

Peter Furlong had learned of his father's death in a factory accident while on watch in an Arras trench.

'Yours?' he asked in a comradely way.

'Still alive and kicking,' I muttered apologetically. It's terrible to feel apologetic for being alive, and more terrible for someone *else* being alive, but at that time it was difficult not to feel that way – there were so, so many dead. He eyed me fishily and drained the dregs of another pint.

On the subject of his own domestic arrangements, Furlong was laconic. A small house in Newcastle, was all he said. When I asked if he was married, he replied with a leer: 'No wife, just women.' I took a long draught of beer to conceal both my embarrassment and my anger at myself for being embarrassed.

We moved on, then, to what he called my 'trade', specifically birds, for he was something of an aficionado himself.

'A score of tippler, two dozen roller, eight blunderbuss and three pair of blue chequer,' he said, or rather declared like a card player showing his hand, and thumped his glass down on the table.

Pigeons. Furlong bred fancy pigeons in a loft at his Newcastle home. All I knew of the domesticated pigeon I had learned from Darwin's *Origin* ('The diversity of the breeds is something astonishing'); of the wild kind, however, I knew a little.

'It is strange, to a city man,' I mused aloud, 'to arrive at the coast and find pigeons – *our* pigeons, the very fellows we know from our rooftops and city squares – dwelling happily on the bleakest and most blasted sea cliffs. It's strange that this is, in fact, their *home*. It's strange to think that here, removed from the business of men, is where they belong.'

'They get everywhere,' Furlong said, with a curious note of distaste in his voice. 'Just like people.'

'Both are what Mr Darwin might call great adaptationists.'

'Mr Darwin. Him and his bloody bunk. There's no *chance* in this world, Mr, Lowell is it. All this, by accident?'

I suppressed a sigh. I could have explained, I suppose. Instead I drank my beer.

'Though I know what he means,' Furlong added with a raised hand, 'about *nature red in tooth and claw*.'

'Tennyson,' I corrected him, and was interested to note that the word came out as two slurred syllables.

Furlong's eyes had taken on a certain glassiness.

'Someone's doing it *on purpose*,' he insisted strangely.

We both looked up, and out, as a sudden breeze off the sea rattled the windowpane in its frame. We could see nothing but the reflections of the gaslights and our own half-reflected faces.

'Much more of that,' Furlong said, clutching his glass, 'and we'll be in the bloody sea.'

I smiled at his fear.

'Hardly. Only a gentle autumn easterly,' I said.

'Oh you think you're so *safe*,' he slurred. 'I'll show you how safe you are. Sand and water. Sand and bloody water. I'll show you. Come on.' He lurched from his stool and, seizing me by my coat sleeve, dragged me from mine. 'Come *on*.'

Clement Holroyd looked up in surprise from his newspaper as we banged through the gate in the bar. He took his pipe from his mouth.

'Now, gentlemen—'

'Fear not, fear not!' I reassured him brightly. He must have thought we were come like Vikings to plunder his cash till or to help ourselves to his pale ale.

'I'm an *architect*,' Furlong roared, hauling open the trapdoor in the floor. A gust of salty cold air came up at us as we descended unsteadily into the cellar. Holroyd's shadow loomed over us as he hovered at the trap, watching us.

'Look, you can *smell* it,' Furlong said with satisfaction.

He meant the sea, the sand and water on which he insisted we stood. And indeed we *could* smell it: though the cellar was dry, the smell of salt was such that seawater might have been swilling about our ankles. Interleaved with the odours of barrel wood and beer, it made a heady atmosphere.

As I blinked in the gloom, Furlong, with a 'Ha!', swung his boot against one of the pub's thick wooden pilings. I felt it quiver, and quivered myself – but the pub did not fall.

'You could knock it down with a feather,' Furlong mumbled with glee. 'You've no idea, you people, no idea.'

'Then the pier is impossible?' I asked, quite fuddled, and Furlong indistinctly replied, 'Everything's fucking impossible till it's not.'

I could hear the yelping of a herring gull.

'Listen,' I said, laying a hand on Furlong's shoulder.

Instead he booted the piling again, like a goalkeeper cleaning his boots on a goalpost.

Holroyd's cellar was long and wide, bigger by a good half again than the footprint of the pub itself, cut cleanly and deeply into the soft rock of the bluff. I walked a little further and became aware, as I walked, that the darkness did not deepen but, rather, grew less. It was not merely a case of my eyes becoming accustomed to the lack of light – not unless Holroyd's pale ale had gifted me with the night vision of an owl, for soon I was able even to discern the stencilled writing on the barrels stacked against the wall. As I soon realised, the double-shuttered outer door of the cellar was open. I saw a fraction of off-white moon; its light made a dove-grey rectangle on the dirt floor. Then, my stomach clenching like a fist, I saw two figures in the darkness beyond the rectangle.

One knelt before the other. They didn't move.

Furlong, who had crept up behind me, was better accustomed to darkness than was I. Every kind of darkness. At my ear, in a coarse whisper, he said: 'Why, it's Mr Novelist getting a chew off of the American lass.' Then he sniggered horribly. My gorge rose at the stink of beer on his breath.

The figure on its knees turned its head. I was transfixed. The moonlight gleamed for a moment on the moist lens of a dark eye. Then the head turned back into darkness. I could still hear the yelping, over and over, of the herring gull. I backed away, pulling Furlong by his arm. As we stumbled up the steps he was still gurgling with laughter.

Once we were restored to the public bar I took him by the shoulders. I wanted to hit him, but I had never hit anybody – and I did not want him to hit me.

'I am leaving,' I told him abruptly. 'I am going home.'

He nodded his head loosely. He either didn't understand or didn't care.

'Aye, aye, aye, aye, aye,' he said. He sounded like the herring gull had sounded.

I took up my coat and ignored Clement Holroyd's puzzled 'Goodnight!' as I walked from the pub. The sea wind assaulted me – it was in truth far more than a mild autumn easterly – but I welcomed it. I felt, indeed, brother to it: a thing of howling and wildness.

Harriet would be at home, I thought. She would surely still be awake; it was barely gone nine o'clock. I imagined finding Harriet in her preferred easy chair, pushing aside her book or embroidery frame, and kissing her in a rude, sailorly way. I would induce her to fondle me as she did on the outbound Bradford train that day. We would make urgent and ungainly love on the sitting-room furniture. It was too much to expect that she would take me in her mouth (a thing that my dear Harriet would sometimes do, but not now, surely, drunk as I was – and having, as I intended, disturbed her reading or embroidery).

As I walked to the road I undertook, clumsily, like a drunk man fumbling with a seaman's knot, to decouple the dark-red excitement I felt (and was loath to deny) from the memory of the figures in the beer cellar. The persistent yawping of herring gulls at roost did little to help me in this endeavour, and yet I tried: to picture Harriet, who was after all beautiful, and not the silhouette – of, there was no gainsaying it, Cordelia Shakes – I had seen kneeling before my friend David McAllister.

I was, of course, disgusted: by myself, by Cordelia and David, by gurgling Furlong and fat Holroyd. Through some sort of psychic osmosis I found myself disgusted by Harriet, too. The gulls' calls repeated in my ears as a bar of music or snatch of song repeats in the head of a man with a hangover – that is, torturously. And yet my arousal could not be denied. I was reminded of the fierce guilt I had felt when, as a schoolboy, some ugly sexual episode from the Old Testament had set the blood pounding in my loins. What sort of boy *are* you? I would demand of myself, locked in a toilet cubicle with tears stinging my eyes. It might have been the rape of Tamar or the harlotry of Potifar's wife. What sort of boy, I would weepingly ask, reads of Jezebel murdered, cast from a window and eaten by wild dogs, and gets a hard-on, as we called it, beneath his school desk?

Of course I came to understand that feelings of this kind are seldom straightforward. Their causes and consequences can be as infinite as those of the weather or the deep currents of the oceans. We shall never understand them; we can seldom control them. Our aim, rather, ought always to be to navigate, to trim or hoist sail, to adapt as a fishing fleet adapts to storms and tides, to *cope*. Thus, heroic and drunk, I wrestled with my lust and my loathing all the way to the road. At which juncture, beneath the indigo lamplight, I beheld a spirit all in white. It was the other Miss Shakes, Eleanor, sent by her father to enquire after her sister's whereabouts.

Were we all to suffer having our mouths stuffed with questions by the turbulent Maurice Shakes? For now the noise of the gulls had ceased and all I could picture in my head was the image of Miss Eleanor Shakes kneeling at my feet and all I could hear in my head was Shakes's plea as I had descended the escarpment: *if you would only ask, sir! If you would only ask!*

It's all Christopher looking daringly at Cynthia across the supper table or Harold drunk in a taxicab because Dorothy won't return his love. It's all well and good, and it's very witty and clever and all that, but I don't see how it's enough for anybody to live off and it doesn't seem like much of a job for a grown man.

Won't tell him that, of course. No doubt I'll simper something about how lovely it is. And it is lovely really, in its way. Oh, I don't know. Books. At the end of it all they're just not real, are they? Sounds daft to say that. The way people go on. But they're not real. It might not bother David McAllister or the fellers from Oxford on the wireless and in the papers but it does me – they're just not.

Set it aside. Sip of tea. It's gone cold, which tells you something, I suppose. I asked him what it was called, this 'work in progress'. He said he never came up with a title until the very last minute, and then he just sort of plucked one out of thin air. But that's the sort of thing he *would* say.

Dad used to read. Serious books about, oh I don't know, The Future and The Way Things Are Going and The Shape of Things to Come. Turned out he hadn't much need to worry on that score. And then he had his shelf of textbooks, 'technical books', he called them – engineering, practical mathematics, all that. His idea of a hobby. I'd sooner collect coins or press flowers but there you are.

Never happier than when he was sat down with a pencil and a puzzle about loads and balances, torque and shear. Tell you what, I'd have liked to see Maurice Shakes come up against Dad on that score. 'Now might I maybe double-check your arithmetic on this point, Mr Shakes? I don't mean to be a doubting Thomas, Mr Shakes, but have you factored in the impact of x on the y of z?' I'd pay a shilling to watch that.

Mother must still have the books. Out of date now, I suppose. Victorian. Do we have new engineering now? New arithmetic? We've certainly got new men.

As for Mother's books. A lot of silly novels about silly women coming to a Bad End. Dad wasn't keen – said it gave her ideas. Gosh, Dad, it didn't half.

Did he read, James? Can't remember. If he did, it was war stories and simple good-hearted tales of simple good-hearted folk. And he read his Bible, of course. Probably not right to say that's a novel. But you can't say it's all real either, can you? Not all of it. Not in this day and age.

I don't suppose James ever doubted a word of it. From James to Jon, what a leap! Whatever the opposite of a leap of faith is.

There's a bit about the war in this work in progress of David's. I heard him say to Jon that it's not a 'war novel', and he said it as though he couldn't think of anything worse in the world than that. As though a war novel was the only thing worse than a war. But there's a bit about the war.

Some folk'd say well, what the hell does he know about that? This clever young fop who's probably never been nearer to France than the end of Skegness pier and never had a wound worse than a paper cut. And you could say he lost his father over there, but then they'd say well, for a start who didn't? And besides, that's his father, that's not him.

They'd have a point. After all, I lost my dad to lung cancer and I don't know the first thing about that, not really.

And you might think I'd be one of those folk saying that, but I don't think I am. Because I think David McAllister does know. Don't ask me how. But from what he says, from what he writes, I mean, in this stupid book, he does.

Partly it's that he hates it. If you hate it, it means you at least understand something about it. But I think he also understands about courage, and cowardice. He knows what a lot of rot it all is, underneath. Not that there's no such things, of course – just that they're not always what you think they are.

Doesn't sound like a hard thing to grasp when you put it like that. But I wish more people understood it.

The most stupid and awful thing about it is that I think David knows more about it than James ever did. James, who was there, saw it all, for two years lived every last nasty, bloody minute of the thing – brave, kind James, who fell out of a troopship and got swallowed by the sea. It's a terrible thing to think but really I think James went right the way through his war without knowing the first thing about it.

Now how can that be?

Pick up the wad of paper again. Daft Harold moping about London. Wet Cynthia having a breakdown over a vase of carnations. I don't know. I want to find out what else this David McAllister knows about.

IX

That day, the day at the technical college when David and I, over breakfast, discussed the loss on Everest of Mallory and Irvine, was the day of what we would later come to call 'the game'. It was an early-season match between local technical colleges, each of middling standard, played on the riverside square at Saltaire Cricket Club, and momentous in no way other than that, between toss and stumps, David and I learned that we weren't really able to do without one another.

The skies were a mottled silver-blue, the sunlight milky and intermittent, the turf of the outfield somewhat soggy from the previous day's rain. Yellow wagtails patrolled the boundary rope. I – a poorish player, picked for the side only three times that season – fielded at deep third man. David, who of course fielded at backward point, had directed me there: 'Deep, but not meaningful,' he had said with a smile.

I daydreamed. I watched girls walking arm in arm along the riverbank. A chaffinch sang in an ash tree just beyond the leg-side boundary. The song of the chaffinch has been likened to the approach and delivery of a fast bowler: the galloping run-up (*pa-pa-pa-pa-pa*), the rhythmic convulsion at the wicket (*papapa*) and then *wheee* (the hurtle of the ball down the pitch); I listened to the chaffinch and watched our fast bowlers, Smith (heavy-footed, thick-kneed) and Clissold (shock-headed, teetering, slender as a plant stem), and could see little resemblance.

All through the morning I hoped that the ball wouldn't come to me – and at the same time I pictured myself leaping to claim one-handed a spectacular and somehow match-winning catch.

When a wicket fell to Clissold or Smith – or to David, who bowled devious leg spin – I clapped my hands and cried 'hooray'. On half a dozen occasions I was required to field the ball: it was wet and hard, hairy with grass clippings, and the heaviness of its five-and-a-half ounces surprised me. My return throws to the wicketkeeper Pinnock prompted chuckles from my fellow fielders; 'Yon lad's got an arm like a limp stick of celery,' a red-headed batsman jeered, and Pinnock, taking the ball on its third bounce, laughed.

I was not hurt; I was used to being held in disdain by athletes of one code or another. I shrugged my shoulders, and watched a wagtail pursue a jiggering crane fly fresh-hatched from the earth.

Yet for all that I was not hurt, it was a pleasure to me – *more* than a pleasure, a heart's leap, a small epiphany – when David, pitching the ball up and disguising the googly, spun the ball past the confident stroke of the red-headed batsman and neatly clipped the bail from the leg-side stump.

'Well bowled!' I cried as the batsman walked mopily from the field, and David waved a lordly hand in my direction.

One might imagine that what I felt in that moment was simply the wide-eyed idolatry of the weaker, smaller boy for the stronger and larger: the house captain who steps in to spare a swot a pounding from a bully, the taller boy from the year above who fetches a kite down from a tree, the big brother who can ride a bicycle, lift dumb-bells and vault a five-bar gate.

There may have been a little of that. My father was no sportsman, handicapped by – no, *characterised* by – a frail frame and a heart with an irregular beat. I had no brothers; I wasn't accustomed to a superman of David's stripe taking *my* part, however obliquely.

But for this same reason, *because* no six-footer had ever boxed a bully's ears on my behalf, because my kite had always remained forever trapped in the tree, I couldn't readily accept that David's dismissal of the batsman who had ragged me was anything in the nature of a favour or boon. Instead, I felt, it must be a *quid* for my *quo*. What my *quo* might be I didn't know, but I had learned from my father that a man who has few physical gifts might yet have gifts of other kinds, and I felt not that David outweighed me but that, rather, we were in some unknown way of equal weight – that each of us was the other's counterweight. Watching the red-headed batsman climb the pavilion steps, I wondered with some excitement what price, in this bargain, I would be asked to pay; I watched David stroll back to his mark, tossing the blood-red ball from hand to hand as he walked, and waited eagerly for the nature of my role in the grand game to be disclosed.

The weir downriver roared. At the river's edge, mallards bickered over bread crusts thrown into the water by two small boys in sandals. A kingfisher said *chee-kee*. Clissold took a wicket, and Smith two, and I again shouted: 'Hooray!' and clapped my cold hands, and the Keighley XI were all out for, I think, a hundred and twelve.

It was fairly clear to me, as I trotted from the field, that David McAllister and I would bat together, that he (batting at three) and I (batting at six) would come together at the crease and that my task would be to accompany him, perhaps chipping in the odd single or off-side two, as he cut, pulled, drove and dashed us to our run target – that this would be my side of the equation we together made.

Perhaps I would shake his hand when he reached his fifty.

In the pavilion, I approached him diffidently as he was buckling on his pads.

'Terrific googly to bag that carrot-top, McAllister,' I said.

'Ah, thank you –' he looked up – 'Lowell.' Buckles fastened, he straightened and stretched his arms up over his head. I heard his elbow joints creak. 'Wasn't bad, was it? Job's only half done, though.'

'A hundred and twelve? I'm sure you'll knock that off with your eyes closed.'

He looked at me oddly, half-smiling.

'Well, let's not forget Howard and Leng,' he said, with a suggestion of reproach. 'With a bit of luck we'll get through this without me having to pick up my damn bat.'

Howard and Leng – our opening batsmen, of course. I'd entirely forgotten about them. In fact, to all intents and purposes, I'd forgotten that there was anyone in our team other than me and David. I felt myself flush; I turned away to rummage in my kitbag.

They stumped past me, our openers, a few minutes later, as they headed out on to the field to begin our innings.

Leng called over his shoulder: 'Put your feet up, McAllister. We've got this in hand.'

David laughed. It felt obscurely like a jibe at me.

Howard said something to Leng about a pint of beer for whoever was first to hit a six into the river (they were both rather tough boys, who were known to sneak into the public bar at the Bee-hive – indeed, Howard, whom I found somewhat frightening, claimed to have bedded the barmaid).

We watched from the pavilion veranda – some leaning on the railing, David seated on the steps, me perched awkwardly atop my kitbag – as our innings began. The conversation was desultory: about the innings just completed, the girls walking the riverside path, Leng's questionable defensive technique, the chance of rain and most of all the monstrous quick who was opening the bowling for Keighley.

'He's a big bugger,' Pinnock said fearfully.

'And there went out a champion out of the camp of the Philistines, named Goliath, of Gath, whose height was six cubits and a span,' I said.

I heard David laugh quietly. It didn't occur to me that, if I heard David laugh, it must have meant that no one else laughed, but I wouldn't have cared in any case.

This bowler was indeed a big bugger, perhaps not six cubits but certainly six feet, wide across the shoulders, with hairy forearms and a thoroughbred's backside. His run-up was perhaps thirty feet and he flung himself violently through the bowler's crease. Clissold and Smith hadn't managed to derive much bounce from the moist wicket, but this boy (how strange to think that he was only a boy!) certainly did: twice in the first over the ball went whistling beneath a batsman's chin.

'This ought to be a lark,' David said thoughtfully.

To me, the probable path of events was growing clearer: Leng would not last long (for his technique was indeed questionable); David would go into bat; Howard, Thorp, Wiley and Pinnock would all fall swiftly before the hairy Keighley destroyer; and I, the last batsman before the team was reduced to its tail end, would march out to rescue the whole show. I wasn't an especially good cricketer, it was true, but I wasn't entirely rotten where batting was concerned. I was obdurate, and technically fairly accomplished; I scored few runs, but made few mistakes. In the circumstances I would be just what the doctor ordered.

Goliath struck in the fifth over, crashing a short ball into Leng's bat handle; second slip took the catch. I think the score was six or seven. Out walked David, tugging on his gloves with his bat tucked under his arm.

'We've not got a bloody prayer,' Leng mumbled, tramping up the steps.

'Least we've got a lad out there now who knows how to move his fucking feet,' snapped Pinnock. In answer, Leng threw his bat down on the boards of the veranda.

It was the Keighley spinner, a small, fat boy in black boots, that took Howard's wicket. Then I felt a prophet's satisfaction when Thorp's leg-stump was dashed from the ground by Goliath's yorker and Wiley, following him in, gloved a good-length ball to gully. David, as these fell haplessly at the other end, batted with grace and scored steadily. The oiled wood of his bat glowed like gold.

I'd seen Pinnock's hands shaking as he was adjusting the grip of his bat handle in the pavilion, but out in the middle he put up something of a fight, fending off short balls with a sort of outraged indignation and snatching panicky singles when he could (it seemed as though David, loping the other way, covered the twenty-two yards with barely half the strides that Pinnock required). His inevitable demise came with the score at seventy-something: a wild outswinger, a swipe, an edge, a lateral leap by the Keighley keeper.

When I joined David in the middle, he greeted me with an unsmiling nod. I kept my face accordingly stiff and stern, though I *wanted* to smile and say: 'It's all right, McAllister. I'm here now.'

It was not Goliath but another bowler, a dark-eyed medium-pacer, who had seen off Pinnock, and so it was this medium-pacer who delivered my first ball. I stepped forwards to meet it as it came up off a fullish length, blocked with impeccable technique, shuddered at the impact of ball on bat and bat on bone, and heard David tensely mutter: '*That's* it, Lowell.' It was the final ball of the over. David's turn to take the strike. I watched Goliath lollop in from the boundary, where he had been fielding without distinction, to the boot scrape in the grass that marked the end of his run-up, thirty feet behind my stumps. I watched the ball work its way round the off-side field, from keeper to slip to gully to point to cover, and then finally out to Goliath, who inspected it cursorily, gave it a brief rub on his flannels, rocked back on his right heel and began his run.

I turned to watch David. It's a fearful feeling indeed to stand with one's back to a giant who is galloping towards you, the thunder of whose footfalls you can feel through the soles of your cricket boots, knowing that you mustn't turn to look – knowing that you must watch, instead, the giant's quarry as he crouches unprotected in his crease. His eyes grow wide. His bat twitches.

The rhythm of the rapid footfalls broke as Goliath leapt into his delivery stride a yard to my left in an industrial explosion of heat, noise and expelled steam: 'Uunk,' as the ball was delivered. *Not at all like a chaffinch*, I remember thinking.

As David lifted his head, the wind blew his hair up from his brow. He rocked backwards – *that's* the way, McAllister, I might have said, for the ball was a short one, spearing into the turf and rocketing, as David's bat swung up and across to meet it, towards his throat. His blue eyes crossed in the effort of following its flight.

This, of course, was David's role in our drama, his dashingly hooked six a complement to my diligent forward defensive. I edged out of my crease, although I hardly expected to have to run: this would surely end up in the river.

The ball met the bat. It was quicker than it looked. It barely kissed the wood. It rode instead the ridge of the bat as David, twisting his wrists, brought the blade round in front of his face.

If he had turned his face away from the ball he might have suffered a broken cheekbone, as Hobbs had at Edgbaston the previous summer. He didn't. He watched it and watched it and at the last moment, arms thrown out and back bent into a C, he lifted his chin, as though he hoped that the ball would skim over the surface of his face, perhaps parting his hair down the middle or shaving the skin from the tip of his nose.

It thumped into his mouth. The bat flew from his hands. And I ran.

In the time it took me to run those twenty-two yards down the pitch to where David crawled coughing on his hands and knees I forgot entirely about our complementarity, our cosmic bargain – but then, when he lifted his white and ruined face to look at me, my heart jerked as if caught in a snare and once again I understood.

I dropped my bat, stooped, pulled off my right glove and picked up from the blood-splashed yellow turf a tooth, a long, clean incisor still attached to a ganglion of pink gum. It was warm in my palm. It reminded me of a strange sea creature, a thing of sharp-edged calcite and vulnerable flesh. Then I looked at David. He remained on all fours, the Keighley keeper bent over him in concern, the close fielders approaching slowly, hesitant and murmurous: 'What a wallop!', 'Are you all right, pal?', 'You copped a good 'un there, lad', 'Christ, I can't abide the sight of blood'.

In David's blue eyes as he gaped at me there was nothing but a terrible animal wildness. The shattered red ring of his mouth was a grisly sight but those eyes were worse.

I knelt beside him. Panic is a strange thing. His breath was a ragged repeated cry.

'Just a blow from a cricket ball,' I said. 'Just a mouthful of teeth.'

Panic is the abrupt realisation of how near we are, *always* are, to horror. There needn't be a war. There needn't even be a cricket match. It's always there, only just beyond a film as easy to break as surface tension on pondwater – indeed, we skate that film as aquatic insects skate upon the water.

And yet a cricket ball in the mouth, broken teeth, blood on a Yorkshire cricket field – these are not things of horror. Intimations of the thing, perhaps, but not the thing itself.

I watched David's eyes (watched the pupils contract and the red recede) and saw, first, that he understood this, and second, that he would not have understood it had it not been for me. Without my banal iteration of what simply and plainly *was*, he would, I knew, have been overwhelmed – he (rather than only his teeth) would have been broken.

He moaned something.

'What's that?'

He made the same noise, more forcefully, and gestured with one upraised finger.

Aweoo. Am I out?

I laughed. David, now dabbing at his mouth with a shirt cuff, furrowed his brow at me. Chastened, I replied: 'No, McAllister. It didn't carry. Not out.'

He nodded. He lifted himself up on to his knees and, planting his bat two-handed in the turf, levered himself to his feet. Blood had drawn a vivid necktie of red down his front and spattered the toes of his boots.

Breathing stertorously, he swung his bat twice in a circle, and then flexed his shoulders. He butted the bat-end twice into the bloodstained crease. I squinted up at him sceptically.

'McAllister, this is folly.'

'There's a game to play,' I think he said.

'Don't be a bloody fool.'

'Get back to your fucking crease, Lowell,' he said, and spat out a gob of gore. I rose, shrugged, retreated to the non-striker's end – until he called me back and held out his open palm.

'Teeth,' he said. 'You picked 'em up?'

I dropped the incisor into his hand.

'Just that one. How many are you missing?'

'Three. Swallowed one. Where's the other? Ah—' he dropped to one knee, picked something up from the grass, slipped it and the incisor into his trouser pocket. 'Now bloody come *on*, Lowell.' He moved unsteadily back to his crease, shook his head, and asked the umpire for middle-and-leg. I heard the disbelieving laughter of the Keighley close fielders.

It *was* folly, of course. David could barely keep his feet. And of course, we lost – David skittled by Goliath, me absent-mindedly run out, Clissold, Smith and the rest of the tail hardly putting up a fight at all, and the lot of us dismissed for ninety-one. Purest folly.

If a man has to be a fool he'd best be a grand fool, the architect Furlong had said.

That moment, of conscious complementarity, of what biologists call symbiosis; that immediate and thrilling knowledge that each of us contained the other, as at the same time the seas contain the land and the land contains the seas – I had not expected, since 'the game', to find it again (for after all I had not found it with Harriet).

*

She turned in my direction – or perhaps she turned towards the pub, in pursuit of Cordelia, and found me in her path. I remember the way she walked, somewhat up on the balls of her feet, springily resilient against the grain of the weather. I remember how her eyes were – I might have guessed, in that first moment, that what I saw in them was pain (indeed perhaps it was). I think we said one another's names: Mr Lowell, Miss Shakes.

It was then that she told me she had been sent to fetch her sister. Uneasily, I said that her sister might not feel inclined to be fetched. Oh, well, she said – she would try, so that she could at least say with good conscience that she had executed her commission.

I reached up to tip my hat at the same moment that Eleanor hit her foot against the uneven kerb. She began to fall and I stepped forwards to catch her. I don't think she would have fallen. I think if I had not moved she would have caught her balance. I did move, however, and in a moment I held Eleanor by her shoulder and her coat lapel, and she held me by a handful of shirt and the forearm of my right jacket sleeve.

In a single small and considered movement she tilted her head and touched her lips momentarily to my open mouth.

I had not, I said, expected to find it again. I found it now, a little drunk, a little wild, a grand fool beneath the last light on the windblown coast road, as after little more than a few seconds' hesitation I moved my right hand from Eleanor's shoulder to the blunt angle of her jaw and pressed my open mouth against hers.

I'm not saying that Dad wished I was a boy. Not exactly. It's not as though he looked at me in my pinny and ribbons and wished I was all skinned knees and snot and bicycle grease, but he wanted a boy, I'm sure about that. I think he thought I was more or less all right the way I was but he would have liked a boy – someone who might have managed a department or overseen a factory floor or captained a trawler (or a cricket eleven or an army regiment). I don't think he was disappointed exactly.

Jon's still out. Sat here thinking about Dad and his puzzles, his numbers, his smart pencil charts and graphs.

It's snagged, somehow, this pier business. Only gently, like goosegrass or a stickybud. But somehow it's sticking. Can't shake it.

Dad might have said you can't trust outsiders. They come in with their fancy ideas and back-of-a-napkin arithmetic but they can't ever really know a place like this – not like we know it. They can't ever know how dangerous our seas can be, our shifting sands, our eroding rock.

I don't think that. There are bright folk everywhere and believe me there's no shortage of thick heads in Gravely. What I think is, outsiders can see risk, can smell danger, just as well as anyone here can – but only if they think to look for it.

When Dad bought me a Hornby Meccano set the first time, I was nine, and he was as excited about it as I was – but the point,

I suppose, is that I was as excited about it as he was. It was the one with nickel finish instead of tinplate. We built a girder crane. Look at that, he kept saying, when it was done. Look what we did. Look at that! The top of it came up higher than my knees. When you turned the handle it could pick up a potato or a jar of mustard.

Dad made a little sign that we pinned to the side of it. Holloway and Daughter Shipyard.

A few years later he bought me the Coronation set second-hand from the lad of a work pal, and he wanted to build a motor bus – I can still see it, the picture in the manual. 'Meccano', it said on the side, 'A Hobby for Bright Boys' – but I was twelve by then and I'd cottoned on.

I saw the latest set in Goldby's the other afternoon when I was buying a toy drum for little Michael Hesketh's birthday (Louisa won't thank me for it but I think it's so funny to see a little one beating a drum). Number 7, they're up to. Braced girders, triangular plates, trunnions, electric motors. Dad would have been beside himself – until he saw the price, at least. Three and six. It's a lot for a toy but of course Dad would have said it's not a toy, it's a system. I heard him say it to Mother: it's a system of mechanical demonstration. He must have got it out of one of the manuals.

I say it to myself now, inside my head, and I can't help hearing it in the voice of Maurice Shakes. My pier is no toy, sir – no, it is a system, sir, a system of mechanical demonstration!

Then I hear Mother's voice, plain as day: men.

Tinker, tinker, tinker. Doing just as they please. Give Mr Shakes a Meccano set and he'd have the pieces tipped out all over the carpet before he's even opened the manual. It's what Mr Aldridge would no doubt call vanity or pride but I call it sheer bone idleness. Anyone can have a dream. It's easy to have a dream. What's not easy is doing the work. Because if you're not doing the work then some other juggins surely is. Someone's paying for your daft dream.

Or else no one is, and what then?

I feel as though I can still feel the hard corners of those little Meccano struts against the soft part of my hand.

X

'He's standing in the street. Right in the middle of the street.'

Harriet, in damask-pink church clothes, was leaning on the doorframe, craning her neck to see beyond the bend of our shingle driveway to the coast road – where, it seemed, Maurice Shakes was standing right in the middle of the street.

She laughed.

'What is he *doing*?'

'I don't know. Playing British bulldog with the churchgoers, possibly.'

'The man is crackers.'

'"It is easier for a camel to pass through the eye of a needle than for a Gravely man to outdo Maurice Shakes at a game of British bulldog",' I extemporised. Harriet laughed, and turned and kissed me – half on the mouth, half on the cheek.

'Let me see,' I said, moving her aside with a hand on her shoulder. I peered out. There, indeed, he was: in the middle of the coast road, greatcoat unbuttoned and flapping, arms spread wide, six-foot staff in his right hand. He was calling or crying out; the breeze brought to us the sound of his voice, but not the sense of his words.

It was a fierce morning, bright and sharp with sun and salt, and hard on a man who had been drunk (and more) the previous evening. I shaded my eyes.

'Is he preaching?'

'Reverend Aldridge won't stand for it if he is,' Harriet said.

She was fastening her grey-ribboned hat. I took my coat down from its hook and shrugged it on. Our agreed plan was that I was to escort Harriet to the door of the church – but no further – and would wait, patrolling the dunes and rock pools as was my habit, until she (or, rather, Aldridge) was done. Then we were to meet David, and the three of us were to take lunch with some friends of Harriet's family. It would all, I had thought, be unobjectionable enough – but of course I had reckoned without Mr Shakes planting himself plumb in the middle of the day's thoroughfare.

'I shouldn't much care to be harangued by Mr Shakes at this hour,' I muttered as, arm in arm, we picked our way along the uneven driveway.

'Not with your hangover,' Harriet smiled, nudging me in my side.

'Well, quite. I've heard of men taking a raw oyster or a whole chilli pepper to cure the morning-afters but I'd defy even them to tackle a draught of undiluted Shakes on an empty stomach, and keep it down.' From here I could see that it was, indeed, the good churchgoers of Gravely that Shakes was addressing. As they drifted down the coast road, he called out to them, jovially it seemed – no tales here, at least, I supposed, of gruesome death in the South Seas (although it was by no means beyond Shakes to tell such tales, and remain jovial).

'Keep him on *your* side,' Harriet said, skipping nervously behind me to take the leftward side of the pavement. I should have done so anyway, of course, the done thing being what it is. But, as we approached the mighty figure in the road, I felt that I should have preferred to walk along the busiest street in London, and bear the petrol fumes and horse dung and drivers' foul language, than to walk this coast road and meet with what I *did* have to meet with.

'Good morning, good morning, Mr and Mrs Lowell!' Maurice Shakes roared.

My skull rang like a bell. I winced, and murmured a politeness in reply. Harriet laughed nervously and said hello. We both kept walking – until Shakes, reaching out, laid a hand on my arm.

I wished I were the kind of man who might have turned and, raising a sword – or, better, a horsewhip – demanded: 'Unhand me, sir!'

Instead I looked down mildly at his hand on my arm and then up into his creased and smiling face.

'In a hurry to hear the good word of the Lord, I know,' he said, and winked outrageously, 'but I'm out this morning spreading tidings of my own.'

'Mr Shakes, I'm afraid—'

He shook me by my arm reassuringly.

'No, no, I'll only take a second, Mr Lowell, Mrs Lowell – all I have to say is that I am convening a meeting, a town meeting. I want to tell you all about my plans for the north bay. And I want every soul in Gravely to come along and tell me exactly what they think of me. Ha!' He barked out the laugh like a seal. 'This afternoon, my dear sir, my dear lady. Two o'clock in, I believe it's called, the old Friends' Meeting House. *Please* be there. It would mean a great deal to me.' Finally, he released my arm, and made a come-by gesture. 'Now go, go. Go to your God!' Again the laugh. 'And please,' he called as we walked away, 'give my love to your Reverend Aldridge!'

It sounded so strange, to hear that word spoken so boldly, so nakedly, on that exposed coast road: *love*.

We had only kissed, Eleanor Shakes and I. But of course, in truth, no one ever *only* kisses. I had held her with one hand in the small of her back and the other on her shoulder blade. She had cupped her warm hands over my ears and her fingertips had moved lightly in the hair of my temples.

'Why *there*, of all places?' Harriet said fretfully as we approached the church.

I shrugged. 'Whalers and Quakers.'

Then I had stumbled away, a sorry creature of regret, mewling apologies. Although *regret* may not be quite the right word.

Had it been merely a matter of bodily lust and pale ale? I did not think so. I do not think so. I recalled it all again, muzzily, miserably, as at the lychgate Harriet recapped our lunch plans (the Heskeths, twelve o'clock, in their home in Sallow Sluice). Had Eleanor said anything, anything at all, as I walked away, telling her (and the coast road, and the night air) that I was sorry, sorry, sorry?

'—and tell David to behave himself.' Harriet reached up to smooth my lapel.

'I'm sure he'll be as decorous as ever.'

She had not, I'm certain. I had not looked back (I don't think I was afraid that she would vanish, like Eurydice; more likely, I was afraid she would still be there).

I kissed Harriet's cheek and watched her walk away along the path that led to the church through a petrified forest of tall grey gravestones. A blackbird alighted on one of the stones, cocked its tail reflexively and flew away. A churchgoer passing by – I think it was Souter the grocer – said, 'Good morning, Mr Lowell,' and I returned the salutation absently. I turned from the church, and began the walk back to the coast road and to the beach. While Harriet bore witness to Aldridge's muscular Christianity, I would, as Harriet was wont to put it, 'do my barnacles'. She had taken the term from a story about Mr Darwin; Darwin's second son George, the story goes, was so accustomed to his father's anatomising that, on being shown round a schoolfriend's family home, he innocently asked: 'And where does your father do his barnacles?'

I had thought it rather funny of Harriet to appropriate the term as a catch-all for my rock-pooling and birdwatching. Now, as I stepped again on to the familiar brown maps of rock that spread out from the Gravely sands, and watched the wind-blown beads of spume roll across the limpet beds and felt the barnacles scuff the soles of my shoes, I recalled another fragment of Darwiniana. In around 1845, having settled at Down House and founded a family, Darwin wrote to his old ship's captain, the doomed Fitzroy, and said (with, I think, much satisfaction): 'I am fixed on the spot where I shall end it.'

He had barnacles in mind, of course – he had little but barnacles in mind for the whole of the 1840s.

I stopped at the edge of the rocks and looked, first north to the little harbour, and then back to the church, and then south and up to the bluff, and the priory and its sad hawthorn. I tried out the words for myself: 'I am fixed on the spot where I shall end it.'

A wave broke on the rocks and the sea ran in little rivers about my feet.

*

Luke Hesketh was a schoolteacher, a local man, reserved and broad-shouldered, rigidly and blackly moustached. I liked him. He taught in a junior position at the Greenbank school, just north of Gravely and just south of Sallow Sluice (the latter being a ten-minute walk up the coast from the former). Two or three times, at his request, I had led his classes on desultory tours of the local countryside – 'Listen closely, children, and you might hear the song of the cock-robin!' and so on.

Luke and his wife Louisa had a child, a son, Michael, who was at this time perhaps two years old. I sipped at the glass of brown ale that Louisa had poured for me and smiled indulgently as the boy capered about the Heskeths' drawing room.

'Has he been bought his first cricket bat yet?' David McAllister asked. 'Or his first pair of football boots?'

Louisa smiled glassily. She had read two of David's novels and, for all Harriet's forewarnings, had been somewhat star-struck by the arrival in her midst of the handsome and garlanded author.

Luke said: 'He may take after his grandfather and be a rugby man, when he's old enough. But for now it's natural history for the lad.'

'Better than games, as Captain Scott said,' I remarked. It had been a great boost to me when, as an adolescent, I had learned of Scott's adjuration in his last letter home to his wife: *Get the boy interested in natural history, if you can – it is better than games.* The next morning I had stridden into school in triumph, and chaffed all the footer first-teamers: 'See! See! Scott of the Antarctic knew his business all right!'

But perhaps the lost captain was too grave an allusion for the company; everyone seemed to mull on the remark rather grimly, until Louisa broke the silence by exclaiming that Michael knew *all* of the birds in the garden.

'He knows more than me, then.' Harriet smiled.

'Yes, but *your* little one will learn all that from Jon,' Louisa said. I saw Luke's moustache stiffen at the impropriety. 'And *you* can teach him – or her! – all the things *you* know.'

'That won't take long.' Harriet gave me a sidelong look and a wry, gentle smile that simply tore at my heart.

I was conscious that Luke – straight-backed in the window seat, jaw clenched, fist tight about his tumbler of beer – was trying to think of something to say to divert attention from our embarrassing childlessness. We had after all been married for two years, Harriet and I.

Of course, David stepped in.

'It's good to see something of the country north of the village,' he said. He was perched beside me on a cushioned form by the fireplace. I noted without much concern that he had already finished his drink. 'I think I've seen all that Gravely has to offer – your village, if Jon and Harriet will forgive me, is far prettier.'

Louisa gave a whooping sort of giggle, like the noise a redshank makes.

'There's less hustle and bustle here,' Luke said, without intending irony. 'Quiet charm, you might call it.'

'Indeed you might. At least' – David raised a finger, and I, seeing clearly what was coming, was filled with an urge to grab at it and snap it in two – 'until Mr Shakes plants his carnival on the north beach.'

Luke's face was a dumb mask of polite incomprehension.

Harriet sighed and said: 'Oh, for heaven's sake. Must that man intrude on our every waking moment?'

As David opened his mouth to reply, little Michael, who had been toddling in the corner, suddenly cried: 'Aooo!' He had, it seemed, bumped his head on the edge of the windowsill.

'Yes, that's exactly how *I* feel about the fellow, too,' Harriet said as Louisa sprang from her chair to snatch up the bawling boy.

Over Michael's noise and Louisa's *hush-hush*es, I explained to Luke, with much internal discomfort, who this Shakes character was, and what he intended for the strand of shore that ran from the Gravely harbour north towards Sallow Sluice.

He nodded imperturbably.

'Such a plan is surely a pipe dream,' he said.

David and I both leaned forwards in our seat and began to frame I-know-better rebuttals ('Ah, you see—', 'It may appear so, but—'). Then we both stopped, and looked at each other, and laughed.

We had been bewitched (or bewarlocked – or, in fact, both). We had drunk too deeply of Maurice Shakes's heady charisma, and that of his daughters; it had fuddled our reason more thoroughly than had all of Clement Holroyd's beer. It took a stout rationalist like Luke Hesketh – innocent of Shakes and his daughters' influence – to slap our faces, clear our heads and restore us to our senses.

'You know, you may be right,' smiled David, leaning back and folding his hands across his waistcoat front.

'When you hear Mr Shakes talk of it,' I said apologetically, 'it seems rather believable. One suspends one's incredulity.'

'Always a perilous undertaking,' Luke said, with the shadow of a smile, which I thought was a bit rich coming from a churchgoer.

We sat quietly for a few moments, and watched Michael, who had been deftly mollified by his mother, lurch about the floor. There was a wooden elephant at Louisa's feet. Michael picked it up and stuffed its head into his mouth.

'Not much meat on that, old boy,' Luke murmured.

I laughed. I liked small children; they always amused me. I liked to watch a sitting baby pick up its own leg as though it were some curious foreign object. I liked to watch the fluid play of entirely unconnected emotions across a baby's face. Did I want one for myself – or, rather, for ourselves?

It seemed rather a daring undertaking – rather a bold venturing forth. But in any case, despite the many and joyous consummations of our marriage, no zygote had yet been forthcoming. Such were the straightforward facts. To Harriet, I suspect, they were rather sad facts; to me – well, to me they were just facts.

David, who seemed preoccupied by his theme, said: 'In any case, we all have the opportunity to hear Mr Shakes put his case to the people in person, as he has called a pow-wow or public meeting this very afternoon. Perhaps we could all stroll down together after lunch and see what he has to say.'

'Where is the meeting?' Louisa timidly enquired.

'The old Friends' Meeting House,' I said.

Louisa said, 'Oh.' Luke clucked his tongue and said: 'Why *there*, of all places?'

I caught David's quizzical look. But it was almost one o'clock. The story of the Gravely Friends' Meeting House would have to wait; it was no sort of story for a Sunday lunch table.

*

'It isn't something that we need to *dwell* on,' Harriet said. 'I'll never understand, Jon, why you always seem to need to *dwell* on things.'

We were on the clifftop just below Sallow Sluice, walking south to Gravely and the meeting. Louisa and Luke had decided not to join us (she had to bath the baby, he had to prepare some schoolwork – and besides, who walks a mile to hear a fool's pipe-dream?). Jackdaws rose and fell from beneath the cliff edge. The day had lost its bright polish, but the sky was still clear.

The three of us walked arm in arm: David, who was never troubled by heights, on my left, Harriet on my right. David smoked a rare cigarette. Harriet's pretty and pale left hand squeezed the crook of my elbow.

It was David, of course, who had started the row.

'So come on, Lowell,' he had said. 'When you mentioned this Friends' Meeting House, it was as though you'd dragged a corpse from the Heskeths' crockery cupboard. There's a story there – I can *smell* it. Tell, tell.'

I had said that indeed there *was* a story, and a good one if not a happy one. And at this Harriet had tugged on my arm and said that bygones were bygones, for heaven's sake, and why should the decent people of the village always have to be re*mind*ed of it, Jon, again and again, when it all happened so long ago?

I had said (mildly) that it wasn't all *that* long ago.

'It isn't something that we need to *dwell* on,' Harriet said. 'I'll never understand, Jon, why you always seem to need to *dwell* on things.'

In any case, as we walked, the story got told.

There were quite a lot of Quakers in Gravely around the turn of the century. They were businessmen, mostly, and good ones; they insured the shipowners, funded the boatbuilders, maintained with diligence and honesty the economy of the town. It was Quaker gentlemen that founded the Greenbank school, a Quaker financier that built Gravely a library and a clock tower. And naturally they built themselves a meeting house, too.

It was a one-storey building, in sandstone, to the west of the town. Two tall arched windows flanked a twin-pillared portico. The door brasses were heavy and fine, the iron railings black and well wrought.

'See, Harriet,' David said facetiously, leaning across me, 'how he paints a picture with words.'

Harriet snorted.

Wealth such as the Gravely Quakers amassed – honestly, diligently – over the years soon begins to chafe against the confines of a fishing village. The families of the Friends began to drift away: to Newcastle, York, Leeds, London, where in the main they flourished (Gravely's Quaker of the clock tower ended up, I believe, with his signature on a banknote).

A few families remained. The Palmers were one such. These were not men of business, or not at least in the watch-chain and stovepipe sense. Leonard Palmer was a boatbuilder – he employed perhaps three or four men in the village. He and his wife had a son, Kenneth. Kenneth was, as it was termed, simple – *not right bright*, they would have said in Bradford. Not an imbecile, far from drooling and helpless, but outstanding among the local boys for credulity and slow wits – and, among boys, that is quite enough. He was born, I think, perhaps a decade before I was, in around '95.

In a grim voice, David murmured: 'I fear for this lad.'

The Palmers and their Friends – 'upper-case eff', I specified – continued to attend the meeting house. For all that there were seldom more than eight or ten present at each meeting, the windows, brasses and railings were kept in good order. This was Kenneth's doing; too cack-handed for his father's craft, Kenneth was instead charged with the maintenance of the building, and each day toted clattering broom, bucket and cloths along the coast road from the Palmers' house on the shore to the west end of town. An easy target, one supposes, for the taunts of those local boys – even as they, and he, grew into men.

'Men can be no better than boys,' Harriet put in.

'Worse, indeed,' nodded David.

The path along which we walked was declining steeply now towards the village. Three black-headed gulls leapt into the air as we crested the brow of the slope. From here, I saw, the meeting house could just about be discerned, down to our right, at the far end of a row of shops whose front windows glimmered weakly in the sun. I stopped on the path and pointed.

'There's the place itself.'

Harriet shaded her eyes with her free hand. 'Are there people there already? I don't want us to be late.'

'We'll see it soon enough,' David said. 'On with the story, Lowell. The boys are growing into men – and there's a war coming.'

David's ear for narrative hadn't deceived him. It came, of course, and when it did, the Palmers wouldn't fight. There were, in the war, Quakers who would fight and Quakers who wouldn't, and the Palmers wouldn't. It was a question of conscience. A man's conscience, if I understand it right, is barely below the Lord God in the Quakers' scheme of things.

Leonard Palmer, in any case, was too old to fight, and went on building boats (by himself, once his hired hands and apprentices had been shipped to France). Kenneth, though, was a strapping twenty-year-old, physically sound and, while certainly stupid, not too stupid to die for his country.

He was not the only Quaker in England to declare himself a conscientious objector. But he *was* the only one in Gravely.

In the summer of 1914, as the local boys – 'Here *they* come again,' David sighed – prepared to join up, the signs started to appear: poorly formed letters slathered clumsily on a board and strung to the railings of the Meeting House. *Nation shall not lift up a sword against nation. Depart from evil, and do good. Seek peace, and pursue it. Thou shalt not kill.*

Each day the boys tore the sign down, and stamped it into bits. Each succeeding day a new sign would be there – and through the window of the meeting house they would see Kenneth, head bent, mopping the boards, or blank-faced up against the glass, wiping down the window frames.

They'd yell foul names at him, I suppose. One day a boy threw a stone through the pane, slicing open Kenneth's brow. He would not have to endure the bullying for long; soon they would be gone, and *he* would be gone, too, he and his conscience, down a mine, or up a fireman's ladder, or in some other way doing peaceable godly service to his country.

Except that, one day in the winter of 1914, their natural cruelty perhaps stoked by that morning's casualty lists, the boys found that stones and harsh words did not satisfy them with regard to the punishment of Kenneth Palmer. I imagine them arriving at this realisation, perhaps gawping at one another in red-faced bewilderment, hearts hammering, fists itching, beneath Kenneth's latest sign.

The well-wrought railings and the door with the fine brasses did not hold them back.

'Spare us the details,' Harriet butted in, with feeling – and so I did, though I knew the details well enough, had been told them enough times by glowering men in pubs, who shook their heads and spoke of a 'bad business'.

'They beat him to death,' I said simply.

They beat him to death – they were brawny lads, fishermen's sons – and then, when he was dead, they carried his body out of the back of the meeting house, and threw it into the beck that ran through the town to the sea.

People said that Kenneth had been killed in a fight. They could hardly, in my opinion, have said anything more foul.

I never learned precisely what happened to the boys. The details I had been told were details of the blows dealt, the hurt done – dispatches from a prize fight. I had been told little of the perpetrators. Packed off hastily to the Western Front, no doubt; perhaps one or two sentenced to terms in some Stockton borstal, or even the old Elvet gaol. It's hardly satisfying to know how unlikely it is that any of them came to anything other than a bad end.

We had paused at the point at which the cliff path veered inland, towards the town.

'I wouldn't have been one of the boys who killed Kenneth Palmer,' said David, squinting out to sea. 'But I'm damn sure I would've ragged him as he went along with his mop and bucket.'

'A bit of ragging never hurt anyone, David,' Harriet assured him.

How my beautiful Harriet knew this I did not know.

'They say we need to restore the population,' says Louisa. White-tipped pink elbow going like the clappers as she whisks the pudding batter. 'I mean, that's not why we had Michael—'

'I know why you had Michael,' I say, and nudge her. I know when his birthday is and I know when their wedding day was, and I might not be Dr Einstein but there are some sums I can do. She gives me the saucer eyes and then giggles. Wipes a floury spot of batter from her chin.

'Oh shush, you. I mean we would have had a little one at some point. But with what they say about, you know, the population – well, you feel like you're – don't laugh.' Sets down the caked whisk. 'But you feel sort of like you're doing your duty.'

I do laugh. I can't help laughing at Louisa sometimes. I'm not being mean. That's what your schoolfriends are for.

'Funny sort of duty.'

'I don't mean that. You. I mean – well, you've not had to do it yet, but it's blooming horrible, Harriet, all the blood and everything. And when you're growing up you think of all the things the men had to go through over there, back then, and you think, what can we do to do our bit? And that's a thing you can do. Have a baby.'

That 'yet' – 'you've not had to do it yet'. Lou said it as unselfconsciously as you like, while bent double at the oven door

142

and swirling the fat in the tin. Never occurred to her that I might never have to do it, that it just might never happen. It's a good thing in her, I think. Call her a Pollyanna if you want but I shan't. It's just hope, isn't it? A thick, pea-soupy sort of hope that you can't see through, can't see beyond, but still hope.

The hope I have – and I have plenty, mind – isn't like that. I can see through it to the other side. And if I wanted I could poke my finger through it like through wet paper.

'I think if people had been a bit less concerned about duty,' I say, 'we wouldn't have a population problem to worry about.'

She doesn't really hear. Concentrating on jug and tin. A gravel-beach roar as the batter meets the fat.

'It's duty,' I say, 'that spilled all that flipping blood. Back then, over there.'

'Oop. Pass us that tea towel, love,' she says. Batter up her forearm. I pass the towel. I want to tell her what a lot of rubbish she's saying but I don't. I want to tell her – and tell the world, while I'm at it – that no one's got the slightest right to expect me to bleed for them.

They might ask, and I might say yes, all right. I might want to. If there's a baby I will. But duty? England expects. Your Country Needs You. If that's its attitude it can get stuffed.

Then Louisa straightens up, pushes her hair out of her face, leans on the counter and says: 'Before, I'd have said you were being the same old hot-headed Hattie, getting cross about nothing. Before Michael, I mean. But I don't now. I feel the same.' Gives me a lovely, guilty smile. 'I think about him growing up into a young man, and I wonder how it'd feel seeing him sent away by the Ministry of War or what have you to risk his life in the middle of nowhere somewhere. No: I don't wonder, I know. I know full well how it'd feel. I'd be absolutely furious, and I wouldn't stand for it.' She laughs and I laugh with her. She reaches out and takes my hand. 'You've been thinking things like that for ever, just out of nothing but your cleverness. But a dunce like me has to have a baby before I can start to understand it.'

'It's not cleverness,' I say, and I mean it, because it's not, and I'm not sure what it is. I feel sorry and I say: 'I didn't think you'd see it that way. I didn't think you were even listening.'

'I was making a pudding. I wasn't doing a calculus puzzle.' Still smiling, but I can see it's her turn to be a bit cross. Good for her. 'I know I'm daft but I can pour a bit of batter in a tin and still hold a blooming conversation,' she says.

I fold my hands in front of me and lower my head penitently. She laughs at me.

XI

We were to sit in deckchairs to hear Mr Shakes speak.

The meeting house, naturally enough, had not been much used since the killing of the Palmer boy. Though its wood-panelled interior was shipshape enough but for dust and deathwatch grubs, the place had long since been denuded of furniture. And so there were perhaps forty folding green canvas deckchairs, carried in from the beach huts (a Mr Hale rented them to holidaymakers in high season) and set out from wall to wall in four tidy rows.

'Ought we to have come in our bathing costumes?' David asked, eyeing the chairs with trepidation.

It occurred to me that perhaps this was, rather than a resourceful contingency, a theatrical gesture by our visiting Barnum, an attempt to lend to proceedings an air of beach-resort gaiety or Riviera charm. Was he to appear in a bathing costume himself? Would his daughters stroll the aisles dispensing candyfloss and cool drinks?

His daughters. They were there, I saw, at the front, reclining side by side in their deckchairs, hatless, Cordelia's red hair shining like a new coin. Nearby, in the same row, the architect Furlong sat with his legs crossed, looking sour. The chamber was around two-thirds full, and resounded with the villagers' grumbling – the word I heard muttered most often was *deckchairs*. People were lowering themselves gingerly into the canvas slings; those already seated didn't *recline*, as the Shakes girls did, but slumped, lolled, lay like dead things. They were, of course, working shore folk; beaches, for these men and women, were places of labour, not lounging, and deckchairs were not their true habitat. Helpless in these deep hammocks, I thought, they would be no more able to rise without help than newborn babies. I thought of babies left out in their prams, exposed to the sunshine – so these good folk of Gravely would be, once Maurice Shakes turned the glare of his rhetoric upon them.

David dropped with a billowing *whump* into a vacant deckchair near the back. I helped Harriet into the chair beside him, and then, sick with misgivings, took the chair beside her.

'Most of these people would have been in church this morning, I suppose?' I murmured to Harriet, looking about me.

She nodded, and lifted one shoulder.

'Most, yes,' she said. 'Though not, of course, the Misses Shakes.'

I translated my anxiety into a nervous pull on my left earlobe.

'Why *of course*?' My voice sounded like that of an adolescent trying to order beer in a pub. 'I thought the younger was an inveterate churchgoer.'

Another half-shrug.

'Eleanor's usually there, yes,' Harriet said. 'But not today. Stop fidgeting with your ear.'

I clasped my hands together in my lap.

It wasn't, I told myself, as though Eleanor and I had sinned. A kiss does not constitute adultery. Whether or not it *feels* like adultery is a different question.

Perhaps Eleanor had decided, the morning after, that she could not pray today.

Or perhaps she had had a headache or an upset stomach, perhaps she had caught a chill from being out so late on the bluff, perhaps she had overslept or been detained by chores, or any one of the thousand reasons why, every Sunday, young women miss church. I told myself not to think like a damn fool. I told myself that she was a modern woman, and an American, what's more – hardly a *flapper* and not so bold as her sister, but still. I told myself that Jon Lowell could no more make a lasting impression on Eleanor Shakes than a man bathing on the beach can make a lasting impression on the ocean.

I peered through the serried Gravely heads. I could see the collar of her grey suit and the nape of her neck, nothing more. This was for the best. I ought not to see more – and yet, for some reason, I longed for her to turn her head, so I could see the line made by her cheek and high cheekbone, and the breve made by her eyelashes.

What did I expect to happen, that day, if we met again, if we spoke?

I heard David mutter: 'By the pricking of my thumbs...' and Maurice Shakes emerged from a side door. Except that he wore no hat and carried no staff, he looked much as he had when he had stood in the middle of the road.

Among the audience there was a momentary upsurge in noise ('Look there!', 'Ah, *here* the feller is!'), and then a descent into quiet: I thought of a wavelet meeting the beach. 'Thank you, my friends, thank you!' Shakes cried, smiling. He clapped his hands twice and then clasped them together, like a man warmly shaking hands with himself. 'Thank you,' he said, 'for coming. I'm sure you all have many questions. If you'll honour me with your patience, I'll say what I have to say, and then afterward you can go ahead and ask me anything you like. But first, let me set out my stall.'

I settled into my seat. I had, after all, heard this speech, this sales proposition, before. I positioned myself so that without moving I could see the back of Eleanor's head. Was this a sin? Perhaps it was – oh, I'm sure that it was, with Harriet's pale hand resting lightly on my coat sleeve all the while, I'm certain that it was.

So I sat and sinned while Maurice Shakes talked.

'There are two stars,' he said, 'by which I steer. One is a memory; the other is a dream.'

The memory, of course, was of poor lost Lawrence Shakes, the coward killed in the war. Shakes told the story in full and with frankness. There were mutters, naturally, at the child conceived out of wedlock; there was huffing and sighing over Lawrence's unmanliness. Perhaps many thought the swine deserved to lie dead in a ditch at Montfaucon. But no one spoke out, and no one left – perhaps Shakes held them pinioned with his charisma; perhaps they hadn't the strength to raise themselves from their deep deckchairs.

This sorry story dispatched, Shakes moved on to his dream – and the people of Gravely laughed at Maurice Shakes's dream. The elderly man seated to my left threw back his head and *roared* at it.

But I don't think there was derision in the laughter. Rather, the people laughed with delight – they laughed like people who were being tickled, and Shakes laughed along with them.

'Isn't it,' he cried, 'tre*mend*ous?'

Again I felt a thrill, as I had on the bluff that evening; I felt the proximity of the dream, with all its colour, its noise, its riotousness – its *awfulness*, in every sense of the word. I wasn't sure how I felt about what I felt. If it was fear, and it may have been, I was somewhat ashamed of it, for what I was afraid of was after all nothing but pleasure. If it was excitement, like the excitement of a boy on his birthday – well, then, I was somewhat ashamed of that, too.

'People will come to Gravely in their hundreds from all over, from the north, the south, the east and west,' Shakes told us. 'They'll come by railroad, by boat, by motorcar – by God, ladies and gentlemen, by the time I'm done people will *walk* to Gravely to see the pleasure grounds we build here.'

The audience tittered. To me it seemed that they, too, were afraid and excited, though I could see that this feeling was not universal: Eleanor Shakes loosened her shoulders, one after the other, as a theatregoer does who is bored or has an uncomfortable seat, and smoothed her hair with a flat hand.

Shakes left the pier until last.

'The grandest in England,' he promised us, and the audience now sat silently, involved, invested in the story and the dream. 'A clear half-mile out to sea, and at every yard along its length a thing of delight, of joy, a sight to make you smile, a wonder at which to marvel, a spectacle to make your jaw drop open.'

As far as I was concerned, these things were already to be found at Gravely; one could already stand on the harbour wall, if one were so inclined, and feel delight, joy, wonder and all the rest – at the daring contests of the terns and pirate birds, the flocks of knots in flight like flags furling and unfurling, the tall clouds throwing shadows on the sea, the sea itself, the sky, the horseplay of grey seals.

But I repented of this sentiment when, at Shakes's throwing open the debate to the floor, the Reverend Aldridge rose amid the crowd like a stage devil from a trap and made the very same point.

'Are the glories of God's earth so mean,' he demanded, a little shrilly, 'that we must bedeck them with baubles for them to seem beautiful to us? Must we rig up cheap painted scenery to block out the light of the sun, obscure the blue of the sky and the green of the sea? Is Creation so poor a spectacle? Must we be given toys to amuse us, as if we were children?'

Shakes, thumbs tucked in trouser pockets, waited until everyone had turned from the reverend to him before he replied: 'What could be more innocent and beautiful, good Reverend Aldridge, than the amusement of a child?'

'I misspoke,' Aldridge snapped back. 'No child, be he as innocent as the day, could fail to see through the charlatanry of this so-called pleasure ground – to which I say, sir, there is nothing more than fool's gold and the profit motive.'

This last seemed to sting Shakes, a man whom I had thought could not be stung (I again felt a dangerous excitement). He did not smile. In a level voice he said: 'There will be no profit for me, sir – or anyway no financial profit.' And then at Aldridge's sceptical snort he added: 'I'll be glad to let you or anyone else look over the books at any time, Reverend. But' – the smile reappeared – 'I'll not stand to have a churchman call me a liar.'

As every head in the room turned to look at the reverend, mine alone remained fixed in Shakes's direction – I waited for Eleanor, in the front row, to turn *her* head, aching to see her face, though those eyes of hers would be not on me but on Aldridge, standing pink-faced and quivering there in his long brown coat. And Eleanor's head did turn, and I drank in the whiteness of her cheek and the wide curve of her nose in profile, and then I found (with a feeling of fear, of *terror*) that her eyes, her dark-gold child's eyes, were not on Aldridge but were indeed on me, directly on me, and in them was an expression I could not fathom. I looked sharply away, down at the floorboards, and then, conscious of my nonconformity, up at the Reverend Aldridge. '*I'll* not stand to have our town brought to wickedness and ruin,' Aldridge said. Someone across the room shouted: 'Hear, hear!' Others laughed.

Shakes, still standing with his thumbs in his pockets, only looked sad.

'You misjudge me, sir,' he said, and shook his heavy head.

Aldridge replied: 'I hope that I do.' Without a further word, he stalked from the hall.

I turned, feeling nauseous, to Harriet. Her mouth was a thin red line and she was nodding stiffly.

'Well said, Reverend Aldridge,' she muttered. She caught my eye, smiled tightly, and nodded again, this time more emphatically. 'Well said.'

'Quite a show, this,' David said, stretching his arms behind his head.

Eleanor had turned back to face her father. Again I could see only her glossy hair, tied into a tight hazelnut, and the light-brown cobweb curls at the nape of her white neck. I was resolved now, of course, that whatever my thoughts on the sea and the sky and the grey seals, Mr Shakes was really quite right, if only because the alternative was for the brown-coated reverend to be right, a notion I could not countenance.

Shakes was looking at the door through which Aldridge had effected his melodramatic egress, though judging by his expression he was looking at something at a far greater remove than that.

'There goes a brave and honest man,' he said.

*

The people of Gravely seemed to relax somewhat once their long-bearded Christian conscience had departed. There was genuine concern in some of the questions asked by those in the deckchairs – 'What will you do to keep out ruffians and the like?' (Mr Stein, our fastidious pharmacist), 'Will this pier affect the shoaling?' (some local herring baron I half-recognised), 'What of the ring-plover nesting grounds on the shingle?' (Mr J. Lowell) – but there seemed to be less tension in the meeting place, less fear. Perhaps it only seemed that way because I was less tense and less afraid.

The voice at my elbow startled me.

'What assurances do you have to offer, Mr Shakes, of the safety of this pier you talk about?'

Harriet. More of Gravely in her accent than usual, I thought. I turned my head to look at her, and at once felt like a man turning a corner in a gallery and coming unexpectedly upon some sacred painting. The strength in her face, the rightness of it.

Shakes, smiling, squinted at her across the rows of heads, hand on one hip.

'Safety, Mrs Lowell?'

As though it were an unfamiliar foreign word.

'This coast doesn't make for easy building. We all know that.'

The look Shakes gave her was level and calculating (Harriet might have called it insolent). He shifted his jaw as though chewing a quid of tobacco.

'I believe, madam,' he said eventually, 'that even ornery nature, even this wild and windy coast of yours, must bend the knee, in the end, to the will and ingenuity of man.'

Harriet opened her mouth and closed it again. I could guess what she'd been about to say: *believing is all well and good, Mr Shakes, but...*

It would have been an awkward sort of thing for a churchgoing woman to say in front of the whole town (even without the vigilant Aldridge present). Instead she said: 'Can you promise that, though, Mr Shakes?'

'I can make you a thousand promises – Mrs Lowell, ladies, gentlemen, I can promise you—'

'That's not what the lady asked,' interjected a man down the front.

Shakes hesitated. The heavy pause of a boulder in slow mid-roll.

David, smirking, caught my eye. *Here's some fun*, his look said.

'Then,' said Shakes, still smiling, moving his hands unhurriedly to take hold of his lapels, 'I will say this instead.' He made a thick-waisted sort of half-bow in Harriet's direction. 'I promise, Mrs Lowell, that I will take every care; that I will move, if I can, with a light step – would you believe, my friends, that I was quite the dancer in my youth? – and that the welfare of your fine town will be uppermost in my mind throughout. I confess, ladies and gentlemen of Gravely, I've grown fond of this damn place.'

He softened the expletive with a self-mocking grimace.

Harriet said: 'Will there be surveys, soundings, that sort of thing?'

'Now, madam, Mrs Lowell—'

'Will it be *safe*, Mr Shakes?'

And from here and there within the crowd – from this lady whose fuchsia cloche hat teetered above the deckchair-back, from that fellow with the peacoat and unshaven neck – came a little volley of supporting noises, of *aye*s and *that's the question*s and *answer us that*s and echoing *will it be safe*s.

Shakes chuckled. Then he rubbed his hand across his jaw and looked up at the ceiling. In another man I might have thought it an appeal to God.

Into the quiet a hard voice from the front said: 'She thinks we're a bunch of bloody amateurs.'

The architect, Furlong. He had, I think, been addressing the person beside him – but he'd said it loudly enough for us all to hear. No one said anything but something changed in the tone or texture of the silence, the way light reflected in a windowpane changes when the angle of the pane shifts.

Shakes, carefully straight-faced, said: 'We'll speak respectfully here, friend Furlong.'

'There's nothing disrespectful in saying that we know our bloody business.' Over his shoulder, to Harriet, and to all of us: 'We owe you no promises. We'll do our work and we'll take our pay. We'll build, and what we'll build will stay bloody built. That's not a promise, that's a fact. We've all of us seen worse things,' he said, with authoritative bitterness, 'than your powder-puff undertow and a bit of soft sand.'

More silence, and in this one I was conscious of a certain heft of expectation. This – with the pinkness deepening in Harriet's cheeks – left me with little other option than to half-rise from my deckchair (itself no easy thing) and weakly begin: 'Mr Furlong, Mr Furlong, I must, I will not—'

Furlong would surely only snigger or deliver some crude

rejoinder. But Harriet was after all my wife and I was after all her husband. I felt a shadow of what it might have felt like to be conscripted to a war.

I was spared, in any case, by a thunderous, wet throat-clearing from the front-right of the room – a whale-noise, a walrus cry. People breathed out; heads turned. Shakes laughed (I wondered if everyone else could hear the relief in the sound).

'You are heard, sir!' he said. 'Speak, please, speak, speak.'

With a drawn-out noise of extreme strain – and, I should think, physical assistance from those sitting beside and behind – Clement Holroyd rose to his feet.

I had known Holroyd as the pub's landlord ever since I had moved to Gravely. He was a huge and revolting man – not, I think, a bad man, but corpulent, inclined (like most of his patrons) to a general and passive lechery, slobber-mouthed and reeking of old pipe-smoke. He stood, now, in the middle of the crowd, swaying slightly from the effort of standing and with his hands planted on his hips.

'If I could turn the conversation to matters of *trade*, Mr Shakes,' he said, and no one could doubt how much more important than weak and womanly *safety* he felt (no, knew) trade to be. 'Is there to be, might I ask, a licensed premises in these pleasure grounds of yours?'

I understood his concern, as our monopoly-holder in that area. Shakes, eyeing the fat landlord shrewdly and theatrically, paused for a moment before he answered.

'Not, Mr Holroyd, in any form that you have ever seen before.' Then he made his seal-like bark of a laugh, performed a stroll up and down the room, wheeled sharply, and cried: 'We will outdo Coney Island on this score, my fellow imbibers, my brother boozers!'

There was a moment's silence. In that silence, I feared for him, but he had not, after all, misjudged, because a moment later the silence broke into scattered laughter and a noise went up, not a cry or a cheer but rather a welter of disparate and jovial noises (hurrahs, jeers, a raspberry) – noises, in short, such as boozers make. For every Christian old maid and stiff-necked nonconformist burgher in Gravely there was a beer-guzzling boatbuilder, coalman, fisherman or stonemason – indeed, there were several more.

Shakes lifted his hands so as to master the crowd's attention.

'At Coney,' he said, 'and I tell this to you true, for I have been there many times, and seen it many times – at Coney Island, there is a mechanical *cow*' – hoots, laughter – 'that dispenses from its mechanical udders ice-cold lager beer!'

General laughter. Even Harriet laughed. David, I saw, had closed his eyes and was smiling, shaking his head in a sort of incredulous admiration.

'We will aim higher, and do better!' Shakes roared in hoarse half-laughter. 'There will be, at the Lawrence Shakes Pleasure Ground, nothing less than a mechanical *bull*.' Loud cheers. 'And it will dispense nothing other than the finest Newcastle *brown ale*!' A roar, as at a football match when a goal has been scored. Smiling Shakes raised his face to the ceiling and clapped his hands together heavily, twice.

A voice from near the front – Furlong's voice, again – said stridently: 'Where from? Its cock?'

It wouldn't be quite true to say that this was a misjudgement, because it didn't seem to me that Furlong had even attempted to exercise any judgement. Silence fell like the suffocating earth of a landslip.

David made a quiet noise of disapproval in his throat. Harriet looked at me and rolled her eyes. In the front row, Eleanor Shakes had turned a fierce scowl on the architect (who was out of my line of sight) – again the white cheek, again the strong line of the nose. The old man to my right said, 'Well, *really*.' From the back a lady's voice cried, 'Shame!'

Maurice Shakes in a state of uncertainty was a strange thing to behold. I watched him carefully, as he waited for quiet, shifting his weight from foot to foot; my guess was that he was deciding between punching Furlong in the mouth, proceeding with his presentation as though nothing had been said or following Aldridge from the room.

We were never to find out what decision he made.

Holroyd shouted: 'Oo-rah!'

He lunged forwards, and his deckchair clattered. I thought that *he* was going to punch Furlong in the mouth. But he didn't arrest his forward, downward plunge. There was a clunk of deckchair timbers, a squeal of wood on wood, a woman's cry, a man's sharp expletive; an elderly couple were spilled from their chairs and sprawled on the floor as Holroyd, one hand grabbing at his chest, fell heavily into the front row. Through the crowd that rose around him I could only see the white balloon of his torso creased by a deckchair strut, and a flailing left hand that opened and closed.

A cry went up for *Reynolds*, Dr Reynolds, the town doctor – but he was not there. A door banged as someone hastened to fetch him from his home on the front. I heard, amid the pandemonium, another name, *Andrassy*, the vet who lived a little way inland and tended to the sheep and horses of the hill farms, but he too was absent from our meeting. And then I heard, from first this quarter and then that, once questioningly and then again urgently, my *own* name – 'Lowell?', 'Mr Lowell?', 'Mr Lowell!' – for was I not a man of science, a man of the scalpel and microscope, an adept of the killing jar?

I rose awkwardly.

'I cannot—' I began to say, to no one.

'Do what you can,' Harriet urged me.

Sometimes a local child would bring to me a badly shot rabbit, a gull with a lamed wing, a bony kitten fished from the sluice. In those cases I *did what I could* – but all too often (more often than I ever let the children know) there was nothing for it but a decisive and terminal scalpel stroke, or a lethal dose of morphia. The kindest thing, as it is invariably called.

David had risen, too. He seized my shoulder.

'You don't have to,' he said.

'I have to do *some*thing,' I said.

Through the deckchairs, no longer in such neat rows. Shakes and another man had manhandled Holroyd to the floor. He lay on his back with his legs apart and his arms splayed. The bottom buttons of his shirt had come unfastened and disclosed the hairy white dome of his belly.

'His heart, I think, Mr Lowell,' Shakes said, looking at me gravely across Holroyd's body as I knelt and reached for the publican's wrist. I could feel no heartbeat.

'I fear there is little to be done.'

'Death,' said Shakes, 'is nothing to fear.' But his expression nonetheless as he looked upon Holroyd's grey face was, I thought, fearful. I felt again for a pulse.

'Nowt?' asked the other man, somewhat plaintively. I looked up at him. Like Holroyd, he had a red face and a fat throat; he might have been the publican's brother – or, then again, he might only have been a regular drinker at Holroyd's pub – only another of Maurice Shakes's *boozers*.

'Nowt,' I said.

The man nodded, and then shook his head. He pulled a handkerchief from his breast pocket and unfolded it. It was off-white and not clean, puckered in one place where (I supposed) a nose had been blown. The man bent and laid the handkerchief over Holroyd's paling purple face.

'RIP, Clem,' he said. 'He was a decent man.'

A morbid piece of theatre. The man extended his hand; I shook it. But we were not at a graveside, not in funeral dress – the body of the fat publican was still warm (I was conscious that I, having felt that last time for a heartbeat, had been the last soul to feel his warmth). We ought to have been calling for help, applying desperate, futile remedies to the dead man, praying to God, or cursing him—

The square of white cotton lay quite still on Holroyd's face. No breath.

The fat man – who, I was coming to realise, was quite drunk – blubbed into his cupped hands. I wanted to tell him to take back his damned handkerchief.

Shakes said: 'Jesus Christ, what a business.'

I felt cold and nauseous. I heard a door bang at the back of the room, and a clamour of voices – the arrival of Dr Reynolds. Too late, too late.

I put my hand on the side-spar of the deckchair nearest to me in order to lever myself to my feet. As I was doing so, I felt a light touch, the momentary touch of a fingertip, on my thumb. I turned and saw the face of Eleanor Shakes close to my own. I almost fell.

'You did a fine thing, Mr Lowell,' she said.

I wanted to ask her what the fine thing was that I had done – but she turned away, dabbing at her eyes with her coat cuff, so I only stood, and turned to greet the breathless doctor.

I said that I almost fell – I had, of course, in another sense, already fallen.

Maurice Shakes had by now taken off his own long coat and laid it over Holroyd's body. Only the publican's feet and hands were visible. The rest of him was a motionless mound beneath good grey broadcloth.

I thought of the *cachalot*, the sperm whale, washed up on Gravely beach all those years ago and doomed to die, for all the boy Aldridge's tears, prayers and buckets of seawater. Here, dead Holroyd had only me – me and the fat brother, and coatless, wordless Maurice Shakes, who stood over the body like a tombstone.

'To a person of superstition,' he says, 'it would seem an ill portent.'

Bad diet and too much ale, more like. I don't say so.

'Just one of those tragic things, I suppose,' I venture.

'And yet the good Lord moves, they say, in a mysterious way.'

I want to say what are you getting at? But you can't start saying that to a vicar. If you did you'd never stop. Anyway I suppose he means the pleasure grounds – I suppose he means that it's against God's will, all this Mr Shakes business. He said as much in there.

He gives me a furtive look and says: 'I waited at the meeting-house door. I heard what you said, Mrs Lowell.'

Crafty so-and-so.

'Well,' I say, 'I felt someone had to ask.'

'Indeed.' There's still a look in his eye. If he wasn't who he is I'd say it was a glint. He sent Alice Reynolds to tell me he wanted to meet me outside the church – and wasn't Alice just dying of curiosity – and now this.

I say: 'Do you think something should be done?'

He rests one hand in his great nest of beard and gives a grave sort of smile.

'Something must always be done,' he says, 'when evil is afoot.'

I think 'evil' is a bit strong but I know that's just the Reverend Aldridge's way. Jon pokes fun. He shouldn't. I think it's part of a vicar's job to talk about evil and wickedness and sin when no one *else will – even when it sounds daft (and I do think it sounds daft when you're talking about candyfloss and stilt-walkers or what have you).*

I don't know about evil but I don't like to see folk being carried away. I don't like to see things not done properly. I think it's all right to act wild but you mustn't lose your good sense.

And if people are going to lose their good sense I don't want them doing it in Gravely.

'I just want everyone to be safe,' I say.

'Safe,' he echoes, nodding. 'The word derives from Old French, salve, *and in its original meaning refers to deliverance from sin and damnation. Salvation, you see, has the same root. And so you see' – that glint again – 'we are working, Mrs Lowell, towards the same end.'*

I'm a bit taken aback. Am I working towards an end? Am I supposed to be? Because I've got a lot on. I've got enough on as it is.

XII

David left; David went home.

'You'll stay for the funeral?'

He'd shaken his head.

'I don't see that it'd do any damn good,' he'd said.

Of course the death of Clem Holroyd had disturbed him; it had disturbed us all. Such a scene, and in such a place.

'I fear that your Aldridge was right,' David had said, smiling lopsidedly and holding his hat in his hand, as we bade one another goodbye at the station. 'I fear the Beast walks abroad in Gravely.' And we had laughed, of course, at the conceit. The reality was that David had a novel to complete, editors and publishers with whom to lunch, a strange London life to which to return.

'I may come back after Christmas,' he had said.

'We may have crumbled into the sea by then,' I'd replied. We had embraced, as the rails whinnied and the train rolled into view. I had helped him with his things and watched him board.

Now I stood in a crowd by the grave of Clement Holroyd. Harriet clung miserably to my arm, a scrap of damp black cloth caught on a tree-branch. A wet salt wind raked the hillside. The Reverend Aldridge, at the head of the grave, spoke, but I couldn't hear what he said – didn't care what he said, didn't even try to listen. The red-faced brother or friend stood, a new handkerchief in his breast pocket, to the reverend's left. Shakes was there, of course. Mr Furlong, Master of the Piers, too. And the daughters, Eleanor, Cordelia, they were there, side by side, across the grave from where I stood with my wife and her heavy-veiled mother, Mrs Holloway – all of them and all of us in black, in unremitting black.

Even Shakes wore black. A part of me had expected him to arrive in extravagant multi-coloured motley – a part of me, I think, had *hoped* for him to do so (if only that we might laugh at him behind our hands).

Eleanor had her hair bound in a broad scarf of black muslin. Each time I looked at her, her eyes were lowered. I supposed she was listening intently to Aldridge's benediction, or trying to. Cordelia didn't look as though she were trying at all. Even when Aldridge declared 'amen', and even I murmured in echo 'amen', *so be it*, for so it was and always is in these circumstances, whether God or anyone else wills it or otherwise – even then, she made no sound, and her face showed no response. Her lips were coral and her skin bone-white.

London called, David had said. The drawing rooms and artists' parties, he added, smirking in self-mockery.

But I'd seen the expression on his face when, as the strong men of Gravely carried the corpse of Clem Holroyd from the Quakers' meeting house on a folded deckchair, he had watched Cordelia Shakes in close conversation with Peter Furlong. In the late light from the long windows he had seen her smile at one or other of the architect's remarks.

I had seen David's expression when, as dead Holroyd was borne across the threshold of the building, Cordelia's sudden laugh, like a light-bulb exploding, had burst over our heads, and we, shocked, outraged, somehow *hurt*, had all fallen silent as though we had been cursed.

*

Six large men of Gravely raised Holroyd's coffin from its supports and slowly, effortfully, lowered it into the earth. Aldridge was shouting over the wind. And seven woodcocks fell from the sky.

One landed in the grass a few yards behind me. The second flailed with a weak cry into the rearward rank of Mr Holroyd's mourners. Two dropped one after the other on to the path of flat-laid stones that led down to the church. A fifth fell at the feet of Maurice Shakes; it struggled, gaping, gasping, to rise, but then subsided. I saw the sixth descend, some way distant, but could not see where it landed. A seventh spiralled with its wings working helplessly down into the middle of the ring of people and, further down, into the deep grave of Clement Holroyd. We dimly heard the clatter of its feet and bill on the coffin lid.

I stepped forwards. I meant, I think, to somehow coax the exhausted bird from the hole. But then I stopped, suddenly too aware of my ridiculousness – picturing myself with muddied knees and elbows, on all fours in my best suit (though not a good suit), reaching down into a grave-hole, chirruping and beckoning at a frightened woodcock.

So instead I did what everyone else did. I stood and looked at the grave, and wondered what was going to happen.

Aldridge, grimacing in the teeth either of the weather or of his conscience, gave a nod. One of the large men who had lowered the coffin picked up a spade. A noise of protest rose in my chest but froze in my throat. I only went on watching: the man dug his spade into the heap of fresh earth at the foot of the grave and, without looking, tipped the spadeful into the hole.

And so we buried the live woodcock with the dead publican. Aldridge spoke the necessary finalities over the pair of them.

In spite of Harriet I confronted him afterwards, the drenched minister, as we walked back towards the town, towards the bereaved pub, towards a cold spread and jugs of barley water and ale.

'I thought better of you, Reverend,' I told him, taking him boldly by the elbow. 'I heard a tale of a boy who wept over a dying whale, and supposed that you were a man of humanity.'

He looked at me. His face was white.

'The bird?'

'The bird. A woodcock, a male. Exhausted. Helpless.'

'I know, Mr Lowell.' Anxiously, he smoothed his damp beard. 'It was – unavoidable. The dignity of the service, you understand. It was not *my* dignity for which I was concerned,' he added hastily. 'Only that of the *rite*, Mr Lowell. And of my office.'

I remembered the cats, gulls and beetles of Withy Passageway and said: 'You are no Saint Francis after all, Reverend.'

'I am no saint, indeed,' Aldridge snapped.

He went on to contend, in shaky, indignant tones, that he had seen such falls of woodcock before – that they always came to a sorry end, the poor exhausted birds: prey to foxes, cats, cruel or hungry local boys.

Then he essayed a joke.

'At least this poor fellow,' he said weakly, knowing even as he said it the wickedness of what he was saying, 'received a decent Christian burial.'

There have been several occasions in my life on which I have felt afterwards that I should have punched a fellow, and this was one such.

'Dignity,' I said instead – and indeed Aldridge stumbled as though he had been struck.

'You spit the word as though it were a blasphemy, Mr Lowell,' he said.

It would not have been quite fair to strike the reverend, in any case. Any one of Mr Holroyd's mourners might have rescued the bird from the grave. I might have – no, should have – myself. If I were to avenge the woodcock through violence I should have to smite, somehow, almost the entire village. And I should have to in some way include myself in the immolation.

'There is no sin,' I said, 'in being ridiculous.' It sounded ridiculous as I said it.

'One thinks,' Aldridge said thoughfully, 'of Christ's humiliations.'

I thought of David – of how David, had he been there, would surely have peeled off his coat and, swearing fiercely, hopped down into the pit, grabbed the bird, thrown it out, and clambered up again, wiping mud and bird mutes from his hands, gesturing impatiently for the reverend to bloody well get on with it—

And afterwards, he would have told me, over beer, that he had never been made to look such a damn bloody fool in his life.

'You know, Mr Lowell, as a naturalist, how the life of a wild creature is,' Aldridge said. 'Look to Hobbes: *nasty, brutish and short.*'

Again I had recourse to Darwin.

'*The clumsy, wasteful, blundering, low and horridly cruel works of nature,*' I recited sourly. 'That is, *I* call it nature, Reverend Aldridge. You give it another name, and kneel before it in worship.'

'You *are* approaching blasphemy now, Mr Lowell.' The reverend looked at me beadily through his silly spectacles. 'Too much time, perhaps, spent in conversation with Mr Shakes, our visiting pagan deity.'

'What you call blasphemy I would prefer to call humanity.'

'Indeed!' Aldridge snorted derisively. 'We laid to rest a man today, Mr Lowell, in case you had forgotten. A *man*. And you harangue me about the death of a bird.'

'Does not your God note the fall of even the merest sparrow?'

'If I have sinned, Mr Lowell, I shall, I am sure, answer for it.'

I left him; I left them all. I went home, returned to my and Harriet's little house, sat by myself in my study with the lights off. I didn't think, or at least didn't think for long, about Aldridge, or about the Shakes girls and their father, or Furlong or Harriet

– about any of those who would now be making inconsequential conversation in the midst of boiled eggs and tinned sardines, tongue slices and cold beef. I didn't think about poor dead Holroyd either. I sat instead, and watching the sky turn to slate-grey, thought about falls of woodcock.

This is a thing that happens on our coast, our east coast. Usually it follows the first full moon of November. The woodcock of Europe, as the cold weather closes about them like a fist, take to the skies – they fly to us, to England. Each bird is no bigger than a jackdaw, as light as a handful of chicken bones. They fly and fly, across the continent, across the unforgiving late-autumn North Sea, and when they arrive they are exhausted – as a man might be who had swum to Kent from Calais, or rowed in a boat from Ghent to Kingston-on-Hull. They are so tired that, on sighting land, they simply fall from the sky.

I had heard the tales from lighthouse keepers up and down the coast (it seems migrating birds are drawn to lighthouses as moths are to flames). A boat found filled with sleeping woodcock one November morning; two dozen gold-crested wrens, tiny as mice, infesting a keeper's cabbage garden; a foreshore littered with the bodies of skylarks and starlings that flew too close to the light, and crashed against the lighthouse glass.

Here was a new story for people to tell. Holroyd's woodcock.

After an hour, perhaps more, Harriet came home. On entering, she called out my name. 'In the study, dear,' I called in reply. She came into the room rather hesitantly; I wonder, still, quite what sort of a figure I made there in the dark study, in my chair, in my shirtsleeves, my right hand resting against a glass of whisky on the desktop. She didn't turn on the light (I loved her for not turning on the light), but came over and sat on my knee.

'All done,' she said.

'A sorrowful business,' I said, and kissed her on the line of her jaw. 'What did they talk of?'

'Oh, you know. What they always talk of. Herring hauls, the price of salt. Your Mr Shakes said some kind things about Mr Holroyd, though he can hardly have known him.'

'Boozers have a natural affinity. Did you speak with the reverend?'

'Yes.' She poked me in the chest with her finger. 'You quite rattled him, you know. It was rude of you, Jon—'

'He is not the Pope of Rome, Harriet.'

'—*but* you were right to be rude. For once. That poor bird. We ought to have done something.'

'I suppose it was only a bird, after all.'

'Mr Shakes didn't think so.'

I drew back in my chair to look at her.

'You mean he confronted Aldridge?'

'No, no. Even that man has his limits, it seems. But he spoke of the business, out of the reverend's earshot. He cited the Buddha, I think, or someone of that sort.'

'He's a student, you'll remember, of all the world's *lidderitcher*.'

Harriet laughed, and pressed her lips against my forehead. Then into my ear she murmured: 'You miss him, don't you?' Her tone was sad. It matched her black gown.

'Who, Holroyd?' I replied, because I was a little drunk, and Harriet laughed again.

'No. David. You miss him, I can see you do. He's barely been gone a week and you miss him.' She kicked her little right foot mock-pettishly. 'You want to go and drink *beer* with him and make jokes about everything and make yourself feel better. Don't you? I know you do.' And again she kissed my brow. 'You can do those things with me, you know, Jon. Apart from the beer, I'll not drink that stuff, but the other things, the talking, the jokes. The laughing.'

I smiled and wanted to drink my whisky.

'I have known David a terribly long time, my darling,' I said.

'Oh, I know, I know. Schooled together in the shadow of the woollen mill. Found together in a basket of willow wands, bobbing in the bulrushes of the River Aire.'

She tousled my hair, and I laughed, though of course this was not true. It was only at technical college, at seventeen years of age, that David and I met – not, in truth, a terribly long time, though it has always *felt* like a terribly long time. Before that, at school, I had few friends. I spent much time reading, and much time bird's-nesting and flower-collecting and grubbing around for invertebrates in ponds and under logs; while I'm sure it would be easy to find a psychiatrist who would tell you that I did these things *because* I had few friends, in order to escape the indifference of my schoolmates, the reality is that the reverse was true. No one, besides me, was much interested in smooth newts and mugwort – and I was always, I think, happy to be alone.

David was not even strictly a Bradfordian; his mother had lived in Calverley, in the far west of Leeds, and it was thereabouts that David had attended school (I had made a joke on discovering this, saying: 'And when they were come to the place, which is called Calverley, there they crucified him,' and he had laughed). It was a place of bloody murder, Calverley – a nobleman of the sixteenth century went mad there, and butchered his own children.

We both attended technical college in order to study the biological sciences, or, rather, *I* was there in order to study them. The biological sciences were an inconvenience to David; he was a crashingly incompetent scientist.

'You are an odd couple,' Harriet said.

'All couples are odd,' I said. 'Except in a mathematical sense.'

She smiled and breathed out through her nose.

'That's true enough,' she said.

We sat there together in the dark, in the room that smelt of seawater and whisky, and I was delivered of a self-fulfilling prophecy: *I shall remember these moments*, I thought. I kissed Harriet's neck. She tasted of coastal rain.

I wondered if I ought to tell her that I had kissed Eleanor Shakes.

Harriet said: 'Speaking of odd couples, Jon, you know that David was – well, was at it with the Shakes girl?'

I heard myself say, with a strange defensiveness, 'The elder Shakes girl, Cordelia, yes,' and I knew that this must lead to my telling Harriet what had happened. What that in its turn must lead to I didn't know.

'A funny business. The woman was as thick as thieves with that Geordie pal of Shakes's today. Is that why David left?'

'I couldn't say,' I said.

Harriet rested her head against mine.

'Poor David,' she said, somewhat derisively.

'David has a heart,' I replied, 'even if it doesn't work quite as ours do.'

'I know, Jon,' she said, and I took it as an apology.

'Do you think he loves her?'

'I could not say, my dove.'

'Well, would you love her, if you were in his place?'

'I don't find her congenial. In fact I find her terrifying.'

A smile, a heartbeat's pause, and: 'The younger sister – Eleanor. She seems less terrifying.'

I thought, fleetingly, of telling her.

In truth I might as well say that I thought of opening the study window and taking flight by flapping my elbows. The thing would have been beyond me. My tongue, my jaw, would have seized in the attempt; I could no more tell her that I had kissed Eleanor Shakes than I could have struck her with a fist.

I cannot abide dismay in others. I would sooner have jumped from a cliff than hurt my Harriet in this way.

I have said already, I think, that I am a coward.

'Less strident, she seems, yes,' I said. 'But strong-minded, still.'

'Do you mean to say that you don't like strong-minded women?' Harriet pinched my earlobe between her teeth, and then laughed, and I heard unease in the laugh. 'Really, Jon,' she said. 'Really.'

'I like *this* strong-minded woman,' I said, and pulled her close to me.

I have never really feared dying. Not the dying itself. We go to nothing, and there is nothing in nothing to fear. But if I *were* to jump from a cliff—

It isn't death that I would fear, I know. It's grief.

Around Holroyd's grave that day – and this, remember, was only Clem Holroyd, the town publican, whom few loved, few would really miss or mourn – I had seen the sorts of faces that would draw me back from the cliff's edge. Harriet's, Eleanor's. Even the red face of the fat brother. Faces creased or broken and crumpled inwards. Faces abandoned.

Such would be Harriet's face were I to form the words: a kiss, my dove, on the clifftop – only a kiss, nothing more.

'I hope I'm the only woman you like, strong-minded or weak-minded or anything,' Harriet murmured into my hair.

'Of course, my dove, my dearest,' I said. 'Of course, of course. Of course.'

Eleanor Shakes is very good-looking. She's not certain about the pork pies. I don't blame her, I shouldn't be either if I was her. Of course I know they're harmless but I'm to the manner born, as they say.

She picks away the aspic and leaves it on the side of the plate. Smiles prettily as Alice Reynolds helps her to a cup of tea from the urn.

I'd say she might be better-looking than her sister. It's not easy to say because Cordelia wears make-up – even today she's got a bit on – and looks good in it and I don't think Eleanor wears any at all. All things considered I think Eleanor's the prettier one.

Still I expect it's Cordelia who gets all the gentlemanly attention. That's fellers for you. Not a clue.

She's getting some now, off that horrible architect or what-is-he. Seems to be enjoying it but of course you can't really tell. You get good at pretending to enjoy it if you're a pretty girl – and even if you're not, I dare say.

What I really want to know is, is Eleanor prettier than me?

I'm almost sure she's not.

No one I can ask, really. Jon'd just say I was the prettier one even if he didn't think I was and if I asked Mother she'd think I had ideas about myself. David McAllister? I hardly know him – and besides I don't think Eleanor's the Shakes girl he's been looking at.

Reverend Aldridge? Ha.

Anyway I'm almost sure she's not.

Should I have gone home with Jon? I know it upset him, those birds falling, it was strange, such a strange thing to happen. A hundred years ago I suppose we'd think it was a sign from God or something and all start looking for the meaning – but what sort of sign is it, what sort of meaning can it have, a dozen chickens or what have you falling on a funeral?

Maurice Shakes is talking about it to Dr Reynolds. Saying something about the sanctity of life, sir, the sanctity of life.

Someone ought to have done something of course but nobody ever wants to be the one who does something, do they?

Here's the reverend. You'd think funerals would be water off a duck's back for a minister but here he looks like he might cry.

Don't cry, Reverend, I want to say. All part of God's plan and so on.

'Your husband,' he says, wafting a sandwich, 'is rather cross with me, I'm afraid, Mrs Lowell.'

'Jon, cross? I'm sure he isn't, Reverend. Just a bit upset.'

'No, no, there's no doubting it.' He does a brave little smile. I smile back. 'I let the poor woodcock perish and he thinks me monstrous.'

You didn't let it perish, though, did you? I think. You did it in, or had your feller with a spade do it in. Makes no odds to me, really, but you might as well be straight about it, I think.

'No one thinks you're monstrous, Reverend,' I say. 'What an idea.'

'You are kind, Mrs Lowell.'

'I'm not. Not especially.'

'It has been a – a rather trying day.'

'I'm sure it has, Reverend. I don't know how you do it.'

He does a grimacing sort of face and I think, oh goodness, he really is going to cry now, and I realise then it's not really the funeral that's upset him and it's not even Jon saying he's monstrous, it's the bird, the blooming bird in the grave.

He thinks he's monstrous, is what it is.

'The dignity of the funeral rite,' he says, fumblingly. Wafts his sandwich weakly. It's going to fall apart if he's not careful. 'We buried a man today, Mrs Lowell. I was only ever thinking of the dignity of the rite.'

I say, let's go and get a cup of tea, Reverend, or something like that.

I sort of hold out my elbow to him. He takes it, his hand tight and warm in the crook of my arm. Hanging on to it like he's drowning.

XIII

In the end I confessed, of course, because in the end we all confess, one way or another, but I didn't confess to Harriet, I confessed to David, and I didn't speak of those moments on the windblown coast road – didn't speak the words 'Eleanor', 'kiss', 'love', 'guilt' – but only wrote of them in a letter, and in a letter in return David said that I was a damn reckless fool and moreover a beast, and that it was the sort of thing he might have expected of a man like himself but not of a man like me, and asked me two things: why I had done it, and (I could read the smirk in his sloppy handwriting) what it had been like.

I couldn't explain to David about complementarity, about me and him and the Saltaire cricket match, without being subjected to an intolerable ragging. I couldn't tell him that I had felt in Eleanor Shakes a strange and lonely and sympathetic kinship, without him telling me that, on the contrary, I had felt nothing but a gallon of pale ale in my belly and a concentration of blood in my loins.

And I couldn't tell him what it had been like – of course I couldn't. And so I answered neither question. I didn't reply at all.

David's letter, the letter with the importunate questions, arrived with us on the morning of November the twenty-eighth. I spent the day closeted in my study, writing a chapter on the breeding of kittiwakes. On the following morning, walking net-in-hand to the rocks through a dismal drizzle, I heard shouts of instruction and warning, and, looking north, saw men swarming over the toe-end of the harbour wall. All through November, since the woodcock moon, they had been assembling: Shakes's men. Shakes's army.

Many, perhaps most, I had met.

Walter Stavanger was an agent of the Newcastle steel company that was to provide the struts and arches for the grand pier of Shakes and Furlong. He had surprised me as I perched at the brink of the Challenger Deep with my shirtsleeves rolled to my biceps. A smart-looking fellow in slate-blue tweed, with a moustache and a neat parting in his hair, he had asked me, with interest and a smile, what I was up to. I had told him – I was hunting for blennies – and he had laughed as though this were the grandest thing he had heard in years. Then he had bidden me a good morning, and continued his stroll along the shore.

Job Wakenshaw dealt in timber, Yorkshire timber, and from his North Riding forests was to furnish Shakes with the planks – six thousand, four hundred of them – on which the prophesied Graveley holidaymakers would promenade back and forth, back and forth, each a tiny human tide. In fact Harriet had made his acquaintance before me; Wakenshaw was a timber dealer of the devout variety, and had been introduced to my wife at the door of Aldridge's church. I had met him over tea one afternoon – and, on learning of the part he was to play in the pier project, I had made a social misjudgement.

'Then through your good offices,' I had said jovially, 'we might all walk on the water.'

Wakenshaw had shaken his jowls at me.

'Oh thou, thou of little faith,' he had rumbled. 'Wherefore didst thou doubt? Were the Christ to call you to walk with Him among the waves, Mr Lowell, I fear you would founder, like Saint Peter.'

I had had little association with Job Wakenshaw since.

The Harrowells, Ted and Arthur, were brothers, young men, steelmen – they did things (I didn't catch what) with steel or iron, and had been brought from Newcastle by Furlong, whom they called *Petey*. Each might, under his skin, have been made from wire; their strength seemed fearsome when I encountered them rolling entwined and drunk down the coast road late one afternoon, but of a different tenor to the obvious, heavy-shouldered might of, say, our Graveley trawlermen. They were trim, neatly built. They seemed somehow to have a soldierly strength.

Their handshakes rattled my skeleton, and they cried jovial things at me in broad city dialect.

'Well met, gentlemen, well met!' I cried, laughing, happy, in response.

I stood beside the beach for quite a while then, and watched them stumble towards the town, each with his arm about the other. The pier foreman and overseer, Mr Wilkie, was pointed out to me in the town one day by Harriet (who, through Aldridge I supposed, knew a good deal more than I did about the workings of Shakes's devilish project); I didn't speak with him, and indeed I never heard him speak. He must have *had* a voice – what would be the use of a foreman without one? – but his face was as flat and unexpressive as the end of a spade and, looking at him, I would hardly have been less surprised by the emergence of words from his mouth than if a spade had bidden me good day. When I heard the clamour from the harbour end, I strained my eyes to see if he was there, finally putting to good use that voice (I imagined a roar like a rasp on metal) that he husbanded with such care, but I couldn't see him.

There were a few Italians, as Furlong had foretold, but they didn't frequent the shore or the pub, and remained mostly in the north end of our town – in the district that I was coming to think of as Shakes's Bay. I had been told their names but had quickly forgotten them.

And there was another, another man brought to Gravely by Maurice Shakes. Neither a north-easterner nor an Italian. This man I had not yet met that day, that day on which David's letter arrived and I saw the men at work on the harbour wall. It was later, perhaps a week later, on a still evening a fortnight before Christmas, that I was made aware of him. I was passing by the pub. Though Clem Holroyd, its familiar spirit, was departed, there was yet a Holroyd smoking a pipe and drawing beer from the pumps in the pub, for it had transpired – after the funeral, with all bar me gathered there for the landlord's wake – that the fat fellow with the unclean handkerchief was indeed Clem's brother, Harold, and that the pub was to remain in the family. There would not be even the least interval in its historic commerce, teary Harold had declared with a brave smile, whipping the cloth from the pump – for as of *now*, he had said, Harold Holroyd's pub was open for trade. So for all that the north of Gravely was alive with new-come Shakeses, Furlongs, Italians and steelmen, here in the south little had changed. I was passing by the pub, with barely any intention of entering, when I heard the singing.

No sheep on the mountain nor boat on the lake,
No coin in my coffer to keep me awake,
Nor corn in my garner, nor fruit on my tree,
Yet the maid of Llanwellyn smiles sweetly on me.

I hadn't heard the song before and nor did I much care for it now, but the voice made me pause, waiting for more. It was a voice of extraordinary resonance; it was as clear to me, there on the clifftop, as though I had been hearing it from the stalls of a concert hall. There was to be no more, however – only a small burst of applause and some shouted words of acclaim. I had a few coins in my pocket, enough for a glass of beer. I walked up the path and pushed open the pub door.

He was a big man – that was the first thing I saw, that he was big, bigger than Maurice Shakes, bigger by far than me. And he was balding. The hair he had was pepper-grey and cut close to his flat-topped skull. He was leaning on the bar with a pipe in his right hand, and as I walked in he looked at me. There was a sort of amusement in his expression.

'Good evening,' I said mildly (as I said everything).

'Hello to you,' he replied, and tilted his pipestem in my direction. I felt dimly as though I had been acknowledged by an emperor. Certainly the men of Gravely – or at least the boozers of Gravely – were clustered about him as though he were a new Caesar. I approached. Had he not been standing at the bar I perhaps wouldn't have been so bold, but as it was I had no other option. I nodded in greeting at the latest Holroyd, and asked for a pint of pale ale.

As the Holroyd drew the beer from the pump, the singer extended a thick-knuckled hand and said: 'Carwyn James. And you'd be Mister—'

'Lowell. A pleasure to meet you, Mr James.'

'Wyn. I'm always Wyn.' His face again warped in amusement. 'A good name, in my trade, Mr Lowell.'

I laughed hesitantly, and guessed, ineptly: 'Perhaps you are in the racing business?'

'I'm a little large for a jockey, Mr Lowell,' James said. Everyone laughed, and I laughed too, though my cheeks burned. (Might he not quite easily have been a trainer or yard owner, after all? I was indignant as well as abashed.) James, though, quickly made me see that there had been no malice in what he said. 'I'm not in what you'd call a regular line of work, you see, Mr Lowell,' he confided. Then he said: 'But let's not talk of my work; I know of *your* work, sir – I read a book of yours, and admired it a great deal.'

No one had ever said this, or anything like this, to me before. I stammered a few thank yous.

'Yes, Mr Lowell, a fine book. *Afoot on the North Sea Coast*, gentlemen,' – now he addressed the men standing around him – 'a grand book about the birds and beasts and sea creatures and so on of this country of yours. It brought the place alive to me, Mr Lowell, before I had even seen your northern sea.'

Wyn James was a Welshman, of course – it was as clear in his accent as it was in his name. I said thank you once more, and asked him if he was a naturalist, too.

'I've climbed to a few gulls' nests in my time, for purposes of robbery.' He smiled. 'Shot a few rabbits, caught a few trout. Boys' business, you know.'

'It's *always* boys' business,' I said. 'Rock-pooling and bird's-nesting and poking for insects under rocks, it's all child's play – and yet, though a grown man, I make it my business. My living, indeed.'

James laughed generously.

'Well, I'm in no position to criticise on that score,' he said, and sucked at his pipestem.

I sipped my beer.

After a little time the conversational mutter of the men gathered at the knee of the Welsh giant began to take shape around a single word, 'song', 'a song', 'another song' – until one of them, a fisherman whom I knew only as Garrety, piped up: 'How about another song, Wyn, before you go?'

And the giant chuckled, and took his pipe from his mouth and said that he really oughtn't as he had to preserve his strength, and shook his head, and began to sing.

It was another folk air, Welsh I supposed, and in a melancholy vein, and as there was little else for me to do I stood and listened respectfully. This was no chore, for again the man sang beautifully. As far as I could gather it was a ballad about sundered lovers – drowned lovers, it transpired, as the one perished in the attempt to swim a fast-running river to reach the other, and the other perished in the attempt to rescue the one.

My thoughts wandered. Music, like beer, often has this effect.

That morning a week before, that rainy morning that had brought a letter from David and busy men to the harbour wall, I had looked south to the bluff, and seen a slender, solitary figure upon the bluff, and recognised it at once as Eleanor Shakes. It is a wonder to me now that I was able so readily to distinguish Eleanor from Cordelia (or for that matter from Harriet, or any of a score of women of the town), but I was – or perhaps I had only made a hopeful guess that proved to be correct. In any case, it was indeed Eleanor.

I had dropped my net immediately on seeing her. I had run across the awkward ankle-deep sands to the foot of the bluff. As I had clambered up the escarpment, I had been nauseated by the supposition, heavy and dull in my stomach, that she would be gone when I reached the top. But she was not gone; she was there, and she smiled, hatless and wild-haired, as I rose to my feet from the cold grass.

Then once I was standing, I hadn't the first idea what to say.

She said: 'Mr Lowell, are you drunk?'

I gaped at her. I stuttered a denial – it was, after all, barely nine in the morning – but she cut me off with a laugh.

'I apologise,' she said. 'I was kidding you, Mr Lowell. It's a bad habit I expect I acquired from my sister at an impressionable age. And' – she looked down at the grass, out to sea, fleetingly at me, and then up at the sky – 'it was in atrocious taste. I was just – I mean, I was alluding—'

'Ah,' I said, and bowed my head as a penitent might.

But the truth was that I was not a penitent. I was not sorry.

'The last time we met,' I said, 'I *was*, as you say, drunk, and I fear I behaved outrageously.' My mouth even shaped itself to form the words, *I am sorry, I apologise, I am so sorry.* I overruled it. I dug a fingernail into the ball of my thumb.

Eleanor was no longer smiling.

'Mr Lowell, I believe we both—'

'I am not sorry,' I said. I said it rather sharply.

She stopped as though I had slapped her and then laughed as though I had said something funny.

David once said to me, in a rakish, tipsy moment, that he regarded every woman (in fact I suspect he said *girl*) whom he didn't court, or kiss or otherwise make love to, as a story untold; not a story that he might have heard or read, or even written, but a story of which he might have been a part – one in which he might have been the hero. Now, hesitantly, I thought: *here is a story – she and I might together make a story.*

But of course in life we are allotted only one story per person, however unreasonable that might seem, and however ardently a person might strive to make it not so. Harriet and I: she was my story, and I hers. It was easy for me, in that moment, as the wind blew Eleanor's hair across her pale brow and she moved a pale hand with an amber ring to sweep it aside, to regret that I had embarked on that story when there was this new one of Eleanor and me to be written, told, lived – but then, there are always other stories.

Eleanor had turned to face the harbour across the bay.

'I came up here to watch the men working,' she said. 'I know that they're not *really* working – even my father wouldn't be so foolish as to begin work in midwinter – I suppose they're only taking measurements and soundings and so on, ready for the spring. But I came up here to watch them, anyway.'

The men on the harbour arm, I could see, were busy with charts and lists and notebooks, and devices of navigation and measurement. One man stood apart, aloof on the steps that led to the brink of the sea wall – the overseer Wilkie, I supposed. He seemed to be maintaining his silence. Perhaps his job required him to see that all went well, and as long as it did go well he had nothing to say.

The wind played merry hell with the work; as we watched, a chart or map was ripped from the grip of one of the men (Furlong, it looked like) and sent skimming away over the white wave-tops. We could hear the architect shouting after it. Eleanor laughed.

'They seem like good fellows,' I said. 'Those that I've met. Good men, I think.' *Inasmuch*, I added to myself, *as I'm qualified to judge.*

Strange, the habits of thought that we had in those days – for whenever I thought of those men and those boys, James, Wilkie, the Harrowells, Wakenshaw, Stavanger, even Furlong, I found myself thinking of them as though they were going to war. Indeed I still do, whenever I think of them.

Dad told me about the clown disaster at Great Yarmouth. It sounds funny, he said, but it wasn't funny. He remembered it. He was there.

'Yarmouth Bridge,' says the librarian. Black hair in a bun. Thirty-odd. Engagement ring. Think I know her. Is she an Endicott? Perhaps I know her sister. Perhaps she just has one of those faces. I wonder if she knows me. She sucks her teeth, fsst, and drops a clothbound book on to the counter. 'Institution of Civil Engineering, eighteen forty-five.'

I pick up the book and ask her if I'm allowed to take it home and she snorts at me. So I sit down at one of the tables they have. Still in my hat and coat. Sixes and sevens. The Endicott watching me. Flop open the book.

Institute of Civil Engineers, it says. Not institution of civil engineering, madam. I feel better. Take off my hat and rest it on the tabletop. Two beads of condensed mist on the crown.

Discussion: The Failure of the Suspension Bridge at Great Yarmouth.

I was in town anyway. I came in to pick up some reels of black cotton for Mother. I have them here, in my coat pocket. I was practically passing by the Mechanics' Institute and I thought, why not? I didn't know if I was even allowed in, not being a mechanic *or anything much like one, but I was, so I thought I'd see. Satisfy my curiosity. Dad used to talk about what happened but he was always talking* around *what happened, really – he'd talk about the famous clown who was to row up the Bure in a barrel, how they came in from their cousin's farm at Stokesby to see it, his dad and his uncle Horace, along the Norwich road, on the back of a haycart, how there was such a crowd of folk ('More than they get at the football now,' he said, 'and they get such a lot at the football now.').*

But never about when the bridge fell down. Never about – as it says here, in this report or discussion, whatever you call it – when a cracking noise is said to have been first heard, which caused a momentary alarm – when about five minutes after this, the fatal catastrophe occurred by the failure of the other rod – when the remaining bar gave way, and that end of the platform, being entirely unsupported, fell into the water.

Seventy-nine people. I don't think I even know seventy-nine people. And nearly all of them kiddies.

It doesn't really take me long to read. There's a lot about welding, unproven iron, scarfed joints, defective casting. One of the men (they were all men) said that the bridge wasn't a proper bridge, but a mere toy.

Seventy-nine. That's the bit that stays in your head.

'It is singularly unfortunate,' it says, this report, 'that the weakest links should have been placed at the point of the greatest tension.'

I suppose unfortunate *is one word for it.*

Flip back to the start, feeling the eyes of Miss Endicott there on the back of my neck. Read through it again. This time I make sure to read the names. Mr Scoles, the architect. Mr Green, the surveyor. Mr Goddard, the contractor. Mr Simpson, the engineer. Mr Cory, the owner.

I don't know if any of them were to blame, exactly. I don't know about blame. But they can't all just have been unfortunate, can they?

I imagine Mr Cory. It says he built his bridge so that people could get across the Bure to a bowling green and a certain pleasure ground. I imagine him with a fat waistcoat and iron-grey mutton chops. Red cheeks and a silver-topped cane.

They've a wonderful pier at Great Yarmouth now. The Britannia. Half a mile out to sea – a clear half-mile. Aunty Grace sent us a picture postcard when they reopened it, a few years back.

'An unusual choice of reading matter, Mrs Lowell,' Miss Endicott says, when I take the book back to the counter. So she does know who I am. I say I don't see anything unusual about it at all. I ask if I'm allowed to look at the other books. Which other books, she says, and I say all the other books. She says she supposes so.

I'll be back, I say.

XIV

'Have you got everything you need? Field glasses, shooting stick, embalming fluid, what have you.'

Luke Hesketh smiled drily. I laughed, and nodded, and said that he could regard himself as my native bearer, and would have to carry home any okapi or kudu I bagged on our journey. Luke and I had arranged – or more accurately Harriet had arranged for us – to take a walking trip while his school was closed for Christmas. There was a tumbledown cottage on the easternmost peak of the moor, perhaps twenty miles north-west, in which we were to camp overnight; we were to walk home to Gravely on Christmas morning.

Harriet was accustomed to spending Christmas Eve with her mother. They'd sing carols together in the little room that was full of seascapes. I always bore the ordeal stoically, I had thought, though my wobbling baritone added little to the proceedings, and I sang (I was told) without earnestness; I understood why Harriet had thought this walking trip a good idea – and I thought it a good idea, too, as Luke was good company, the moors in the snow would be splendid, and we might see peregrine, northern diver, hen harrier – who knew what else.

I was warmly and happily clad in rather worn tweed. Luke wore rust-coloured corduroys and a heavy sweater. We stood in the white sunshine at the foot of the path to Marlowe Moor and admired one another.

'Gosh, but our wives are lucky women,' I joked.

Luke hitched his haversack higher on his shoulders and led the way out on to the moor.

We walked in file, as the path was narrow. The wind, when it blew, was north-easterly and bit with a Baltic sharpness, but it hardly did blow, and the new sun – it was barely past eight – warmed our necks. The air was full of pipits. Luke whistled hymn tunes as he walked.

I knew it well, this seaward flank of the moor. After so much strangeness it was good to be alone (or as near as dammit, for Luke, bar his whistling, was silent as we walked) in a place of familiarity. For half a mile or so I entertained the unnerving notion that at any moment a Shakes or a David or a Newcastle steelman might spring from the black heather bents, and force new strangenesses upon my days – but the moor, the air and sky and birdsong of the moor, soon rinsed me clean of it. A young curlew wailed nearby.

We stopped for sandwiches a little after noon. We knelt in the bents by a stone wall and Luke unwrapped the paper from two rounds of bread slathered with the autumn's jam. While we munched, I asked after Louisa and Michael.

'Yes, the boy is coming along very well,' Luke mumbled through his mouthful.

'And Louisa?'

Luke made a sort of shrug, said: 'Yes, I suppose,' and took another bite of bread.

I was curious, and offered rather impertinently: 'The child, I imagine, takes over somewhat.'

He gulped his bread and squinted at me. He seemed amused.

'Takes over?'

'Yes. I can only speculate, of course, but is it not the case that, while you are "only" husband and wife, the, the mutual affection' – under Luke's dark gaze I balked at the word 'love' – 'is, one might say, undiluted? But, when a third arrives, the affection is, perhaps, diverted? Towards the child, I mean? And away from the wife, or husband?'

Luke smiled.

'Mutual affection?'

'You think me mealy-mouthed. Love, then.'

At this Luke set down the remainder of his sandwich and laughed.

'You sound like a schoolboy, Jonathan. How strange that you are a married man.'

In the silence that followed I listened to the sad ululation of a curlew nearby and *felt* like a schoolboy – an unpopular schoolboy, who is bad at games and doesn't understand the jokes.

'I've blundered,' I said, looking meekly at Luke, seeking for a clue.

'Not at all. I'm sorry. I wasn't laughing at you.'

You were, too, I thought – but didn't say so, and instead only nodded.

'Love. It's such a funny thing to think of.'

'Funny?'

'Oh, I don't know.' Luke shoved his sandwich wrapper back into his haversack and swung the haversack on to his shoulders as he clambered to his feet. 'Love, for Louisa! I mean, not that she isn't a terrific girl – but love? Like in the poems and things at school. That's not how it *really* is, is it?' He looked at me. 'Is it?'

I looked at my feet.

'I had always thought so,' I muttered.

'Well!' said Luke, and laughed loudly – awkwardly, I think – and the curlew, wherever it was, answered him with another *oh-oh-oh*.

We walked on, he in front and I behind.

That the marriage of Luke and Louisa Hesketh should be something other than a covenant of love – however quiet, however undemonstrative a love – was to me a hammer blow. It seems so foolish, now, that it should have struck me so forcibly, or indeed that it should have shocked or even surprised me at all – but it did, then. To not love one's wife! This was a great and terrible idea.

I thought of the boy, Michael. Did Luke at least love the boy? I daredn't ask.

As we walked, he whistled 'God Rest Ye Merry, Gentlemen', and I remembered that it was Christmas Eve, and found myself wondering: if Luke Hesketh did not love Louisa Hesketh, and considering all that followed from that, what after all was the *point* of it being Christmas Eve?

The moor was silent, the heather black and the sky clear and blue by the time we reached the ruined cottage. It had four walls, just about, and no roof; black ferns drooped from the wall tops and a bare warped elder scraped against the stone. We picked our way inside, stumbling on the rubble and bracken.

'It'll keep the wind out at least,' Luke said, stooping to gather broken elder branches. I thought him optimistic but didn't say so.

'Little chance of snow, thank goodness.' I sat on a stone and loosened the drawstring of my bag. I had brought cheese, potatoes, corned beef and whisky, which I had thought would be festive. I did not feel at all festive now, but still I was glad of the drink.

While Luke expertly made a fire, I prepared the food. It felt as though we were the last people – no, the last *things* – left alive. As though the war hadn't ended when it did, ten years since; as though, instead, it had somehow found its blundering way here, to the windblown peak of Marlowe Moor, and laid all to waste. I felt cold, footsore, hungry, empty.

We threw two potatoes into the fire to bake in their skins. Then we arranged ourselves in our sleeping bags as best we could, and as near to the fire as we dared, and took a tin cup of whisky apiece, and drank to a merry Christmas. I cut slices from the cheese and corned beef to eat while we waited for the potatoes.

'A splendid feast,' Luke said.

I asked him why he had married Louisa. He looked at me with patient amusement. I saw that he was a good teacher.

'It's what one does, Jonathan,' he said. 'And she was a fine-looking lass, Louisa, when she was younger.'

His face in the firelight appeared terribly old, as faces do when lit from beneath, but Luke Hesketh had never seemed so – so *childish* to me as he did in that moment. I'd seen him playing silly games with Michael – acting at being a horse or a dog or a pig – and he had seemed, nevertheless, a man, far more a man than I; but now, for all his stern moustaches and his skill at fire-making and his cup of whisky, it seemed to me that *he* was the schoolboy and I the grown man.

I thought of my love for Harriet. I thought of Eleanor Shakes. These, I thought, are not childish things.

'It's going to be bloody Baltic when this fire goes out.'

'Worse things happen at sea, old man.'

The thing is of course that Luke Hesketh, back then, *was* a child, or anyway barely more than that. Twenty-three, twenty-four?

And I the same.

We sat and shivered and ate tepid, hard potato out of charred skins, and drank, and talked – easily, even merrily, after three or four cups of whisky. I remembered that I liked Luke. I forgot, for the time being, about Luke and Louisa. When the fire went out, it *was* Baltic, and we drew the strings tight on our bags; I pointed out which constellations we could see (it was freezingly clear), and then, rather drunk, we made owl calls to one another in the dark, howling with laughter in between hoots. Before we fell asleep we once again wished one another a merry Christmas: 'A bloody merry Christmas to you, Jonathan – a damn merry Christmas!', 'Luke, a happy Christmas to you, too, most sincerely, a very bloody merry Christmas to you, Luke.'

*

I awoke briefly before dawn to the sound of Luke being sick (he was unused to drink), and then slept until around seven. I sat up in my bag to find a light drift of snow covering my feet.

'Christmas day,' I said, to no one in particular. Luke groaned in his bag. My head ached. I wished David were there. I wished Harriet were there. I wished for a hot breakfast.

I stood and stretched. The blue-white sky burned my eyes.

'In your sleep,' Luke said from behind me, 'you said "Eleanor", you said the name "Eleanor". More than once.' A laugh, utterly mirthless. 'There's your true love,' he said. Lapwings tumbled laughing down through the sky as we descended the snow-striped moor. The air was cold and steely on the tongue. My tweed coat felt too thin, my bag too heavy, my boots too tight.

There's a legend about lapwings. The legend says that each lapwing is the soul of a Jew who jeered at Jesus Christ as he bore his cross along the road to Golgotha, reborn as a bird, in punishment. If this is true, though, the lapwings haven't learned their lesson; they haven't learned a thing. Still they laugh and laugh – and, this Christmas morning, I was in no doubt that they were laughing at me.

I led the way, this time. Luke, muffled in a scarf, followed me in silence. The sea far ahead of us was the colour of wet slate.

Harriet would be at church, of course. Everyone would be at church, bar the Shakeses. That ham actor Aldridge would be distilling the Christmas spirit. I shivered at the thought of it. A church in December is a cold place; we had had our fill of cold old stone in the ruined cottage, Luke and I.

I wondered where Eleanor would be. Perhaps walking on the beach. Perhaps peeling potatoes or preparing a turkey for the oven.

The lapwings rose again from the heath and chorused their derision.

Back in the town the two of us parted warmly, with hand-shakes and good wishes, for we were friends, after all; I didn't think less of *him* for learning that he did not love Louisa; he and I had got drunk and made silly owl calls together, and while such a thing might not quite give you the full measure of a man, it is something – it is no small thing.

Gravely smelt of seaweed and boiling root vegetables. As I walked up the driveway of our house, I hummed a carol in spite of my headache.

Harriet was in the kitchen. She wore a belted dressing-gown. Smiles, kisses.

'You survived the trek, then?'

'Yes. By the skin of our teeth. We thought we should never see home again.'

'Oh, you hero. Merry Christmas, Jon.' Another kiss, and then: 'Did you see him? On the promenade?'

'Who?' (Though I should have guessed.) 'I didn't come along the prom.'

'Mr M. Shakes Esquire, naturally. He was on the prom as we all left church. And do you know what? He had with him an organ grinder and an ice-cream man. Italians. The organ played carols. And ice cream! In December.' She laughed, for once amused rather than appalled by Shakes's audacity. 'That man always has to be the centre of attention.'

'He isn't the centre of my attention,' I said – for I suspected that beneath her dressing-gown Harriet was naked. She smiled, and said: 'Nor mine,' and slid her arms around my neck. I unlooped the knot of her dressing-gown belt.

'My hands are as cold as ice,' I warned her.

In answer she took my right hand and pressed my fingers into the bristly softness between her legs. She shuddered and laughed.

'You'll soon warm up,' she said.

'Happy Christmas, my dear,' I said.

Although on the long walk down from the moor I had been dreaming chiefly of a plate of fried eggs and sausage, I was not about to protest. Harriet lifted herself on to the tabletop and we made love. I am not being coy; 'made love' is the correct term. It was sex, of course, we copulated, of course, but we made love, too. It *was* a kind of love, I think.

Harriet's kicking left foot knocked an empty gravy boat from the kitchen counter and we ignored its smashing on the stone flags. That's a kind of love.

'Jon,' she said, insistently.

'Harriet,' I said, and just as I said it, 'Harriet', the image – no, not only the image, the odour, the taste, the *essence* – of Eleanor Shakes arose in my mind. And I thought: well, all right. If Luke Hesketh didn't love Louisa Hesketh (such was my logic in the moment) then what of it if I loved one woman and lusted for another, or vice versa, or lusted for two women, or loved two women? What of it? It felt, for a moment, like a liberation.

Harriet's strong fingertips dug into my buttocks and she climaxed with a staggering whimper. I looked at her. Her glorious eyes were open but she looked at the ceiling, not at me.

And in *this* moment my logic said: well, Jon, if – as it turns out – you can make love to your wife and think of Eleanor Shakes, why, then Harriet can just as well make love to her husband, to you, and think of another.

And the image, not the essence, only the image, of the long-bearded Reverend Aldridge rose into my mind.

'It was like Christmas came early that year, of course,' she says. 'Came early and stayed around for longer, too. All through November, December, on into January, on into spring, even: lads coming home. Sons, husbands, brothers. Boyfriends,' she adds darkly. 'My goodness, there was nothing like it. Like when trawler crews made it through a heavy sea or a lifeboat's put out and come back safe – like that, only a hundred times more, a thousand times.'

'Despite all those that didn't come back,' I say. Really just to see if she even remembers.

'Aye.' She nods distantly. 'And in a way that made it more special. Of course it did. They knew how lucky they were, you see. All those not coming back, never coming back. Oh, goodness, you could see what it meant. Mothers, sisters, wives. They all of them realised all at once, like it'd hit them with a hammer, how much they cared for those lads.' Her active little eyes settle on me for a moment. 'Fathers, too, for that matter, Harriet.'

So now I see why she said she wished Dad'd been here to see me coming home. Bradford was my war, was it, Mother? The fellers of Bradford my Boche. And my marriage my Armistice, I suppose, or my Versailles.

I'll take her to mean that, until I came back to Gravely, she didn't know that she cared for me all that much. And as for Dad, who died before I went away let alone before I came back – well, he died not knowing whether he cared for me at all.

Merry blooming Christmas, Mother. I take a big drink of my tea. It's nothing I'm not very well used to (both the veiled criticisms and the horrible tea: both mother's milk to me).

She doesn't remember James, anyway. That's clear. Can I blame her? I hardly remember him myself.

I wonder, when Mother goes off to strain the gravy or something, if the boys came back different. I wouldn't know, because back then I only really knew one boy and he didn't come back at all.

I suppose they must have seemed different because of the war. They'd have grown older in the trenches, lost limbs or picked up bullet wounds, killed men, seen dreadful things. But maybe it wouldn't just have been that. To the people here, I reckon they'd have seemed different because they'd been so far away; in a different country, away beyond the sea, France, Belgium, the Dardanelles, what have you. To people here – who've seen plenty of young men die, seen plenty of limbs torn off, felt plenty of grief and fear – that's every bit as strange as a war.

XV

We had feasted, inasmuch as our means allowed (a small chicken eked out by bacon and a superfluity of sauces, mashed potato, carrots, parsnips, and plum duff); we had read to one another at the fireside, from Christmas books; we had retired exceptionally early to bed, with all that that entailed – and yet all the day I was haunted, like Scrooge, by a ghost of Christmas present. Mine, like that spirit from Dickens, was long-bearded (though not so merry). On Boxing Day I awoke feeling nauseated and irritable.

Hail spat fiercely against the window glass. On the roof, the querulous herring gulls mewled in the teeth of it, and I pitied them. I thought of the woodcock in the landlord's grave.

But when, late in the morning, I finally stepped outside, I found that peace had returned. I walked down the driveway to the seafront in a watercolour wash of pale-blue sky. The road, the pavement, the red-brick seafront houses seemed fiercely clean, like a well-scoured pan. I breathed deeply. A pair of carrion crows flew low over the weed-strewn sand. Crows form lifelong pair bonds – but they are not necessarily monogamous. I have always felt a sort of weary sympathy for those who seek in nature examples of a Christian life.

I walked along the road and then crossed the damp beach to the foot of the bluff. I sat there for a while, on a rock. I watched turnstones potter at the tideline. I watched a young girl chase after a rubber ball. I thought of Eleanor, her serious eyes, the taste of her mouth, but then thought, just as inanely, that this was perhaps only likely to invite further haunting. I watched the turnstones, poured a measure of tea from my Dewar flask, eyed the clouds, which were once more thickening. I sipped the tea and tried to think of Harriet.

Then I noticed that the coast road, previously deserted save for the odd promenader or workman, was growing busy with people. They were headed north, not hurriedly or in a panic, as if there had been floods or riots to the south, but with purpose and direction, certainly – like people walking to a football match or a fair. I shifted on my stone to watch. The odd snatch of laughter or shouted jocularity reached me against the wind.

Church? It was no hour for a service, surely. Some popular spectacle, then. A whale on the beach? A wreck off the north bay?

Of course I knew really where they were going. They were going to Maurice Shakes. I knew not why, I knew not where – but they were going to Maurice Shakes. And so I stood, stowed my flask and field glasses, and went too.

This was hardly a human tide, but only a broken stream of people, mostly men it seemed, a few alone, some in jovial mobs of more, along the coast road to the harbour. Most faces were familiar; though I wanted to ask where we were all bound, and why, something stopped me – something more than simple shyness. I feared engagement with those men. Perhaps I thought of them as Shakes's men.

I saw the fat landlord Harold Holroyd, the godly timberman Job Wakenshaw, the Harrowells, again arm in arm. And I saw strange faces, too – the faces, I mean, of strangers, a strange sight indeed in Gravely, once.

Aldridge I did not see. Did I want to see him? Was this not why I was here? Why else was I marching to the beat of Shakes's drum? If you would seek godly men you had better go to where the devils are.

Eventually I summoned the guts to take a sauntering townsman by the elbow and ask: 'What's all this, then?'

The man (I knew his face but not his name) looked at me in surprise.

'Ah, now then, Mr Lowell! Do you not know?'

'I do not. Evidently, I'm in a minority of one!'

'It's a match-up, Mr Lowell. The big American feller has fixed it over at the harbour.'

'I had guessed our Mr Shakes must be involved!'

'Is that his name? The one with the daughters.' He winked clumsily. 'Aye, it's his making. Some sort of publicity stunt, I dare say, but still it ought to be a good ding-dong. I've a florin on the Taff, mysen, though I don't hold much hope of seeing it again.'

And once again I was the schoolboy who did not know the rules and did not understand the jokes.

A 'match-up'? A foot-race, then? Swimming? Chess?

It would have been so simple to ask but how could I ask?

'Best of luck to you and your florin,' I said weakly.

'Aye, thank you, Mr Lowell. Good morning to you!' He tipped his hat and I stopped by the roadside, feeling very small and lost.

I have never been good in crowds. I have watched knot and turnstone fly across the sea in vast flocks that furl and unfurl in an unthinking unity at which I could only marvel. I have seen military men drill without hesitation or misstep in the same awesome uniformity. In each case I have wondered at the harmony and shuddered at the mindlessness.

At the harbour, in any case, it seemed I should find answers.

There was more cloud in the sky than blue as we passed the church. I walked at the shore-side of the road as we approached the blasted grey steeple, anxious lest Aldridge should be at the church door, haranguing the masses – *go back, go back*, as the red grouse cries upon the moor. But the church was quiet. Perhaps Aldridge was within, praying for our souls.

As we approached the harbour I became aware of music: an organ, playing a tune I didn't recognise (though the fisherman walking beside me began to whistle an accompaniment). The men up ahead were slowing their pace; we began to bunch, there in the road where the in-butting harbour wall forced a kink inland. We craned our necks to see. The whistling fisherman resourcefully scaled a pile of empty lobster pots for a better view.

'There he is,' he called down, grinning. 'There's our lad.'

I made my way, murmuring polite apology, to near the front of the crowd (townsmen, back then, would quite readily step aside at the sound of a better-spoken voice). I peered over the cloth caps to see a man standing in a space that had been cleared amid a clutter of pots, nets and other paraphernalia of the trawlermen. The man's head was shaven and he wore a clean white singlet. His hands were bound with bandages and he bobbed on the spot, smiling and throwing punches at the air.

'Our lad'? It still took me a moment to realise – such is the power of context. This was Carwyn James, the sweet-singing Welsh giant.

'Put your money down, boys!' he roared, grinning round at the men. 'This is a walkover. Did you ever see a wop who could fight?' He fired a fierce one-two at an imaginary opponent. 'I'd give bloody Primo Carnera a run for his money, if they'd let me fight him, and this boyo, I tell you, is no Carnera!'

The men – there were perhaps fifty of us here, and more up ahead – clapped and cheered. A few produced coins or banknotes.

A prize fight, then. I had never seen one (the nearest I had come was watching sixth-form boys scrap at school). And this Wyn James, a prize fighter. I suppose I shouldn't have been surprised. I suppose a less sheltered man would have guessed it right away.

I stood uncomfortably among the jostling, bantering workmen of Gravely for a few more minutes, watching Wyn duck, weave and shadow-box, and then, skirting the Welshman's makeshift training arena, made my way deeper into the shadows of the harbour.

Here, the high harbour wall cast a wide, dark shadow. I had to find my way with care: the trawlermen's rig that was strewn on the flags shared the space, now, with a different kind of workmen's clutter – a theodolite here, a sheaf of steel scaffolding poles there – and I felt rather like an archaeologist picking his way through the strange treasures of a pharaoh's tomb. The bulk of the prize-fight crowd was up ahead, in sight of the sea, where I supposed the bout was to take place, so here I had leisure to catch my breath and collect my thoughts.

This had become, I saw, a sort of shanty town. Huts – solidly made by capable men, but huts, still – lined the wall beside the road. Some had windows. These, I suppose, were for working in, for poring over sounding charts and lists of figures. Others seemed like the meanest conceivable sleeping quarters. I could imagine an army being billeted here.

The place was horridly littered. Discarded food wrappings lolled in what breeze there was, and glass bottles, upright or on their sides, empty or half-empty, beer or whisky (but mostly beer), were all around. They chimed much as the masts of boats chime in a crowded harbour. There was a smell of stale drink and urine.

As I moved through the gloom I had a wary feeling I had seldom felt before in Gravely.

'So how do you like Shakestown, Mr Lowell?'

I spun at the sound of the voice: she was behind me, so I suppose she had been following me. Cordelia. She stepped from the sunlight into the shadow, a slight figure in a dark red dress, green coat and cream cloche hat.

At her approach, quailing inside, I removed my hat and said: 'Good afternoon, Miss Shakes. A real workers' campground.'

'A slum.' She smiled through the word. 'Or so your good church ladies would think it.'

'It could,' I conceded with a silly bow, 'be better kept.'

'Here for the fight?'

'I simply followed the crowd and found myself here. I suppose I shall stay for the spectacle.'

'You should. Father assures me it'll be a *real good rout*. And you men do so love that kind of thing.'

I laughed.

'I am a logical disproof of your assertion. I am a man, or a near enough approximation – but I have no appetite for bloodshed.'

'Oh, I don't know, Mr Lowell.' She was beside me now, and took my elbow. 'You kill your pretty little creatures readily enough.'

'Come, now. With the killing jar there is no blood, no suffering. For a wild thing, Miss Shakes, death is more often than not a mercy. And besides – that is science.'

'So, they say, is boxing.' She tugged my arm. 'Come. Let's go and watch.'

I had little choice. We walked arm in arm out of the shadows of the camp – Shakestown, she had called it – and towards the furthest knot of spectators, who were gathered about a cleared space where the great north spur of the harbour wall met the land. Some stood, some perched on the steps cut into the wall, others lounged on the ground as if it were midsummer. Many held glass bottles or steaming fried food folded in paper.

'You are a different man,' Cordelia said, 'when David – when Mr McAllister is not here.'

I shrugged, but I was surprised.

'I *feel* different, for David is a good friend. But I had not supposed the difference was noticeable to anyone else.'

'Not to just *any*one, but to me.'

'How, then, am I different?'

She stopped, so I stopped. She turned to face me, so I turned to face her. The low pale sun, south-east of us, whitewashed her left cheek and glinted wintrily in her left eye.

'I guess I imagined, when I met you, that David was the – the reckless one' – she smiled – 'and you looked after him. I imagined you were the staid, wise fellow who held David's arm when he was looking to stray – the wise voice at his ear.'

'But?'

'No, not "but". I'm not saying that you don't look after him, Mr Lowell. But it's clearer to me now that he looks after you, too.'

Slightly irked, I half-turned to squint out at the sea.

'You speak as though we were children,' I muttered.

'No, you're men, only men,' she said, and laughed. 'Don't take it amiss. It's nothing but a girl's dumb thoughts, after all. It's just you seem less – less *complete*, without David.'

'If my wife were here, I might perhaps seem more whole.'

'Ah, dear Harriet,' Cordelia nodded. 'Maybe.' But she was not, it was clear, convinced. She led me on towards the crowd.

People turned and looked at us as we approached. If Cordelia Shakes wished to impress or frighten me by demonstrating how – in her high-heeled shoes and coral lipstick – she could turn men's heads, she had failed, for my own Harriet invariably had the same effect (in more comfortable footwear, at that).

Besides, this was Gravely. It did not necessarily take a great deal to turn men's heads, in Gravely.

Perhaps, though, Cordelia wished to show me something else, something that *did* impress me, and not favourably. Perhaps she did not intend to show me it – but I saw it anyway. Scandal. In men's expressions: alarm, fear, even horror – Miss Cordelia Shakes had become scandalous.

It may be that the scandal was her walking arm in arm with a sea creature like me.

It was scandal that made the local men look away almost as soon as they had looked (and then they would look again). It was scandal that held their tongues; had this been Harriet, we would have been wished a dozen 'good afternoons', a score of 'merry Christmases', by now. We were not.

But while the Gravely men, the men whose faces I knew even if I didn't know their names, were fearful, there were, from strange men, catcalls, leering sniggers, a shout of: 'Clara Bow's here, lads!'

Scandal is about danger. Our men, the men of our town, knew about danger, knew far more than most, for were they not by and large trawlermen? Barely a day passes but a trawlerman sees death an arm's reach away. The new men – steelmen, riveters, men of the furnace and scaffold – surely knew danger, too. But they knew something more: Shakes's men, who were older than ours, had seen the war, and danger to them, I supposed, was no longer what it might have been.

Our men were superstitious (one thinks of the credulous fishermen who followed Christ) – our men would not tempt fate. These other men, these older men, had seen fate do its very worst. They had seen what fate might do without the least invitation.

Cordelia Shakes, in any case, was indifferent.

'We'll see all right from here,' she said, climbing two of the granite steps to lean in the sunlight against the harbour wall.

Indeed we would, for I was taller than most Gravely men, and so, in her heels at least, was Cordelia. From here we could see the cleared, roughly circular space, dusted with sand. The crowd formed a horsehoe around the space; at the furthest end the land fell away and there was only a twenty-foot drop to the lapping waters of the harbour. A dramatic backcloth for Shakes's drama. Gulls rose and fell beyond the harbour wall.

In the middle of the sandy ring stood two men: Maurice Shakes, of course, richly suited and in a tweed baker's cap, and the Italian, the 'wop', whom Wyn was to fight. He was, perhaps, six feet tall, less bulky than Wyn but by no means slender, far younger, beetle-browed and olive-skinned. He was not a heavy labourer; I might have thought him a sailor or soldier (but then, I might have thought Wyn James a racehorse-trainer).

Shakes, circling at a slow walking pace, held up two worn pads of leather, bristling with horsehair where the leather had split, and the young Italian, bouncing on his toes, pounded them with his bandaged fists. All the while, with the Italian's thumping as percussion or punctuation, Shakes kept up a stream of commentary.

'See, there, my boys – see (oof!) the left hook that will put your old Welshman on his proud posterior. *That's* it, Enzo, my lad (urgh!). Did you ever see such a prodigy, my friends, did you ever witness such a miracle of physiology? He seems to walk on air, doesn't he? He moves likes a dancer, but (hey, boy!) he strikes like a snake. I hear some of you fellers (humph, hurr!) are throwing away your hard-earned sterling on that goddamn valetudinarian from the Valleys, is that right? Well, you go ahead, my fine, foolish boys (oof!) – but don't come complaining to Maurice Shakes when this figure from a Correggio canvas has old Taffy begging for a merciful end inside of three rounds!'

And so on.

The Italian, Enzo, did seem fearsome – to fearful me, at least. He skipped limberly from foot to foot, and when he threw a punch the muscles of his bare arms contorted dramatically. He was dressed much as Wyn had been, in singlet and leggings. He was perhaps nineteen or twenty.

I glanced sideways at Cordelia. She was smiling, in a somewhat curious way, and her eyelids were half-lowered. I followed her hooded gaze and saw that she was not, as I had assumed, smiling upon the handsome and athletic Enzo. Peter Furlong stood at the far side of the ring, smiling back.

Then she turned her head, as though to look at me – but she did *not* look at me, but instead looked past me, or through me, with a different smile, a warmer, a softer and a sadder smile. I did not turn, I did not have to turn, to know that Eleanor Shakes had joined us on the sea wall.

'Your father has such vision,' says Alice Reynolds.

I wonder what it must be like to have a father like that. It's not that Dad didn't have any imagination; it's more that he never saw, really, how the things he imagined – I mean, look at Holloway and Daughter Shipyard – might have anything to do with real life.

Other way round with this one's dad.

'He is an adventurer, I'm afraid,' says Eleanor, 'with all the good and bad that that implies.'

'We don't mind buccaneers in these parts,' says Alice. She's from Ripon. No business talking about 'we' and 'these parts'.

We're walking along the coast road, going nowhere. I was putting out the washing when they came by the end of the drive. Arm in arm. It was Alice that called me over, of course. Take the air with us, Harriet! Take the air. I've been taking this same air since the day I was born. I've no need to go high-stepping up and down the coast road to take some more. But I could hardly say no, and anyway I think I like Eleanor Shakes, or I want to like her, or she intrigues me or something. When I did join them – I came up on Eleanor's side, and kept the crook of my arm out of reach of Alice's hand – Eleanor gave me a little smile that had nothing at all to do with Alice.

There are birds – would they be skuas? Jon would know, of course – chasing each other across the sky. Who knows what it's about. Food *or territory or something. It's Eleanor who points them out. Alice says they're enough to make one dizzy ('one', honestly). I say, like one of those fairground rides, and Alice says that – with no disrespect to Mr Shakes! – those contraptions always make her awfully nervous.*

Eleanor – still watching the skuas, if they are skuas – says: 'My father would say that the things that make you nervous are the only things in life that are really worth doing.'

Alice, and I have to admire her sometimes, says: 'But what do you say?'

She laughs, does Eleanor. The dizzying birds rise and plunge two hundred feet or so above the grey sea. The light is lovely on her face. She says oh, I don't know. I don't like to be frightened, she says, but I admit I do quite like the feeling of butterflies in my tummy.

Then she looks at me and says: 'Do you say that here, Harriet? Butterflies in your tummy? Or is it an American phrase?'

I say no, yes, we get them here, too.

There seems to be a lot of men about, suddenly. A young lad, Mildred Grieve's son I think, comes past us, headed somewhere in a hurry. Two fellers I was at school with – but not the sort I'd dare speak to with Alice Reynolds in tow – come jogging after him. Three rough-looking out-of-towners, laughing together (at us?). As we turn, with the road, towards the bluff, I look over my shoulder and see that something's happening – or all these men think something's happening – at the harbour. I'd not heard about a ship coming in or going out. Nothing out of the ordinary, anyway. I say as much. Alice says she's not heard anything, either (and crikey, you should see how much it stings her to admit that). We both end up looking at Eleanor, like supporting players in a stage musical.

'I think father's putting something on,' she says. Is it embarrassment, in her face, her voice? A sort of tightness. 'Some silly show or something. I shall probably head over there a little later. Someone,' she laughs, without meaning it, 'ought to keep an eye on the man.'

Well, you'll not get Alice Reynolds along to anything she's not already invited to. So sorry, dear Eleanor, but just so much to do, she says; isn't everything, she says, always such a whirl?

Not always, Alice, no. But I say I'll head home, too. It's not a lie because I will go home; it's just that I'll go out again. I'll go – it makes me feel silly, almost dizzy; God, of all things it makes me happy *to say it! – to work.*

XVI

One evening in the cold early spring of 1926 I led my new fiancée up to the moors above Baildon, beyond the jolly racket of the Shipley Glen fairground and away from the steep rocks where climbers in sweaters and long socks practised their heel-hooks, pinchers, slopers, crimps. Hand in hand we walked through dry, rustling waist-high ferns beneath the pealing of lapwings to a place where the path faded to nothing and the mossy wall of a disused quarry hid the view of the smoke-blue town. Here, I set Harriet on her knees (not roughly, but not gently, either), hoisted the snug hem of her cheap tweed skirt over her bottom, and pulled down her ivory underpants. She waited quietly while I unfastened belt and fly buttons, and then I – for want of a better word (or perhaps for fear of it) – took her, as a savage might. A polite savage, of course, a savage who would not stoop to bullying or rape, but a savage yet. I was savage enough to not care about the three-inch rip that my manhandling had opened in the seam of her skirt or about her stockings, which were bloodied and torn to bits at the knees (they had to be knotted into a bundle and discarded among the ferns). I was savage enough to not care until some time afterwards whether the sound of her cries had carried to the parents and children walking home from the fairground.

And this, I might say, was no isolated incident. Would they have been shocked, our neighbours, there in Bradford, or later up in

Gravely, if they knew how we were with each other, Harriet and I? We were married, after all – and that there were no children, that our coupling was not good, godly procreation, was no fault of ours.

I wonder which would shock them more: that, beneath a holy blue sky, I ravished my wife on her hands and knees on an April Sunday (a Sunday!) – or that, on the Gravely sea wall, I took Eleanor's hand in mine, and held it, and held it.

I know now and knew then, of course, which would be thought the more fearfully scandalous. But that, at the time, was less important to me than which of the two made *me* the more afraid. Which caused the greater frenzy in my chest. Which filled me with the fiercer feeling.

We stood side by side in a row on the granite step, Cordelia, me and Eleanor. Our hands – my left, her right – were concealed by the skirts of Eleanor's pewter-grey coat. We hadn't yet spoken; we had begun to, of course; our mouths had formed 'good day' or 'ah, hello' or 'Mr Lowell' or 'Miss Shakes', but we hadn't spoken because we had been overwhelmed by a roar from all about us as Wyn James, jogging lightly on the balls of his feet, entered the ring.

Above the ballyhoo I could hear Shakes crying out: 'Here he is! The Welsh Goliath, the champion of the Rhondda! Welcome your gladiator, boys!'

Wyn, smiling, squatted at the edge of the ring as a boy I didn't know fastened the laces of his liver-coloured gloves. The young Italian, Enzo, danced from foot to foot, fists circling, with his eyes on the bent Welshman.

The men catcalled, shouted support, whistled, cracked baffling jokes in impenetrable accents. I could hear little above their din but above the smell of onions and beer and the smell of the sea I could smell Eleanor. My empty stomach rolled like a lobster pot in deep currents. It was at this point that I took her hand. I didn't take my eyes off the fighters and Maurice Shakes, their impresario. I just felt carefully for her hand, felt it, took it; at first it shaped itself to fit mine, but then sought to move – when I held fast to it (become again a savage) it relented, and remained.

It was cold and dry and soft, and the fingers were slender without being bony.

It was Enzo's turn to have his fists tied up in gloves, and Wyn's turn to jog on the spot as Shakes, red-faced and beaming with his foolish cap tilted far back on his head, shouted on and on.

'These, my fine lads, are warriors worthy of the name,' he yelled. 'In the east corner, you see Tenente Enzo Baldini, heavy-weight champion of the Eye-talian army' – this drew a few jeers and jokes – 'the fastest fist in Campania, mighty as Vesuvius! Watch for his right hook, fellers – it comes out of nowhere and like a kiss from a Naples *bambolina*, it's *bang!* and you're on your knees before you know what's hit you. Lay your money down, boys, lay your money down!'

Baldini's broad back was turned to us. He raised his ungloved fist in a salute of sorts. I wondered how much of Shakes's publicity spiel was true. If he was indeed a lieutenant, this Tenente Baldini, he was a young one – a brave one, I supposed. Too young for the war but old enough for much else.

'And in the west corner, fellers, gentlemen!' Shakes, sweat darkening his suit despite the seasonal chill, persisted over the fresh uproar of shouts, argument and betting talk. 'In the west corner, why, a giant of the Welsh hills, a very Rhudda Gawr, a colossus carved of Pennant sandstone.'

I grudgingly acknowledged that Shakes had, at least, done his homework.

Eleanor's hand stirred in mine. My heart tumbled in my chest – but she did not remove her hand, only shifted it into a new position (now it felt colder, as when one turns over a pillow in bed).

In my head, full of self-recrimination, I sought to approximate David's voice: *you're a grown bloody man, Lowell, for Christ's sakes.*

Shakes was not done.

'I do not speak lightly, gentlemen, when I speak of warriors,' he cried, 'for I invite you now to show your appreciation for Captain Carwyn James, late of the Royal Welch,' he jabbed with his finger at the air for emphasis, suddenly no longer smiling, 'DSM, MC, the *hero*,' he bawled, 'of Mametz Wood! Show your appreciation, boys! Here's Captain James himself. Let's have you now! Let's have you!'

The applause was dense and drenching as an ocean wave, deafening, irrestistible. Of course it was – Distinguished Service Medal, Military Cross, the hell of Mametz, of course it was – but amid its thunder I watched Wyn James, who had ceased to limber up and now leaned close to Shakes. How small Shakes seemed!

Nothing could be heard above the din. But I watched Wyn's impassive face and in the motion of his lips I believe I read: 'We said we wouldn't speak of that, boyo.'

I might have been wrong.

Cordelia turned to me and made a wide-eyed face, so as to say, mockingly, *what larks!* I smiled – and yet she was there, we were all there. In the secret pleats of the grey coat I squeezed Eleanor's hand, and she squeezed mine in reply.

It was only when the applause finally ceased – not abruptly, as at a concert, but as reluctantly as the ebb of a tide – that I realised, really realised, that these two men were to fight each other. They came slowly, unhurriedly, to face one another in the middle of the makeshift sand-strewn ring. Their hugeness struck me anew. When I squeezed Eleanor's hand now, it was from fear.

There'd been fights at school, of course. Bust noses and black eyes, neckties torn, shirts and coats dishevelled. Faces red with tears and mucus. Shouting boys (but when, at school, are there not shouting boys?).

I had never fought – I was often shoved, hit from time to time, ran away a great deal – but I had seen fights. I supposed this would be rather different. I thought of David's bloodied mouth on the Saltaire cricket field. As bad as that?

I had seen excerpts from one or two prize fights on cinema newsreels. Dempsey? Willard? But those were just pale shapes moving here and there on a charcoal ground. If there was blood it did not show. If there was pain it was cinema pain, far-off, mediated Hollywood pain. This would not be like that. I didn't know what it would be like.

For a moment the thought occurred to me that ladies should not be here. It was not, after all, a carnival, a sideshow jape. It was, bluntly, a fight. It was no place for ladies.

The thought would have troubled me once, I think. It would not trouble me now. It did not trouble me then. Where might a woman not go? What might a woman not do?

With one fingertip I brushed the surface of Eleanor's fingernail. It was as smooth as the inside of a seashell.

The two men banged their hands together. It seemed so sudden. I wanted to hide my eyes but didn't. Enzo, the Italian, threw a punch so quickly I barely saw it until it connected with Wyn's face, and Wyn's head was jolted backwards. The Italian backed away quickly and covered his face with his fists; Wyn spat blood on to the sand, nodded (seemingly to himself) and moved warily forwards.

Shakes, who I understood was acting as referee or umpire in the contest, tracked the circling motions of the two fighters with a broad smile upon his face. All about us, men hooted and yelled. Eleanor's fingernails dug into the back of my hand. Through her thumb I could feel the beat of her heart.

The crowd maintained an undulating mutter of encouragement and commentary, now crying out in excitement, now falling quiet in anxiety or awe, now murmuring wonderingly at this fellow's skill, or that fellow's strength, or the pugilistic technique involved in this or that punch.

At my ear Eleanor said: 'This is fearful.'

There was a tension in her voice; not a quaver or a throb, but, rather, the firmness of a string drawn taut but not twanged.

I did not trust my own voice enough to reply, but if I had I would certainly have agreed, for apart from the physical sensations of noise, bodily scents, the bleak wind off the sea, the chalky sunshine and Eleanor's hand in mine, fear was all I felt. Love? Perhaps I felt love. I don't think I was able to tell. If there was love it was washed as with watercolour in the light of fear.

'Smite the wop bastard, Wyn!' someone yelled hoarsely at my side. There was a tolerant sort of laughter in response. I thought 'smite' an odd word – but then what did I know of what men yelled at prize fights?

Wyn bobbed and ducked. The Italian pranced and jabbed. There had been no more blood since that first shocking initiatory wallop. Across the ring I saw Furlong, in the swaying front rank of spectators, grinning and gesturing and shouting (I felt sure) foul things. He looked up at us – that is, at Cordelia – as much as he watched the fight. Cordelia's face was turned away from me, and I couldn't see where she was looking.

Baldini bounded from his left foot on to his right, and drove his left fist between Wyn's raised forearms and into his chest. I heard Wyn's grunt of pain (a sound never broadcast in the silent newsreel fights). He stepped back to steady himself, took a glancing blow on his cheek and returned the Italian's compliment: a mighty blow of his right fist that landed square in the middle of Baldini's face. More blood, new blood, the younger man's blood – it dripped in gobs down his chin as he swayed beyond another punch and danced unsteadily back towards the sea. Wyn, to my surprise, did not pursue him. Evidently this was a long game, a contest of stamina and will in which strength had to be preserved, discipline maintained. A war of attrition (one might have thought we had learned the folly of those). We were to be there, it seemed, for some time.

It would be easy to say that this mattered not a jot to me, so long as I was holding Eleanor Shakes's hand in mine – but it was not so simple. I knew that I would stay. Because of Eleanor? Because of my slight acquaintance with Wyn James? Perhaps I was compelled by the sordid drama of Furlong and Cordelia – had she, did she, would they? Or perhaps I had sporting blood in my veins after all.

Shakes, with a wave of his arms, called a halt to the first round of the bout, and the noise of the crowd rose in a drawn-out note of relief. I turned my face to the ocean and breathed in deeply.

'Is it over?' Eleanor said, bewildered.

I squeezed her hand – and then I had to release it (as it fell from my hand I felt as though my stomach fell from my belly in the same moment) because Cordelia turned with a laugh to face us, loose hairs streaming across her flushed face.

'Over? My goodness, Eleanor, use your head. Do you think they pay Jack Dempsey half a million dollars to spar for two minutes? There's *hours* to go yet.'

A tease, surely (hours?). I managed a good-natured smile.

'Father is enjoying himself,' said Eleanor. Her knee brushed mine. I don't know if it was meant. It didn't matter.

'That's what father does,' Cordelia replied drily.

'It's what *everyone* seems to do, in these parts.' The words had a heft to them.

'Pleasure, dear sister, is not a dirty word.'

It sounded like a dirty word, though, the way she said it. I remembered what Shakes had said, up on the bluff: *pleasure, the greatest thing of all.* I remembered what he had said after that, too – about Eleanor and Cordelia – about his daughters.

'Are you enjoying the fight, Mr Lowell?' Cordelia asked me, blinking in the wind.

'It's rather a bloodthirsty business.'

'*Isn't* it just.'

'I'm not sure I quite see the point.'

'You're a naturalist, Mr Lowell. Isn't conflict, competition, the fight to the death, the only way anyone gets anywhere? Survival, the phrase goes, of the fittest. They tell me it's the law of the world.'

'Of the animal world, yes.'

'We can't all sit quietly in the mud getting along with one another. Otherwise we'd never get *out* of the mud.' She grinned at me. 'We have a thing in the States, Mr Lowell, called *aspiration*.'

'Obedience to the laws of the beasts does not seem like much of an aspiration to me, Miss Shakes, if you'll forgive my saying so.'

The round toe of Eleanor's shoe poked my foot: I considered it a round of applause. Cordelia shrugged.

'Touché, Mr Lowell.'

We stood for a while in silence, watching the crowd mill restlessly, the fighters rinse their faces and chests, a man with a cart dole out portions of fried sausage and onion. *Quite a pleasure ground, Mr Shakes*, I thought.

I saw Furlong slurping beer from a bottle.

'You ought to discuss your views on the survival of the fittest with Mr Furlong there, the architect,' I said, rather daringly. 'He has no time for Mr Darwin's mechanism. He sees, I gather, a positive purpose in the world.'

Cordelia looked at me briefly with mild surprise, then turned away and gave a stark laugh.

'I'm acquainted with your Mr Furlong,' she said (and I wanted to say: *he's not* my *Mr Furlong*). 'The man has spent too much time in my father's company.'

I frowned.

'I thought your father was quite unequivocally a sceptic, where higher powers are concerned.'

She gave me a sardonic look.

'You misunderstand me, Mr Lowell – as ever. What I meant was that a man who spends too much time with Father often ends up believing that *he* is the higher power.'

Eleanor, at my left shoulder, laughed guiltily, as though she could not help it, and I, pincered, laughed along, and then the crowd noise surged once more. I looked back to the ring, and saw that the fight had resumed. Someone yelled, 'H'away, Wyn man!' Eleanor took my hand.

What are you, Jon, for Christ's sakes – fourteen years old?

David's voice in my head again.

It went away again soon, in any case, to be replaced by fear as the terrible bout wore on. After half an hour the two men looked, not really as though they had been in a fight (though each wore the odd bruise, the odd graze) but as though they had been worn away. I thought of the disintegrating foundations of our town, of our disintegrating island, when I looked at them both: heads rubbed red-raw by the friction of rough leather, bodies stooped, reduced, faces withdrawn like crabs into shells.

'How long can they go on?' I murmured, more than once, but no one answered.

Throughout, the small movements of Eleanor's hand played on me as though I were the keyboard of a piano.

Near the beginning of the seventh round (or sixth? fifth? eighth?), Wyn shuffled forwards, threw out his fist, missed his target, brought his hands back up to his face, but not quickly enough – young Tenente Baldini, tired I suppose of merely enduring, tired of being so *tired*, countered with a fast right hand to Wyn's jaw, a lumbering left to his ribs and another left to his face – here the crowd screamed, Eleanor yelped and I (the coward, remember) looked away.

I could tell by the ululations of the crowd that punches were still being delivered, and were still connecting – still? *Still?*

I mustered courage and looked back. Wyn was still on his feet.

I don't know if he was a good fighter or not. If he had been as successful in the business as Shakes had implied then this might have been why: this capacity, this inhuman, harrowing, heart-breaking capacity for hurt; this capacity to endure and not fall.

He held one hand over one eye, and with the other gamely fended off the flying fists of the ever-oncoming Italian. He was bent almost double. I saw fresh bright blood on the sand. Baldini – taller anyway than Wyn – beat down upon him as though his hand were a hammer and Wyn an anvil.

Cordelia held her hand over her mouth. Furlong, still at the front of the crowd, bellowed and waved his fists. 'Crowd'? No, this was a mob now. The noise had reached a new level, but I could no longer read its character: joy, exultation, anger, fear, bloodlust, I didn't know.

Fall, I wanted to shout. Fall, Wyn, or yield, withdraw, cede the field, *surrender* if you must, for God's sake. But he continued to stand, as best he could, while Baldini's punches thundered into his face, neck, skull top, ribs, kidneys, guts...

Shakes stood by, as I supposed his job required.

'Can't he stop it?' I quavered.

'Stop it?' I had earned another scornful smile from Cordelia. 'I'd like to see him try.'

'Fall!' I cried aloud, at last – but no one heard me, save Cordelia who laughed, and Eleanor who squeezed my hand, and a few fellows stood round and about me, who either sneered or scoffed, or made some jibe ('Dr Lowell's got a fiver on a sixth-round KO,' one barked – so it was the sixth).

Wyn fell as Baldini threw a heavy overarm right-hand. He fell, so the punch missed, and Baldini's arm over-stretched, and the *tenente* stumbled to one side, rubbing at his shoulder. It did not matter. Wyn had fallen. A great cry went up all about me. I was jostled, shoved. Eleanor drew closer to me – so, for that matter, did Cordelia. Through it all I could see Wyn James on his knees and elbows, forehead pressed to the sandy stone. Dark blood spread from his forehead. It formed a pond and in a way it looked as though Wyn were a terrible red monster stooping to drink from the pond.

The Italian still clutched at his shoulder, swearing at the sky through a sweat-streaked, blood-streaked grimace; I supposed he had suffered a dislocation. Then he held out a hand and shouted furiously for someone to cut him out of his gloves.

Shakes was besieged. It would have been worse, the deluge of yelling, gloating gamblers greater, had Wyn won, for I believe most of the Gravely men in attendance had backed the Welshman (wanting, I think, to get one over on Mr Shakes, the bombastic 'Yank').

The men who converged on Shakes, hands outstretched for their winnings, were by and large Shakes's men. Furlong, pie-eyed from drink, was among them. I don't understand betting, but I suppose Shakes – laughing and bantering at the heart of the maelstrom, passing out coins and banknotes with good grace – came out the winner by a distance.

In the ring, Wyn James was being helped to his feet by a slender boy in a dirty white shirt.

I felt Eleanor move a half-step nearer to me as, with the rush of the crowd subsiding – leaving us on the sea wall like things left behind by the tide – Cordelia made her way down the steps to a spot by the lobster pots where Furlong, on one knee, was forcing the cap from another bottle of beer. He looked up, slack-jawed, at her approach, and then laughed and stood, and, stepping forwards, pushed an arm about her waist and impressed his open mouth on hers.

She beat with open hands a couple of times at his shoulders. Then they both, for want of a better word, surfaced – both laughing. Cordelia slapped Furlong's fishy face lightly and straightened the sit of her cloche hat.

'There's Furlong collecting his winnings,' someone roared. There was a spatter of joshing applause. 'Do we all get a go?', 'That's *my* sort of fairground ride' – that sort of thing. I watched Cordelia's face, which was never still, either mock-scowling at Furlong, laughing at the men's seedy jokes, glancing out the open sea or looking back, almost expressionless, at Eleanor. In fact she looked back at Eleanor more than once.

'I'll fetch her,' Eleanor said. I turned and saw that her face was pale, her closed lips narrow.

I put a hand on her forearm. 'Are you sure?'

'Of course. I'm her *sister*, Jon.'

She brushed by me and descended the steps. I would have followed but that a voice not far away said, 'An unedifying spectacle, all in all,' and I looked and beheld David at the foot of the steps. He smiled weakly. His hat blew off – a sudden gust from the sea – and I caught it, with a neat slip-fielder's reflex grab.

'What on earth are you doing here?' I asked, pushing out a dent I had made in the crown of the hat.

He gave me a sour look.

'I was invited, would you believe.'

He sprang up a step, and I went down a step, and on the middle step we shook hands. I glanced over my shoulder and watched Cordelia and Eleanor walking away to the north, arm in arm.

At the library they're sick of the sight of me. I'm sick of the sight of them, too – them, their old-fashioned jackets, their old-fashioned collars, their moustaches and cigar smoke, their looks when they think I can't see them (or even when they know I can), those engineers and architects and whatever they are, those men. That place and its grey light and its smell of beeswax and newspapers. Miss bloody Endicott. Sick of all of it. But it must all be looked into.

Erosion. Friction. Live loads, dead loads. Metal fatigue. Bridge scour (a lot about bridge scour). Tidal drag. Tensile strength. Oxidisation – that's just rust. Compression. Decks and abutments. Then there's the other stuff, the stuff that's like reading a sensational novel. Trains plunging into icy rivers, bridges giving way at county fairs, a pontoon bridge collapsing under the weight of a Boy Scouts troop, whole buildings falling into abandoned mineworks. Sick of it. But it has to be done.

Later Reverend Aldridge and I talk about sin. He tells me about sin a lot – well, of course he does, he's a reverend, my *reverend, whatever that means exactly; my soul's his to worry about and I'm grateful that he does worry about it (someone should).*

He goes on about wicked pleasures and godless diversions, about putting away childish things. He says there's darkness gathering – which even I think is a bit much for a pleasure ground. Today I muttered something like I don't see any harm in good clean fun.

Because I don't, as long as nobody gets hurt, and once in a while I can't help saying so. But the reverend got angry and said there was nothing good or clean about – about whirligigs and organ grinders.

I didn't laugh but it took all my effort not to. I deserve a medal. He means well, of course.

When you look at it, all at once it seems a miracle anything ever stays up. A miracle anyone's left standing. I'm not like Reverend Aldridge, it's not the fun that bothers me – even if it's not good and clean, I can't say it bothers me much. I suppose at the bottom of everything it's about trust, isn't it? And trust is tied up with other things. Trust is tied up with fear.

XVII

'If you fear getting hurt,' Wyn said to me, later, eyes still swollen, head bruised, lips torn, 'you have no business stepping into the ring.' He smiled and added: 'No lasting damage done.'

But that was to come. Now, with the fight just over, the sand of the ring still wet with the Welshman's blood, David and I hastened away, southwards, in the van of a regiment of men – mostly older, mostly local – heading back along the coast road, towards Holroyd's. Many more had remained behind, in 'Shakestown', to carouse with Maurice Shakes.

We had a great deal to talk about, but neither of us said anything.

The shadows of the west-swarming silver clouds marbled the damp beach. White sanderlings ran to and fro with the waves. A great black-backed gull stood on the rocks further along, facing the ocean, opened its bill and barked.

I glanced sidelong at David as we mounted the path to the pub.

'Here?' He mustered a half-smile.

I nodded. Here the kiss.

'A romantic spot,' David said. 'Small wonder you couldn't help yourself.' He held open the pub door and followed me in. I heard him sigh, as though with relief; for myself, I felt a leavening or loosening in my spirit, as though a belt had been unfastened.

I barely thought of Harriet. I was shaken, by the fight, by the touch of Eleanor's hand, by Cordelia and the architect, by David, here again all of a sudden – I felt in need of strong drink.

Holroyd, jogging in breathless behind us (for he, of course, had been to see the spectacle, too), at our request poured whisky from an unlabelled bottle into two heavy glasses. We drank, and called for more, and hurried with the new drinks to the small table by the window.

We sat, and exhaled.

'Well, well,' David said, and laughed. The laugh was wondering, amazed, bewildered. I shared the sentiment, but did not laugh.

'Invited, then?' I prompted finally.

'Oh. Yes. You knew, of course – my address? Where to send the invite? I'd assumed you passed it on.' He sipped his whisky. 'I've been wondering whether or not to thank you.'

'Well, don't. Nothing to do with me.'

'Oh? Hm. A letter found me, in any case. Strongly worded.'

'Strongly?'

'Saltily. Saucily.' He could not contain a smile. He shook his head and looked out of the window. 'These American girls.'

'I'm a little surprised that was enough to tempt you back. Though I haven't read the letter, of course.'

'You'd blush to your roots, old man.' He sighed, shrugged. 'But it's true, my iron resolve wasn't quite at its most formidably ferrous. After I got home – back to London, I mean' – David, like myself, has never quite known where he means by 'home' – 'I embarked on rather a racket.'

'The Christmas season, of course.'

'Well, that, too. But not just that. The fat man's heart attack. The damn Quaker boy – it stayed with me, Jon, that bloody story, I'll tell you. And, you know.' The eyes he turned on me over the rim of his whisky glass were the same eyes – older, dimmer, not so brightly blue, but the same – as I'd seen on the cricket field that day at Saltaire, when we'd been boys. There was less blood, or anyway less of David's blood, today. Less pain? I couldn't say. And we weren't boys any more.

'The damn girl,' he said, with a smile that twisted into a sort of sneer: at her, at himself.

'She's very beautiful.'

'We sat at this table, didn't we?'

'You say it as though it were fifty years since. It was September.'

'We sat here and I let her bewitch me.'

'There are no such things as witches,' I said.

'The man of science speaks,' David laughed. 'Anyway. I went back to London, and did my best to drown myself in gin. Didn't quite pull it off but by God I gave it a good go.'

I smiled.

'How is the new novel coming along?' – at which David, as I had hoped he would, roared with laughter, rocked back in his seat and drew glances from the drinkers about us by banging his hand on the table.

'You can guess! It's not a novel. It's a chapter, and a short chapter at that. My publisher despises me with a rare passion.' He raised his eyebrows. 'Another excellent reason, if I'd needed one, to take myself up north for a little while.'

'You owe him money?'

'Well, yes, of course, some, but that's the natural relationship between writers and publishers. Debt one way or another. We drink away the advances they give us. They chisel us out of the profits we earn them. It's the way of things.'

He finished his drink, stood and signalled over the heads of the other drinkers for Holroyd to bring more. 'Beer,' he called, 'and whisky.'

'Your racket isn't quite done with, then,' I noted, feeling rather prim, and smiling to soften the remark.

'A good racket is *never* done with.'

I felt that there were many in Gravely now who would second that motion heartily.

We returned to Cordelia, to why she had summoned him. I said that perhaps she was a siren, luring him here to be dashed on the rocks. I said that he should have stopped his ears with wax or lashed himself to the mast.

'You wouldn't understand,' he replied, meaning it kindly.

'I think I might, you know,' I retorted, meaning by it a great many things.

It was dark by four. David, chin propped on hand, stared vacantly at his reflection in the window. At last, I thought of Harriet. I wondered what she was doing. I supposed she would be at her mother's, or her mother would be at ours. Or she might, it occurred to me, be with the bearded minister – a St Stephen's Day Bible class, or something of the sort. Perhaps it was to just such a pious gathering that dear Eleanor had led her sister after the fight (or, as I had come to think of it, with skewed perspective, the beating); godless though I was, I quailed at the alternative – my Eleanor led somehow by Cordelia to a drinking party of steelmen and riveters in Furlong's grimy digs.

'Shall we go to Bible study?' I said to David. I was a little drunk, of course.

'It's as good a plan as any,' David laughed. 'My Scripture is a bit rusty, though.'

'Follow me, and I will make you fishers of men.'

'If the blind lead the blind, both shall fall into the ditch.'

'Let not your heart be troubled.'

We left the pub with our arms about each other's shoulders, bound for the Reverend Aldridge's Bible class.

*

As we walked to the vicarage we sang to keep warm, an old hymn from our youth, 'Father Hear the Prayer We Offer' (I have always been attracted more to hymns that plead with God than to those that exalt him). An early barn owl sailed by us on the landward side, silent and white. There were plenty of people on the cold road: stragglers, like us, from the fight, heading to or from the pub, and of course the usual traffic of a winter's afternoon in Gravely, workers, couples making calls, three children in best clothes running behind a dog.

'Where is this Bible class?' David demanded as we turned away from the sea. 'Do you mean an *actual* Bible class? Is it with that terrible reverend of yours?'

'It may be,' I said. 'We are taking something of a leap of faith.'

'Oh, Christ,' said David.

'Be of good cheer; it is I, be not afraid.'

The passageway that led to Aldridge's door was unlit and quite black. I hesitated at the end of it.

At worst, I thought, I am trespassing temporarily on our minister's Boxing Day afternoon. There is no crime in that. I shall find Aldridge alone with Bible and teacup, and bid him good afternoon and best tidings of the season, apologise for my intrusion and retreat. I shall go home and find Harriet there, or if not there, at her mother's.

At best, I shall find three shining faces (and one bearded one) uptilted from pages of Scripture, surprised and smiling upon me (or not, in Aldridge's case – and Harriet's, come to that). I shall find the Shakes girls.

I didn't think very carefully about what might happen after I had found them. This, I have found, is an effect of strong drink. I supposed – I think – that it was sure to be terrific fun.

Or perhaps (this is in all honesty more likely) I did not care, as long as I was in Eleanor's company and the Reverend Aldridge and his God did not have my wife to themselves.

It was David, in the end, with an impatient hand in the small of my back, that propelled me into the dark passageway and up the steps to the threshold of the vicarage. A weak lamp burned over the door. David looked haggard – he might have been thirty-five or forty – in its light.

'Will she be here?' he asked leadenly.

I, all at once fraught with misgiving, said that I did not know. David made a face and rang the doorbell.

*

Mary, Aldridge's maid, was slightly known to me. There was a story there – a tale of adultery, or in any case a damned near thing, during the war, with a local cripple while her husband fought (and died) in France. I didn't know the details. I supposed, in employing her, Aldridge thought himself terribly Christian.

She opened the door and looked on me with delight.

'Mr Lowell!'

'Mary.' I doffed my hat. No, it wasn't quite delight; it was, I think, relief.

'You've come for Mrs Lowell, of course,' she babbled. At my elbow I could almost hear David's brain at work – reading the characters, figuring out the story.

'To see my wife, yes,' I said, smiling in my puzzlement, 'though you say it as though I am here to carry her away across my shoulders, like Menelaus come to Troy.'

She trilled a silly laugh, and disappeared down the corridor.

'A curious woman,' David murmured.

'I suspect we don't know the half of it.'

'You frightened her with your erudition.'

We followed the bewildering maid down the hall, and were shown, with strange smiles and bows, into a sparse parlour. A bookcase, an aspidistra, a stack of sheet-music on a wooden stool. My wife. Aldridge.

'Jon!' cried Harriet, and then: 'David!'

She smiled. Note that. Note the order of events.

The reverend rose.

'Mr Lowell! How good of you to stop by.' For some reason he shook my hand, and then David's ('Mr – Mackay, I think?'), and then David shook Harriet's hand, and I kissed Harriet's cheek, all the while wondering what the devil was afoot.

No Shakes girls. More pertinently, no Bibles. Just a pocketbook at Harriet's side, which she closed abruptly.

'Mrs Lowell and I were discussing a point of – of Scripture,' Aldridge said.

'Right up our street!' said David.

'I thought you might have been holding a Bible study class,' I said, trying to find my way, 'but I note an absence of fellow students. Not to mention Good Books.'

'Yes,' said Harriet, frowning at me. 'The reverend was good enough to allow me to intrude on his free time. I had some particular questions with which to pester him.'

As Aldridge shaped his mouth to humbly protest, David nudged me and said: 'You ought to've asked Jon here. He knows his Bible back to front.'

Harriet smiled.

'The next time I have a question about the habits of the sea worm or the blue-clawed crab, I shall be sure to ask my husband – if I can find him. But for spiritual matters, I prefer to consult someone who knows the Bible the right way around.' Having thus neatly skewered me, she lifted her chin at David and said: 'Surely you can't have tired of your beloved London already, David? When a man is tired of London – and so on.'

'I don't believe the Great Cham ever came to Gravely.' David grinned, rocking on his heels with his hands in his pockets. 'For there is, in Gravely, all that life can afford. Only today, we witnessed a heavyweight contest equal to anything one might find at Whitechapel or Bethnal Green.'

Aldridge stiffened. He eyed us penetratingly, eyes burning a holy blue behind his spectacles.

'A prize fight?'

David, grinning, nodded.

'As brave and bloody a prize fight as I ever saw.'

'Oh, really, you *men,*' Harriet murmured with distaste, lowering her eyes.

Aldridge said: 'Mr Shakes.'

'Naturally.'

The reverend's anger took me by surprise. From the bookcase he took a Bible; from by the hearth he snatched up a stick. David and I parted like the Red Sea to allow him through and then chased after him as he stormed down the hallway.

'Do you intend to thrash him?' David laughed.

'Someone ought to have thrashed the fellow a long time ago,' Aldridge snarled over his shoulder, and charged bare-headed out into the darkness.

*

'What were you thinking, Jon? What are you *doing* here – except filling Mr Aldridge's house with beer fumes?'

David had gone after the vengeful minister; Harriet and I were in Aldridge's hall, which rang still with the reverberations of the slammed front door.

'I – I was looking for you, of course, my dear.'

'Don't "my dear" me.'

'Harriet. Come on, now. I was simply—'

'If you could hold your beer,' she said, 'it wouldn't be so bad.'

She took her teal coat and blue hat from the stand. With the hat in one hand she struggled with the coat, but wouldn't let me help her. Finally she got it on and planted the hat without ceremony on her head. She looked so beautiful my stomach turned over.

'Why am I,' I quavered thinly, 'the one at fault in this?'

'In this? In what?'

I waved my hands helplessly.

'You, here. Him. Whatever you're doing here.'

On her catching my meaning (though really it was something less than a meaning), her blue eyes flared like gas flames.

'You wouldn't understand, Jon.' She looked as though she were about to sneeze. 'I do love you,' she said, 'but you can be so – so *stupid* sometimes.'

'A drink or two with an old friend, stupid?'

'It isn't about that.'

'Then it's about the mysteries of the Holy Spirit, I suppose. In which case I once again confess myself an' – realising too late what I was saying, I choked on the word – 'infidel.'

She opened her mouth and then closed it again. I still wonder what it was that she was going to say.

'Harriet,' I said.

She made for the door, shook off my hand from her arm, shook her head, opened the door, threw herself out into the night. In the lamplight she was bright, for a half-second, bright blue, bright teal, and then she was gone. As I stepped over the threshold to follow – hearing her quick footsteps along the passageway – I heard Mary, the maid, behind me in the hall.

'I was glad when you came, Mr Lowell,' she said, 'but now I wish you hadn't come at all.' And she raised her eyes to the heavens.

I turned back to the open doorway, to the passageway beyond the empty pool of lamplight. I ran – cursing the minister's addle-headed maid as I ran – to the street, but there was no one. No, not no one – a drunk man singing on a bench, a gentleman in a tall hat bicycling by – but not Harriet, and not David either, nor Aldridge nor any sign of any of them.

The drunk man stopped his song, and lurched on his bench.

'All gone running off,' he yelled at me. Shook his head. 'All gone running off.'

I watched the man on the bicycle pedal round the corner and out of sight. I stepped back into the passageway, bent double, pressed my forehead against the whitewashed wall. My throat filled and I vomited. Watery stuff: all beer. I straightened, breathing hard.

All gone running off.

I pictured Aldridge, seized with a fit of holy passion, blood-flecked and beating upon Maurice Shakes with his stick. Could my wife love a man like Aldridge? Aldridge, for his part, loved a God who allowed whales to die on beaches and woodcocks to perish in men's graves.

Home, I thought. And then: no, not there, for home would be an angry Harriet, and if it was not an angry Harriet, it was only shelves of books, and a typewriter, and jars of dead crabs, drawers of dead beetles, labels in Latin, the stink of taxidermy, the sourness of the killing jar. Not there. Not now.

And so I replaced my hat on my head and wiped a smear of vomit from my shirt front, and I went back to Holroyd's, not to drink, but to go up the backstairs to the guest rooms, and to knock, be called in, enter and gaze upon him: the great and terrible Welsh god, Wyn James, who peered back at me blindly from deep within a red-blotched head swollen to the size of a barrel, and said 'Is it Mr Lowell?' And I said it was indeed, and touched his hand, and hoped he was not too badly hurt – and he told me that if you fear getting hurt, you have no business stepping into the ring. 'No lasting damage done,' he said.

Jon will think I've gone mad. Or he'll think goodness knows what. Well, let him. If he wants to be a blooming fool then let him.

It's lowish tide. From here the sea sounds impatient to come in.

Don't know where they went. David, the reverend, I don't know where to find them, if I even want to find them, which I don't.

No doubt there'll be a set-to. Men shaking their fists at one another. It's funny – not funny ha-ha, the other sort – that there's nothing about that in the Bible. Thou shalt not fight. Thou shalt not spill blood. It's just killing that's not allowed – which is a bit rich, anyway, when you look at the rest of the book.

Though it's more than a book, of course, and you shouldn't expect it to be just common sense. If it was just common sense we wouldn't need it, would we?

I don't like the idea of the prize fight, anyway. Where was it? Round about here? Too dark to see any bloodstains but it must be like a butcher's block or one of those sacrificial stones like the one at Stonehenge.

That's what it feels like, to me, in my head, and that's why I don't like it. It feels like a sacrifice has been made. Everything that was silly and absurd and laughable seems more serious than it really is; everything seems dark.

I don't know quite why Reverend Aldridge has such a bee in his bonnet about it, though. I think really he's just blowing off steam.

There's some'd say he's a reverend, he's not got any steam to blow off, but he has, of course, and anyone who'd think otherwise doesn't understand much about religion. Or about men or about anything.

So the reverend will catch up with Maurice Shakes – tonight, tomorrow, whenever – and they'll 'have it out', I suppose. They'll say a lot of tough things to one another and make themselves feel very important and principled and all that.

Nothing'll be settled. Not now, I mean; not here. In the end, as the Reverend Aldridge knows all too well, everything'll be settled, reckoned up. Weighed in the balance, as they say.

There's footsteps. A feller coming. Shrink back against the sea wall. Stones cold as iron through the tweed. Don't know if I want to be found.

Sea still making a great noise out there. It's only the sea, Harriet.

'Hello?' calls David. Then, after a few more footsteps: 'Hello!'

Must have seen me. The moonlight must have given me away.

XVIII

He spoke of whirligigs and turnabouts. He spoke of wolves, elephants and a Wild Man of Borneo. He spoke of 'shoot the chute'. He spoke of Babe Ruth and Harold Lloyd.

'Whirligigs. I know a beetle of that name.'

Wyn smiled. 'Chairs, Mr Lowell, suspended from long chains, in which you sit to be whirled at great speed about a carousel.'

'My goodness. And "shoot the chute"?'

'It's a sort of water-borne plummet, as I understand it, you see. You sit in a canoe, and descend—'

'At great speed, of course.'

'Of course! You descend at high speed down a steep watery chute. I suppose the effect is like paddling over a waterfall on the Zambezi or similar. Very exciting.'

'For those that enjoy peril.'

'I fear you must include me among that foolhardy number, Mr Lowell,' the boxer chuckled. Then he grunted at some consequent pain in his head or body.

I leaned forwards uncertainly and asked if I could do anything for him. He asked me to go downstairs and fetch him a glass of beer. I did so (Holroyd was glad to oblige, having won heavily by betting on the *tenente*). He struggled to lift it to his lips; I helped him, and then – after only a moment's hesitation – wiped the froth from his rough chin with my shirt cuff.

I asked about Babe Ruth (a name I didn't know) and Harold Lloyd (a name I did: a bespectacled, comical man, often in peril in films).

'Celebrities,' Wyn said shortly. 'The Ruth fellow plays baseball, for what that's worth, but celebrity is the principle. Publicity. People queueing for a photograph with Mr Lloyd. Reporters flocking to see Mr Ruth posing with his bat on the pier.'

'I dare say people *would* do that,' I said glumly.

'Now, Mr Lowell,' Wyn chided. 'You wrote in your book of once walking to Redcar on a fisherman's report of a grey phalarope on the beach.'

I laughed – for indeed I had. Worse, the phalarope had left by the time I arrived.

'A novelty is no bad thing,' the Welshman added.

I thought of Eleanor and Cordelia.

'Each thing according to its own merits, Mr James,' I said.

As for the wolves and elephants, these, Wyn told me, were to be transported to Gravely from a menagerie in London – along with who knew what other exotic fauna, for the education and entertainment of the general public. I couldn't, I admit (and admitted to Wyn), suppress a tremor of genuine excitement at this prospect.

'A moth-eaten dog and a shaved boar,' Wyn predicted, intending to jibe good-naturedly at Maurice Shakes, and I laughed along, but in fact I did not think Shakes a charlatan. I thought him honest – whatever else he was.

I thought that if Shakes had promised to bring wolves and elephants to Gravely then bring them he would.

There was a fad at that time for allowing weeds to grow in one's unmown garden, for leaving one's hedgerows untended and one's rambling ivy unchecked. There was a fashion, that is, for wildness.

I thought that a very poor sort of wildness. It reminded me of those young men – there were, I gathered, several in David's

London set – who affected unkempt hairstyles and untidy dress. Some, David had told me, went to the trouble of applying a thick grease to their hair, or of snapping off waistcoat buttons, in order to achieve the desired effect.

Where is the wildness in keeping one's gardener idle (cursing you and your fashionable weeds, no doubt, over a pipe of tobacco in his shed)? Where is the wildness in unkempt hair when one has the wherewithal for a rack of ivory-backed hairbrushes?

It all had something to do with the war, I suppose. But I disdained those pantomimes of wildness. Wildness that one chooses, I thought, is no wildness at all.

Maurice Shakes's wolves would be caged and his elephants chained, of course. But he would bring wildness – wilderness – to Gravely, I thought. Indeed he had already brought it.

For completeness's sake, feeling weary as I said it, I prompted Wyn: 'And the Wild Man of Borneo?'

'Black chap,' Wyn said. 'Bone through his nose. Loincloth. Will perform native war dances to frighten the ladies, that sort of stuff.'

I sighed, and nodded.

'You oughtn't,' Wyn said, groping for my sleeve and squeezing my forearm, 'begrudge folk their entertainment. However foolish it seems to you, Mr Lowell.'

I looked down at his battered, blind face.

'As long as it is only foolishness,' I said, 'I've no quarrel with it, for we've all done our share of that.'

'What else could it be?'

'Our good reverend believes it rank wickedness.' It was funny: I'd forgotten Aldridge and his vengeful stick, forgotten Harriet and David for that matter, since I'd arrived here.

Wyn made a questioning face, in response to which I told him about Aldridge's opposition to Shakes's pleasure grounds –

his misgivings, his talk of sin, his dramatic exit from the public meeting, his fierce revulsion at the prize fight.

'He sounds like a bloody prig,' Wyn said with some heat.

'That is what he is,' I said – but I did not say it easily.

'I dare say Mr Shakes will bring him round.'

'I believe not.'

'Then I dare say Mr Shakes will simply walk over the top of him.' Wyn said so with the thumping finality of a knock-down punch.

I wondered what sort of retribution, what sort of punishment, a man like Aldridge was capable of delivering. Muscular Christianity was the minister's game; I wondered, when it came to it, what that might mean, what it might permit, what licences it might grant.

I had for a moment a fanciful idea of Aldridge pounding a bloodied Shakes with the club end of his stick, like Bill Sikes murdering his Nancy.

'It's hard to imagine Mr Shakes losing a fight,' Wyn murmured.

It was hard to imagine you *losing a fight, Mr James*, I thought to myself.

I sighed and said: 'Well, the righteous battle will rage until the summer, I suppose.'

'Not so long as you think,' Wyn said. 'The plans for the pier foundations are finalised. Mr Furlong has been burning the midnight oil and I am told his masterpiece is complete. The work schedules have been drawn up.' He laughed shortly – in helpless admiration, I think, at the boldness, the recklessness, the indescribable folly of the man, if indeed Maurice Shakes *was* a man and not a pagan god or an incarnation of a force of nature. 'Our American friend will not wait for time and tide. The pier will be up by the end of March.'

Through his swollen eyes he could not see the astonishment in my face – but he laughed again at what he read in my silence.

*

I took my leave of the blinded boxer, who had begun to nod, at around seven o'clock. With a polite 'good evening' to Holroyd and the drinkers at his bar, I stepped out into a night of bitter black clarity. Stars sprawled over the withdrawn North Sea.

Harriet, I thought – I ought to find Harriet, and David, too. They had gone after Aldridge, and Aldridge had gone after Shakes, which meant the north bay, or thereabouts.

I thought of the sheds and shadows of Shakestown, as Cordelia had called the workers' place by the harbour, and I thought of wilderness.

The beach was not the quickest way to the harbour, especially at night, when one had to pick one's way in the darkness over the breakwaters and between clumps of rock and watery depressions, but it was the way that I went: across the beach – *my* beach. I knew it well enough. I felt sometimes that it was all I knew.

*

A beach does not seem rich with life on a winter's night, except to one who knows, and of course I did know, did know that in the lee of the bluff crabs were lurching lengthwise from pool to pool across the barnacled rocks, did know that beneath my feet the sand roiled with invertebrates, did know that towards the harbour the slick foreshore was crowded with roosting sanderling, did know that out upon the waves – far out now, at low tide – black-headed gulls slept, bobbing in constant, lulling motion.

One seeks out certainties at times of worry. In my place David would, I suppose, have taken up a book, or a bottle. I might in fact have taken up a bottle myself but there had been none to hand and, besides, I still felt queasy.

I stopped, halfway across the beach. I looked out into the night in the direction of the harbour. In the darkness – as though scratched upon the darkness – I saw the pier.

Another vision. It was a vision, I recalled, that brought that poor girl, all those centuries since, from Barnoldswick to Gravely Priory and its ravenous monks. And see how *that* ended. My vision of Shakes's folly can hardly have been less vivid than hers of Christ and the angels.

I could hear the tiny murmuration of limpets binding to the drenched timber of the pilings. I could smell the mops of green *Ulva* weed.

A fancy, a fantasy, yes. But if you had told me six months before of Italians brought to Gravely to crank organs and sell ice cream, I should have said that *that* was a fancy and a fantasy, not to speak of Holroyd's death and the woodcock fall, of David ensnared by Cordelia Shakes, of Luke Hesketh drunk and hooting like an owl on the high moor – all, I should have scoffed, fanciful and fantastical, yet all now shown to be true. Of Aldridge, raging out into the night. Of Eleanor. Of Jon Lowell and Eleanor Shakes holding hands while a Welshman had his brains beaten out by an Italian soldier.

I wouldn't have much cared to encounter the sort of person whose mind would conjure such fancies. I dare say that if I had ever moved to literary London with David I would have encountered plenty such.

The end of March? The man was mad. But that did not mean that he would not do what he said he would. Madmen can achieve much, in this world.

Turning my face from the sea, from the not-pier, from the pier-to-be, I continued across the lonely beach.

*

A narrow, brown-crusted iron ladder climbed up from the north extremity of the beach – where sanderlings muttered and shuffled in their sleep – to the south spur of the sea wall. This I shinned up nimbly, of old a dab hand at the ascent (and usually encumbered by field glasses and specimen cases, too). At the top I paused. I had few clues. They had sought Shakes, directly or otherwise, but where he might be I had no idea. In his home? I didn't know where the Shakeses had taken lodgings, except that I knew it was in the north bay, and that wasn't much help. The northern part of Gravely was a disordered shambles of narrow streets, picturesque and easy to get lost in: fishermen's cottages, smokehouses, boat sheds, a few Victorian terraces enjoying grand views on the slope up to the moor and, closer to shore, a handful of bitterly unprofitable guest houses. The whole tangle petered aimlessly up the coast almost to Sallow Sluice.

There was no pub out that way. People drank, as I understood it, in one another's kitchens. There was the church. Aldridge might have dragged the lot of them there, to repent of their sins (or perhaps, having committed the bloody murder of Maurice Shakes, he would be there alone, begging his God for mercy). I turned left at the end of the sea wall, away from the shadows of Shakestown and towards the sandstone steeple. Underlit off-white by the sparse street lighting, it put me in mind of a solitary fish hanging in a smokehouse.

I approached the doors. No light within that I could see. I tried the door. It seemed fast but I was not well versed in the workings of church doors. Was there a latch or a hasp, or failing that, a knocker? Or a doorbell?

Perhaps the church doors opened only to the just at heart. In which case I supposed that the righteous Aldridge would, as a rule, have the place to himself.

I rapped half-heartedly with my knuckles, expecting no answer, and got none. I turned about in exasperation.

It was not, of course, only ignorance of the terrain that kept me from venturing far into the ginnels and shadows north of the church. It was fear, too. I am a coward – I have said so. I retraced my steps to the harbour wall, and rested for perhaps a minute against the cold stone. I looked north.

Shakestown. A fancy, of course, a moment of whimsy on the part of cynical Cordelia Shakes. It was hardly the St Giles rookery there, in the shade of the sea wall: a twenty-yard stretch of sheds and shelters where working men did their honest work, talked their honest talk, drank their honest beer. In Bradford I had walked every day through worse places. I'd grown up in a worse place. In Bradford you would find worse on a plot of gardeners' allotments.

And yet there was something in Shakestown that filled me with dread. There was no dread for me in the rough stuff of men's talk (awkwardness, anxiety, self-consciousness, but no dread); there was certainly no dread for me in work (I earned a living for two), nor in beer.

One dreadful image: Cordelia Shakes, stepping from the sunlight into the shadow in a dark red dress, green coat and cream cloche hat. Something in what I felt for my friend David McAllister – and something in what I felt for Eleanor Shakes – quailed at the image.

But in any case I was resolved to pursue my wife (and the minister my wife was pursuing), and so I gulped a boldening breath of cold air and started along the sea wall. The darkness became darker as I walked. Naturally it did, for the wall behind which I passed blocked out the starlight and the moonlight – but in normal circumstances (had I been out mothing, say, or hunting for bats) no darkness would have inspired in me such a craving for light and space. I longed for the broad, cold, simple sky. I believe I even reached out to my right, to the east, and touched the sea wall with my fingertips as I walked (sometimes a wall, even as it encloses us, can reassure us by reminding us of what is beyond the wall). The tin roofs of the Shakestown lean-tos hummed softly in echo of my footsteps.

When I came to the end of the shadows, I knew, I would first probably stumble over a rabble of strewn ropes and lobster pots, and second have to cross the 'ring' – have to step upon stone flags still messy with sand and prize fighters' blood.

On consideration I found that it was not so much the thought of the blood on the stone flags that troubled me (I imagined it marking the stone like a port-wine birthmark); rather, it was the blood that had seeped *between* the flags, into the thin, sandy, salty soil there, for this might nourish some determined plant or other, and this notion in its turn brought to mind the nun's hawthorn, up there on the bluff. Green life sprouting from the wet-rotted fruit of wickedness.

A medieval legend told that the timber from which was made the cross of Christ was taken from a tree that grew from seeds planted beneath the dead tongue of Adam.

All of which was foolishness, of course, for there was not sufficient soil on the sea wall to nourish the meanest weed. I don't suppose the top man at Kew could have done it, the fertilising properties of blood notwithstanding. If a botanic monument to the evil of Maurice Shakes were ever to grow here it would require a true miracle (and, then, one would have to consider it a wicked waste of a miracle). I stepped out of the shadows, stepped awkwardly over a pot that stank of uneaten bait, and entered the ring.

A peal of laughter swept across the flagged expanse, such that I thought it might sweep me into the sea, like a great wave, and I staggered from one foot to the other, and looked, and saw my Harriet, with her arms about a man.

I could let it all go hang. Let him do as he pleases. Nights like this I feel like it. What's it my business what that noisy walrus does with his money? But it is my business. I know I sound like the reverend but it is.

He goes on, this feller here, on and on. All this clever talk, it's all we ever do. On and on like the jabber of birds, and birds don't know they're born, don't know they'll die, either; don't know about love or sex or marriage or happiness, and what's more – and I could blooming well envy them this – they don't know that they don't know.

What good is it, talking, after all?

I know more than one feller who'd tell me it's speech and reason that separates us from the animals. A lot of rot. A lot of bloody rot.

This feeling I've got here, now, in the bottom of my belly, in the hollows of my ears. There's no one can tell me that any bird or crab or monkey feels that. I've heard birds talk – it's all the damn things do – and I've seen a seagull drop a crab on to rocks to break the poor thing's shell.

But this? They don't know a blind thing about it.

I suppose they know fear, right enough. Hit a pan with a spoon and watch the sparrows go up in a panic. That's not this. It's bigger, this, bigger, deeper, more complicated. Older.

It's tied up with love and you can't tell me an animal knows a lot about that. It's why we talk so much I suppose. To drown it out. To make something we can hide behind. We don't talk about *it, crikey no – that wouldn't do.*

We're just so afraid. I'm just so afraid.

David here talks, and talks, and talks.

XIX

'Lowell!' David roared, and the sea roared with him. He was propped against the sea wall, holding my wife in an awkward clinch. He beckoned vaguely. 'Come, you bloody wet fish, you bloody crusted barnacle. Come here! You unshelled limpet, you.'

Harriet laughed.

'This isn't,' I said, carefully crossing the boxing ring to where they perched on the sea wall, 'quite how I expected this evening to conclude.'

'Tell us, Jon,' my wife said, smiling rather fiercely. 'What did you expect? Bloodshed and melodrama, is that it?'

'Or another prize fight!' David again. 'Hugh "Christ's Soldier" Aldridge, stripped to the waist and having it out through twelve rounds with "Coney Island" Maurice Shakes! God, I'd pay to see that.'

I took a hesitant seat on the stone wall. The cold sea wind raced up the back of my shirt and coat and turned me to gooseflesh.

'Did you catch him?' I asked mildly.

'We did.' David, his laughter ebbing back to a weary smile, rubbed thoughtfully at his chin. 'Or anyway we caught *up* with him.'

'Too late,' said Harriet.

She was sitting sideways on the sea wall, her back against a step, with one leg extended along the wide wall top. Her hat lay on the floor by a coil of rope and rocked in the wind. Her tightly fastened hair shone like wet stone in the moonlight.

'So there was a confrontation,' I surmised.

David smiled at me.

'Was there ever!'

'A holy war?'

'Something of that sort.' He caught my eye, still smiling, and I wondered for the first time if he was quite as drunk as he seemed. But then David had a knowing quality even when sincerely and authentically drunk.

'May I be told?' I prompted. 'Come on. Sing the ballad.'

'Sing, O goddess, the anger of Achilles, that brought countless ills—' David began.

'In prose, please.'

'—upon the Achaeans. Many a brave soul did it send hurrying down to Hades, and many a hero did it yield a prey to dogs and vultures. Oh, very well, you clammy bounder.'

'You may begin,' I humoured him, 'with the clash between Agamemnon, the Greek warlord, and godlike Achilles.'

David laughed. Harriet glowered at us. I was stealing David back from her.

David – in an outrageous impropriety – patted her stockinged knee and, addressing me, said: 'When we found them they had already collided. Out here – or anyway, just a little way along. Your minister steaming northwards at a rate of some knots, and Mr Shakes standing in his path there' – he gestured vaguely – 'like a sitting duck.'

'Or an iceberg.'

'Or, as you say, an iceberg. One or the other. *Mr Shakes*, the minister roared. And when Shakes, smiling – he's *always* smiling – turned to face him, well, I wouldn't quite say the minister lost his nerve, or regained his temper, but his fury seemed to sort of diffuse, somehow, on contact with the fellow. I'll tell you what it was like, here's an analogy—' He stumbled a little over 'an analogy', grinned at himself, shrugged. 'It was as though a man had a full pail of water and wished to drench the Rock of Gibraltar with it – and so he flings the pail, a good thorough fling full of vigour and purpose – and finds that, after all that, his pail is empty but the rock is hardly wet at all.'

'He looks in the pail and thinks, but where did all my water go?'

'Precisely, Lowell, precisely. Thus your minister. He had as much rage as he could hold—'

'—but it wasn't enough to drench Maurice Shakes.'

'Exactly exactly exactly,' David said. In an absent manner he patted Harriet's knee again. This time I looked somewhat askance at him. He didn't notice.

'Shakes was out here looking at the sea wall and the harbour,' he said. 'Sizing it up, I suppose.'

'Blueprints in one hand, iron girders over one shoulder, rivets held between his teeth.'

'Ha, quite. I think he likes to contemplate the sea, our Maurice Shakes.'

'One never knows what one might see on a beach after dark.'

'Mm? Well, Shakes turned to greet Mr Aldridge – *good evening*, he said, or something of that sort. Polite in that way he has. Aldridge faced him with one hand on his hip and the other holding his stick, and he rapped the butt of his stick on the ground. Shakes made some crack about Moses, I couldn't follow it.'

'Where were you during all this?'

'Hanging back. Loitering warily.' David shrugged. 'I don't know about Harriet here but I was catching my breath. Anyway we didn't hang back for long, or anyway your dear wife didn't.'

'Don't you "dear wife" me,' Harriet put in.

'No. Well.' David blinked and rubbed at his face. 'Aldridge said something hostile about the Moses gag, which hadn't gone down well with him at all, and then he lifted his stick – purely as a rhetorical gesture, I think, but at this point Harriet gulped two or three times like a landed fish and then shouted *Reverend Aldridge*!'

We both looked at my wife. She glowered from one to the other of us and said carefully: 'It was all very undignified. I wasn't about to stand for it.'

'Quite right!' David laughed. 'Quite right! Can't be having such unseemly seems. Scenes. Unseemly scenes. Quite right!' His hand hovered over Harriet's knee, as if to clap it jovially, but then he seemed to rejoin his train of thought and instead raised and wagged an upright index finger. 'That, though,' he said, 'was where the battle was properly joined.'

I glanced at Harriet.

'Not much of a peacemaker, eh, my dove?' I murmured.

She ignored me.

'We moved into the fray – well, we had to, of course, after that clarion call,' David went on, settled now into the groove of the story he was telling. 'Aldridge turned around looking exasperated. No vicar likes to be interrupted while tearing a sinner off a strip and it seemed he was no exception. *This is* my *concern, Mrs Lowell, Mr – ah*, he says. I say McAllister and he nods and says, *all the same, it is no concern of yours.*'

His impersonation of Aldridge's taut tenor voice was rather good.

'So, knowing the two of you, I assume you trusted in his good judgement and left the pair of them to their own devices.'

He smiled.

'You jibe at us cruelly, Jon. Besides, it was our civic duty – our Christian duty, come to that – to stay with them, and prevent any bodily violence.'

Again the mental image of the mismatched pair squaring up in a prize fight.

'I don't think there can have been much danger of that.'

'Well, in any case, Aldridge was peeved at us, and Shakes, well, he stood there catching flies for a minute' – he dropped his jaw open gormlessly in imitation – 'and then said *Mrs Lowell! Mr McAllister!* – which of course we'd been over already with the minister.'

'A pretty poor standard of conversation, so far.'

'The way the poor bugger looked at us we might've been avenging angels swooping down on him. Instead of a half-cut writer and a Gravely housewife.'

'Discombobulating in its own right, I should imagine.'

'Perhaps, but the look on his face – well, we bade him good evening, and Harriet here made a beeline for the minister.'

'Naturally,' I said – but she was still ignoring me.

'She said there was no need for anyone to make a scene. Aldridge said that he was not making a scene, he was taking a stand – which I thought quite a good ad lib. He added something about godless immorality and Harriet said that not everything had to be black and white, and he said *on the contrary, Harriet, on the contrary.*

'She said it wasn't worth all this. She said there were far worse things than a prize fight to worry about, and he turned to her – he'd been looking at Shakes all this while, you see – he turned to her and he had a face like out of a film, and he said yes, he knew there were, much to his regret.'

'Very much the tormented preacher, then.'

'Very much. Though I imagine it's hard to be a preacher *without* being at least a bit tormented.'

'Come on, then. What next?'

'Well, Harriet had given Shakes his "in" there, you see. A salesman like Shakes is always on the lookout for an "in". At the mention of the prize fight his face had lit up like Blackpool—'

'Appropriate.'

'—and he lunged forwards and grabbed Aldridge's forearm.'

'And flung him into the sea?'

'Indeed not. The earnestness was coming off him like cologne. Enough to make your eyes sting. I know the Americans are sincere folk but bloody hell. *The fight, sir?* he said.' David's accent was a little off but I let it go. '*Where is the immorality in a fight, a test of strength and courage? My good Reverend*, he said, *how can an event, an honest sporting event, that brings such joy to hundreds of your townsfolk, be counted a sin?*'

'That old dialogue again.'

'He never wearies of it. And then the other fellow's turn. Why cannot we be content with the blue of the sky and the gold of the sun? Why must we drink beer and have sex with ladies, why cannot we be content with the whip and top and the sherbet fountain?'

Harriet woke from her reverie to laugh shortly. I blinked at her.

'A laugh, my dearest? At the good reverend's expense?'

'He's a good man, the best of men,' she snapped back.

I was momentarily afraid that she might in her bitterness add 'and I am not your dearest' – but she did not. Instead she again turned her face to the ocean.

'Actually, Aldridge went straight to the heart of the matter this time.' David was holding his hat in his hands. He turned it thoughtfully as he spoke. 'He manoeuvred into a sort of side-on position – you could see he was trying to establish an "I am the preacher, thou art the congregation" set-up – very much a priest craving a pulpit. In fact it's a wonder he didn't climb on to the sea wall – he turned side-on and said to them both: *We must consider the condition of our mortal souls.*'

'What cant.'

'I don't know as I'd go that far, Lowell – but I share your sentiment.'

'Cue a Maurice Shakes disquisition, I suppose.'

'Oh, yes. And a good one, too.'

'Oh, Lord.'

'*We are all immortal*,' he said.

'That's a new one for him.'

'I know. Wait, it gets better. *We are all immortal*, he said, *for when there is nothing before, and nothing after, how can we ever in good sense speak of an end or a beginning?* With a few "sirs" and "my good Reverends" thrown in, of course. The idea being that if life has no beginning and no end then it has to be infinite, and we all therefore have to be immortal.'

'Oh gosh. Do we *have* to be?' I creased my brow for a moment. 'I'm too tired to think. Is it nonsense?'

'Too drunk, more like. I wouldn't say it's nonsense. It might even be damn clever but I'm not sober enough to judge either. I read a mathematician. I forget why but I read a mathematician who says there are big infinities and small infinities. *You* ought to know this, Lowell. Man of science like you.'

'If I were a man of science I would know it. I'm not. I'm a man of worms and lice, kelp and wrack, shrimps and anemones—'

I stumbled over the word 'anemones', and David pointed at me and giggled. 'We're as bad as each other,' he said.

'Maurice Shakes's philosophy in a nutshell,' I observed. Harriet – for once not ignoring me, perhaps forgetting to ignore me – laughed again, and I preened a little.

'That *daughter* of his,' she said then.

I froze. I don't think my exterior showed it but inside I froze.

'The daughters came up next in the conversation,' David explained with a pained expression. 'Aldridge questioned the example father Shakes was setting his little ones.'

'Well, it's a sight too late for that eldest one,' Harriet muttered. 'A slut. And as for the youngest...' She rolled her eyes somewhat stagily. 'What a *prig*.'

Addressing his hat, David said quietly: 'With Maurice Shakes for a father, it's hard to know how one would expect them to have turned out. They both reached their majority without being despatched to the loony-bin – I wouldn't call that a bad effort, in the circumstances.'

Urgently wishing to no longer speak about the Shakes girls – particularly, of course, about that priggish younger daughter, but also, as a kindness to David, about the elder, the slut who had (I feared) snared his heart – I asked them quite mildly how, amid all this drama, David had come to get stinking drunk.

David said: 'Poor Harriet here became a little overwrought.' He lifted his eyes to mine. If there was a meaning in his look I couldn't read it. 'Tears, et cetera. If I were one of those fellows who say *you know how women are* I'd say, well, you know how women are, but as you know I'm not. All I know is that part-way through the muscular double-talk going on out in the middle, your Harriet started to weep.'

I looked at my wife, who was already looking at me.

'I hate to see good people needlessly upset,' she declared, jutting her chin.

'It does you credit, my sweet.'

'And so the chivalrous Mr Shakes,' David said, 'did the decent thing and produced a bottle of whisky from his coat pocket. That ghastly Canadian stuff he carries around like a pocket watch.'

'Ah. Well, that explains it.'

'At this, Aldridge took fright. A tip for the future, Jon: if you wish to ward off the Reverend Aldridge, keep a bottle of Scotch about your person. My removal of the stopper sent him scurrying for home.'

'Reverend Aldridge did not *scurry*,' Harriet said.

'Striding, then. In any case off he went, no blood having been shed but honour satisfied, I think, on all sides.'

It hung in the cold night-time air, that word, 'honour', like a coin spinning on a tabletop, and it seemed that we waited for it to stop and for the echoes of its hum and clatter to die before we resumed our conversation. I spoke first.

'Shakes did not stay to drink with you?'

'No, he, too, quit the field. He looked tired.'

'I'm not surprised. I can think of few occupations more exhausting than being Maurice Shakes.'

'And so we did the honours ourselves, here at ring-side. Though in fairness I should admit that I did most of the damage myself.'

'Most?' Harriet, weakly indignant.

'Very well, very well, nearly all, in truth. Your abstemious wife, Lowell, took barely more than a medicinal snifter. And so the cup was drained, the evidence flung into the sea, and that brings us up to date.'

'I see,' I said.

Harriet – showing me a flash of ivory underwear – inelegantly swung her legs down from the sea wall. Her shoe heels clicked on the stone. She drew in a breath, and covered her eyes with her hand.

'I know *that* feeling,' David murmured sympathetically.

'*None* of you know how I feel,' Harriet said.

I was thinking of what she had said about Eleanor being a prig. I was thinking about holding Eleanor's hand – here, right here, just across the bloodstained boxing-ring, only that afternoon. Harriet had rubbed me to a climax before she had ever held my hand.

'There are only two of us, Harriet,' David said. 'You mean *neither.*'

She now placed both hands over her face.

I took her hand in mine when I proposed marriage. Can that have been the first time? No. No, for there had been cinema trips and tea shops, tram rides and brief, secret moments on other people's settees. But I suppose that after that encounter in the train carriage a squeeze of the hand had less capacity to overwhelm the heart.

Of course, I had kissed Eleanor Shakes before I had held her hand – almost before I had *met* the poor girl. So what did it matter?

It mattered because I could not, quite, picture Reverend Aldridge kissing my wife (where would the beard go?). I certainly could not – or, rather, was certainly able *not* to – picture him in undress, and in the throes of sexual ecstasy with her. I could picture him holding her hand in his. I could picture that very readily. It took a great effort of will *not* to picture it.

I looked morbidly at Harriet's white hands – a pale-tan mole here, a blue vein here, a wedding ring there.

'I'm cold,' David decided.

Of course he was cold; it was perhaps ten o'clock on a winter's night on the North Sea coast, and none of us in proper winter clothes – but I was not cold, did not feel the wind off the sea or the bite in the air at all, did not in fact feel anything much, besides a bewildering, directionless anger, like that of a crab in a glass jar (which might be as afraid as it is angry, but is no less angry for that).

David reached over and put his hand on Harriet's thigh.

'Come on, old girl. Time we all went home.'

I slewed forwards unsteadily, one long stride and two short steps, swung my fist, and hit unwitting David on the nose. He grunted, blinked, swayed and remained seated. He raised his wrist to his nose and I saw blood on his cuff, black in the moonlight.

'Bloody hell, Lowell,' he said irritably.

I was no Tenente Baldini. He was no Wyn James. This was no victory.

A man with dirty hands sitting astride a fallen tree like a nervous jockey on a horse he can't handle. I'll tell you, my first thought wasn't: 'Here's a husband!' But I don't suppose it ever works that way, not really.

First time I fell in love in Bradford, I fell in love with Manningham Park. Silly but there you go. If you can love a place, I loved that place (maybe I still do, too). There were flowers and birds and ducks and I couldn't for the life of me tell you their names but you don't have to, do you, if all you want to do is look at them, see the pretty things they do, the daft things, the bad things. You only need to know their names if you want to study them (or save them, like Jon with those plovers or what-is-it in the north bay – or, come to that, kill them, like Jon with his poison jar and his neat labels).

Trees I wasn't bad at. Oak, ash, elm, beech, birch, hornbeam.

I loved the open spaces of sky between the trees – even if it was never much of a sky, being in Bradford. I loved the little lads who'd have wrestling bouts or play cricket on the lawns, and the little lasses with bits of leaves and moss making houses for pixies or Mister Mouse or whatever daft thing it'd be.

I loved being able to walk up the slope through the avenue of evergreens and gawp through the box hedges at Cartwright Hall. Imagine living there, motorcar and servants and all.

That's what I'd been doing, that day. Head full of ideas about fresh-cut flowers on the table and a girl to light the fire for you every morning.

'Entomology,' he says. I'd half a mind to shout for a policeman.

Then before I knew it I was in love twice over. First the park, then him. Or does it multiply, maybe? Loves timesed by itself – love squared. I think a place you love does have that power. Is that a good thing? Doesn't sound like one.

Now little Michael's up to his elbows in a rock pool. I'm worried he'll get stung by an anemone or bitten by an eel or something but Louisa's hardly bothered. He could be hanging by his ankles halfway up the bluff and she'd not pay much mind. I suppose they get to two years old or thereabouts and you start to take it for granted. They're just there. Until they're not of course but it doesn't bear thinking about. He's a nice little boy. We're perched on the rocks, trying to ignore the wind.

'They wouldn't let it happen, would they,' she says, 'if it wasn't going to be safe.'

'Who's they?'

'The government.' She knows that sounds silly so she sniffs and says: 'I mean the town council. The authorities.'

'You'd think there'd never been an accident in this country.'

'Well, they happen. But no one could have known, could they? They're accidents, Harriet. They just happen. If people knew they would have done something.'

'It's amazing, really – all these brilliant men, engineers, architects, and it turns out afterwards none of them knows a thing.'

They've come down for the afternoon, Louisa and Michael. It's nice to see them. I shouldn't have said anything about Mr Shakes and his scheme. I wish I hadn't.

Louisa looks tired but I bet she thinks I look tired, too. We're both just getting older, that's all. The seaside doesn't help. Sea air. Puts years on you.

The Woodcock

His little bottom's up in the air. Sandals scraping the wet sand. In up to his shoulder, rootling for something. A crab or what have you. I nudge Louisa and say, look at him. She looks, and smiles, and says he loves a rock pool, that lad.

I can't help it. I shout, 'Take care, Michael!'

I shouldn't say that. I don't want to make him afraid. Louisa gives a tolerant little laugh.

'He's all right,' she says.

And he is all right. He straightens up and waves a hand at us. Bright-green lock of seaweed round his fat wrist. Something in his hand, I can't see what: a hermit crab, a periwinkle, a whelk, a shrimp.

He gets up and comes running over, pat pat pat his little feet on the sand, and he holds it up to Louisa. I still can't see what it is and she says ugh or yuck, and tells him to put it back. I ask if I can see it, please, Michael. So he totters over and holds up his open hand.

It's just a piece of bladderwrack, brown and cold and glossy with seawater.

I tell him it's lovely and he smiles. Then I say, 'You had better not let Mr Lowell see what you've got. He'd very much like a thing like that.'

Michael looks at the seaweed and then looks at me, and he says, for dinner?

I don't laugh because little ones don't like it when you laugh at them. Who does? Instead I just say no, for his collection – Mr Lowell collects pretty things from the sea, all labelled and in glass jars. I don't say all dead but I think it.

He asks me what it is, the thing he's holding, and I say it's bladderwrack, and he says blatterjack, and this time I do laugh, and Louisa says it's getting a bit nippy, let's go and find a cup of tea – which is all right by me.

XX

I saw, over the course of the next week or two, that gulls and wading birds coming in from the sea banked over the north bay and veered away, and would not land there, as though the bay were cursed. There was no curse, of course – only unfamiliar men, unfamiliar noise, unfamiliar work.

At the height of the Great Fire of London, Samuel Pepys observed pigeons seeking to return to their familiar haunts in the city's roofs and gutters, even as these were ablaze. The pigeons suffered burned feet and singed feathers for their folly; our Gravely gulls were wiser, and stayed away from the place they used to know, seeing that it had become strange.

I was as wise (or as craven) as the gulls. For some days I could not bring myself to look upon the north bay. Even to mount the sea wall was beyond me. When I sat in study on the beach or walked upon the bluff, I averted my eyes.

David was all right, despite the slap (really it had been barely more than that); we quickly resumed our companionable friendship. Harriet, too, returned to normal – although the question of what was normal no longer seemed straightforward to me. I don't suppose it did to her, either. On beaches further up the coast, the sands were treacherous, inconstant, changing with each tide and without safe places to stand; I thought about those beaches a lot, at that time – and about the erosion of the land by the grinding of the sea.

One morning, as I was assembling my rock-pooling kit (and anxiously eyeing the darkening sky), Harriet, with a passing remark, ended my exile from the north bay.

'I see,' she said, wiping breakfast crumbs from the kitchen table, 'that the revolution has begun.'

I looked up from refreshing my killing jar with ethyl acetate. 'Revolution?'

'Your friend Mr Shakes.'

Something under my heart rolled like a large stone stirred by a riptide.

'The pier?'

'Not much of that yet, no. I went for a look yesterday while you were out with David.' (We had taken a walk – and a bottle to share – to Sallow Sluice.) 'Not much of a fairground yet but you can see where the fairground's going to be.'

'Not a fairground, my rose. A *pleasure* ground.'

'Of course. In the name of the poor brother.'

She sounded unwontedly satirical.

'There is much amusing about Maurice Shakes,' I said, buckling my satchel, 'but I shouldn't have thought to include the death of his brother in that.'

'No, of course.' She flashed a penitent smile over her shoulder. 'It was more – well, there is something absurd about grand gestures, isn't there?'

'To an Englishman, yes,' I agreed.

After that, I could hardly continue to treat the north bay as if it were a leper colony. Cowards suffer from curiosity, too.

*

It was not yet dawn when I left Harriet in bed and ventured out on to the sands. The sea was a far-off stripe of dark grey-green and above it the first dull light of day had almost overwhelmed the bright points of Pegasus. The cold was savage. My trousers flapped about my knees as I held on to my hat and made my way north. A redshank, exploring a seam of flyblown seaweed, ignored me as I passed. To the south-east, in the lee of the bluff, a slim cormorant held out its wings as though in supplication.

I reached the ladder and scaled it. From the top I looked back at the coast road and thought: why didn't I walk that way? I would at least have got less sand in my shoes.

The answer was twofold. One, I knew and loved the beach, *my* beach. Two, walking across the beach meant not walking past Aldridge's church.

I cut back along the harbour arm to the mainland and turned north. At the point at which the sea wall rose to enclose the shadows of Shakestown, I paused. It had never looked darker. The smell of stale drink, cut timber, rusting iron and derelict crabbing kit had now become familiar, and I jibbed at it. But the north bay – whatever I would find there (what did I *think* I would find there?) – exerted its own pull, which I found hard to resist. I went on. It was not, I suppose, quite as dark as I had imagined; it did not take me as long as I had feared to reach the light.

Where before one had stepped from the footway along the sea wall on to an unmade path, a shallow bowl of knotty heath on one's left and a short descent of shingle to the sea on one's right, now one stepped from the footway on to the surface of the moon. Or so it appeared. It was as though a wrathful god – seeking vengeance on gorse and heather, stonechat and meadow-pipit, rabbit and weasel – had reached down and simply ripped away a fistful of Gravely. A long, wide slope of pale soil was all that could be seen. A white-tipped severed tree-root wagged in the wind.

Of course, I reasoned, the town still stood, civilisation endured, Shakes had not reduced us quite to ruin. Here where the heath had once been, the coast road, which at most places closely hugged the shoreline, made an inchworm's loop inland, returning to the sea after a half-mile or so of eastward diversion. I stood now in the middle of that loop, knowing that beyond the low brow of the slope the road was still in service – hearing, indeed, the clatter of a horse and cart emerging from the town to the south and following the road eastwards – but wondering, at the same time, how on earth it *could* be. Standing in that swath of lamb-grey vacancy it seemed impossible that the church still stood, the road still worked, carters still drove horses, and just a little way north the road still wound its way back to the shoreline, bringing Gravely with it.

The little bowl of heath, hemmed in by the ocean and the road, had always, I reflected, been a wasteland, a wilderness. It was a wilderness now. But there were, I thought, different kinds of wilderness.

To my left, at the south side of the grey expanse, an acre or two of cleared land had been given over to what might have been a railway yard, if railway yards, in addition to wheels, struts, lengths of iron and steel, steam boilers, flues, tools and riveted panels, were customarily strewn with things from dreams. Each was neatly strung with an inked cardboard label. I stirred myself and walked over to the nearest: a contoured sheet of metal cut into the shape of a dolphin (whether white-beaked or bottle-nosed I couldn't say). The likeness of a dolphin had been painted on to it only moderately well. The dolphin was candyfloss-pink, and grinning.

I stood with my hands on my hips and surveyed the other artefacts. I felt as though I were acting in a burlesque of Carter at Tutankhamun's tomb, with me as the awestruck archaeologist.

Here, a wheelless automobile cut in two longitudinally, painted with gold paint and surmounted with a dragon's head, similarly bisected. There, a fifteen-foot arch constructed from green iron seahorses. Here, a wing-backed easy chair to which a dozen stuffed, plumed birds had been glued or stapled. There, a segment of railway line corkscrewed about a silver pipe as wide as a man's height.

All awaiting the expert ministrations of Peter Furlong. Hands that can build a pier could, I supposed, build anything – even these Surrealist contraptions.

A birdwatcher is highly attuned to the signals of his peripheral vision. Something now stirred in mine. I was facing away from the sea, examining a stack of swing chairs fancifully ornamented with characters from Lewis Carroll. Some distance to my left was the inland bend in the road, and a break in the roadside hedging that afforded access from the road to the heath – or rather, to where the heath had once been. A figure had just passed through the break.

I could not say for sure why I took a furtive rightward step into the shade of the Wonderland chairs (a purse-lipped mock turtle peered at me dyspeptically). And I could not say, either, why, on seeing that the figure stepping purposefully across the cleared ground was Harriet, I did not move – did not step out, and cry 'hello' and wave my hat. I remained where I was, quite still.

She was looking for me, of course. Perhaps I ought to have left a note; perhaps I had overlooked some necessary chore before going out; perhaps she had been preparing breakfast and was bringing a bacon sandwich; perhaps she was merely curious as to where I was. Anyway I waited until she passed behind the hulk of a carousel and swiftly doubled back towards the sea wall.

Something about the emptied heath, the empty sea (and something about myself, no doubt). Together they fostered a sense of dislocation, and of people and places out of joint.

I did not want to be seen. I did not want to see Harriet.

Turning back to the path to the sea wall, I observed that, beginning a little way above the tideline, pairs of pale timber stakes had been sunk into the earth and shingle at measured intervals, each pair perhaps fifty or sixty feet apart. They proceeded down to the susurrating grey breakers and no doubt beyond. I had missed them on my arrival, thanks to the low light and the angle of my approach.

They were the engineers' preparations for the pier, of course.

Again the black vision before my eyes. An iron boot planted on the Gravely shore.

A 'field expedition', the reverend called it. I like that. Sounds serious, like a serious thing. As though I'm a serious person – not some silly housewife, only good for getting the brush-off from the men who sit on councils and committees, writing letters no one replies to, worrying myself sick about something no one else seems to give a bloody fig about.

Except Reverend Aldridge, of course. You can say what you like, but he cares.

When you stand here now you can almost imagine it – almost step into Mr Shakes's crackpot dream. Now he's wiped it clean of straggly shrubs and spiky weeds, you can almost see his silly funfair. In a way it looks satisfying, like when you take a damp rag to a school blackboard all cloudy with chalk dust and bring up a clean wide stripe, glossy as new paint. I suppose he'd say that's what this was, a grubby board, nothing written on it. Wipe it clean! Start again – with a blooming roller coaster or what have you.

But maybe there was something written on it, only it was something he couldn't read. There was something written like a hard equation or Egyptian letters and only people like Jon could read it.

If only people like Jon can read it, then what's the point in keeping it, Maurice Shakes might say. There aren't many people, he'd say, like our Dr Lowell. He'd not be wrong there.

Besides, it's what people like to do now. Where did that old stuff get us? To a world war and a million men dead, that's where. So boo-sucks to the old stuff, let's make new stuff, let's make everything new...

I don't know. You've got to worry about chucking the baby out with the bathwater, haven't you? But if you've got too much bathwater, more than you know what to do with, enough to drown in or to flood your house, maybe you don't think about the baby. That's an awful way to say it, but still.

Jon gets cross with me if I wake the cat from his sleep. I watch Josephus sleeping curled on the tatty wicker chair he's made his own and even though I can see how peaceful he is – he's so peaceful, so free of fretting that I could cry – I somehow, at the same time, can't abide his peace.

So I poke him, make him blink open his cabbage-green eyes and mouth at me enquiringly; I cajole him from his comfy chair and badger him into chasing a cloth mouse or leaping for the curtain-pull.

'Let him be,' Jon'll say, looking up from his book. 'The poor chap gets little enough peace and quiet.'

But that's not what Josephus the cat is for, I think.

Making notes in this daft little pocketbook. 'Funfair parts unshipped', 'clearance of herbiage'. I don't know what I'm doing really but I'm glad I'm doing something. Knowledge is power, Dad would have said. Learned that from the library gates. 'Pier staked out,' I write – I mean, you can see where the pier, the 'boardwalk' as he calls it, will go. We'll see.

Poking about here gets me to thinking on the Shakes girls. I was mean about them the other night. Firstly they might not be a slut and a prig, and secondly if they are it's unkind to say so. Most of all, you've got to ask what chance did they have? With him and how he is. I don't believe in destiny or anything but a father isn't far off the same thing.

A sea-pie (Jon calls them oystercatchers but each to their own) comes flying in, low down and flapping fast, doing a sad sort of shouting as it circles the bay. The pier'll be on your doorstep, too, my lad. But you'll get used to it.

I just stand here for a bit, shivering but not wanting to go anywhere, just looking out at the sea. Lots of white horses, and those black ducks again, going up and down, up and down.

The thing about a pier – a thing I knew before all this, the obvious *thing about a pier – is that it's practically a bridge. Of course it goes nowhere in particular but other than that it's a bridge. And I think when they start building this one, in spite of myself, in spite of the reverend and all the rest of it, I'll be sort of disappointed when they stop.*

All at once I have a really queer picture of myself, so queer I laugh out loud; I imagine myself, wild-looking, in clothes like a tramp or a mad person, out on the end of Maurice Shakes's half-mile pier, shouting at the workmen as they pack up their tools: 'Don't stop now, *young man! Why are you stopping? Why, if you kept at it, you could be in Holland or Flanders in no time! Don't stop now! Where's your sense of adventure?'*

Given myself the proper giggles. Here's the sea-pie full of misery by the sounds of him and here's me, all by myself and laughing fit to bust. Crackers. Especially in the present circumstances.

XXI

My first thought, when I saw her from the road, was: *where the devil have you been?*

It was unfair. I had seen her go, after the fight, before David appeared – I had seen her walk away arm in arm with her wanton sister, and I had not gone after her. Should she have sought me out? Called at the house, perhaps: 'Hello, Harriet – is your husband at home? We held hands at the prize fight, and have much to discuss.'

I had no office save the beach, the bluff, the moors. I kept to no routine. She might have found me at the pub – but where was the good in that? Cryptic conversation in shot of wagging Gravely ears.

Perhaps I should have gone after her. Maurice Shakes would, I suppose, have taken great pleasure, genuine pleasure, in a married man knocking at his door and asking permission to pay court to his younger daughter.

No. We were helpless. We are all helpless of course, but in this matter we two were more helpless than most.

Eleanor was intent on her book. I hoped that it was not a Bible but knew that it probably was. This was a bright day, a day of glassy sea and gleaming sand, frost on the inland moors and ice in the water butt. I was warmly wrapped in coat, scarf and hat, out that day to hunt for winter thrush flocks in the hilly farmland south of the bluff.

I felt each current of the air. I felt the earth alive with creatures and the sea alive with fish. I felt beneath my feet the motion of the earth. A robin sang in the trees beside the road and it was my song, sung for her.

Her coat was camel-coloured, her dress lemon yellow. I looked for a hat and saw it, narrow-brimmed and campion-pink, perched on a nearby rock. Her hair was bound up tight. As I watched, the wind riffled the pages of her book, intruding on her reading, and as she turned them back I felt their thinness through her fingertips (Bibles, being wordy, are printed on the thinnest of paper).

The Reverend Aldridge had asked more than once, in confident rhetorical vein, how it could be that, if there was no loving God, we were allowed to live in a world of such beauty. I had always wondered, conversely, how it was that, living day to day among beauty, we ever found anything beautiful.

I had never found anything as beautiful as I found Eleanor Shakes, viewed from a distance, reading the Bible on a rock, in a lemon-yellow dress.

I stood in the road like an idiot.

'Stay there much longer and you'll grow moss, Mr Lowell,' some wag called from a passing bicycle.

For all that I believe in a man's free will, I believe with just the same certainty that it was impossible for me to not act, that day, on my desires. I am no philosopher, except in the sense that our forefathers considered a philosopher anyone who peered in rock pools or cooked chemicals in crucibles or watched the stars.

As I skirted Challenger Deep, newly refreshed by the just-gone tide, I glanced into the water and saw there only the reflection of high white clouds.

Eleanor looked up as I approached. A sort of well-bred alertness showed in her face first, and then – I think – happiness.

'If it isn't Mr Lowell,' she said.

Had I expected coyness or embarrassment? No – not in her, and for once not even in myself, for I was just as clear-eyed and unblushing as I bade her good day, removed my hat and said: 'May I sit with you?'

'Of course.'

I chose a solid, smooth-edged boulder to Eleanor's left. Her pink hat sat in between us, as though it were a subject for our study and consultation.

'I'm sorry to intrude on your reading,' I said.

'Not at all. I was finding it rather hard going in any case.'

She wafted the book apologetically. I leaned forwards to inspect its cover, and almost slipped from my boulder in surprise. *The Sea-side Book: An Introduction to the Natural History of the British Coasts.*

'My goodness! W. H. Harvey.'

'You know it?'

'Very well. When I was a boy I could recite whole chunks from it.'

'The fellow knows a lot about the sea.'

'Well, there's a lot to know. I corresponded with him once – I probably still have the letters. Some detail pertaining to the breeding of seahorses.'

'I haven't got to seahorses yet. I'm stuck on polar currents.'

'Dash polar currents. Here you are cupped in the very hands of Gravely bay and you're seeking education from a book. Come on.' I stood. 'Practical study is the way. Time to get your hands dirty. Or wet, rather.'

She looked up at me for a moment with a rather savage smile.

'All right,' she said abruptly. She set her book down beside her hat and hopped to her feet. 'Give me your crustaceans, your arthropods, your jellyfishes yearning to breathe free.' She unbuttoned her camel coat and slipped it off. Immediately I saw her bare arms come out in goosebumps. 'Brrr. My goodness. Where do we start?'

I laughed.

'You can kneel there.' I pointed to the brink of the pool. 'No weed, no barnacles.'

She lowered herself dutifully on to her left knee, folding one arm about her right shin and resting her chin on her right knee as she peered down into the water. I wondered at her grace. At her kneecap as the sunlight gleamed on the fine-latticed fabric of her stocking.

I skipped the pool rather deftly and took up a position across from Eleanor, kneeling on both knees like a schoolboy. I could feel seawater seep into my trousers.

I bent over the silver water.

'Are we to make a bridge?' I heard her say gently.

I looked up. Her brow was an inch from mine.

I bit my lip and thought of things I might say, about perhaps what sort of a bridge we might be – a Bridge of Sighs or a Bridge of Hearts? – about what gulfs we might span, what a structure together we might make, how sound our balance and tension, how perfect our complementarity—

But the words in my mind again summoned the black vision of the pier and so I didn't say them. Instead I leaned a little further forwards, knees chafing against the rock, and lifted my face so that it confronted hers. I felt her breath on my chin. If she had blinked I would have felt the draught from her eyelashes – but she did not blink. Only after a moment did she lower her eyes from mine.

'You are married, Mr Lowell,' she said gently, like a doctor or priest delivering sad news.

My head wanted to be bowed. My mouth wanted to say sorry. I said: 'That's a legal term, Miss Shakes. A legal and a religious term.'

'And you think you stand outside the authority of both? Is this anarchism, Mr Lowell?'

'I mean only to observe that in itself it says nothing about – about—'

'Love,' Eleanor said. We looked sadly at one another across the rock pool.

'It's *meant* to, of course,' I added. 'But the fact is that it doesn't.'

'No.'

Something stirred in the water. We looked down. No, not in the water – something above us, and only reflected in the water: a black-headed gull, aimlessly elbowing its way this way and that through the cold air above the beach.

Eleanor touched the water with her fingertips, and both gull and sky broke into ripples.

'So what lies beneath, Mr Lowell?' she said. 'What terrors of the deep have you to show me?'

I had already dragged off my heavy coat and now I rolled back my sleeves.

'This is the special joy of the rock pooler,' I smiled. 'One never knows what treats the tide will leave behind.'

The seawater, as I plunged my hand into the bladdered weed of the nearside shallows, was perishingly cold, as cold as death – and as always it felt strange to feel at once such a quickening of life. Shrimps sprang from the groping of my fingers. A small fish glanced against my wrist. When I touched the periwinkles on the nearside rock I could feel them redouble their grip.

I levelled my palm, reversing my elbow like a leg spinner, and ran my hand gently beneath the ridge. Weed-ends tickled. I felt through the water a familiar sort of motion, the awkward mechanical scamper of a running crab, within the span of my hand. I closed my fingers about its shell, and drew it with a snort of satisfaction from the water.

It regarded me with disdain and wheeled its fists at me.

'What a beast,' said Eleanor drily. I wondered if she meant me or the crab. 'Is this where you gut and clean it, and mount its head on a plaque in your study?'

I considered my study, with its rows of labelled jars and butterfly cases, and concluded that perhaps she was not far wrong.

'A common shore crab,' I said, as she peered at it curiously.

'Does he pinch?'

'Like a devil.'

'You really are very brave.'

'I can hold a bee or wasp, too,' I boasted with a smile. 'It's quite simple, if you take the right approach.'

'All right, enough posturing. Put the poor fellow back.'

I returned my hand to the water and released my hold. The crab sank to the bottom of the pool, took swift bearings and trundled back into the weed.

'You see?' I said. I was – as I often was when rock-pooling – mildly exhilarated. 'There's a lot you can learn on a rocky beach.'

'Evidently.' Eleanor grinned at me. 'My turn,' she said. 'I'll come up with a conger-eel or a barracuda, you'll see—' She shifted her small feet on the rocks, perching on one hip and propping herself on one hand. For a moment I saw her face – her wide eyes, her just-parted lips – reflected in the water.

Although I watched what happened next from a distance of just two or three feet, I was as helpless to prevent it as if I had been, not just on the other side of a rock pool, but on the other side of the sea. By the time my brain and body had registered one event in the disastrous series the next was unstoppably underway – and so on.

I saw the hand on which she was resting slip on the green weed. I saw the heel of her hand scrape across a field of grubby barnacles, and I saw the stripes of vivid red blood they raised on her white inner wrist. I heard her draw in a sharp breath. I probably made some useless sort of sound myself.

I saw her twist, one leg trapped beneath the weight of her body, nothing before her but cold air and cold water, nothing within arm's length (nothing within a half-mile) to grab at – save me. I felt the waft of air as her other hand snatched at nothing beneath my chin.

I saw her hand lunge for the water as if it expected to meet with resistance there – and, finding none, keep going. I saw Eleanor's head trailing a loose lock of brown hair drop in a helpless arc, the arc of something falling from flight, towards the sharp edge of rock at my side of the pool.

I cried out. I saw her head miss the rock. She plunged face-first into the pool, drenching my shirt front and trousers, sending icy seawater swirling over her shoulder blades. One foot, loosed by the tumble, waved in the air. Her left arm, wildly swung, found a purchase on the pool's edge, and almost at once – though it did not feel like 'at once', not at all – her face reappeared, streaming salt water, gaping, gasping, droplets exploding from her eyes as she blinked. I felt her clawed hand briefly on my knee as she fought her way upright.

At last – too late – I seized her by her shoulders, and held her steady, held her safe. The water falling from her face and hair clattered in the pool. With a quivering hand – the bloodied hand – she dashed a clef of dark wet hair from her face, and shook her head.

'Are you all right?' I demanded.

She gasped, heaving in air, and banged her fist on her sternum. She had been in the water for only a second; her breathlessness was the effect of cold, of a sudden ice-cold drenching as from a prankster's bucket, not of any prolonged lack of oxygen. Rather manfully, I shook her, and asked again if she was all right.

'I'll live,' she said weakly. She was laughing.

I acted out a short charade of indignation: what the devil was so damn funny, she might've had her brains dashed out, frightened me half to death and look at the state of my trousers, why couldn't she have been more careful—

But under the gravely humorous look in Eleanor's blinking eyes I couldn't sustain it. I grabbed hold of her right hand – almost pulling us both into the pool as I did so – and lifted it to my lips; I kissed the red scratches made by the barnacles' shells.

'Ouch!' she said, and then, reprovingly, 'Mr Lowell.'

'My goodness, I love you, my goodness,' I murmured over her scratches.

She made a small noise; a small exhalation through her nose.

Why this unbecoming excess of sentiment? (How David would have laughed at me! The David of our youths, anyway.) Love, of course, but not only love. Thankfulness. To whom or what? To God? No: to nothing and no one.

Those who say that one cannot give thanks to no one are mistaken. I gave them, dozens of them, that morning. They drifted out into the North Sea. They sailed up into the empty February sky.

'I shall have seen a thing or two when this is over.' A line I remember from one of his letters. He'd hardly seen anything when he wrote it – he'd not left Hartlepool, where they'd sent him for basic training. Still the line runs through my head while I peel the potatoes. *I shall have seen a thing or two when this is over.*

It makes me think of the blood inside the skin of my thumb, dark-pink and pressed up against the dull side of the knife-blade.

Leave the potatoes in a pan with water. Towel my hands, take two minutes to fasten up my hair and make sure I look respectable. You'd think if there's one person you wouldn't have to bother looking respectable for it's your mother, but no.

A bit of sunshine out but not much. Changeable, the sky. Clouds coming and going. Must be blowy all that way up there.

'I've been thinking about the reverend's sermon,' she says, the first thing she says.

Takes me a minute to remember what it was about. Obviously I know generally what it was about. But specifically.

The noise of his voice makes me tired. Just thinking about it.

'Adam,' she says.

'Oh, him.'

'Adam's curse. In the sweat of thy face thou shalt eat bread, till thou return unto the ground.'

She's as bad as Jon, only she doesn't do it to be funny.

'Well, *what about it?*'

'Work, Harriet. The Reverend was quite right. Work isn't a curse, it's a blessing, he said. A man ought to work. I'm glad,' she says, 'that you found a husband who works for his living.'

Meaning, of course, either that she's not glad at all, or that my husband doesn't work for his living, but only goes bird's-nesting and splashes about in rock pools. Probably the second, but with a bit of the first, too.

The Reverend's sermon, I remember, was just 'the Devil makes work for idle hands', dressed up. And I remember thinking he had a bit of a nerve, saying so.

We're walking up the high street. She needs thread and fish, I need soap and a cabbage.

Louisa Hesketh pops out of the ironmonger's holding a bit of railing. Sees us, smiles.

'For the railing,' she says, waving it. 'Good morning, Mrs Holloway. And how are you, Harriet?'

Mother makes her excuses, potters off to the haberdashery. I say I'm very well. Louisa, pink-cheeked under her blue knitted hat, does a face as if I'd said 'I've got cholera'. I guess why before she takes a step closer to me and says in a sort of squeaky whisper: 'I'm going to have another baby!'

Well, I say the things you say. I'm happy for her, of course I am. It's a happy thing. Not always, not everywhere, but here, now.

'Still doing your bit,' I joke, and give her a sort of nudge. She does a daft grin and for a minute I think I'm going to get the giggles again.

Cordelia Shakes in a copper-coloured dress walks by on the other side of the road and our heads turn as though she's holding both our noses on a string.

'I've heard some things about that one,' Louisa mutters.

'You're not the only one.'

I'm not my mother. I've got nothing against Cordelia Shakes. But I've not got the giggles any more.

'I think Jon is in love with one of the Shakes girls.'

No: *I don't really say it. I try it out in my head. My tongue practises the steps in my mouth, but I don't say it.*

XXII

I have never seen a stranger February.

At all hours – whether I was birdwatching at first light or gathering seaweeds before bed – there emanated from the north bay a terrific din, or rather *many* dins, from a varied portfolio of clangs, roars, whirrs, vocal clamours, mechanical music, rhythmic bangings, drillings, hisses and rowdy singing. Gravely was, of course, not a funeral parlour; we did not demand quiet. Trawlermen and crabbers yell and sing and laugh and row – we knew that. We never expected our boatbuilders to muffle their hammers or fish-traders to silently pass around bills of sale instead of bawling out their wares and prices. Gravely was a place of life.

In mid-February the north bay – or Shakestown, or Mr Shakes himself – took its first life: that of the soldierly metal-man Arthur Harrowell, killed in an accident of riveting or welding (I shrank from the details). I was told that Maurice Shakes and the overseer Wilkie accompanied the remaining Harrowell brother, Ted, back to Newcastle for the burial. The brother did not return; I suppose he was replaced.

I could no longer ignore the pier. It was, for one thing, no longer a ghost or a premonition or only a mad American's dream; it was a real thing of pilings and girders, extending into the deep grey swell beyond the harbour, still frail, a preliminary sketch, perhaps not yet what anyone in Southend or Skegness would call a pier – but a real thing. One could see it from the beach. When *I* stood on the beach I could see nothing else.

'It might be nice,' Harriet suggested tolerantly to me as we walked one day along the coast road, with the insistent pier on the edge of our vision like a fault in the eyeball, 'to be able to stroll on a pier. Entertainments and such. Toffee apples. Barrel organ. I might not mind that, if it's safe.'

'Chaps on stilts are a new one on me. I thought it was just going to be fried onions and grievous bodily harm.'

'It's no good just being sniffy, Jon. If you want it to turn out right, and have a say in what they *do* there, you have to get involved. Like with the government and so on.'

'Yes, democracy did us such a lot of good, didn't it? It was going tremendously well, I thought, right up to the war.'

'Talking to you, Jon,' she said, 'is like talking to the reverend, sometimes.'

She said it only to sting me.

The reverend, the righteous Aldridge, was still around, of course, eternal and unchanging, except that perhaps his beard grew a half-inch or his pious Christianity, through regular exercise, grew a touch more muscular.

How would one exercise Christianity? Through temptation, I suppose.

Shakestown grew. The sheds and lean-tos crept out from the shadows of the road by the harbour wall and began to colonise, in unplanned fits and starts, both spurs of the wall itself and the barren edges of the cleared heath where the devilish Furlong rigged his contraptions. Two latrines, crossed by a plank, were sunk into the ground near the brow of the slope. What I began to think of as 'old' Shakestown, the sheds in the dank shadow of the wall, remained much the same. Perhaps in fact – in spite of the gradually lightening evenings – it grew darker.

Mr Shakes's stunts continued. One day there was a bloated opera singer with bad skin and a waxed moustache bellowing arias outside the church. On another day a champion sprinter from Billingham raced a point-to-point racehorse over ninety yards along the sea road. Sensationally, an Italian restaurant opened in the town (few Gravelians dared to eat there, but many gathered each night at the windows to gawp).

When one day Harriet and I were walking to her mother's house and passed a tall, olive-skinned fellow with a wooden leg, I remarked that Mr Shakes was attracting all sorts of exotica to our town.

Harriet snorted and said: 'Exotica, Jon, isn't the half of it.'

In response to my enquiring look she widened her eyes meaningly and said, '*Girls.*'

I presumed that she didn't mean the Shakes girls – but, with that subject remaining a sensitive one (to say the least), I declined to pursue the point. Only a few days later was its significance – which of course I had guessed blushingly at – fully revealed to me.

I was at the north end of the beach at dusk, sitting cross-legged upon a blanket and watching the wading birds gather to roost. A flock of knot in flight over the sea moved against the sky like the flexible sable of a painter's brush against a canvas. I became aware (with a little annoyance) of human noises above me, at the top of the corroded ladder at the south extremity of the sea wall. No one worked there at this hour; it was surely too dark, in the shadows there, for anything productive to be done.

The noises – though I did my best to ignore them – recalled to my mind my encounter (it seemed like a century before) with David and Cordelia on the beach – and, then, my first encounter with Maurice Shakes.

I looked around, half-expecting to see Shakes squatting beside me, chuckling in approval, and perhaps asking to borrow my binoculars.

The noises went on as the wading birds gathered. A man and a woman, certainly. Sometimes an indistinct word or two. A whimper. Murmurs most often. A loudly spoken curse. Quiet. A flight of turnstone descended to the beach. A man's laugh.

For some minutes then, everything was quiet, and I tried to concentrate on the birds, squinting in the gloom to make notes – *Turnst.* c.7, *Oyst.* 4 – and a clumsy sketch in my notebook.

Above me and perhaps ten yards ahead of where I sat, the rusty ladder chimed dully as a shoe struck the top rung. I looked up, and dropped my pencil.

A lady in high-heeled shoes was climbing down the ladder. She wore no stockings and as, in order to facilitate her descent, she had pragmatically hitched her full burgundy skirts right up about her waist, I could see that she was very evidently not wearing bloomers either. Her bare and shapely white buttocks jutted out in frank profile against the sky. From what I could see of her face she appeared heavy-jawed but not unattractive. A cloche hat with a feather in it crowded her dark-coloured curls about her cheeks, and the short, pale sleeves of her gown were embroidered with dark diamonds. Her legs and arms were muscular.

I didn't think she was a Gravely girl. One would think that if I had seen her about the town I would have remembered.

Much later than I ought to have, I looked away. When – sooner than I ought to have – I looked back she was trotting down the beach to the sea, still holding up her skirts with a hand at her hip.

For an awful moment I thought she was going to plunge suicidally into the surf, and I would have to run and rescue her, and thus endure all sorts of embarrassments. She did not. She stopped at the water's edge, rather daintily removed her shoes, waded out until the water was calf-deep and squatted.

She was washing herself. I looked away again. The birds – just feet from the woman – were utterly unperturbed. I stared determinedly south, at the bluff and the outline of the priory, until again shoes rang on the ladder rungs. I counted them – I knew that there were twenty-six rungs – and on the twenty-sixth I looked up. All I saw was a sweep of burgundy skirts at the edge of the sea wall. I heard a weary sigh, and then footsteps heading towards Shakestown and fading rapidly to nothing. I gathered my things, folded my blanket into my satchel and went home.

I said nothing of my encounter to Harriet. I would not really have been telling her anything she did not already know, and I had done nothing wrong – or nothing much (I oughtn't have looked). But I said nothing. Saying nothing to Harriet had become something of a habit.

I'd seen Maurice Shakes only briefly. I think it was shortly after the death of Harrowell. He was standing alone up on the bluff, and it looked as though he was watching the birds. What birds there were that day, at that time, were a desultory lot – the odd gull, the odd rock dove, the odd wader – but it looked as though he was watching them anyway. It was mid-afternoon; I had just left the pub. A sort of fellow-feeling must have taken hold of me – for how often had I stood just there, freezing in the wind, watching birds from the bluff?

'Mr Shakes!' The words leapt from me.

He turned, and lifted his broad-brimmed hat in greeting.

'Mr Lowell. You find me studying the avifauna. A poor student, of course, beside you. Now tell me – the hurrying, frantic little birds at the water's edge, the little white wading birds – what are those?'

'Sanderling,' I told him.

'Of course.' He was, I saw, holding a small flask. He took an unhurried drink from it, and screwed back the cap. 'Will they return, do you think?'

'Return? The sanderling?'

'*No*. The – the ring plover, will they come back to breed? In the north bay?'

I laughed.

'One might perhaps take up residence in one of your whirligigs, if it has a strong stomach. Or nest between the ears of your mechanical cow. Otherwise, I think not.'

He was looking at me quizzically, and I returned the look. Then he nodded.

'Of course. You don't know. I forget, Mr Lowell, that your natural range seldom takes you north of the sea wall.' He smiled.

'I'm sure I'm missing out, Mr Shakes,' I said stiffly.

'Oh, that you are. But I'm not talking about the pleasure grounds – although, my God, sir, we are doing something splendid there. I mean north of there. The beach.'

North of there? North of the scraped heath there was only the coast road and the straggling far end of Gravely; seawards of the road was nothing but muddy foreshore, all the way, more or less, to the cliffs of Sallow Sluice.

'Beach?' I echoed dumbly.

'Indeed.' Shakes rocked on his heels. 'Do you know, Mr Lowell, a small headland, beyond my grounds, to the north, where the coast road kind of kinks inland, just a little, leaving the headland, which is overgrown with elder and I don't know what – though I'm damn sure you do, sir—'

'I know it. A nightingale nested in the elder once.' Don't tell me, I wanted to say – you have razed the elders to the ground, and installed all the conveniences of a bathing beach.

'How glorious! Well, just beyond the headland, in the crook of its shoulder if you'll permit me, sir, there's a beach.'

I contradicted him flatly.

'No there isn't. There's a rubble of mud and rocks. There was a landslip there years ago. There isn't a beach.'

'There *wasn't* a beach.'

I looked at him and not for the first time saw that I was looking at a god. Not a very good sort of god but a god nevertheless. With one hand he had smeared away the heath. With the other—

'I did some reading, sir. *Common Bird Life of the North Sea Coast*? Your own, of course – damn, sir, there's no need to blush' – I cursed myself – 'I read your book, and learned what your ring plovers desire in a nesting place – and by God I built them one.' He beamed. 'A clean shingle beach, fifty feet across. Sixteen ton of shingle barged down from Durham.'

'You – but—' I blinked, and rubbed my eyes. 'But how did you know there ever was a nesting place there?'

Again the quizzical look.

'Your memory fails you, Mr Lowell.'

I stared stupidly until he prompted me: 'The meeting of the townspeople, sir. You particularly requested that these poor birds not be dispossessed. Did you think I had forgotten? Or not listened? Or not given a damn?'

I remembered, at last.

'Yes. Yes, I thought one of those.'

A great bark of laughter.

'There's no getting by you, Mr Lowell. I just couldn't stomach it. I had little choice but to wreak a little havoc on their old place, you understand – this is a small island of yours, and a fellow has to fight for what breathing room he can get! – but I couldn't stomach the idea that I'd – that I'd done them wrong, you see.' He snorted. 'Makes me sound like a goddamn fool, Mr Lowell, but there it is.'

He was looking down at the beach in the direction of the sanderlings but his focus seemed to be some way beyond the beach. Then he glanced at me sideways.

'Remorse can be a great motivator, sir,' he rumbled. He extended an open hand northwards, out over the bluff edge, indicating the north bay, and the pleasure grounds. The Lawrence Shakes Pleasure Ground, of course. Lawrence, who went to war at his brother's command, and perished.

I thanked him sincerely for his thoughtfulness over the plovers, and bade him good afternoon. He remained on the bluff, watching the birds from beneath the shelter of his wide-brimmed hat.

Then of course there were the Shakes girls.

I saw Cordelia before I saw Eleanor. That is, after our escapade at (and in) Challenger Deep, I did not see Eleanor until March. I saw Cordelia on, I think, February the twenty-fifth.

David and I were walking in town. I had met him off the York train – he had had some business down south, which had taken him from us for two nights – and, instead of going home directly, we had wandered up the Gravely high street. He had remarked on the Italian restaurant, glowing and aromatic in the grey, which had led us on naturally to the town's new-found (or new-arrived, new-imposed) cosmopolitanism.

I, indulging a fleeting mood of schoolboy juvenility, had told him about the whore on the beach, and the roguery of Shakestown.

'The workers' sheds, by the sea wall? Looked as innocent as a granddad's allotment to me. Just a place for horny-handed sons of toil to smoke their pipes and consult their charts. But you say it's sort of a sink of iniquity.'

'I say so because it's true. A proper St Giles.'

'Should we go and have a look?'

At once I felt challenged and hesitant, and regretted my worldly swaggering. I glanced at my pocket watch.

'I think Harriet's making tea—'

'It's barely five, man. Come on.'

He hooked his arm through mine and we turned towards the sea. The sky was riven with long, steel-blue reefs of cloud.

'They may still be working,' I submitted meekly.

'Then we'll stop for a little chat and a pipe of baccy,' David shrugged, 'before proceeding home to dear Harriet's stew or chops or whatever it might be.'

'Fried liver.'

'Fried liver, then. Show some backbone, my boy. This is your town, Lowell, for goodness' sake. You've every right to wander wherever your legs take you.'

Actually, I wondered if my legs *would* take me to Shakestown again. Whether they'd fail me, simply give way, as we broached the shadow of the sea wall.

We slowed as we passed the church.

'Would you look at that,' David laughed uneasily.

Someone – and we both guessed who – had stuck a large poster across the parish noticeboard beside the church door. The letters printed on it were tall, black, well spaced and uppercase. *I AM NOT COME TO CALL THE RIGHTEOUS, BUT SINNERS TO REPENTANCE.*

'Go on then,' David murmured.

'Matthew nine.'

'Honestly, Lowell, you ought to go on the boards with that routine. You'd slay them.' He shook his head, and we walked on.

Was he thinking of Kenneth, the simple Palmer boy, the backward son of the boatbuilder, beaten to death for preaching peace by Gravely boys more fierce and warlike than he? I couldn't see how he could fail to be. *I* was.

David would have ragged young Kenneth, he'd said. He'd have ragged him like I ragged Aldridge (though I did it behind his back, as befitted a coward).

The hooped toprails of the rusty ladder. The muted beat of waves against the sea wall. A coil of damp rope lying across the path.

'Though I walk through the valley of the shadow of death, I will fear no evil,' David said in melodramatic tones, 'for thou art with me.' Then he laughed lightly.

'I *am* with you,' I said, 'for all the good that'll do you. Here we are. Shakestown. Enter at your own risk.'

David, hands in pockets, stepped over the rope, humming softly to himself. His nonchalance was forced, of course; there was nothing to fear in Shakestown, he knew, and yet he felt afraid, because my fear, my terrible coward's fear, had transmitted itself from my heart to his. That was how it was between us.

'I see no murderers lurking in the dark,' he said, peering about him. 'I see no fleshpots. I see no opium dens.'

The serpent, I thought, is the most subtle of the beasts of the field. But I didn't say so – I had tired of our parlour game.

'Well, you wouldn't.'

'It's just a row of shacks, Lowell.'

'Yes. Did I say it was anything else?'

'You muttered darkly of painted Jezebels.'

'Yes, but they aren't permanent fixtures.'

'Hm.' David rolled an empty beer bottle under the sole of his shoe. 'You know,' he said, 'I could at this moment simply *devour* a plate of fried liv—'

A woman cried out. There was simply no doubting what sort of a cry it was. David and I looked at one another. He lifted an eyebrow theatrically.

'There she blows,' he said – and I thought instantly of Maurice Shakes, on the slick red deck of a whaler in the lee of the Falklands, vomiting up his faith as his comrade tumbled from the whale's gut.

'David—' I said, for of course I had recognised the voice. I wondered that he had not. Later I understood that of course he had.

He turned and took three purposeful strides in its direction, towards the far end of the terrace of buildings and lean-tos. I heard an ill-fitting door bang and bang again. Brief words in a man's voice and then she stepped out.

It all recalled my evening on the beach, with the sanderlings and the whore, and yet it was not the same, I was not the same, *she* was not the same.

Footsteps coming our way.

'David!' I shouted.

'Oh, shush, Lowell,' he snapped impatiently.

I'm not talking to you, *you damn fool*, I thought.

The footsteps hesitated. David havered uncertainly, poised on his front foot. Then they came on – she must have heard me, she had to have heard me, but she came on anyway. Her clothes were dark and her face pale, her mouth a fine black line, her eyes black marks, soot marks.

I shrank back. I stumbled, in fact, back across the rope, back out into the open. I looked out at the seal-grey sea. It offered me nothing. Beyond the harbour the black frame of the part-built pier bridged the sea to a distance of perhaps four hundred yards. I reached out and touched my fingertips to the stone of the sea wall.

'You did get my letter, then,' Cordelia said.

'I did,' said David. 'It – it piqued my curiosity.'

I could not stay. How could I stay? I could not leave. How could I leave David now, after all, with her, with Cordelia Shakes?

So it was that as night fell – a cold night, bitter, sharp with moonlight and salt sea spray – I was to be found high up on the sea wall, above the tin roofs, sitting with my knees drawn up to my chest, trying not to listen but listening, shivering, shuddering. There but not there. Gone but not gone.

Can't sleep. They won't let me alone. I close my eyes and all I see is dead James and poor dead Arthur Harrowell. I don't know which face is which any more.

I only met him once, I think. Just a how-do-you-do and a tip of the hat (he was wearing a boater, at this time of year!), on the coast road when I was out with Jon. A grinning, joking, frightened soldier boy.

Drowned, I suppose, in fixing pilings or riveting iron. Though I don't know; Jon never thought to ask.

Before we came to bed I laid out my clothes for tomorrow. Widow's weeds. Jon saw but said nothing. People'll think it's funny, if I see any people, but I may not, I may just stop at home. Widow's weeds for a daft Geordie lad I barely knew? Mad.

They were vulgar, for a while. I remember Mother saying so. For a time, with the war, it was as though everyone was in them. All the men in uniform and the country's womanhood swathed in crêpe. It lost, Mother said, its significance.

I don't see how it did, I don't see how anyone's grief is made any less by anyone else's, or even everyone else's. And besides that I don't give a damn. I'll wear widow's weeds tomorrow for Arthur Harrowell.

They were all in the war, Jon said. The men. They all fought. Arthur can hardly have been out of combinations so I don't suppose he did. But the rest.

That's not all, though. From what I've heard Peter Furlong's name is mud in Newcastle. Just whispers. Reading between the lines. I've letters from Consett, Newburn, Willington Quay. No one goes into detail but no one's got a good word to say. They all tell me I can put my trust in Newcastle iron, though. For what that's worth, coming from them.

I wrote to one of the union men. He told me they're a right crew, Mr Shakes's men. Time in prison, some of them. Deserters. Run out on their families. You don't have to be a saint to build a pier, to rivet together iron, I know that, just like there's not many saints in the fishing fleet, or anywhere really – anywhere where there's fellers. Even writers and rock poolers have their weaknesses, God knows.

Still, you wonder, don't you? It adds up.

Or else I'm just a gossip and a scold and no better than Mother. Here I am fancying myself one of those muckraking journalist sorts. But maybe I'm just a daft lass writing letters.

XXIII

'Who was it?'

The affected casualness, the forced air of the Bloomsbury bohemian well accustomed to maintaining a dozen love-affairs at a time, was plangently unconvincing.

'Not that it's your business, Mr McAllister—'

'*Mr McAllister*, is it, now?'

Either he couldn't hide his hurt or he could no longer be bothered to try. There was a short silence. Perhaps they whispered and I didn't hear. Perhaps they touched hands or kissed. The barred clouds were descending like a portcullis to the horizon.

'David.'

'I think it is my business. I think—'

'You could have made it your business.'

'Dammit, I—'

'You could still.'

That well-educated American voice (I had once thought it fearless) rang like a hammer on steel and multiplied the silence that followed.

David said something into the silence that I couldn't make out, but I heard the last word: 'Furlong.'

'You don't understand. You don't understand a thing.'

'You're bloody right, I don't. That bloody dirty scaffolder—'

I expected her to butt in with a correction, defend Furlong's professional reputation – 'He's a goddamn *architect*!' or something – but she didn't.

'Why?' David asked.

'Why what?'

'Why bring me back here, Cordelia? Why would you bring me back here and carry on – carry on *carrying on* with him, right in front of my face, right in front of everyone, with that—'

'Don't talk about him,' Cordelia said.

'—with that *bastard*. I mean, I'm no angel, I'm no monk.' I thought of the monks of Gravely Priory. 'I know how it is, really I do. This is the modern world and all that and I don't see why it should be any different for girls than it is for fellows, I mean with sex and things – but—' He stopped abruptly. I suppose the lipless face of Furlong had arisen before his eyes, rendering words impossible.

'You don't understand a thing.'

'You said that, darling.'

'Maybe you would, if – well, if you had a father like I have and a sister like I have. Maybe then you'd understand.'

'My father died.'

'I know. That's why you turned out so terrific and I—'

It was her turn to fall suddenly silent. Tears, I imagined. I wondered if David reached out to dry them with a handkerchief or if he just stood and watched her cry.

He murmured something that the noise of the waves obscured.

'It's too late,' she said.

Absurdly, it occurred to me that it *was* rather late – Harriet would wonder where we had got to, and the liver would be getting rubbery from over-cooking.

'For us?' – in the strangled voice of a character in a melodrama, which of course he was, as we all were.

'For me.'

'My God, anyone would think it was the bloody 1860s. You're not—'

'It's too late, David, for me to be the woman I should have been' – David began to say something rather heatedly but she carried on – 'for Eleanor's sake, for my sister's sake, David. Can you understand that?'

There was a long pause during which two waves rolled heavily against the sea wall.

'No,' David said.

If, in truth, I had ever been trying not to listen, I was doing no such thing now. I even leaned to my left, cocking my ear to these terrible voices of Shakestown. She had spoken of Eleanor; she had brought Eleanor into this. I ached and felt nauseated. The cold sea wind and the hard stone. Cordelia and Eleanor.

'It's too late for me to go to your pretty little seaside church and study the Bible with your ridiculous minister.'

'Well, why the devil would you want to?'

'It's too late for me to pretend I give a good goddamn about God and goodness. It's too late to pretend I care one bit, in this damn mess of a world, David, about who fucks whom.'

'Cordelia. Darling.'

'Because I don't, David, I simply don't. That's my father's gift.' She made a noise, a noise that began (I think) as a derisive laugh and as it filled with tears became more like a bird's cry, the cry of a crow or a gull. It was eerie. 'My inheritance,' she said.

'Your father's a freethinker,' David argued gently. 'I'm sure he's no saint, but I don't believe he's a wicked man.'

She snorted.

'You don't know a thing,' she said.

'I'm sure I don't.' He sounded nettled. How odd for David to be rebuked for naivety!

When, after a pause, Cordelia spoke again, the words came in a hurry, in an urgent clatter, thick with glottal sounds.

'Eleanor needed me to be the woman I ought to have been, and I'm not, I can't be – but the woman I *am* can't just watch Eleanor become what I became, and she doesn't know what the hell to do, I mean *I* don't know what the hell to do, except, except—'

Her voice tailed off, subsumed by David's ocean-like murmuring. Did he take her in his arms? I guessed that he did. Did he understand what she had said?

Did I?

It seemed so odd, so improbable, the idea that my dear Eleanor might come to speak, act, feel, think like Cordelia. They looked rather alike, and their voices weren't dissimilar, but beyond that, one would hardly have guessed them sisters.

Bile rose in my throat. Eleanor had kissed a married man, of course.

I fought an urge to reach down and knock with my fist on the corrugated iron roof below me: 'Are you talking about me? Do you mean *me*?'

The idea that she *wasn't* talking about me, that there was some other fellow somewhere leading Eleanor astray, didn't bear thinking about. If it occurred to me at all I instantly dismissed it.

David's murmuring went on for a little while. Then there was quiet. A tawny owl cried *ke-wick* from the trees beyond the road.

I heard David say: 'Now,' in a manly, authoritative tone. I pictured him taking Cordelia sternly by the shoulders (I remembered holding Eleanor by her shoulders over the rock pool as she laughed and dripped seawater). 'Now, darling. Talk to me. Tell me what you mean. Tell me what you need.'

'I need her to *see*,' Cordelia said. Her voice was tightly wound. 'I need Eleanor to *see*.'

'To see – what a fallen woman looks like?' Mockingly, now. But Cordelia must have nodded, in silence, because David snapped: 'Oh, for Christ's sakes.'

'I need her to see how ugly and rotten it is, because my God David it *is* ugly and rotten, when you're *in* it, when it's what you *are*, it's ugly and rotten and awful. It's not about it being *wrong*, my God, I don't even know what that means – but it's just *awful*, David, and she thinks it's so beautiful and splendid and wonderful, I know she does.'

'What the hell does she know about it?'

'My damn fool sister is in love with a married man,' Cordelia said with sudden acid clarity, 'and it's going to tear everyone apart.'

David paused. I wondered if he knew where I was – if he thought I'd gone home to Harriet, or if he guessed I was nearby, if he suspected I was eavesdropping from behind a lobster pot or in in the shadows of the Shakestown shanties.

My belly ached and my throat felt as hard and dry as stone.

'Eleanor,' David said firmly, 'can make her own mistakes.'

'Oh, really?' She laughed shakily. 'Do you know, David, how many mistakes a woman is allowed to make in this world of yours?'

'This is—'

'—the modern world, yes. O brave new world! Only it's the same, David, it's the same mean, hateful, vicious, brutal world it always was. Let Eleanor make her mistakes, see how the world treats her, see what you do to her.'

'I don't—'

'Oh, God, I don't mean *you*. Or maybe I do. Why not? It's all the same.' She gulped fiercely and a momentary whimper escaped her throat. 'My goddamn father, he's *made his own mistakes*, hasn't he, and see what that's gotten us! A crackpot fairground a thousand miles from home. Or Uncle Lawrence, my God. The fruits of our father's mistakes.'

'Your father, I gather, didn't see your uncle's indiscretion in such a bad light. The flowering of physical love between two young people, he called it.'

The words fell into a barren silence.

'The flowering—' Cordelia began thickly.

'Of physical love, yes. The kindling, if I remember rightly, of new life. Your father's words, on the day we met.'

In a cold voice Cordelia said: 'You don't believe my father is a wicked man.'

David hesitated. He knew the story, it seemed; he was reading ahead.

'I didn't, no. But I fear you're about to disabuse me of that notion.'

'That depends. You may still think him merely a freethinker.' A pause. 'I'll put it very simply. Grace Derbyshire *was* carrying a baby, but it wasn't Uncle Lawrence's. It was my father's. There you go.'

I could almost hear the typewriter keys rattle in David's head.

'He would have kept the child,' he said.

'He would! A child by his brother's intended. He'd have raised her as our sister.'

'Had she lived.'

'Yes. She died, I don't know how. It doesn't matter. She lived barely a week.'

'And Lawrence—'

'Sent to France, to war, to *die*, for my father's convenience. There's your freethinker, David.'

After a moment David said: 'The child is one thing. The child – forgive a writer's instinct – *fits*. But the brother. Lawrence.'

'Oh, don't kid yourself, David. My father proclaims pleasure to be his creed, but it's *his* pleasure he serves, and only his. Freethinking! Selfishness, that's his religion. Thou shalt have no other gods before Maurice Shakes.'

'I think,' David said slowly, 'I understand things somewhat better now.'

'But you *don't*, David!' A swallow, a half-sob. 'Because he's still here, isn't he? He's done all right, in spite of it all. Shakes is still standing. And where's Grace Derbyshire? For that matter, David, where am I?' She let out a juddering breath. 'Believe me, darling, because you'll never have to find it out for yourself – there's no vengeance in heaven or earth like the vengeance your world takes on a woman who makes mistakes.'

David, uncomfortable, I guessed, with the high emotional pitch, sounded somewhat bored when he said: 'It's not *my* world.'

'Oh of *course* it is,' Cordelia sneered.

In the quiet the sea bore down again and again on the sea wall and the shore, eating away at Gravely all the while, and a late starling flew in a flurry over my head, calling out alarms. My frozen hands shook in my pockets. My feet were numb, my buttocks dully sore from the stone.

Shakes was no less a god – for weren't all gods selfish, and weak, and wanton with human life? But a darker god, now; perhaps a more ancient god.

I sat shivering in the trade wind and listened to the silence below. It must have been dark down there. Were they kissing? Touching? In one another's arms? Staring coldly at one another? Did either weep?

David said: 'So you let Mr Furlong fuck you in a workman's shed because you fear Jon Lowell will break your sister's heart.'

Cordelia's laugh, while my stomach lurched, was helpless, hopeless, humourless and ended in a cracked sob.

'Something like that.'

I was saying to myself: *I shan't, I shan't, I shan't.* I promised that I wouldn't. Again, some might say that one can't make promises to no one. Or perhaps just that promises made to no one will not hold.

David kissed Cordelia. I'm sure he did – something in the sound of the silence, its texture and timing, told me so – and then Cordelia said: 'Save me.'

'I thought it was Eleanor who had to be saved?'

'Oh, God, I don't know, darling. I'm so tired.'

'Cordelia, my dear—'

'If you can't, I don't, I can't.'

I don't know if David said nothing or if he said something that I didn't hear.

'Please,' said Cordelia.

Again, in reply, the ambiguous quiet.

How's your landlady, Lowell? I don't know why I found myself thinking of that evening in Bradford so long ago. Because of the cold, perhaps. I thought of the girl in the hat and dark stockings, David's girl, whoever she was – I never saw her after that night. Did David break her heart? I expect he did. I wondered if anyone saved her, or if she even needed saving. Perhaps David saved her from something worse. I wondered if I saved Harriet, or if Harriet saved me.

I wondered what salvation even *was*.

'It's you, or—' Cordelia said.

David said: 'You can't *threaten* me, darling. With your unhappiness. Your ruin, even. You can't threaten me with it. It's not of my making, Cordelia. Can you see that?'

'For God's sake, David, I'm not threatening you. What I'm telling you is a fact. You can like it or not.'

'I don't like it.'

'Well, then, you can do something about it.'

'But *how*, for the love of God?'

I could picture it: David and Cordelia, arm in arm, boarding the train to London, he in a fine suit, she in a good hat, to marry (or not marry – it wouldn't matter), to live together scandalously, riotously, hilariously, the novelist and his American lover; I could *see* it, I could see their happiness, their complementarity—

And I wondered again about salvation. I wondered what the use of it was if, in saving the one, we lost the other.

'Do you want to – to come to London?' David said, as though with a great effort. 'With me?'

Well, of course she bloody does, you damn fool, I thought. I tried to picture Cordelia's face. I found I could only picture Eleanor's.

'David,' Cordelia said.

David could tell the story. Of Cordelia's heart, that is – David could see it, feel its struggles, delineate its many motions, tell its story. David's a writer. He could do it and perhaps one day he will.

'Come with me,' he said, with a sort of urgency, perhaps, even then, sensing, through her coat, her dress, her white skin and her ribs, the uncertain retreat of Cordelia's heart.

'But *then* what?' she said.

'Then – I don't know then what. But nobody knows *then what*.'

'It's all too rotten.'

'Cordelia, my dear, it's—'

'It's rotten and ugly and I can't bear it, David.' Cordelia drew in a long, ragged breath, making a sound like the cleansing withdrawal of a wave from the beach. Then: 'No. No.'

'No what?'

'David, I – when I asked you to save me—'

'I can, Cordelia. Just come away. No more father, no more Furlong. No more bloody Gravely. Just come away. It's all you have to do.'

David's sincerity was painful (because it was David's).

'It's too late. It's too late.'

'But why? Tell me why.'

'I think it was always too late. Right from the start it was too late. I shouldn't have brought you back here.'

'I'm glad you did.'

'You won't be.' A shuddering breath, perhaps the ghost of a laugh. 'You won't be, my darling. Damn this place. Damn Maurice Shakes. Damn you, my love – you can't help me, David. I thought you could but you can't. Damn you all. There: a pretty curse to end with.'

'End? But—'

I half-expected tottering footsteps, a vanishing wail and a terrible splash as Cordelia flung herself into the sea. I had been in something of a reverie, there on the sea wall with my head resting on my knees, frozen but absorbed, horridly absorbed in my eavesdropping; I had to remind myself that I was not listening from the flies during a stage melodrama, that these were real people whose hearts were breaking down there in dark Shakestown – that, for Christ's sake, it was David, my David.

Then there were footsteps: hers, not his, confident, or anyway loud and brisk and even-paced, headed north, away from him, and I heard him sigh, and sniff. I waited. He loitered on the spot. Another sigh. A word like 'ohh' or 'aye'.

Finally, in a low, embarrassed voice: 'Lowell?'

I unfolded my legs, stretched them, shivered. I was more aware than I had been of the drop to my left, to the sea. I waited. Why did I wait?

'Lowell?' David said again. More boldly, more bravely, this time. 'Come out, come out, wherever you are. You bastard.'

On my hands and knees I leaned down as best I could. My neck was cricked. I called: 'I'm up here. On the sea wall. David? I'm up here.'

There was a short, joyless laugh, then a bang, a scrape, a curse (another one), and David appeared, elbowing himself upwards, over the rusted edge of one of the iron roofs. It groaned beneath his weight. He looked up at me sourly. His face was so pale – but then faces in moonlight are always pale.

'You stupid sod. Communing with the seagulls?'

'I – I'm sorry,' I said.

'You heard all that rot, then? Well, there it is. I'm sorry you were exposed to it. Now come down, for God's sake. Unless you enjoy clinging to walls like a bloody limpet. Let's see about that fried liver.'

'Limpets,' I said, beginning to crawl back along the wall, 'cling to rocks, not walls.' I said it for form's sake, in aid (vainly) of the restoration of normality. David chuntered something at me – gratefully, I thought – and dropped from the roof.

When I rejoined him on the ground he slung an arm about my shoulders.

'There's always a certain satisfaction,' he said, 'in coming to the end of a chapter.'

'Even when the plot has taken a tragic turn.'

'Tragic? Come off it, Lowell.' He ruffled my hair. 'Come off it,' he said again.

That other memory from Bradford – at the college, at break-fast, that conversation of poor lost Mallory and Irvine. *We haven't got time to cry and wear black armbands, Jon, because we've got things to do ourselves.*

Yes, well, I thought now, as we walked home to Harriet and our ruined tea. There comes a time in life, I thought, a sort of tipping point where the things that you have to do *are* the things that you want to cry about. The same things. So how does one not cry?

Well, by not doing the things, I supposed.

To mollify Harriet we called into town and bought two par-cels of fish and chips. Harriet – who never much cared for liver, and bought it only because it was cheap – was duly appeased; the three of us ate, drank beer (Harriet had cordial), talked little, read until bedtime.

In the morning I worked dully at my microscope and David remained in bed. Harriet went out to the shops. She returned while we were having mid-morning coffee and announced sensationally that, by all accounts, Cordelia Shakes had run off in the night with the architect Peter Furlong. They had been seen boarding the milk train to Newcastle.

I looked at David. Harriet looked at me and then at David. David studied his coffee and drank a mouthful (though I had only just poured it from the pot, and it must have scalded him).

'Well, well,' he said. 'Bad news, I imagine, for the pier. I gather he was a sound architect.'

Then he laughed. He laughed like someone doing a very good impersonation of David laughing.

A face I didn't expect.

'Harriet. How do you do? Is – is Mr Lowell here?'

She holds her hands cupped in front of her as if she's praying. We've had many people come to the door in this way. Schoolboys mainly.

Did you not see him on the beach? I want to say. You must have passed him on the road.

'Good afternoon, Eleanor. No, I'm afraid Jon's out – working.' *Roll my eyes because of course, Mother, it's not real work, is it?* 'Can I help?'

'Oh, goodness, I don't know.' *She parts her cupped hands and I lean forwards to peer inside. In May I'd've bet you a pound to a penny I'd see a fledgling's gape, probably a baby blackbird, but it's February, and this is a mouse.*

Looks dead.

'Oh, dear me. Poor thing. Is it—'

'It's awfully cold.'

I usher her in, saying that we can perhaps give it a little warm milk, and anyway she should wash her hands. I'm wondering how long she wandered around looking for a dead thing to bring us. For a fraction of a second I wonder if she killed it herself.

In the kitchen Josephus the cat is noisily devouring the rubbery liver of the night before.

'I don't know how he stomachs it,' I say, kneeling to fetch a dish from the cupboard in which to lay the mouse. I line it with an old dishcloth and Eleanor puts the mouse on the cloth. She does it very gently even though she must know it's dead.

Josephus looks up from his clammy liver, and goes 'wiaowp' enquiringly.

'Not for you,' I say.

Eleanor's looking at the mouse as if it's going to do something. It's not, I'm quite sure. Its yellow front teeth are bared and its eyes are shut. It looks as if it's perishingly cold but I know from experience – two years as a naturalist's wife – that all dead things look like that.

We set the dish on the table beside the stove. I point her to the sink and soap, and I put the kettle on the hob. Prepare tea.

It's odd, this.

We say nothing much in particular until I pour the tea into the cups and then Eleanor, taking hers from the countertop, says: 'I'd like to know you better, Harriet.'

She blows on the tea.

'That's nice.' Smile as if it is nice. 'But why me, Eleanor?'

'Because,' she says, 'you're important.'

Am I? I had no idea.

'Shush,' I say.

We sit and talk. Josephus, sated with offal, curls up on the boards beneath my chair and sleeps. Eleanor asks me about my life, about where I come from – just about here, I say – and where I've travelled ('To Bradford,' I say, and explain where and what that is, and she laughs at me; I like that she laughs at me).

She tells me a little bit about America. No, not America; not like some boaster in a silly novel, arms flung wide: 'Wide open plains! Towering mountains! Verdant forests! Herds of buffalo!' Not about all that but about her home town, its people, its buildings, its birds; her school, her church. What she remembers of her mother (not much).

I tell her what there is to tell about Gravely. What I remember of my dad.

She watches as much as she listens, this one.

Then she goes from looking at me to looking at the wet tea leaves left in the bottom of her cup.

'I hope you're not going to read my fortune. That'd be embarrassing.'

'No.' Laughs, looks up. 'I like,' she says, 'to see clearly.'

I take her cup from her and put it with mine in the sink. I feel, as I run a bit of tapwater into the cups, that there's something I have to say or ought to say to her, some perfectly right thing. I can't get hold of it. That is, if it's there at all – if there even is such a thing.

'Does it help you think clearly?'

It's just a daft thing to say. But it's the right thing, too.

'Gosh, no.' She laughs, loud and throaty. 'I haven't found anything that helps with that.'

'Let me know if you do,' I say.

A little while after that, she goes. She leaves the dead mouse with me. I tip it into the bin (despite the keen interest of Josephus the cat) and sit down again on the second-best kitchen chair. Seeing clearly is something, I suppose. It's not quite being honest. It's a sort of one-way honesty, which I suppose is better than no honesty at all.

We didn't mention her sister once, it occurs to me.

I sit and listen to Josephus lick the last traces of the liver from his bowl.

XXIV

David went on a drunk, of course.

He retired to his room after coffee, and when at perhaps one o'clock I met him on the stairs he was noticeably tipsy. With a hand on his forearm I advised him to stay out of Harriet's way. He nodded carefully, and went out.

In his wake Josephus the cat circled in the hallway and mewed at me.

'Very well, sir,' I said. 'Come on, then.'

The cat followed me to the kitchen and I fed him some fish trimmings on a plate.

For the rest of the afternoon I worked: I dissected a beadlet anemone (*Actinia equina*), wrote a magazine article on the nesting habits of the ringed plover, composed two letters to scholarly journals on questions pertaining to *Crustacea* and *Chelicerata*.

Near teatime, Harriet came in. She was wearing a skirt of teal tweed and held an empty glass in her hand.

'On the booze, my love?' I said lightly (I was in the middle of an anatomical preparation).

To my surprise she stepped quickly to my chair and kissed me on the mouth, deeply and with intent. What was still more surprising was that she *had* been on the booze; I could taste it on her lips and tongue. Whisky?

'Why is my entire household steeped in spirits at four o'clock on a Thursday afternoon?' I asked, even as Harriet undid my fly buttons and I wiped preserving fluid from my hands with a cloth.

She didn't answer. We made love noisily and uncomfortably on the varnished boards of my study.

'*Jon*,' she cried, at one point, and it sounded somehow like a question, so I said 'Harriet, Harriet,' as though it were an answer (what else could I say?).

After, she kissed me and left the room. A few minutes later I heard her leave the house. Josephus the cat sidled into the study and I leaned down and scratched his little scalp. I never saw Harriet again.

*

Strolling south on the coast road a little later in the day, watching for oystercatchers and thinking about Shakes, Cordelia, Furlong and David, I saw Job Wakenshaw, the stout and godly timber-dealer, coming the other way. I touched my hat brim politely, not expecting him to stop (we had not met since my gaffe about Christ walking on the waves).

'Mr Lowell,' he said, stopping abruptly and touching his own hat (an ill-fitting trilby).

I sought a little desperately for small talk, and of course there was only one decent subject for small talk: the long finger of sea-sprayed black iron thrusting out from the north bay behind me.

'How go the great works, Mr Wakenshaw?'

He disliked my flippant tone, and glared a bit, but evidently the man was feeling full of himself.

'Passing well, sir, passing well. My boards go down today upon the pier ironwork.' He smiled in a hard way. 'You will smell the forest as you stand beside the sea. It is one of the joys of laying timber, Mr Lowell. The smell of sap and split wood. It transports you.'

Fearing that he was growing poetical, and somewhat – again – forgetting myself, I gestured to the pub from which I assumed he had come and said jovially: 'Celebrating the occasion with a drink? Why not!'

I suppose I should add that after my unexpected intimacy with Harriet I had had a glass of whisky myself. More so as not to feel left out than for any restorative purpose.

Job Wakenshaw's complexion darkened a shade.

'No, Mr Lowell. Mr Holroyd had sent word that he requires timber for new storm boards. I was measuring the apertures in question.' He produced a sprung metal tape measure and twanged the tape rebukingly at me. 'I do not imbibe, sir. *Wine is a mocker, strong drink is raging, and whosoever is deceived thereby is not wise.*'

Of course I was on him at once.

'Proverbs twenty.'

'You know your holy book, sir.'

'I do.' I licked my lips, and added: 'But to me, Mr Wakenshaw, I fear it is not holy.' I touched my hat again. 'A good afternoon to you.'

As I walked on I marvelled at myself. Of course my general lack of Christian piety was well known in the town, but had I ever gone so far before? I thought not. I didn't know if I was a freethinker but in any case I felt liberated. This is Shakes, I told myself. This is Shakes's doing.

But which Shakes?

*

At six I found David. There was no great art to my finding him. He was in Holroyd's pub. There were four fishermen at the bar, and a young man and his girlfriend at the table by the window. The massive Holroyd brother manned the bar and greeted me with a purse-lipped nod. David was at a table in the far corner, facing the wall.

'Good afternoon,' I said, joining him.

He didn't look at me. He wasn't looking at anything.

'It's you, of course,' he said.

'Yes, 'fraid so. How goes the racket?'

'Well, I'm drunk,' David nodded, 'so in that respect it's going terrifically well.'

'And in other respects?'

He wobbled a hand held horizontal to the table.

'Only so-so.'

'You're brooding.'

'Well, of *course* I'm fucking brooding, Lowell.'

I remembered that crack about black armbands and said: 'I suppose life goes on.'

'Life. *Life*. Life,' David said, and laughed. At last he looked at me. His blue eyes wavered with a drunk's strabismus. 'Speaking of life, how's your wife?'

In conversation with drunks one expects non sequiturs.

'Very well,' I said. He missed the impishness in my tone.

'That's life, isn't it, that's your precious life all over. A wife, a very-well wife in a little house by the seaside full of jellyfish and lobsters. That's a man's life, Lowell, isn't it, Lowell, a life for a man.'

Holroyd brought me a glass of beer I had not asked for. I thanked him and paid him and took a mouthful.

'Where is she?' David said.

'Now? I don't know. She was out when I left. Paying a call or something, I imagine.'

He gurgled.

'I haven't forgotten, Lowell,' he smiled, unpleasantly.

I drank more beer. I hadn't forgotten either.

'Dear Harriet and Mr Christ-on-the-Cross the vicar, at Bible study without a single Bible to their name, not a scrap of Scripture between them, I've not forgotten it, Lowell.'

'Most scholars know a great deal of the Bible by heart. I do, and I'm not even a vicar.'

'And the housekeeper, that funny old bird, how *odd* she was when you turned up. I saw that, that wasn't missed, that was *significant*, I thought, Lowell.'

'I know you're drunk, David, but—'

'Oh, I know.' He nodded, or in any case his head lolled on his neck. 'I'm overstepping the mark. I'm taking a jolly old liberty. I'm sorry, Lowell, I am, but anyway.' He took a slurp of whisky. 'The interesting thing is from a dramatic perspective, that is, *my* perspective, Jon, as a thrilling and bold young novelist, Jon – which one of them do you doubt?'

'Harriet is my wife.'

I said it and I knew how weak it sounded. The words on my tongue felt as fragile as a wafer.

'And you're her jolly old husband.' He laughed throatily. 'And *he's* a jolly old vicar, for Christ's sakes. Literally and figuratively for Christ's sakes. You'd think you could trust at least *one* of them, wouldn't you, but there it is.'

I should of course have ignored him. Ignored him or taken him outside and had a fight with him.

'David, I—'

'Jon.' He slapped a hand on the tabletop. 'My God, Jon Lowell, you're my friend – are you my only friend? – you're my *only friend*, Jon Lowell, you bloody ragworm, and I'll not stand here or sit here and watch you be made a bloody fool out of.'

I was the boy who was bad at games. I was the funny man racing pink-faced to the shore with binoculars and rock-pooling net.

'A fool?'

'We're all fools, Jon, we're all fools,' David said largely, with a gesture.

If there'd been anybody there that I wanted to fight, I would have fought them. If there'd been anybody there but David and Holroyd and the fishermen and the young man with his girl. I would have fought Maurice Shakes, I think. I would have fought Aldridge. I would have fought Furlong.

It's terrible when one feels that one would fight if one could fight but one can't. I drank my beer, *dragged* at it, took it into my throat like a sinkhole.

*

Earlier in the day – between Job Wakenshaw and David McAllister (this was a day of meetings as well as of partings) – I had encountered the Welshman Wyn James. I was at the top of the beach, idly birdwatching; he was passing by. He hailed me: 'Good Mr Lowell!'

He was dishevelled, red-faced, sweaty despite the biting wind.

'You haven't been fighting?' I asked, bewildered, and he laughed.

'Only with missus nature,' he said. 'She's a rough one, Mr Lowell, never gives a man a fair chance. But we got her down, at the last. We got the wood laid and lashed. Your pleasure grounds have their pier.' Another laugh. 'Your Mr Shakes has his folly.'

Not just a prize fighter, not just a war hero and a pub singer, of course, of course. This Wyn James was one of the men. I wondered at my own stupidity. Of course, a man must work; a prize fighter's purse must go only so far. Would a rich man – a man with Jack Dempsey's half-million – travel from the valleys to Gravely to be beaten senseless by an Italian half his age? No, he had come here to work; prize fighting, I supposed, paid his bill at the bar, and pier-building did the rest.

I ventured a question I had not dared ask Job Wakenshaw.

'I hear your Mr Furlong has left us.' I said it without the least wink or nudge, thinking *poor Cordelia!* (and thinking, then, what a strange thing that was to think). 'Has this not impaired progress?'

Wyn pushed out his lower lip and shook his head.

'No, no, we've a good bunch of lads, a smart bunch of lads,' he said. 'Pete Furlong left us his plans and measures in any case.'

'I'm glad he won't be missed.'

'You're right, he won't.' He made a face. 'Far as I could tell he was a sound architect, he knew his iron and his steel – but that's only as far as I could tell, Mr Lowell, and I can't tell very far, being only a labourer, only muscle.' He grinned again, and flexed his arm, so that his biceps bulged against the fabric of his coat. 'Yes, he knew his trade – but I'm afraid the war did something to him.' He gave me a knowing look that made me feel older than I was (older than I am now). 'Of course the war did something to us all, Mr Lowell. But to our Mr Furlong – well, I don't know. Something in his mind. Or something in his soul, if you're that way inclined.'

I told him with a polite smile that I was not that way inclined and he said ah, well, then, it must have been just his mind, then, just the poor soul's mind.

*

'I'm bloody furious for you, Jon,' said David. 'On your behalf. I'm livid, do you hear me? You poor damp cold sea creature, Lowell. In your place I'd have beaten that damn preacher black and blue.'

'In my place you'd never have got married.'

'No, and wouldn't have had a cat, either, wouldn't have had one in the house. But this, I would not have stood for, Jon, this I could not have borne.'

Harriet was a good wife. I loved her. I was proud that she was my wife and proud that I loved her.

'David, you had better stop now, I think.'

I was beginning to feel the effects of the beer (I was on a second or third glass) on top of the whisky I had drunk earlier.

'Stop? I'll tell you who had better stop, *she* had better stop, *he* had better stop. Damn it all, Jon, you ought to stop them. To think of all that bloody rot about you and Eleanor. You were going to ruin her life, or she was going to ruin yours, or some fucking thing, I don't know, I don't remember.' *Yes you do*, I thought. 'I'll tell you who's ruining whose life, Jon. It's not that little Eleanor thing. It's not you, Jon, it's not you, I'll tell you, it's not, it's not.'

'David, please—'

'It's *them*,' he hissed. His bulging eyes would have been amusing in different cicumstances. 'Them,' he said, 'with not a Bible between them. You tell me where she is now, Jon Lowell, and I'll shut up. You tell me where she is now.'

*

Mary's story? The story of Aldridge's odd maid? I had probably heard many versions of it; such are a small town's stories. Her husband – some years younger than her – had gone to the war, and been killed, I never heard where. There had been a liaison with a visiting man, a salesman or civil official, or something of that sort. Scandalous in itself, of course. But what compounded her crime was her failure to ensure that her husband was properly dead before falling in love with the salesman. It was said that the fellow had been seen leaving her house – no, her *husband's* house – on the morning the telegram boy arrived with the black-edged telegram.

I wondered about her story. I wondered about all the stories, the monks at the priory, the murder of the boatbuilder's boy, all of them, and this one, too – mine, hers, his, ours, I don't know whose. The story of the rock-pooler's wife. The story of the minister's passion. The story of the fat American's fairground.

All of these stories made a noisy discord in my head as I pushed past Mary into Aldridge's hallway.

'Mr Lowell, please!'

'She's here, isn't she?'

He appeared in the parlour doorway, in shirtsleeves, tall and spare as a cricket bat, russet beard bristling, the glare of his spectacles hiding his eyes of innocent blue. He told Mary to go away; she cavilled and he told her again, in ringing be-sure-thy-sin-will-find-you-out tones, and she went.

'What has happened?' he demanded.

'A great deal, Mr Aldridge, a great deal!' I may have shaken my fist at him. Absurd, absurd.

He eyed me as if from a great height, though he was barely taller than me.

'You had better come in, Mr Lowell,' he said. 'I will have Mary make tea, if you wish, and we can talk.'

'I don't want tea.'

'Ah, well, I am accustomed to a cup at this hour – so I shall just ask Mary to make some, and then I shall join you.' He indicated the parlour door with an open palm. 'Please,' he said.

I was – what was I? Disarmed, perhaps, but then I had been disarmed when I arrived, when I had left David in the pub, I had been disarmed all along, I had always been disarmed. Or rather I had never been armed. I had always been defenceless.

I sat obediently on a chair in the parlour and studied the grain of the floorboards. The floorboards put me in mind of that afternoon. I had to close my eyes and think: *yes, yes it* was *only this afternoon*. The inner bone of my left elbow was bruised. My shoe heel had left a half-moon scuff on our floorboards.

Aldridge joined me with beads of tea in his moustache and a cup in his hand. He seated himself opposite me and held the cup one-handed in his lap.

'What has happened, Mr Lowell?' he asked me again.

I felt like a schoolboy. I ought to have felt like a bully.

'Where,' I said, 'is my wife.'

There was no need for an interrogative note. It was, after all, a statement: a statement that I did not know where my wife was, and that I believed he did.

He was watching me rather closely.

'At home?' he suggested gently. 'Or at her mother's, perhaps?'

It only occurred to me later that either of these things might for all I knew have been the case. I hadn't been home for some hours; I hadn't been to her mother's, to Mrs Holloway's, at all.

I think somehow I felt that that was beside the point. I thought constantly of the Bible-less Bible study. I felt that what I was seeking was – to frame it as Aldridge might have understood it – a deeper truth.

'No,' I said.

'Have you checked?'

'I don't need to.'

Aldridge smiled slightly.

'The just shall live by faith,' he said.

'Don't talk to me about justice,' I said. I lifted my hand to my face to scratch an itch there and found to my surprise that I was not scratching an itch but wiping away a tear.

'What would you rather I talked to you about?'

'I don't know. What do you talk to Harriet about?'

'Faith. Fear. Sin. Weakness.'

'Me?'

'Sometimes.'

'You must laugh your bloody heads off.'

Aldridge lifted his chin and as the reflected light shifted on his spectacle lenses I saw his blue eyes slowly widen. He blinked. Then he lowered his chin to his chest. His beard crumpled against his shirt front and his eyes vanished again behind the light.

'Perhaps I have been naive,' he said.

'I don't doubt it,' I replied sharply – but I felt uncertain.

'You think I'm a hypocrite.'

'I know you're a hypocrite.' I swallowed down the hardness in my throat and tried to master myself. 'I remember the woodcock.'

I expected him to look puzzled, or to stare at me as though I were mad, or perhaps to smile horribly and ask: 'How much have you had to *drink*, Mr Lowell?' But he didn't. He inclined his head forwards a little.

'I remember it, too.'

'You—'

'It pained me, Mr Lowell.' Now he smiled, showing his small white teeth through the trailing hairs of his moustache. 'It pains me still. You don't believe me? I tell you it's true.' He took a drink of tea, looked out of the black study window which now showed clean-edged streaks of rain, looked back at me. 'I am not blind to suffering,' he said. 'I was indeed the boy who, as you heard, spent a long, sad day on the sands washing a beached whale with seawater – in vain, alas. And I still *am* that boy.'

'That bird meant nothing to you.'

'Other things meant more.' He removed his spectacles and bathed me in his blue gaze. Judging by the thickness of his lenses I don't suppose he could make out much of me across the three or four yards that separated us, but the gaze – and the high, white, troubled forehead and, by God, even the trembling auburn beard – unnerved me nonetheless.

'Dignity.'

'Sanctity.'

I wondered that he could say it – that anyone could say it – with such seriousness.

'The sanctity,' he went on, 'of the burial rite, of a man's transition from this life to the next, of a man's rebirth in Christ.' He replaced his spectacles. 'These obligations matter, Mr Lowell. Perhaps they matter more than anything. Not just in death, but in life, too.' The blue eyes glared briefly. 'Think of marriage, for instance.'

'That's bloody rich.'

'Marriage—'

'You wouldn't know a bloody thing about it.'

Aldridge leaned down, nodding vaguely, and placed his half-empty teacup on the floor. Then he sat back in his chair and folded his hands over his belly.

'We were not,' he said, 'discussing a point of Scripture.'

This was the breaking of the wave I had been waiting for. How long had I been watching its dark swell, feeling in my blood and skin its deep approach? My gut turned to salt water. I gaped, and struggled to breathe.

'Except in the most oblique sense,' the minister added, watching me closely. 'Except in the sense that all discussions are discussions of Scripture.'

'A – a tryst, then,' I managed to stammer.

I thought he might strike me. He wanted to, I was sure. I waited for him to snatch up his stick. His folded hands gripped each other.

'Mr Lowell, I see that you are in some distress,' he said. 'But I will ask you to remember that I am a man of the cloth.' He watched me some more and then, when I failed to answer, when I simply sat there like a drowned man, he said: 'In return, I will tell you the truth.'

I smiled weakly.

'Will it set me free?'

He didn't have an answer, or, if he did, he didn't give it. He held up a forefinger, and then quietly left the room.

*

A leather folder lined with green canvas, a little scuffed at one corner. Inside, papers: typed correspondence, newspaper cuttings, handwritten notes in Harriet's hand (loose, wiry, brisk – almost hasty).

I looked up at Aldridge and found that he was smiling on me with a benignity I found powerfully offensive.

'There are several more,' he said.

'What the hell is it?'

'Her work.'

'What the hell do you mean, her work?'

He would not be provoked by my profanity. He gestured, smiling and silent, at the folder.

I lifted out the first sheet in the sheaf.

Dear Mrs Lowell

I stared at my own name. Lowell. The third 'l' was somewhat faint on the page. It was strange to read my own name – Harriet's name, of course, but my own name, too, my own name *first* – and not know why I was reading it.

It was not a long letter. *Entrepreneurial spirit. Terrible tragedy. Competence and rigour. Groundless concerns. Every confidence. Sidney Makepeace, MP.*

I looked from the letter to Aldridge and from Aldridge to the next sheet in the folder, which was covered over with pencilled calculations of some sort – feet, tons, degrees.

'Harriet did this?'

'Indeed.'

'What—' I shuffled awkwardly through the pages. More letters, some drafted in pencil in Harriet's hand, some typed (some addressed to *Mrs Lowell*, some – many more – carbons of Harriet's own letters, to a Mr Longshank at the Admiralty, a Mr Middleton on the town council, a Mr Corke-Bennett on the Committee for Public Safety, a Mr Slatters at the Constructional Engineering Union; to the *Times*, the *Chronicle*, the *Courant* – in snatches I read of 'grave danger', 'public well-being', 'sound construction', 'flawed design'). 'What is it? Is it to do with – has it to do with Mr Shakes?'

I was being, I suppose, obtuse. Aldridge nodded, his fool's beard wagging gently.

'Mr Shakes's enterprise on the seafront, yes,' he said.

'She has been trying to stop it?'

Again the gentle, encouraging nod – as though I were a not-very-bright Sunday schoolboy, stumbling his way through the sons of Jacob or the inheritance of Manasseh.

'Your wife and I formed,' he said, 'a sort of union, I suppose.'

I might have struck the man then. That is, if I were going to strike him, that was when I would have done it. I didn't, of course. He must have seen my Adam's apple bob in my throat or my eyebrows pinch together, or discerned some other pusillanimous sign of warning, because he then said: 'Perhaps not a union. A united front, rather. A coalition in pursuit of a common goal.'

'Harriet had nothing against the pleasure grounds.'

I glanced down again at the file. The papers had fallen open to disclose a newspaper clipping. 'Great Tragedy on the Bure.'

'Quite, Mr Lowell, quite,' simpered Aldridge. He turned from me, adjusted the sit of his trousers with a fastidious tug and lowered himself into one of the straight-backed chairs. He crossed his legs in a show of ease that I did not find convincing. 'Will you sit? It will make it easier to handle the papers.'

'I've seen enough of the bloody papers.'

'There are many more. Two more files full.'

'She'd no objection to the damn scheme. The funfair and so on. Even the pier. She couldn't see the harm.'

'In spite of my best efforts, yes,' Aldridge said. He shifted slightly, without, I thought, really meaning to – something shifted in his upper body, his chest and shoulders, something in him, something *structural*, seemed to stiffen or strengthen, and he said, 'It's a wicked and a sinful undertaking, Mr Lowell; a folly, yes, but a wicked folly, a godless and mocking foolishness. It speaks to the weakness of man, not his strength; it calls out, this risible Babylon, to his baseness, to the baseness in us all. These toys, these dancing mannequins – these low, low, loathsome things.' He paused, pressed his lips together, let out a breath that was almost a whistle. Then he glanced at me over his spectacles and his moustache stirred almost playfully. 'But I could not, for all my ardour, persuade Mrs Lowell of this.'

Good old Harriet, I thought, like a loyal bloody fool.

I lifted the folder. A couple of loose leaves fell to the floor.

'What's this, then? You talked her into it, I suppose – against her better judgement.'

'I was, I *am*, concerned for men's souls,' he said. 'Your good wife, Mr Lowell, was and is concerned for—' Again he hesitated. I suppose he was about to say *men's bodies*, or something like it – he hesitated, in any case, and said: 'For, let us say, the corporeal salvation of the townspeople.'

It was the newspaper clipping that had drifted to the floor. I bent, and picked it up. *Dreadful Accident at Yarmouth. Great Loss of Life.* May, 1845. I dimly remembered Harriet, or Mrs Holloway, speaking of it – a great-uncle, or a second cousin, was present, or almost present, or lost.

I was conscious that I *could*, had it been necessary, have recalled the inheritance of Manasseh (for the children of Abiezer, and for the children of Helek, and for the children of Asriel, and for the children of Shechem), but I could not for the life in me remember anything more about the Holloways and Yarmouth.

The fine newsprint said something about iron, and something about iron founders.

I looked up at Aldridge.

'And so,' he said, 'though our motivations differed, our object was the same, and thus' – he touched the pads of his fingertips together unpleasantly – 'we came to work together, against the common enemy.'

He meant Shakes, of course. He did not mean me.

'A plot, then.'

'Of sorts.' Aldridge beamed.

'But it failed.'

'Did it, Mr Lowell?'

'Well, there's a damn big pier poking out into the sea and so yes, I should say so.'

'Would you be pleased, had we failed?'

That 'we'.

'You still hope to thwart the man? What will you do, dynamite the bloody pier?'

'Mrs Lowell, your wife—'

'I know who she bloody well is.'

'Your wife believes that he may yet be reasoned with. She has grave doubts concerning the pier, you see – its, its *structural integrity*, and suchlike. She believes Mr Shakes will in the end yield to what she calls "hard facts".'

'And you? Do you think Mr Shakes will yet yield?'

'I pray that he will.'

'Oh, well, then the thing's in the bag,' I said, less lightly, more bitterly, than I had meant to.

'You have not,' Aldridge said, 'answered my question.'

He was right. Would I be glad, were some government inspector to close the project down, to still the whirligigs and rope off the pier, over this-or-that infringement of this-or-that ordinance or by-law, some minor breach of Section something of the Such-and-such Act? It would seem a painfully ill-fitting end to a project like this – to a mission like this, for a man like Maurice Shakes. What then, if instead Mr Shakes were to fall dramatically dead, struck down (by a heart attack, as with the publican Holroyd, or a stroke or aneurism – or by a lightning bolt, flung by a laughing God) as he was poised before a great crowd to hammer home the final rivet in the pier, or cut the ribbon on the helter-skelter? What then? It would at least be a gripping conclusion to the drama.

I would not be glad. It would, I think, be a relief, an enormous relief.

'It would make no odds to me,' I told the minister, more or less honestly. Then I said: 'I should like my wife to be happy.'

'Of course, of course,' said Aldridge, and in his reedy, canting tone I heard a deep sea of meaning.

*

I left him. I left him to his damn folders and files and letters and carbons and tragedies clipped from newspapers and his 'we' and his 'union' and his damn smiling 'Mrs Lowell'. That busy ghost Mary held the door for me. The weather on the coast road was turning fierce, the easterly air wet and turbid. I felt rather sober – rather *too* sober. I wanted to drink but did not want to face David. 'You were vanquished!' he might cry, rising and pointing. 'Vanquished by that queasy cleric, Lowell, that tufted equivocator, that bearded jellyfish. Sent packing' – he might laugh – 'by the vile and creeping Vicar of Gravely!' Or whatever else it might be. And what could I say in reply? 'You were mistaken, old man. Mr Aldridge met with my wife only to pen letters to Parliament, to discuss load-bearing limits, to consider, you see, the corporeal safety of the townspeople...'

I did not want to face him, and he would still, I was sure, be at Holroyd's. Instead I walked to the top of the bluff, and there stopped.

It's a sorrowful thing to sit on the grass in the dark and look at the yellow-lit windows of a warm pub. I turned my back to Holroyd's, and faced across the bay, blinking in the sea weather. I could not tell the noise of the sea from the noise of the wind. A white bird – a fulmar, I thought, by its pinched-off nose and starched-stiff wings – drifted by in the darkness; I felt I might almost have reached out and grabbed it, it flew so near, but I knew that the bluff edge fell away not far in front of me, and in this gloom it would have been folly to move far.

It was, of course, not far from this spot that I had kissed Eleanor Shakes, or that she had kissed me. I thought about her, and her father, and Mr Aldridge, and my wife. I looked at the pier, from here a thumb's-length of black in the charcoal dusk, a darkness within the darkness.

He *had* vanquished me, of course. I had without the least doubt made a silly fool of myself in Aldridge's drawing room and he had seen me off pretty smartly. He had not, I suppose, in the circumstances, been unmerciful.

I wondered what, if anything, he would say to Harriet. *There was a rather amusing misunderstanding with Mr Lowell...* No. Not 'amusing', for all his smirks and simpers. *I had a rather unfortunate conversation with your husband. Mr Lowell had fallen prey to the most lurid of misconceptions.* I would come out of it looking a damn jealous drunken ass, in any event, which of course was nothing but my just deserts.

I hadn't asked the only question to which I'd really wanted to know the answer. I was glad I hadn't.

Why didn't she tell me?

I couldn't have asked that of the Reverend Aldridge – I couldn't have had him guessing at the answer as he stroked his beard with his fingertips, and the cursed Mary hovering behind the door all the while.

I suppose she thought I would laugh. I don't suppose she was wrong.

If it were someone else (someone else's wife) – Louisa Hesketh, say – I should certainly have let drop a few irreverent remarks. Civil-engineering seminars with Saint Hugh of Withy Passageway? I should certainly have laughed.

I lifted my left hand and, with my own white thumb held sideways, blocked the pier from view. When I lowered my hand I seemed to see lights on the pier, two (I thought), in motion, slowly intervolving, like the lit bulbs of female glow-worms. I blinked and looked away.

Perhaps she thought I would laugh or that I would not understand. Perhaps she thought that I – closeted with my limpets, my crabs, my killing jar – simply would not be interested and would not spare the time to listen. Perhaps my Harriet thought it was unwomanly, or unwifely, to do as she had been doing – all these letters to strange men (for they were, I imagine, all men).

In fact, I realised, shivering on the bluff, it did not much matter to me which of these was the case. What mattered was that I did not *know* which of them was the case. I did not know. She was my wife.

I climbed falteringly to my feet, feeling the emptiness, the vacancy, before me, beyond the bluff edge. I may indeed have reached out a hand, as if to take a fistful of it. I took a few steps westwards and when I was standing more or less on the spot where Eleanor Shakes and I had kissed that night I said out loud, 'I am sorry, Harriet,' without saying what I was sorry *for* (it might have been so many things) – but I was sorry most of all, I think, for that not knowing, which I felt violently in my stomach.

This idea that there was some *thing* between us – a pane of smoked glass, a yard of fog – that Harriet could see and I could not – I found this hard.

I looked once more into the pit of the bay and at the pier and again saw or seemed to see two lights amid the thickening weather, now three-quarters or four-fifths of the way along the pier, appearing to twinkle (not glow-worms now but twin stars). Mr Shakes's hard-pressed workers toiling late, chasing a relentless schedule; rascally boys on a perilous exploration; bold sweethearts in search of a secret place.

I did not care for this last idea. In any case I was no longer thinking much about the damn silly pier. I buttoned my coat and took to the coast road, headed for Shakestown.

*

The rainstorm blowing in off the sea nearly bowled me off my feet as I ran, cold, chafed, struggling to breathe, from the shelter of the sea wall and across the boxing ring. Ahead, to my left, the part-assembled things of the fairground, laid about like brass instruments abandoned by their band, muttered and rumbled beneath the rain. Beyond all this, beyond all that was left of our lonely heath and shingle beach, were the houses of the north bay, and Maurice Shakes.

I had had the notion, I think, that I would come to Shakestown and there find Shakes himself, half-lit by lightning or St Elmo's fire, howling like a devil among the bars of scaffold, on the sea wall shaking a fat fist at God, calling to the whales, reeking of whisky and sin. Of course there was no one. In the darkness I had trodden on a discarded beer bottle and staggered, thumping my shoulder into a scaffolding pole, and all the iron of Shakestown, which was already roaring in the rain, had roared louder, as though angry. I had fallen to all fours as a snakes' nest of cold wet rope tangled my feet. Grit burned my palms; my shin was nastily barked.

I stumbled onwards (as I have done so very, so terribly often).

I did not know what I hoped to do with Mr Shakes when I found him. I don't know now what I hoped to do and so I suppose I shall never know. To seize him by his broadcloth lapel and say – what?

'Do as my wife says', perhaps. His laughter at that would drown out the storm.

I was, I think, still jealous. It was not the mad satyric jealousy that David had somehow stirred up in me (my Harriet, and him, *Hugh*: the idea now seemed beyond mad, fantastical, a drunk's dream or a Maurice Shakes vision); I was jealous now – and no less stupidly – of Harriet's privacy, her confidentiality, which ought to have been only mine and hers, but had instead, it seemed, been shared out with Aldridge, and Shakes, and dozens – hundreds? – of others. Had they been nearby, those others, those aldermen and safety inspectors, those gentlemen of the press, that fat MP, those damned *correspondents* of hers, well, I should have liked a strong word with them, too – but so far as I knew they were not nearby; there was only Maurice Shakes, and so it was after Maurice Shakes that I went, lost and weeping amid the unbuilt fairground rides.

I would, I thought, be having strong words with Harriet, too, when I got home (or when she got home). I wondered what they would be. I remember wondering if I would still feel sorry.

The breaking waves surged over the path and I danced preposterously as the seawater soused my shoes and socks. In the wild darkness a bell – some part of a whirligig or carousel – rang a cheerful, tinny diphone, over and over. And then when she appeared, picking her way towards me through the rushing surf, I almost laughed. I felt myself begin to laugh, and thought: *you have gone mad, old fellow – you have lost your mind, Jon, old man*, as the silly bell rang and rang.

It took her some time to see me. She was concentrating on finding her way (and I was glad of it – the muddy shore was not safe. In fact I called out to her: 'Take care!' but over the sea and rain and wind she didn't hear).

'Jon?'

She was barely twenty paces from me. Her white face was scalded pink by the weather. A bonnet was bound tightly about her head and its knotted ribbons flailed in the wind.

My first instinct was to run to her (I pictured myself as she would have seen me, in my heavy, drenched clothes, splashing clumsily through the breakers) and – what?

I didn't run to her. I waited, panting, on the swirling path, until she came to me, and then I grabbed her by the shoulders, and shook her. *Where is he?* I cried.

Her gaze was steady enough. She laid her hands on my forearms.

'Who? What's the matter?'

'Him.'

'Do you mean—'

'Your father, Eleanor, your bloody father,' I shouted, and let go of her shoulders, and turned, exasperated, to face the sea. Salt air tore through me. I thought, fleetingly, wildly, of birds overhead, driven ahead of the gale, stars blotted out, the world askew. I heard her say, 'I'm looking for him.' Then she took my arm, her hand folding hard inside my elbow, and close to my ear she said: 'My gosh, it's so *exciting*, isn't it?' One of her ribbons lashed my cheek.

I don't think I was excited.

*

The muddy breakers shuddered the beach, and further off, the waves of the true ocean made a bass thunder against the sea wall.

I helped her, almost dragged her, with my arm about her waist, the little way from the shore to the boxing ring, and together we hunched behind the wall where, weeks before, I had held her hand in the secrecy of her skirts.

'Where is he?' I asked again. 'Why are you looking for him?'

She said she'd had word from a crabbing boat (or so it called itself) just come in up the coast, some rogue from the cottages beyond the north bay, that worse weather was blowing in, and quickly – word had come in, via the slipway, the backyard wall, the Shakes's landlady, a Mrs Tice, that it was no night to be out on the front – no night, Mrs Tice said, to be out at all.

'I think he thought it would be tremendous *theatre*.' Eleanor was almost smiling. 'He has a meeting. With some *campaigner*. Public safety or temperance or something, I'm not sure. Some concerned citizen.'

'Harriet.' Again I looked to the sea; I looked out, east, into the darkness, and then back over my shoulder. I could see the pier. I could no longer see the lights. 'Eleanor, your father is with my wife.'

And for a moment her face lost all its expression, like a face falling into a sneeze; and then it folded gently into something like pity, and I saw that she had taken me to mean something else entirely. *That* must have happened before, and I wondered when and where – some whaler's wife at New Bedford, perhaps, or the wives of stilt-walkers or hotdog sellers at Coney Island.

'I mean – I mean Harriet is the concerned citizen. Harriet is the campaigner.'

A funny thing to say – a funny thing to hear myself say.

Eleanor looked as though I had slapped her, or said a foul word or bared my behind.

'They're on the pier,' she said. For they were, of course.

*

I wondered about Maurice Shakes; I wondered why he had come here, why he was who he was (or tried to be) – what he was fighting for, or fighting against. What the hell he *wanted*.

'They'll be on their way back, if they're not back already.' Her right knee was pressed hard against my left as we crouched in the wall's inadequate lee.

'That bloody fool.'

'Mrs Lowell's a smart lady. She knows—'

'She should have damn well known—'

'It's getting worse. Jon, it's getting—'

'I'll go and fetch them. I'll—'

There was a lurch in the earth, in the fabric of the earth. Eleanor's right hand closed reflexively on mine, her left snatched at my coat. There was a new note in the braying, groaning organ-chord of weather and sea. With my hand in Eleanor's I stood, and as I stood the noise met me like a wave.

Such was its volume, its vastness, that I at first thought that the bluff across the bay, eaten at, eroded, had at last given way, and crumbled to the sea, the priory falling to a rubble of rock and bone and hawthorn-root, Holroyd's pub sliding, subsiding, collapsing (I remembered the collapse of Clem Holroyd among the deckchairs). Squinting that way, I could make out only gradations of darkness against a dark sky. The wall, the sea – and the bluff. Still standing, after all.

In my mind's eye I saw two figures, one tall, the other less tall, on the bluff, silhouetted. A father and a daughter; the father, with animated gestures, showing – no, showing *off* – to the daughter the site of his soon-to-be-realised pleasure grounds, pier and all.

Looking down and north we could see it as straight and black as a minor piano key. As we watched, brave and clutching one another at the battlement of the sea wall, we saw, now at its furthest end, for God's sake, that so grandly boasted-of half-statute mile out at sea, the two lights – two yellow lanterns, it was clear now, hanging, still but not quite motionless, imbued or cursed with a human restlessness, in the darkness.

I thought my heart would stop in terror at Eleanor's sudden scream beside me, *Father*, a piercing, far-carrying yell, not a cry from the heart, but rather the cry of a practical woman, frank and honest as a foghorn; the yell of a woman telling a fellow not to be such a damn fool, to stop being an idiotic child, to act, dammit, like a *man*—

And then my heart *did* stop. I'm convinced it did, I swear it did, for all the biology I learned at that damn technical college.

The black piano key was at once played upon. The two lights broke apart. One, moving swiftly, shifted shorewards, then stopped; the other dithered, chased after the first, stopped with a sudden blurring judder, lurched again towards the first.

It was not easy to tell black from black. I must have yelled something – I *must* have. The new note rose from the chord, through the chord, like a whale from the sea. My ears ached at it. Eleanor again shouted: 'Father.' The finger of the invisible player pressed down upon the end of the pier.

The lights – together now – moved sharply away from us.

'Harriet,' I said, but I didn't scream it or even shout it, I only murmured it into the water-beaded collar of my coat.

A sidelong surge in the darkness. Heard or felt or seen. I could not tell what yielded first, what gave way – could not say, then or now, how what was lost was lost; how the pier sank into the sea. Only that it did.

Only around five fathoms hereabouts, I had said. *Quite deep enough for me*, I had said. Quite deep enough. The lights went out.

Eleanor's weight, the full weight of her wet, shivering body, was suddenly upon me. Her arm smothered my face. I thought at first that she was clinging to me for support, for help, to keep herself from falling in a swoon, but she was not. Her weight, though not much, was enough, just enough, to keep me from doing what I all at once realised I was trying to do: climb on to the sea wall, and throw myself into the sea.

'We will prevail,' Aldridge had said to me, before I left. 'Trust in that.'

So they had, I suppose.

What are you afraid of? That's the question. It's always the question.

What would James have said, if I'd ever asked him? He might have said 'nothing', with one of those laughs that fellers do for daft girls, but he'd have been lying. He was scared of getting shot, I bet. Not when he joined up maybe but I bet he was in the end. Poor soul. And he was scared of God, that God of his. He loved Him but he was scared of Him. Why wouldn't you be? I've read the Bible and it's enough to put the – well – the fear of God into you. Sounds funny but it's true.

What's Jon afraid of? Heights. Big dogs. Who knows what else. Dying? Goes without saying, I suppose. Even our Mr Aldridge must be afraid of that. He'd say otherwise, and no doubt have some line of Scripture to back it up, but I'd not believe a word of it.

Mr Shakes, now. He might be different.

I wonder what he felt when poor young Arthur Harrowell fell in the sea and was drowned (I know, now, what became of Arthur: Alice, who got it from Dr Reynolds, said he hit a cross-strut on the way down, and it took half his head away). I wonder if it was any different to what the reverend felt when that daft bird fell into the grave. I let the poor woodcock perish, he said.

You did, Reverend. You bloody did.

Oh hell, I don't know. The wind's getting up. I don't much like the look of the sky either but I've come this far. How far, really, Harriet? Not far, but almost far enough.

The black-headed gulls are getting busy out on the water. Food, of course. Fish. Only thing they care about. Like our little Josephus.

The stupid thing is I know what he'll say. He'll wave his arm at the view and tell me it's a great grand thing. He'll stamp his big foot on Job Wakenshaw's fine pine boards and knock his stick against that Mr Furlong's good Newcastle iron. He might talk about love: about the love he has for his fellow man. Or he'll go on about joy, pleasure, freedom; what it costs, and what it's worth.

We'll have all this, and then there'll be me here with my list of numbers and calculations and by-laws and Acts and letters from this, that and the other – and really I'll only be thinking of poor Arthur Harrowell swallowed by the sea, and I'll only be thinking of him because underneath I'll be thinking of James. My poor simple stupid James who went to war and drowned. I'll be thinking of him and I'll just be afraid.

What are you afraid of? If he asks me I won't know where to start.

He might surprise me. Maybe he'll just lean on the pier rail, spit in the sea, and ask me what's life, Mrs Lowell, without a little goddamn risk?

Epilogue

David still tells me to come to London. I never shall, however much he calls me a damn hermit crab.

The birds here are different. I found that disorienting, at first, until I came to realise that for one thing all birds are very much alike and for another all birds are rather different.

I wrote as much in a letter to David once and he – reading too much into it, like the critic he is – replied that I was a bloody misanthrope.

We ran from the sea wall and the boxing ring, Eleanor and I, with the rain and much else shrieking at our backs. We found the people of the town (not all, but many, four or five dozen) coming towards us, drawn by the terrible sound of, first the slippage of the seafloor, the sundering of the foundation, and then the pier giving way, its scaffolding surrendering, its pilings shifting fatally in their bed of sand and water. A lifeboat was summoned, its crew mustered – I saw by rain-riddled lantern light the drenched and warlike faces of Reynolds the town doctor, Carwyn James, Mr Wilkie the silent overseer – but how could a lifeboat put out in such a storm? For the rain and wind had, impossibly, worsened. How sad that the pier had fallen so early, I heard someone remark, later, for if it had only held out an hour more, even the worst kind of fool would have known better than to be out on it.

I wasn't sure what kind of fool Maurice Shakes had been. Nor Harriet, come to that.

Few boats or ships pass by here. I see hardly any, though I spend much of my time on the beach and rocks. They must have frequented our choppy northern waters once – an abandoned lighthouse stands on the promontory – but something changed, something, I suppose, to do with currents, or winds, or the shoalings of cod or haddock (I have never truly understood the ocean, the *real* ocean; the shore has always been my habitat).

The letters from David – insulting, brilliant, human, enquiring, showing appalling penmanship and, I expect, worth a quid or two once David McAllister has drunk himself to death – are not the only letters I receive. The postal deliveries are haphazard up here but nevertheless I maintain what the biographers call a wide and varied correspondence. Apart from anything else there is my work: articles, monographs, manuscripts (I publish from Edinburgh, now, rather than London, but the content is much the same – still too many damn invertebrates).

Luke Hesketh, once in a blue moon, sends dourly witty missives from Sallow Sluice: funny stories of his schoolboys and (less often) his son and daughter. And the Reverend Aldridge writes to me.

I believe Aldridge thought himself terribly brave for conducting the funeral service. I don't know. Perhaps he was. I'm not sure, myself, that I should *want* to be brave enough to be able to stand over a drowned girl's body and speak – however wisely, however learnedly, with however much bloody pity – of mercy and grace.

I went because I wasn't strong enough not to. I gather that some people are driven by momentous tragedy into the arms of religion. Where Maurice Shakes vomited up his faith, others, looking on death or disaster, are swallowed by faith, engulfed by it.

Not me. When I give thanks – and sometimes I do – my thanks are still to no one. I still make promises to no one. I still say sorry to no one (I still *am* sorry to no one – sorry without object).

Afterwards I spoke to Harriet's mother, Mrs Holloway.

'When she went to Bradford,' she said, tiny on the settee in that little room of bad seascapes, 'it was fellers I was worried about. I thought, there'll be fellers, you watch. And of course there was, Jonathan, there was you, wasn't there?'

'There was, I'm afraid, yes.'

'Aye, well, that can't be helped now. But I thought her being wed would make her safe. And I thought her coming back up here would make her safe. I thought we could look after her, Jon, me and you.' She looked at me out of a face that seemed sunk into itself, funnelled inwards, drawn tight and pinched fast by sorrow. 'But she wasn't. We couldn't, could we?' she said.

Would Harriet have been safe here? There are fellers in the village but that's six miles south-east. Here on the brink of Scotland there is very little danger from fellers. There's the sea, of course. There's always that. But then there's always something.

'We could not, no,' I agreed, looking steadily at a washed-out watercolour of Fossmouth lighthouse.

I've thought once or twice about the correspondence that Harriet received – in the course of her campaign, her work, all those letters she was sent. They did not come to the house, for I would have seen them (I was not always attentive, but I would surely have seen *some* of them). They must have been addressed, instead, to the tall house at Withy Passageway – they must have been addressed 'care of the Reverend Aldridge'.

I was poised over a Gravely rock pool, net poised, a day after the funeral, when this thought occurred to me. Mrs J. Lowell, care of the Reverend Aldridge. I let my quarry (a pipefish, *Syngnathus acus*) get away.

I have one of Aldridge's letters before me now. Propped against a jar of seawater and vermilion seaweed. In it – as in all his letters, and there have been many in the course of the last eight years –

the minister writes (in a shapely hand) of forgiveness, judgement, God's justice and salvation. He seems to want something from me but I don't know what. If it's in my gift he can have it, for all I care.

Maybe he wants me to tell him more about Harriet. Maybe he wants to know what she liked for breakfast, what novels she liked to read, how she looked when she was nineteen, what underwear she wore. Maybe he wants to hear my tall tales about our sex life.

I think Aldridge might love Harriet now that she's dead even more than he did when she was alive. Christians have this talent, of course.

Josephus the cat – a different Josephus the cat, in fact Josephus the cat the third – walks uncertainly into my study, walks in a circle on the rug, and then comes and butts his head against my shin.

'Hullo, old man,' I say.

He mews, and I reply, 'Well, quite.'

There is no Lawrence Shakes Pleasure Ground at Gravely. How could there be, without its guiding spirit, its pagan god? The unbuilt Mangels machines, the labelled components of whirligigs and 'shoot the chutes' and whatever else, were crated up and shipped back to America. The steelmen returned to their cities up the coast, Wyn James to the Welsh valleys, the Italians to Glasgow.

Wyn wrote once. He explained that he would not be writing again because he had never got the hang of writing (I suppose he had dictated the letter to a helpful postmaster or some such).

There is no pleasure ground and so there is no memorial to poor Lawrence Shakes, killed at Montfaucon. But what of his brother, what of the fecund and insatiable Maurice Shakes? To him there are many memorials.

I am one, I think: me, my grief, my joy; my being here (on the one hand), my being anywhere (on the other). Eleanor, of course. Cordelia? I don't know what became of Cordelia and I suppose my not knowing is a memorial, too.

The pier when it stood was Shakes's memorial and it's still his memorial (now that its iron lies buried in silt on the seafloor and its timber washes up, bleached and worm-eaten, on remote north-eastern shores).

From Luke Hesketh I learn that ringed plovers still nest in the north bay. They might be a memorial to Shakes but I prefer to think they are a memorial to themselves. I don't want Shakes taking credit for them – for their scrapes in the shingle, their harsh songs as they skim the wave-tops, their dark-speckled eggs.

Has Harriet a memorial? A memorial suggests the possibility of forgetting. I need no memorial to Harriet – nor does her mother, nor does poor Mr Aldridge. There's a gravestone, in Aldridge's churchyard, should anyone need it.

'She's safe now, anyway,' Mrs Holloway said to me.

The safest thing, then, is never to be born, I thought. I didn't say it aloud, of course.

I wrote to Eleanor. Not long ago, and for the first time since I sold the house and moved up here. The letter found her, not in Gravely but in London, a suburb in the east of the city.

What did I say in it? I was honest, perfectly honest, but really I said very little.

I *am* a damn clammy sea creature, a cold thing from a rock pool, an invertebrate or a hank of seaweed. The safety I sought here and found here might just be the mercy of the killing jar.

But Eleanor wrote back. She, too – following my example, I suppose, as in a dance – said very little.

I had too much foolish humanity in me, after all, to forget about Eleanor, and I think (or dream, or worry) that perhaps one day – though today it seems as unlikely as my learning to breathe underwater – I might find the humanity to ask her to join me here; to marry me; to (the words still sound absurd) love me.

David McAllister is to blame for that. David is to blame for a great deal. It's funny to think of one's life as dependent on a cocky boy being hit in the face with a cricket ball, but then it's funny to think of one's life as dependent on *any*thing, even though of course one's life always is.

I fold Aldridge's letter back into its rain-marked envelope and stow it in a drawer. I sit back in my chair. I sigh, not unhappily. Harriet would have said – perhaps looking up from her sewing, perhaps only glancing sideways from the next pillow along – it was the sigh of a man with the weight of the world on his back; and I would have said something in reply about it being only a breath, my darling, only the outward breath one has to make if one is to make an inward breath.

She would have said I was a loon.

I look at the rather ancient crab, *Portunus puber*, pickled eternally in a jar on my desk. The crab looks back at me.

Acknowledgements

I'm deeply grateful to everyone whose guidance and friendship helped to shape this novel. In particular, I must thank my first reader, my mum, Mary Smyth; Louise Boland and Urška Vidoni at Fairlight, for taking the thing on and never giving up on it; Owen Booth, Carys Bray, Rebecca Machin, Jon Dunn and Peter Buckman, for their wise and generous feedback; Emma Rogers, for her wonderful cover design (the woodcock on there, I learnt, comes from a French dictionary of 1888, under the entry for *bécasse*); Alom Shaha, Fiona Gell, Rebecca Nolan, Rob Palk, Clare Fisher, Francy Wagstaff, Emma Townshend, Jenn Ashworth and Rachel Connor, for in their various ways helping me to be a writer at a time when it hasn't always been easy to be a writer; and Frin, Genevieve and Daniel, my miraculous family, for everything.

About the Author

Richard Smyth is a writer and critic. His work has appeared in the *Guardian*, the *New Statesman* and the *Times Literary Supplement*, and he is the author of five books of non-fiction. He was shortlisted for the BBC National Short Story Award 2021. He lives in Bradford, West Yorkshire, with his family.